FROM SLAVE TO

NATIONAL HERO!

THE LEGEND OF

NANNY

The Greatest Jamaican

Maroon Chief

Second Edition

By

COLIN C. REID

From Slave to National Hero!
The Legend of Nanny

Historical Fiction: ISBN 978-1500468996
Cover design by Scott Bennett
Author's photograph by Patty Tam
Printed and bounded in Canada

Disclaimer

This is a fictional account of the life of Nanny, the Jamaican Maroon Chief. While the events described and some characters may be based on actual historical events and real people, the overall saga is a work of fiction by the author.

"From Slave to National Hero: The Legend of Nanny" is solely for entertainment purposes and is never intended to be used as historical facts. Any resemblance to real persons, living or dead is purely coincidental.

<u>DEDICATION</u>

Dedicated to the memory of my dear mother, Iris Matilda Reid;
a courageous lady who taught me to believe in myself and dream big.

ACKNOWLEDGEMENT

As a young boy growing up in Jamaica I always enjoyed listening to stories about Nanny. In those days every Tom, Dick and Harry had a 'good' story about Nanny and her many victories over the British.

I always imagined her as this larger than life African woman who, with the help of her audacious Maroons, broke the back of the mighty British military machinery. These stories and more gave me a real sense of pride in my ancestors.
The Diaspora is forever grateful to the many storytellers who have kept the sagas of this amazing woman and other heroes like her alive for generations.

I would like to thanks the many associates, colleagues and friends who have helped to make this project a reality.
To Rovina Subryan and Crystal Thureson who have burnt the candles at both ends to edit the manuscript. To my good friend and colleague Scott Bennett, for the many hours he spent editing and preparing the manuscript for the publisher. To my friends and colleagues Cecilia Kwon and Ardeen Taffe, for their support and advice along the way. To Safia Bartholomew, who had confidence in this venture from the beginning, and who kept me focused on the big picture.

To my niece and author Pauleanna Reid, for her encouragement. To my brother, Paul Reid and family. To my wonderful in-laws Mark and Lieta Depass and my good friends Joy and Lambert Watson; for the many hours we spent discussing Jamaican politics and heroes like Nanny. This and more provided me with invaluable fodder for the story. To my nephew, attorney Che Claire; for our many stimulating discussions and your assistance in preparing the legal framework for the novel.

And most of all, I would like to thank my wife Joycelyn and son Seargeoh for their love and support and putting up with me for so many months during the writing of this story. I would especially like to thank Seargeoh who created all the art work for the novel. I am eternally grateful for his advice and encouragement. I will forever cherish those precious moments we spent working together.

Part One

In the Beginning...

Chapter 1

Kaka-rook-koo! The roosters crowed their early morning greeting, breaking the stillness of the cool hazy morning and rousing the sleepy African village. Visibility was limited as the thick white soupy mist blanketed the entire valley, while dew water drenched the surrounding foliage. This quaint little African village was slowly coming to life with folks rustling around in their tiny huts, while others gathered firewood outside to boil the morning tea. For the older women of the village the night was rather long, waiting in anticipation of the birth of Mada Poku's grandchild. Mada Poku, or Mada P as she was affectionately called by everyone, was the renowned spiritual leader of the Ashanti tribe. Some people claimed that she had great mystical powers and was able to speak with the dead. No one dared to question Mada P. Her words were more significant than even the Chief's because of the belief that her profound wisdom came directly from their great ancestors. As the sun struggled to break through the thick murky fog a single piercing cry of a newborn baby broke the silence. Inside the hut Mada Poku quickly cleaned the baby as it continued to wail at the top of its lungs.

The people rushed out of their huts with excitement and jubilation towards the hut where the newborn baby was crying.

"That must be a baby boy," one elderly woman said. "Because for one thing, only boys take so long to be born."

"And where did you get that from?" another woman asked. "Have you forgotten how long Miss Della's granddaughter took last year? It was like the baby didn't want to come out."

"I believe that the young mothers are not resting enough," another mother of three daughters added.

"They're always out enjoying themselves so the poor babies are tired, tired as hell, and that is why they don't want to come out."

"Is there anything that you don't know Miss Know-it-all?"

"Lawd woman, give it a rest! So early in the morning and you've started flapping your mouth already; like it never gets tired. A man's ears can't even get some peace and quiet. Everywhere you go you're always talking," a man said, seemingly annoyed after his wife had dragged him reluctantly over to see the baby.

"I only hope it is a boy baby," a little old man sitting before his hut nearby said. "Mada P needs a little boy around here to help her, she's getting old."

"So what's wrong with a girl child?" a voice sounding like his wife came from deep inside the hut.

"Woman, don't ask me any question!" the man snapped back.

"But it is true," the wife continued. "You men always want us to have boy babies and you know full well that you don't do a darn thing around here. You're saying that Mada P needs a boy, ah! What a joke! We both know that she can only depend on a girl."

"Woman, don't bother me so early in the morning," the man said, raising his voice in frustration. "By the way, what happened to the tea that you had promised me woman? Why is it taking so long?

"Now, do you see what I mean? You've just proven my point. There you're sitting down on your rump and waiting on me to bring you your tea."

"This woman talks so much, from morning until night. I wish that she would just shut her mouth," the man uttered under his breath.

"What're you mumbling about, out there?" she shouted. "You're always mumbling to yourself. You need to stop it! It is a bad habit." And on and on she went.

The little hut was neatly decorated with flowers and ornaments to herald the arrival of the baby. In the centre of the room the young mother rested quietly on a little bed after wreathing all night in pain. Crouching around her bed were her mother, aunts and other elderly ladies of the tribe, humming quietly as they wiped her brow and cleaned her body. Mada Puko cradled the baby in her arms, and as the sun came up, she looked intently into the baby's face and declared, "You look just like my grandmother, identical to her. Those eyes remind me so much of her."

Turning to the other elders she said, "The child looks like she knows me already. She looks like she understands everything that I'm saying. This child must be my grandmother, come back to life! I can already see the power in her. She, like my grandmother, will lead our people one day. The world will know of her and about her one day; you mark my word."

"We believe you Mada P," the other elders echoed. "We will help to train this child so that she can take her rightful place here in our tribe."

The young mother laid still on the bed listening to the elders and her mother talking about her baby as if she was not there. She wanted so badly to hold her baby in her arms but they only allowed her to hold her for a short time before Mada Puko took her back and passed her from one hand to another; each elder spending some time to pray over and bless the little child.

"This baby!" Mada Poku declared, holding the baby up to the light. "Shall be called Nanny, after my grandmother. Like my grandmother, she will lead our people when the time comes. She will do great wonders that this world has never seen; and will lead her people with wisdom and conviction."

"This child is really special," one elder whispered to another. "I've never seen Mada P so worked up over a birth, and I've seen her deliver hundreds of babies over the years."

"True, true," the other woman concurred. "This one is very special."

As the morning sun came up, more and more people arrived at the hut to pay their respect to the newborn. Many brought gift baskets of fruits and vegetables, ground provisions, honey, and grains.

Preparations for the evening celebration to welcome Nanny into the tribe were progressing well. Some women prepared the vegetables while others pounded maize into a fine powder. The men skillfully skinned the goats as the dogs hung around lapping up the fresh blood. Kids were organized in groups to collect all the garbage and trash around the celebration square. Everyone was in a joyful mood, singing merrily as they worked to get things ready for the afternoon festivities.

All throughout the day leaders from the surrounding tribes arrived bringing gifts, extending greetings and paying their respect to the newborn babe. The Chief of a great Northern tribe, a good friend of Mada Puko and the Chief, on hearing of the impending birth, walked for two days to pay his respect. He brought with him a small herd of goats as a present for the child. When the people saw this they were amazed, because they knew how powerful this Chief was.

As the afternoon approached the people got ready for the festivities. Families began arriving and choosing their spots on the square. The Chief arrived with his entourage; and after greeting Mada Poku, with the baby in her arms, and the other dignitaries, he took his seat at the north end of the square, signaling the start of the celebration.

The drummers came out in great numbers with drums of all shapes, sizes and colors. As the drummers pounded energetically on their finely tuned skins, sweat ran freely down their bodies giving them a distinct glow. The elite bunch of talking drummers were the envy of everyone as they played their instruments with such finesse; broadcasting the good news to all who would lend an ear.

Dancers of all ages took to the square dancing rhythmically and gyrating to the infectious beat.

The young kids moved effortlessly to the rhythm while the older folks rocked steadily to the beat. The youth dancers showed off their dancing skills to the amazement of the crowd, turning, spinning, dancing in circles and showing off their impressive talent.

Mada Poku lovingly passed the baby from one elder to the other, each elder praying over the baby and giving their blessing.

The baby's mother Nige' could hear the distant laughter and the rhythmic drumming from the square as she laid uneasily in her bed drifting in and out of sleep. She wondered to herself what was so special about her baby. Why was her mother so excited about her baby? She had heard her mother saying that the child looked exactly like her grandmother and that her baby was in fact her great-great-grandmother reincarnated. This was too much for Nige' and she promised herself that she would talk to her mother about it in the morning, as she drifted off to sleep again.

The musicians played non-stop throughout the festivities. The dancing continued until late into the night. And at the end of the celebration, everyone went home feeling fortunate that they had been there and able to witness the arrival of this precious bundle of joy.

Chapter 2

Nanny spent most of her early years with her grandmother, Mada Puko. When she was a baby, Mada Puko would often go over to her house in the morning, and as soon as Nanny was awake, she would take her from her mother, give her a bath and then dress her for the day. After she was fed Mada Puko would take her back to her house where they would spend the entire day playing, singing old tribal songs and Mada Puko speaking words of comfort and blessings over her. Whenever she had to travel, she would bundle Nanny carefully and lug her on her back. Nanny never cried or made a fuss as she enjoyed being out on the road with her grandmother.

As Nanny grew older Mada Puko taught her the tribal language and the magic of numbers. The girl was a very fast learner and by the age of two she was able to speak fluently in both her tribal language and the official language of the Ashanti. Everyone was astounded by this child. Some people said that she had healing powers because whenever she laid her hand on the sick they always felt better.

Nanny adored her grandmother very much and made every effort to please her. She knew that Mada Puko woke up early in the mornings to pray and commune with the spirit world so she readily jumped out of bed before her mother and father were awake and dashed over to her grandmother's house to worship with her.

Mada Puko walked around the hut while she chanted in tongues calling upon her ancestors to protect their tribe from the evil white devils from across the sea. Her chants got louder and louder, with more power and anger as the prayers progressed.

"They've come here with their big dirty ships and weapons to steal our people and corrupt our people. Oh great ancestors what are we going to do? We're losing our brightest young people to these white bandits. We've tribes turning against tribes, selling to these wicked people, why? Why? Oh Mada Kuzo! Oh my glorious ancestors help us this day! Take this cup of poison away from us!" she chanted.

"We've got to stop these white devils from coming here and taking away our children. Where they're taking our people, we do not know. None of them has ever come back. We've got to break this cycle of misery for our people. But how can we do that without your help Mada Kuzo?" she cried out in a loud voice, with tears running down her face.

"I just hate those white devils with all my heart, Mada Kuzo! I hate them for what they're doing to our people. Help us this day, oh great ancestors! We're waiting patiently for your deliverance."

At the end of her devotion, Mada Puko and Nanny would both sit down and wipe away beads of sweat; all the while fanning with anything they could find to keep cool. After, they would wash thoroughly before going off to prepare breakfast in the kitchen. That was the best part of the whole morning for Nanny because her grandmother made the best breakfast in the village.

After a mini feast, Nanny followed Mada Puko out into the village to work among the people; caring for the sick, the dying and those giving birth. However, on some days Mada Puko would get into a frenzy chanting and stomping around the hut for many, many hours without stopping. With tears streaming down her face and her body washed in sweat, she cried out over and over to her ancestors for help.

Young Nanny loved chanting with her grandmother. She would hold onto the end of her dress and stomp with her around and around crying out for help from the spirit world.

"White devils, burn them up!" Mada Puko chanted loudly with Nanny chanting meekly along in her little voice:

"White devil must die.

White devil brings misery.

White devil brings sickness.

White devil brings death.
White devil is evil to the bone.
Burn their boats,
Burn their ships that take away our people!
Rid us of the evil ones."

Mada Puko wiped beads of sweat from her face with her rag. Nanny never took her eyes off her grandmother. She watched her every move and memorized all the chants and tribal songs.

As Nanny grew older she wanted to spend more and more time with her grandmother to learn about the problems plaguing their people. Mada Puko hid nothing from her and taught her everything that she needed to know.

"Gamma [Grandmother], you're always chanting about white devil. What is white devil?" young Nanny asked one day.

"White devils my child are those pale skin people who come here in their big ships from way across the seas," Mada Puko began.

"So where do they come from Gamma?" Nanny asked innocently.

"Nobody knows my child. They just appear and load up our people on their ships and leave. They are evil people my child, pure evil!" Mada Puko emphasized, shaking her head in frustration. "They're dangerous people child! Very dangerous! Never trust them! Some people say that they're cannibals, but I'm not sure. They seem to act like cannibals though, because whenever they take away our people they never come back; so nobody is sure."

"But why do they want our people so much Gamma?" Nanny asked, opening her little hands.

"I don't know that either my child, but one day I'm going to find out, if it is the last thing I do before I die," Mada Puko promised. "Imagine this child; they come here and take away our people in their big ugly ships and we never see them again. It's like our people just dropped into a giant sink hole and vanished. And the bad thing is that they keep coming back again and again for more. They're never satisfied!" Mada Puko stressed.
"And another thing, these people talk through the two sides of their mouth. They have no truth in them! Never trust them my child, never trust them. Do you hear me?" Mada Puko exclaimed, opening her eyes widely and looking Nanny squarely in her face.

"Yes, yes Gamma," Nanny stuttered, realizing that what her grandmother was saying must be important, but unable to understand what it meant.

"Your generation will change things for all of us my child. Our generation made the big mistake of trusting these people, but your generation will know better and will fix the problem," Mada Puko predicted.

"What do you mean by fixing the problem Gamma?" Nanny asked innocently.

"When the time comes my child, you will know and I'm sure you'll do the right thing," Mada Puko reassured her. "The most important thing that you have to remember is never trust them blindly. Never agree to anything without thinking it through carefully because they're very clever my child, and never let them pressure you into any agreement before you're ready. Are you listening to me child?"

"Yes, yes Gamma," Nanny replied tongue-tied; not fully understanding what she was hearing.

Nanny was never really interested in playing with kids her age. She was more interested in sitting down and talking with the senior folks in the tribe. She enjoyed listening to stories of days gone by and would sit at their feet to learn.

By the age of ten Nanny was working full time with Mada Puko in the village casting out demons, giving bush baths to the sick, prescribing different herbal medicines and acting as a medium for people who wanted to contact their dead relatives. As Mada Puko grew older she allowed Nanny to take on more responsibilities and assisted only when she was needed.

Nanny loved serving the people and woke up every morning at the crack of dawn ready to begin her day. She worked from morning until dusk helping the people who were sick in body and mind. Sometimes she became so exhausted that her grandmother would have to insist that she take a break.

In late spring the tribe was attacked along their western border by a neighboring hostile tribe. The skirmish lasted a day and a half, causing many casualties. Mada Puko, Nanny and several elderly women treated and cared for the returning warriors out in the open square. As the day progressed more and more injured warriors were brought in from the battlefield. Nanny and the other women worked all day and night treating the wounded. At day break, Nanny was so exhausted that Mada Puko insisted that she get some sleep. But after a few hours she was back in action treating the injured.

"I couldn't sleep Gamma. When I thought about all this suffering, I had to come back."

The battle ended quickly but it took Mada Puko and the ladies a couple days to take care of all the injured warriors.

While working, Nanny saw an old woman in a full flowing white dress walking effortlessly in between the injured, sometimes stopping momentarily to comfort a dying warrior. She touched their foreheads with her finger and gently breathed on them. Suddenly she stopped, turned her head towards Nanny and smiled, then continued moving among the injured. Nanny ran quickly over to Mada Puko and whispered in her ears what she had seen; not wanting to alarm the other elderly ladies.

"She is here! Thank Massa God!" Mada Puko exclaimed, as if she was expecting her. "She has really come! I was wondering how she was taking so long," Mada Puko said, holding Nanny's face tenderly in her hands. "That is my mother my child. Her name is Mada Kuzo, the greatest prophetess and medium this tribe has ever known. She always turns up whenever we have a disaster or when a disaster is about to happen. She has never abandoned us. No sir! Never! Many times we find ourselves in deep trouble like this one here and she just turns up and helps us. I'm so happy that you've seen her child!" Mada Puko said excitedly. "This proves that you're the one. When Mada Kuzo comes around, I know everything will be alright. She always knows what to do," Mada Puko said, holding Nanny's hands and looking tenderly into her eyes.

"Now my child, this is where the fun begins. I've taught you all that I know. There's not much more that I can teach you. I do not have many of the gifts that you have. I'm surprised at some of the things that you're able to do now at such a young age. You remind me so much of my grandmother. I see so much of her in you. I'm releasing you to my mother, your great-grandmother. She will teach you from now on. Trust her child and you will do wonders. No matter what trials you may face, trust her and she will get you through it."

Nanny was confused. Many questions popped into her mind. What kinds of problems could she be facing in the future that would require her great-grandmother's help? When would her great-grandmother contact her again? Would she be able to talk with her?

"Do you hear what I'm telling you child?" Mada Puko asked, holding Nanny by the arm to get her attention. "Pay attention my child; this is life and death we're dealing with."

"Yes Gamma," Nanny said nervously, not knowing what else to say.

"My mother has been my spiritual guide for a very long time," Mada Puko continued. "And she has never let me down. You will learn many things from her, I know you will! She will take you to places that you can only dream of!"

Suddenly a few patients began moaning and groaning in pain which caused Mada Puko and Nanny to turn their attention back to the sick.

"Let's get back to work," Mada Puko suggested. "These sick warriors need us."

As Mada Puko worked feverishly among the sick, her thoughts flashed back to the day that her mother died. She looked very weak and frail; a far cry from the bold, larger than life charismatic leader who had served her people for over fifty years. No one questioned her judgment. She was so powerful that even on her death bed, in her frail condition, she commanded respect. With a forced whisper and a slight wave of her hand, she ordered everyone out of the room except Mada Puko.

"Puko, my Puko," she said, in a rasping whisper between short gasps of breath. "You must continue to help the people, the people, the people, the people," her voice trailing off. "Serve them well. Never forget them. Our family has been serving our people for hundreds of years and we need to keep passing the torch to the next generation. I'm on my way out to be with my ancestors but I will never leave you. I will be over on the other side looking out for you and our people. And when it is your time my dear I will be right there to meet you just like my mother and all of my ancestors who have gone on before are right here beside me now, waiting to take me home. I love you with all my heart Puko. Remember, take care of the people. They need you. I'm now passing the torch over to you. You're now in charge. Make your ancestors proud." And with that her head fell to one side, her eyes closed and she was gone.

There was weeping and mourning for the next seven days in the village following the death of Mada Kuzo. Now everyone looked to Mada Puko for leadership.

"Ohh! Ohh!" an injured warrior wailed, bringing Mada Puko back to reality. Sometime later, Mada Puko's thoughts again drifted back to her childhood.

Her mother took her everywhere with her. She met numerous kings and chiefs from several tribes, and travelled to many distant regions. She witnessed her mother healing people, treating people with all types of sicknesses, and diseases. She especially liked when her mother took her to those sessions where she acted as a medium, passing on messages to people from their ancestors.

Mada Puko remembered that as an only child she grew up rather quickly. Lots of people were always around the house. They came from near and far; people desperate for help or just to know their future. Young expectant mothers wanted to know whether it was a boy or a girl. Some people even came to find out what the planting season would be like. Mada Kuzo never turned anyone away. She believed with every fiber of her being that serving the people was the highest order of living. Mada Puko kept hearing those words over and over all her life, and although at first she did not fully understand, as she grew older, she found herself embracing this philosophy. She was becoming her mother, and loving it.

She recalled the time as a little girl when there was a plague in the village. Many people were dying daily and there was no remedy available. Mada Kuzo worked tirelessly, sometimes getting only a few hours of sleep per day; treating the sick and trying to find a cure for this terrible disease. After a few weeks she started showing signs of exhaustion. Young Puko was sent to live with her aunt while her mother continued to work from morning until night.

One day news came that there was a special herbal plant, far up in the mountain that could cure the disease. Everyone became excited and hopeful that the end was near. Young Puko remembered hearing her mother telling the anxious people that the plant had the cure for the disease but that it grew only in special regions, high up in the mountain. She explained that after the plant was harvested the juice had to be extracted within twenty-four hours as the quality deteriorated rapidly after that time and became useless.

"Then that plant can't help us," one old lady said, shaking her head. "Because only birds can reach up there and get that herb."

"Why are you so negative Miss Dhotti?" another elderly woman asked. "Leave everything to Mada Kuzo; she will find a way, she always comes true," the lady said with confidence.

"Yes! I agree," chimed in a short middle aged man. "We believe that Mada Kuzo will call upon the spirits to help us."
Mada Kuzo gave a nervous smile and implored everyone to call upon Massa God to help them.

That night Mada Kuzo told young Puko about her plan to harvest the plant. It seemed impossible at first but she had grown to believe everything that her mother told her without question.

The next morning, to everyone's surprise; lying in front of Mada Kuzo's hut were several large bundles of the freshly cut plants ready to be prepared and juiced. The people became very excited all the while wondering how the plants got there, but no one dared to ask.

For the remainder of the morning Mada Kuzo and the ladies prepared the plants, extracted the juice and gave it to the sick. The medicine began working almost immediately. Some patients were up and about before the end of the day. Mada Kuzo worked non-stop until the last patient was treated. She was so exhausted that when she eventually went to bed she slept for over twelve hours.

Over supper one evening young Puko looked at her mother and asked, "Did you really turn into a bird and fly up to the top of the mountain Mu'ma [mother]?"

"Yes my child," Mada Kuzo replied boldly. "It was not difficult. Our ancestors have been doing it for generations. You too will be able to do it someday. Look at me; I can change into any animal I want to right now. If I can think it, then I can transform into it. I will teach you these things when the time is right. In the meantime you must never ever reveal this or anything else you learn to anybody, understand?"

"Yes Mu'ma," young Puko said.

Suddenly her thoughts were interrupted by an excited Nanny.

"Gamma! Gamma!" Nanny called out from across the room. "Over here," beckoning her to come over towards her. Mada Puko refocused her attention and hurried over to find out what was the matter.

"Mada Kuzo is back!" she said excitedly. "She is over there with the patients," pointing her finger across the room. "What must I do? Should I go over there to her? Will you be going over there?"

"Calm down child," Mada Puko said, raising her hand. "Don't go to her; let her come to you."

They watched intently as the old lady in white moved with urgency among the sick, checking especially the very sick and badly hurt.

"Something is not right," Mada Puko pondered. "Mu'ma looks worried. Something terrible is about to happen."

"How do you know that, Gamma?" Nanny asked, trying to understand her grandmother.

"I just know my child, I just know. She looks worried. Something is not right. I wonder how much time we have?" she asked, not expecting an answer.

Suddenly the old lady looked towards them and with a troubled look on her face, raised a crooked finger and made a gesture for both of them to follow her.

In a short while, Nanny found herself flying through the air with her two grandparents.

"Wow," she thought, with her mouth wide open. "We're flying! But where are we going?"

"Stay focused Nanny!" Mada Puko cautioned, knowing exactly how she was feeling and remembering the exact words her mother had said to her on her first flight.

"Yes Gamma," Nanny replied, trying hard to keep her focus.

"Leave the girl alone," Mada Kuzo rebuked Mada Puko, with a smile.

"But that was exactly what you said to me when you took me up on my first trip," Mada Puko protested.

"That was then, I know better now," she defended her remarks with a pleasant laugh. Both ladies laughed while Nanny smiled to herself as she enjoyed the whole experience. All of a sudden she felt this deep love for this charming old lady.

"You've done a wonderful job with this child Puko. I'm so proud of you. I wish you had spent more time with her mother though when she too was a little girl, but I understand what was happening at the time and frankly, you did your best."

"Thank you for saying that mu'ma. I needed to hear that from you. All these years I thought that I had disappointed you," Mada Puko said.

"You could never disappoint me love. I'm always so proud of you and grateful that I was the one chosen to bring you into this world."

"That daughter of mine was a challenge from the day she was born, do you remember?" Mada Puko asked.

"Yes, I remember. I was there, remember?" Mada Kuzo reminded her. "Who do you think was there keeping everybody awake throughout the night? I didn't allow anyone to get sleepy. I just blew on them and that would revive them so that they could continue helping you. Did you know that we almost lost that poor baby many times during the delivery? Of course you wouldn't know that because you were in so much pain. I had to breathe into her a few times when she stopped breathing. And because she was early, her lungs were not fully developed so she was very, very weak. I never left her side for the first six weeks of her life. I had to make sure that she was developing properly."

"I thank you mu'ma for being there and delivering my daughter. When I saw you moving around I knew everything would be alright. I knew that you would make sure that me and my daughter would be fine. Your words of encouragement in my ears always soothed my pain."

"I loved that little girl with all my heart, but she wouldn't stop crying," Mada Kuzo laughed. "She cried all the time, sometimes for many hours. It used to drive me crazy," she laughed.

"I loved when you came around because you played with her and she would stop crying," Mada Puko added.

"Well I had to come," Mada Kuzo replied. "Because my mother insisted that I come and stop the baby from crying. Yes, my mother is with me all the time, just like I'm with you."

"It was a big joke when people would see her suddenly stop crying and begin laughing and playing by herself; turning her head from side to side and giggling in the bed," Mada Puko remembered. "Sometimes people asked me who she was playing with, but I would just tell them that she liked to play by herself. Some people however realized that she was playing with somebody from the spirit world."

The conversation continued as the women flew way above the tree tops. Meanwhile, Nanny couldn't contain her excitement at the thought of actually flying through the air with her two favorite relatives. At first she was scared to look down at the forests rushing by below at breakneck speed, but with a little encouragement from both ladies she learned to relax and enjoy the scenery.

Mada Kuzo headed south towards the sea with Mada Puko and Nanny trailing behind. Nanny noticed clouds of dust as hundreds of wild animals headed north and thousands of birds anxiously flew away from the ocean.

"What is happening Mada Kuzo?" Nanny asked, looking concerned. "Why are the animals and the birds acting so strange?"

"Look way over yonder in front of us," Mada Kuzo instructed, pointing out to sea. "What do you see?"
Nanny suddenly gasped.

"A storm is coming our way!" she exclaimed.

"This one is worse than a storm my child. This one is called Atbecwe. It is bad! Old people call it the devil from the bottom of the sea. It is like a giant wall of water travelling towards land. And when it comes ashore, it destroys everything in its path. It takes anything that is not tied down right back out to sea. Puko, you have to go back and warn the people. They have to leave immediately and go up into the hills or they will all be washed out to sea by this time tomorrow."

"So that is why the animals and the birds are so agitated and moving north," Nanny reflected. "They know that the Atbecwe is coming and that's why they're fleeing to higher ground."

"That's right child," Mada Kuzo said. "Puko, this little girl is so smart," she observed.
"Now ladies we have to return to the village and prepare the people. We have lots of work to do before this thing comes ashore tomorrow evening," Mada Kuzo declared. "Get everybody out: men, women and children. Get the sick warriors out first. Leave nobody or animals behind because this

Atbecwe is the biggest I have seen and I have seen many. Nothing will be spared. Everything will be destroyed. But remember, I will be here to help you. Nanny, you work with the young mothers and young children. Help them to get organized; and calm down the children. Puko don't let them stop until they reach the North Pass, because anything below that will be washed away out to sea."

Mada Kuzo saw the worried look on Mada Puko and Nanny's face.

"Don't worry, everything will be alright!" she said with a grin. "Just get the people moving by tonight and we will not lose a single soul. Go to the Chief and tell him to start warning the people," Mada Kuzo instructed. "Listen ladies, I have to go; do as I say and by tomorrow evening all of your people will be safe." And with that she was gone leaving Mada Puko and Nanny to finish the journey home.

They travelled in silence, each person reflecting on what they had seen that afternoon. Nanny wondered if they could move so many people in such a short time. She looked down and saw the animals and birds making their way swiftly away from the coast, and out of arms way. Would they be able to get the people to respond accordingly?

At the village, the farm animals looked agitated as if they knew that something devastating was about to happen.

The dogs howled continuously while the chickens jumped up and down and flew around nervously. Although most people went about their business oblivious of the impending danger, some elderly folks wondered what was happening when they saw their animals acting up.

Mada Puko met with the Chief and informed him of the coming danger. He quickly summoned his top leaders and they started rounding up the people. Young musicians began vigorously playing the talking drums and blowing the abeng horn to warn the people of the approaching danger. They also broadcasted messages to the surrounding villages to warn the people. People quickly gathered in the center of the village to receive instructions from the Chief.

Within a few hours the entire village was evacuated with the people taking what little possession they could carry, along with their animals.

Mada Puko and Nanny walked with the people all night to get to the North Pass. Nanny worked tirelessly with the young mothers and kids throughout the night, helping to keep them safe and occasionally providing a little relief for the mothers.

The following evening, as Mada Kuzo had predicted, the giant waves came ashore grabbing everything that was not tied down and taking them back out to sea. The water rose quickly to the top of the trees, covering all the huts. As Mada Kuzo had predicted, everyone at the pass remained safe.

Mada Puko was grateful that her mother had come to warn them. She knew that if her mother had not come, only a hand full of people in the village would have survived.

The water subsided slowly and returned to the ocean carrying everything in its path and leaving total devastation.

Slowly the people returned to the village to see what was left of their homes and belongings. The Chief built a big bon fire in the centre of the village and invited everyone to gather and give thanks to God and show their gratitude to Mada Puko for issuing the warning that ultimately saved their lives.

Chapter 3

There was a great deal of work to be done. The men worked tirelessly to rebuild the huts while some repaired the canoes to take them back to sea. Still others formed groups and travelled far inland to cut down trees.

Young women and children worked daily in the scorching sun preparing the fields and replanting crops that were destroyed. Many neighboring tribes, who were not affected by the flood, made donations of food and building materials to assist in the recovery program. Some tribes even sent volunteers to assist in the rebuilding of huts and the cutting down of trees in the forest.

Mada Puko worked alongside the people in rebuilding their homes and preparing the fields while Nanny took care of the younger children, so that the mothers could work.

The people worked hard from sunup until sundown; day after day, to rebuild their village. No one thought about the danger lurking in their midst. It happened one evening when some of the young men from the village were returning from the forest after a long day cutting wood. The men didn't have a clue that they were being watched. They joked about and were having a good time when suddenly they were pounced upon by a group of ruggedly looking men with spears and clubs. After a brief scuffle, they were all subdued except for a slim, fleet footed youth who escaped and dashed off like the blast from cannon; not looking back, and dodging their spears. The young man ran as fast as he could all the way to the village.

He was quite exhausted when he arrived in the village square. His desperate cries for help instantly brought everyone rushing towards him to find out what was wrong. The Chief, upon hearing the report sprang into action immediately. He instructed his specially trained talking drummers to send out urgent messages to everyone around to begin the search for the men before they were taken out of the area. He dispatched his elite teams of trackers to expeditiously comb the forest to find the men, as time was against them. There was weeping and wailing in the village as mothers, wives and children cried openly for their love ones.

Everyone became extremely worried for these young men. They all knew that if they were not freed from these captors, they would be marched down to the sea coast and placed on the big ship never to be seen again.

Nanny became quite worried when she heard the news. She knew many of the young men who were captured. She was especially worried about her good friend Odeo. She had known him for a long time and was very fond of him. Mada Puko also knew Odeo and his parents and grandparents very well. In fact she was the one who had delivered him at birth.

As darkness approached Nanny hurried over to Mada Puko and whispered into her ears.

"Gamma, we have to do something for Odeo and the other men or we're going to lose them to the captors. We won't be able to find them during the night, and by daylight they could be miles away."

"So what do you suggest child?" Mada Puko asked, knowing exactly what she would say.

"We have to travel out there and look for them now!" Nanny exclaimed.

"Sounds like a good idea, my child," Mada Puko said. "But before we go you need to understand something. These slavers, as they are called, are very dangerous men, so I don't want you taking any unnecessary risk; do you understand?"

"Yes Gamma, now can we go?" Nanny begged.

"Ok, meet me behind the hut," Mada Puko said. "I don't want anyone seeing us when we leave."

Minutes later Mada Puko and Nanny were flying through the air in the direction of the forest. They peered over the vast terrain looking for any large movements of people. They travelled to the east and then to the west. They circled the north section and the south section, but the group was nowhere to be found.

"This is like searching for a flat stone at the bottom of the river," Nanny said, sounding frustrated.

"Maybe we have to call upon Mada Kuzo for help. Surely she will be able to find these men."

Suddenly Mada Kuzo appeared in their midst which caused Nanny to yell out in fright.

"I'm so sorry I startled you child, but I heard what you said and I'm here to help. Let's go over on that side and find these slavers and teach them a lesson," Mada Kuzo said, pointing to the east.

A short while later, Mada Kuzo stopped in mid-air and pointed below, indicating that she had found the men.

Nanny couldn't wait to go down and rescue the men.

"Come, let's hurry down there and rescue Odeo and the others," she said, trying desperately to control her excitement.

"Nanny, do you remember what I said about those men?" Mada Puko addressed her, opening her eyes widely.

"Yes Gamma, I remember and I promise to be careful," Nanny replied meekly.

"It looks like the slavers heard the talking drums and the whole lot of people searching for the men; so they have hidden them inside those caves down there until nightfall. They will then march them throughout the night until they are out of the area without anybody seeing them," Mada Kuzo explained. "Maybe we should go down there as crows so that we can get up close to the slavers and find a way to free the men."

Everyone agreed, and in a flash three crows flew in formation towards the trees. Soon they located a giant tree with large branches extending outward above a cave. Mada Puko counted two guards at the entrance with spears in hand.

"Nanny, you keep an eye on these guards out here while me and Puko will go inside and look around," Mada Kuzo instructed.

The two ladies became invisible and casually walked by the guards without a hitch. Nanny felt like her heart was about to jump out of her chest. Here she was alone, sitting on a branch directly above these two guards while her two grandparents were inside. She wished that they had taken her along so that she would not have to face this all by herself. But what was she really afraid of? The guards didn't even know that she was there. One of the guards was not much older than her and she wondered how they could live with themselves knowing that they were selling their own people to the white devils to take away on their big ships.

Suddenly she was jolted out of her thoughts when she realized that the guards were talking to each other and pointing up at her. She felt very uncomfortable and slightly troubled. She had to remind herself constantly that they were not seeing her as Nanny, so there was nothing to worry about.

Meanwhile, Mada Kuzo and Mada Puko wandered deeper inside the shadowy cave and began looking around. The captives all sat against a rough wall with their hands tied behind their backs. The ladies examined each person carefully to see what condition they were in.

The men looked confused. Some were covered in blood while others bled from different parts of their bodies. A few men had their mouths swollen and teeth missing while some had scratches and bruises all over. One man, who was moaning quietly, had a big open laceration across his back. He looked like he had lost a lot of blood and would not make it home without significant help. Mada Puko deftly placed her hand on him and immediately the bleeding stopped and the wound started drying up.

Sitting across from the men were the guards armed with spears unaware of what was taking place around them. Some of the men continued moaning quietly, ignoring the slavers' orders to be quiet or else be killed.

The two ladies moved stealthily among the men, soothing and administering healing to the injured. Mada Puko searched and found Odeo at the far end of the line. Fortunately he only had an open wound on his forehead, a swollen lip and a cut on his knee, otherwise he was fine. Mada Puko gently passed her hand over his wounds sealing them.

"Are you ready to take them?" Mada Kuzo asked with a sly grin on her face.

"What's the plan?" Mada Puko inquired.

"Well, if we attack them openly, they might retaliate by killing the captors," Mada Kuzo said. "I think it is best that we put them to sleep, then release our men and take them home without anyone getting hurt."

28

"Ok, let's do it," Mada Puko affirmed.

The ladies calmly moved over to each guard and gently touched the back of their necks, putting them to sleep curled up on the ground. Mada Kuzo walked outside the cave, and finding the two guards sitting near the entrance, quietly and effortlessly put them to sleep as well, before waving up to Nanny.

Slowly the men wobbled out of the cave rubbing their hands and checking their wounds. When they finally realized that they were really free, they began jumping up and down hugging each other with joy. Nanny felt overjoyed when Odeo eventually came out limping but otherwise fine.

The men gathered around and talked for a few minutes among themselves and then hurried on their way home. Although they were astounded at their good fortune, they did not wish to stick around, fearing that the guards might wake up and try to recapture them.

"Do you think that they will be able to make it back home on their own?" Nanny asked, thinking mainly about Odeo.

"They should be fine," Mada Puko said. "And we'll stay with them until they are out of danger."

"My two favorite ladies," Mada Kuzo called out. "The time has come for me to leave you. Walk good and protect these men, until we meet again."

"Walk good Mu'ma," Mada Puko said.

"Until next time Gramma [great-grandmother]," Nanny added. And with that, she disappeared.

The men walked for hours in the dark without stopping, for fear that the slavers might catch up to them. They all helped each other along the way.

A little after midnight the men arrived at the village to find all their relatives and friends waiting anxiously for them. Then the celebration began. The young people came out into the square and began dancing and singing to the beat of the drums. The talking drummers relayed the good news to their friends and allies in the surrounding tribes and thanked them for their support. Shortly after, talking drums from the surrounding tribes began sending congratulatory messages to the village.

The Chief met with all the men and their families, hugging them and telling them how happy he was for them. Rumors spread rapidly that it was

Mada Puko who had rescued the men but no one had any proof and neither ladies was talking.

Mada Puko and Nanny quietly slipped out of the celebration and retired to bed, drifting off to sleep to the pulsating sounds of the Ashanti drums.

Chapter 4

As Nanny grew older she became more aware of the troubles of the African people. Everyone was becoming scared to leave their village for fear of being captured and sold to the slavers. Nobody trusted outsiders. Tribes that were once close allies had now become enemies; and the main reason was the high demand for people to supply the slave merchants.

"Are you still thinking about the slavers my child?" Mada Puko asked Nanny one day when she was sitting by herself in a corner, lost in thought.

"Yes Gamma," Nanny replied, snapping back to reality.

"You're too young to be worrying about things like that my child," Mada Puko told her.

"But somebody has to think about it Gamma," Nanny said. "To me, it looks like all the old people have put their hands in the air and given up."

"Don't say that my child; many people like myself are really concerned, hoping and praying that things will change," Mada Puko said, feeling somewhat guilty because she didn't have a better explanation.

Nanny scratched her head as she thought for a while.

"Gamma, I don't understand. How did we get into all this mess?" an innocent Nanny asked.

"It's a long story my child, with lots of blame to go around the world and back. But the bottom line is greed, pure and simple greed," Mada Puko acknowledged.

"Gamma, I wonder where the white devils are taking all these people on their big ships? I knew many of the people who were taken away and I have seen the pain and suffering on the families left behind. Every single day we hear another family holding their bellies and crying out in pain. Why Gamma? Tell me," she cried. "It does not hurt only that family Gamma, it hurts all of us."

Mada Puko did not know where to begin. The situation was not easily solved because there were so many tentacles to this wicked serpent.

"We have to do something Gamma; we can't just sit around and do nothing."

"It is good that you want to help my child, but remember that this situation did not start overnight and it will not be solved overnight or with the snap of the fingers. The system of kidnapping is well organized and firmly established in the society."

"Gamma, do you remember one morning, not long ago, you were telling me that the white devils would only stop coming and taking away our people when all our tribes refused to sell our people, and instead join forces to chase them away from our land?"

"Yes I remember my child, but the white devils are not the only ones to blame. We as a people are just as guilty. Greed and selfishness will cause us to do ugly things my child, ugly things."

Nanny scratched her head as she realized how complex the situation was and the great dilemma that the common folks had found themselves. Change would not be easy or readily accepted by many of the tribes, especially those that had depended upon this trade for so long.

Mada Puko knew what Nanny was thinking and although she liked her enthusiasm, she was worried that she might do something or say something to upset some people. She had taught her well, but that was as far as she could go. The girl had a mind of her own and she had proven over and over again that she was not afraid to use it.

"Gamma, you say that timing is everything! Well, when is the right time to fix this problem?"

"That is a difficult question my child because we don't control all the elements in the problem. What I mean to say is that I don't know that even if the ships stopped coming to our shores tomorrow, that the slavers would stop capturing our people and selling them," she tried to explain. "In some tribes the young men prefer to go out and plunder villages, capture people and sell them rather than cultivate the land; something that their ancestors had done for generations. The white devils now provide them with weapons and food in exchange for slaves. With these newly acquired weapons the young thugs are becoming more daring in their raids on villages, killing at random and taking whatever and whoever they choose. Sometimes they capture even the Chiefs and their families and sell them to the slavers. These criminals show no mercy and respect nobody; a far cry from the good old days when the elderly were honored. It is getting so bad now that some of these tribes are becoming more and more dependent on the white devils for their daily food; a real disgrace in a fruitful land like Africa."

Nanny observed that the society was not only losing its young men and women in record numbers but the community was quickly losing its ability to sustain itself. This was cause for serious concern. The society was imploding at a rapid rate and no one seemed to care.

One night in a dream Nanny saw the entire countryside looking bare and devastated. The people had stopped cultivating the land. Starvation was everywhere. It was every man for himself. No one shared what little they had. People walked around as if in a daze. Everyone was suffering. New diseases were crippling and killing the people. Hungry children, covered with sores and distended stomachs, lay on makeshift beds as helpless mothers waited for them to die. Many children were taking care of their younger siblings because their mothers and fathers were either captured by slavers or died from one of the new diseases.
Then she saw her village being attacked and plundered by a ruthless invading tribe from the North. Many of the young men, women and children who were healthy were hauled off into captivity. The chief and those people who they did not need were subsequently killed. The village was then burned to the ground.

Nanny jumped up out of her sleep, quickly ran to Mada Puko's room, woke her up and told her the dream. "What do you think is the meaning of this dream Gamma?" Nanny asked.

"I'm not surprised my child," Mada Puko said, now fully awake. "Things are getting from bad to worst. Our society is in grave danger and our ancestors are worried."

"But what can we do Gamma?" Nanny asked, somewhat bewildered.

"Well my child, the problem lies squarely with our leaders," Mada Puko began.

"Some Chiefs have ignored the problem for a long time because they are benefiting directly or indirectly from it. Many of them even have their own raiding parties who go out and capture innocent people and sell them to the slavers. Without our leaders denouncing the practice, the problem will persist and the society will continue to suffer."

"Then somebody needs to talk to these Chiefs, Gamma!" Nanny exclaimed, wringing her hands. "Somebody needs to tell them that time is running out for our young people, our community and our land."

Mada Puko thought for awhile then looked at Nanny and asked, "Would you like to be that somebody?"

"Me?" Nanny asked, with a surprised look on her face.

"Yes you," Mada Puko replied.

"We have a three-day Family of Chief's Conference coming up a week from tomorrow over at Cassia Gully Settlement. At these conferences all the Chiefs of the confederation come together to debate issues and develop plans that will benefit all our communities. Would you like me to get you on the program so that you can speak to them for a few minutes?"

"Yes Gamma!" Nanny shouted with excitement. "I would love that! The Chiefs need to know that they have the power to change the situation."

"Now my dear, take it slow," Mada Puko cautioned. "It will not be an easy sell. Remember, many of these Chiefs have invested heavily in the trade. Their economies are highly dependent on trade with the white devils. Don't be surprised if some of them jeer you or worse, walk out on your little speech. Are you prepared for that?"

"I'm not worried about that right now Gamma," Nanny said casually. "I believe that somebody needs to start the conversation, and that person might as well be me."

Nanny held Mada Puko's hands gentle as she said, "Gamma I love this land with all my heart and I don't like what I'm seeing right now. We're draining the land of all of our young, brilliant people in order to build up the white devil's lands, somewhere across the sea. It makes no sense Gamma!

No sense! So I will do whatever I can to help to turn things around," she said.

"I remember when I was a little girl you used to pray every day to Massa God to rid our land of the white devils. Do you believe that Massa God is listening to us Gamma? Why does he allow this to continue? Surely he must know that the white devils are evil and up to no good? So why doesn't he just destroy them forever, so that we can go back to living the way our ancestors used to?"

"Those are difficult questions my dear," Mada Puko said. "And I must admit that I don't know the answers. But what I do know is that Massa God will never gives us more than we can handle," she emphasized, gently patting Nanny on her back. "Ok," Mada Puko continued. "This is what I will do my child. Tomorrow I'll talk with the Chief about putting you on the program, as I always travel with him as part of his delegation. This will give you an opportunity to talk to all these very powerful leaders."

Nanny smiled and hugged her grandmother affectionately. Over the next couple of days, Nanny wrote her speech over and over again, making changes as she tried to frame her arguments to appeal to the various Chiefs in attendance. She reflected on what Mada Puko had said about those Chiefs who were in the trade itself. She chose her words very carefully so that she would not offend them. She remembered Mada Puko telling her that, 'you will catch more flies with honey than with vinegar.'

The night before the conference Nanny tossed and turned in her bed as she rehearsed her speech over and over in her mind.

'What if they walk out,' she thought. 'What if I freeze up on stage and no words come out?'

She wondered if she had bitten off more than she could chew this time.

Morning could not arrive soon enough for her. She was up at the crack of dawn and had everything packed for the long trip.

After a big breakfast, Nanny and Mada Puko joined the Chief and his delegation on the long journey. They arrived some time later to find Cassia Gully bustling with Chiefs and dignitaries from all the surrounding regions. People hurried to settle in and prepare for the opening ceremony.

Nanny was scheduled to speak that afternoon. As she looked around and saw the many powerful leaders she began to sweat all over. She held on tightly to her grandmother's hand for dear life, just like she did as a little girl when she was frightened.

Suddenly she heard a voice in her head saying,

"Nanny! Nanny, this is Mada Kuzo. Listen to me carefully my child; don't be afraid, you will be fine. I will be standing right beside you all the time. What you have to say is very important for everybody to hear. Our nation is in turmoil. We over on this side are very worried about the kidnappings and sale of our people, and we see you as the only one trying to do something about it; and we appreciate it. We will do everything we can to support you."

"Ok Mada Kuzo," Nanny said, responding to her. "I'm so glad that you've come. I thought that you had forgotten us."

"I will never abandon you my child," Mada Kuzo reminded her. "You know that I love you very much."

Just then Nanny heard her name being called to go up on stage. Before she stood up to walk up on the stage, she quietly leaned over to Mada Puko and whispered, "Mada Kuzo is here! She will be on stage with me," gently squeezing her hand.

"Thank Massa God," Mada Puko whispered, smiling back at her.

Nanny began her speech by extending greeting to the Chiefs and thanking them for allowing her to speak. She then recounted a joke about Chiefs to great laughter. That got their attention and made her more relaxed as well.

First, she invited her audience to think back to a time before the white people arrived in their big ships. She spoke of a time when everyone lived in peace and harmony. Food was plentiful. Tribes respected each other and did legitimate trading. People actually liked each other and cared for one another.

"Those were the good old days of our ancestors; where peace and prosperity reigned for thousands of years."

After, she encouraged them to skip to the arrival of the white people. She painted a grim picture of mistrust, fear and suspicion among the people. She debunked the myth that trading in human lives was good for business. She then delved into the agony of human trafficking. She brought to light the ugly side of the trade, the side that no one wanted to talk about.

Next, she took them on a journey into the future where she described a society made up mostly of the very young and the very old, where people sat around starving because no one was willing or able to work the land, a society that was unable to feed itself and just waited on the big ships from across the sea to bring them their food. She made the analogy of this new society as a crocodile eating its tail to survive.

In closing Nanny challenged her audience to face the facts and resist the temptation to do what was easy; but instead to think of the long term effects on their communities, and do what was right or face a dismal future for their children and grandchildren.

At the end of the speech, Nanny was given a standing ovation. The audience clapped and cheered. This was the first time that some of them had heard the facts as she had presented it. Mada Puko was so proud of her granddaughter. Everyone said that she would be the next Mada after Mada Puko.

However, not everyone was happy with what Nanny was expounding. Some Chiefs now thought that it was a big mistake to have given this little girl permission to speak. They thought that she was just going to go up on stage, say a few words, give them a bunch of laughs, and then they would get back to the business at hand. But what she had done was to put that nonsense into the heads of those bleeding heart Chiefs. 'Something had to be done to nip it in the bud,' they ruminated

For the next two days Nanny became extremely busy; answering questions, talking to various heads of tribes and conducting workshops. She felt like she was making progress and that the leaders were actually listening.

At the end of the conference, Nanny was quite exhausted but satisfied with the progress that she had made. She left with a new found hope that some leaders were beginning to understand the ramification of doing business as usual. She looked forward to working with many of them in the coming weeks.

On the way home Mada Puko, the Chief and the other delegates were in high spirit. They had accomplished many of the things that they had set out to achieve at the conference.

Suddenly, as they drew near to the village they saw big black plumes

37

of smoke rising in the air. Mada Puko felt a giant knot in her stomach. Everyone in the delegation became worried for their family. The smoke grew thicker as they came nearer.

As the village came into view, there was a collective gasp. Every hut was on fire!

Chapter 5

The entire village was deserted. No one was in sight. Dead bodies lay all around; in the village square, on the road, and in the burnt out huts. Some bodies were badly damaged; some had missing limbs, while others were decapitated. Blood was everywhere.

The Chief's palace was burned to the ground and all of the staff was dead. Nanny ran over to Mada Puko's hut and found that it too was burnt to the ground. She tried desperately to salvage a few valuables items but her grandmother held her back.

"It's no use my child, everything is gone," Mada Puko said. "Run over to your parent's hut and see if anybody is alive." Nanny ran quickly over to her parent's burning hut to find her mother and father both dead. She searched desperately for her five brothers but they were nowhere to be found. Then it dawned on her; oh no! The boys, young! Sold to the slavers!

"Gamma, come quickly!" Nanny shouted. "Mother and father are both dead and I don't see Cudjoe, Accompong and the rest of the boys. It looks like they were kidnapped. Gamma what are we going to do?" Nanny cried out loudly, holding her stomach.

"Whoever did this will pay dearly," she promised.

Mada Puko hugged her tightly and tried to console her. "I know how you feel my child," she said. "It hurts so much, but we have to help the people who are still alive. Come; let's join the Chief and his team. We have to spread out and search for survivors."

As they searched among the rubble they found an old lady lying in a pool of blood at the back of a partially burnt out hut.

"What happened Elder Qoeji?" Mada Puko inquired, cradling her blooded head into her lap.

"Water!" the old lady whispered, barely holding up. Mada Puko beckoned to Nanny to bring over some water for her.

"Massa God bless you," she whispered, gasping for air between sips. "They came out of nowhere. A lot of them with muskets shooting, wielding machetes and spears," she tried to explain.

"Who they didn't murder, they took with them in chains. Wicked! Wicked! They showed no mercy! No mercy," was her last words. She slowly leaned her head to one side, and was gone. Mada Puko gently passed her hand over her eyes and closed them before wrapping the body in cloth.

Nanny turned to Mada Puko and cried, "I have to go after these slavers and bring back Cudjoe and the others before they sell them to the white devils!"

"But you can't go all by yourself Nanny. It could be dangerous," Mada Puko protested.

"I'll be fine Gamma, I'll be careful. I have to find them! They are the only family I have left beside you."

Mada Puko thought for a moment then said, "Ok my child, Massa God go with you; go and find your brothers, but be careful."

"I will Gamma," Nanny promised, and with that she slipped away. Moments later, she was flying through the air towards the coast.

Tears flowed down her face as she thought about her brothers, from the oldest Cudjoe to the youngest Quao; suffering at the hands of those brutal slavers. She wondered if they were together or were separated. And young Quao, so sweet and gentle, her favorite little brother, she was so worried about him. Her mind flashed back to when they were kids. She was the one who played with him most of the time when he was a baby. She enjoyed feeding, bathing and cleaning up after him. Her mother chided her sometimes for pampering the boy so much, but she merely smiled and said that he was hers.

As they grew older their relationship grew even closer. He visited her everyday at Mada Puko's house and made sure that she was alright. She remembered speaking to him on the day that she was leaving for the conference. He was so worried for her safety and wanted to accompany her. She smiled when she thought how protective he was of her. He acted as if he was the older sibling and needed to protect her.

As Nanny scanned the skyline for signs of the slavers, she thought back on the good times she had had with her brothers. Although she spent most of her time living at Mada Puko's home, she was never far away from her brothers and played with them regularly. She was sometimes called a tom boy because she wanted to play all sports and go on hunts in the bush with the boys. She was very competitive and refused to give up even when she was facing defeat. The boys respected her for this and eventually everyone wanted her on their team.

She thought about Cudjoe whom she admired a lot. He was the strong one. The one you could depend on to protect your back. He was loyal but very outspoken. Many times he got into trouble with their mother because he told it like he saw it. Then there was Accompong, the joker of the pack. He was able to see the humor in everything. No one around him could remain sad for long. He always had the whole family laughing whenever they met at family functions. He was also a great story teller. He told tribal stories to kids through comedy.

When Nanny thought of all the brilliant people of the tribe who were killed or now captured and on their way to be sold, a flood of hatred welled up in her heart.

"When will this madness end?" she questioned. "How can we ever build a society that will take care of itself? We're losing our brightest minds, our artists, our musicians, our builders, our hunters, our leaders, our mothers, our fathers, our religious leaders, everybody we need to make our tribe prosperous. This is an evil system, very evil. Who decided that this was our destiny? Who gave anyone the right to subject another person to untold suffering? Someone needs to stand up for the weak." Through clenched teeth Nanny cried, "I have to do something about this. Something needs to change. Someone needs to strike back at the heart of the white devil's society. I need to find their leaders and tell them that what they're doing to our people is wrong. I have to convince them to change their ways. Now, if they refuse to listen then we will bring the war to them." The more Nanny thought about it the more she knew what she had to do.

She thought about Mada Puko and how she would manage without her. But she knew that this had to be done.

Suddenly, looking ahead, she saw a long line of men and women with their hands tied behind their backs and wooden forked poles tied together linking their necks. The children, with their hands tied, walked obediently beside their parents. Some mothers had their babies wrapped in cloth tied to their waist.

The kidnappers were heavily armed with muskets and spears. Some had whips which they used without mercy on those people who walked too slowly.

As Nanny drew nearer to the long line of captives, she could hear the cracking of the whips and the wailing of the people. The children cried openly and held onto their mothers for dear life. Some kidnappers took their role very seriously, keeping guard with their muskets and leading the captives at a fast pace while others laughed and joked around as they inflicted pain on the helpless people.

Nanny wept as she witnessed the suffering of her people. She felt the urge to destroy the kidnappers and free her people but she knew that this was not the right time. She remembered Mada Puko telling her that 'timing made the difference between success and failure.'

She swooped down from the sky and circled the chain gang in search of Cudjoe and the rest of her brothers, but they were nowhere in sight. She wasn't sure if she should rejoice or be sad because she didn't know if she would be able to hold back if she saw any of those kidnappers abusing any of her brothers, especially Quao. She just knew that, that would not be good because she would probably lose her temper and destroy all of them; which would ultimately wreck her plan. She wondered if they were farther east of this group or they were already placed on the ship. She hurried along in the direction of the coast scanning the surrounding landscape for any signs of the captives.

At the beach, Nanny couldn't believe what she was seeing. A large number of men and women bound in chains; some without even a stitch of clothes were waiting by the water's edge to be placed into small boats. The crude little canoes packed with captives made several trips out to the big ship anchored outside the harbor.

The enormous, rust colored ship looked creepy and menacing. Nanny sensed a heavy presence of death and suffering surrounding the vessel. On board she felt the presence of hundreds of ancestral spirits moaning and groaning.

'The ship is well haunted and the white devils them don't even know it,' Nanny grinned to herself.

Meanwhile the kidnappers moved guardedly around the captives using their whips occasionally to get some of them to sit quietly and wait. Nanny searched everywhere for her brothers but they were nowhere in sight.

"They must be on that big ship already," she uttered in disgust. She took a deep breath and looked towards the ship.

'The time has come for me to meet the white devils in his world,' she said to herself as she flew out to the ship and eventually landed on the main mast.

"Then, were you planning to leave without saying goodbye girl?" a smiling Mada Kuzo asked.

Nanny jumped with fright when she saw her great-grandmother.

"No! No! Mada Kuzo, I wouldn't do a thing like that." Nanny uttered sheepishly.

"Of course you wouldn't, because your grandmother just sent me to take you back home. She wanted to come herself but she was too busy burying the dead and taking care of the living. She said that she needed your help badly at home, but I believe that deep down she is worried that you're too young to face the white devils all by yourself."

"But I would not be alone, Mada Kuzo!" Nanny replied, trying to sound convincing.

"I know that you will be with me all the time and if I get into any trouble I know I only have to call on you. Am I not right Mada Kuzo?" Nanny inquired, looking like the little girl again.

"I suppose so," Mada Kuzo replied reluctantly, knowing full well that the girl had made up her mind to go after the white devils and there was nothing that she or Mada Puko could say to change her mind.

Mada Kuzo then decided that it was time to have a serious talk with the girl.

"You might think that you're here to avenge only your brothers, but it is much bigger than that my child. You might be asking yourself why you

43

were given so many powers. Right now you could destroy all these white devils on this ship with the snap of your fingers. The poor fools wouldn't know what hit them," she laughed.

"But listen, the point I am making is that you have been given these awesome powers by your ancestors for a reason. That's right, you were chosen by your ancestors long before you were born. You were chosen to help to bring an end to this evil system of slavery. Yes, you have more powers at your command than you can ever imagine. But with it comes so much responsibility my child. Look over there to the east, what do you see?" Mada Kuzo directed.

"Wow!" Nanny exclaimed. "Are they for real?" she asked, when she saw a legion of warriors assembled on the hillside.

"Look over there to the west, what do you see?" Mada Kuzo continued.

"Thousands of warriors!" Nanny exclaimed.

"Look to the north, what do you see?"

"Wow! Many, many warriors!" Nanny cried.

"Look to the south, what do you see?"

"Again, more warriors! I'm beginning to get the picture Mada Kuzo!" she said excitedly.

"Yes child, they're all here at your command ready to help you. Just call on them like you call on me and they will respond."

"I've always wondered why I got it and my brothers didn't," Nanny volunteered.

"You didn't have to do anything for it my pet. We chose you before you were born," Mada Kuzo reassured her.

"We knew that this day would come when we would have to give you this talk," Mada Kuzo said.

"You've been a very good child and we're so proud of you. Your ancestors foretold these times long ago, and in their wisdom, recognized the need to find someone to lead our people out of bondage and speed up the process to bring an end to the suffering. Everything is working according to plan. You might notice that among many of the legions of warriors were white people, yes white people! Not white devils like those down on the deck of this ship. These white people you will meet will be part of the solution instead of part of the problem. So remember that my child. Some of these white people you will meet will genuinely want this brutality to end just as much as we do; so don't ignore them, they will be your allies, work with them and give them your support. But for the ones like those on this ship; use your powers as you wish," she said firmly.

"Baby," she continued. "You have a lot of work ahead of you. You will have to restore pride back into our people who are now being taken across the seas. The white devils treat them like wild animals; and they will remain a minority in the white devils' world for a very long time and suffer though a system that will tell them who they are and what they are capable of doing. They will live in confusion and lose their faith in humanity and will need some capable persons like you to get them through the valley," she told Nanny.

"And do you want to know something my pet? The funny thing about all this, is that the white devils don't realize that change is coming and that they will have to come to terms with the rising tide of our people in their midst. They're taking all of our brilliant minds into their lands and they don't expect our people to shine wherever they are. We're a great people my child, and we will exceed all limitations placed on us. We will control their sports, their music, their foods and their entertainment. We will excel in knowledge and make some amazing discoveries to help mankind," she continued. "Baby girl, the white devils meant us evil, but our people will show them that they can't keep us down; we are overcomers. It will take many generations my child, but our people will eventually rule the white devil's lands and take our rightful place in that society," she smiled.

"A time is coming in the future my baby, when our people will become the majority in the white devil's land. What they're doing right now; stealing all our greatest minds and taking them to their land to provide cheap labor is a mistake, a grave mistake, and they will pay dearly for it in the years to come," she said, with confidence.

"One more thing my child, be patient with your people, they've been through a lot, and they won't know who to trust," she cautioned.

"My pet you will be known throughout the whole world long after you're dead and gone. They will write poems about you and your people. They will sing songs about you. Kings and Queens will hear about you. Scholars will study your methods. Your name will be on the lips of storytellers for generations to come."

Nanny sat quietly, thinking about all that Mada Kuzo had said.

"Tell me Mada Kuzo," Nanny asked. "Why did our ancestors wait so long to send somebody to help our people?"

"Timing my child, timing is everything. Nothing happens before the time," Mada Kuzo commented.

"Ok girlie, let's go down on the deck and find your brothers; we will continue this conversation another time."

Chapter 6

The ship was old and rickety like it had seen better days. The giant sails now lowered, flapped obediently in the warm West African breeze, minding its own business as the human misery played out around the ship. The wooden deck was scrubbed clean. Sailors in wide brimmed hats competently fixed ropes in place, adjusted the masts and mended the sails. Some sailors briskly brought on water in round wooden barrels and stacked them away in the bottom of the ship. Standing alert all around the deck were burly guards with muskets and swords. Some looked towards the shore, keeping an eye on the arriving boat loads of captives while others paid special attention to the activities on deck. A short middle aged man dressed in white, with a colorful wide brimmed hat, stood on the deck with a long telescope in hand looking towards the land.

"Who is that one in the full white clothes and pretty, pretty hat Gramma?" Nanny asked Mada Kuzo.

"You don't have to whisper my pet because nobody can see or hear you," Mada Kuzo reminded her. "That is the man in charge; they call him the Captain," Mada Kuzo explained.

"Do you see how he is looking into that long shiny thing there? It is called a telescope. He is checking to see if any more boats are coming. If he doesn't see any more out there and there are no more captives coming down the path, he will begin getting ready to leave. They don't like to stay too long tied up around here because when they anchor in the bay they are like sitting ducks. They prefer to be out on the open seas with their illegal cargo."

Moaning and groaning filled the deck as the people suffered immensely. The men, with only a piece of cloth around their waist had their hands tied behind their backs and their legs shackled in iron. Each new arrival was held down by one or two crew members while another one fitted the iron onto their feet and hands. After being fitted with their irons, the captives were marched in a single file downstairs to the holding area, under the watchful eyes of the guards. Some men cried out in agony, not caring who was listening, as the whips cracked on their backs and they are shoved and kicked for no apparent reason. The white slaver with the huge, black whip in hand, laughed haughtily as he inflicted the brutal punishment on the men.

"I think I would lose it Gramma if I saw that man whipping any of my brothers and laughing like a stupid hyena on top of it."

"Let's go downstairs my pet," Mada Kuzo indicated, ushering Nanny away from the dreadful conditions on deck, "But don't be too alarmed at what you will see down there," she cautioned, trying to prepare Nanny for what was to come.

As they sauntered down stairs Nanny felt the thick, heavy, murky heat quickly wrapping around her body and suffocating her. The strong, foul smell of stale urine and feces was more than Nanny could take. Although Mada Kuzo had tried to warn her, there was no way that she could have been prepared for this. She retched uncontrollably as all of her insides screamed to come out. In all her years working with the sick and the dying, she was still not prepared for this squalor. She held her breath for a while covering her nose to keep out the stench, but this was only a temporary fix. She knew however that she had to adjust quickly to this bizarre reality if she was to be of any use to her brothers and these desperate men.

"Relax my child, you will soon get used to it. The same thing happened to me the first time I came down here. I nearly left my whole insides on the floor," she smiled.

"So you have been here before?" Nanny asked surprised.

"Oh yes, I've been down here before, but that is a long story which I will tell you about one day. Right now, let's go and find your brothers."

As Nanny surveyed the poorly lit hold she was shocked at what she saw. The ceiling was no more than six feet high with three levels of shelves fastened to the wall. The men were chained hands and feet and packed so tightly together that they had to be lying on their sides all the time; like sardines in a tin.

The nonstop cries of agony were unbearable. The moaning and groaning! The retching! The vomiting! The urinating! The defecating on themselves! Utter nastiness!

Some men cried out for water, while others called out to their Gods to come and rescue them. A few looked like they were going out of their minds, rolling their eyes around in their heads as they banged their bleeding heads continuously on the irons, the poles, the walls or any other hard surface they could find.

As Nanny walked around she saw some of the men that she had grown up with; their faces bathed in sweat, and showing genuine fear and panic.

"Oh my God Mada Kuzo, they won't make it! They will all die before they reach the white devil's land," Nanny exclaimed, with her heart pounding like it wanted to jump out of her chest, while tears ran down her cheeks. "This is cruelty! This is inhumane! This is unacceptable! They can't treat human beings like this! This is wickedness!" she cried.

"Calm down child," Mada Kuzo chastised her sternly.

"Get a grip! Look!" she said harshly; and then paused when she saw the shock and horror on Nanny's face, and felt her trembling uncontrollably. She quickly lowered her voice and said, "I'm so sorry for being so hard on you my pet," she apologized. "I didn't know that it would affect you so much. Forgive the old lady," she said with a weak smile. "But Nanny, please listen to me carefully, this is very important."

She now had Nanny's full attention. 'Mada Kuzo never calls me by my real name, it is always child, baby, pet or something else but not Nanny, so this must be very important,' she thought.

"Some of these poor souls will die on the high seas my pet; it is a fact of life, but most of them will make it. The healthy ones will make it for sure while the sick and the weak ones might not. That is it plain and simple. But never forget that we Africans are a very resilient race of people and we will do whatever it takes to survive. Don't you worry too much, ok?"

"Yes Gramma," Nanny replied, trying to make the adjustment.

"And another thing, with you travelling with them everything should be fine. You take care of the big things and the little things will take care of themselves. Do you understand?"

"Yes Gramma," Nanny said, wiping her tears with the back of her hand.

"Look over there to your right my pet," Mada Kuzo pointed. "There is Cudjoe, and Accompong, then look over there to your left, there they are: Johnny, Cuffy, and Quao. Let's go over to them. They're dying to see a friendly face." Then she stopped Nanny abruptly in her tracks and said, "Now my dear, I don't want you to go over there to meet them with any crying. They have enough trouble on their plates right now to handle any more. Just greet them like everything is not all that bad, understand pet?"

"Yes Gramma," Nanny said, trying her best to mask her true feelings.

As Nanny approached them from afar, a feeling of joy came over her; all the darkness and evil seemed to melt away like fat in the fire. She walked towards them, then stopped abruptly and looked back at Mada Kuzo.

"Can we become visible so that I can hug them properly and let them know that we're here? Can I? Can I?" she asked, sounding like a little girl begging to pet an adorable puppy.

Mada kuzo saw how happy and excited the girl was and knew that she couldn't say no. "Go ahead my pet, I'll be right over here. They won't know that I'm here."

Nanny nervously approached her brothers, being careful not to startle them. Her heart was breaking into a million pieces as she observed the dehumanizing conditions that the boys were in. They were packed so tightly that they looked like they were suffocating. Nanny's heart skipped a beat when she saw her youngest brother Quao. He looked the worse of the brothers. He looked weak, dehydrated, pitiful and confused as he moaned quietly to himself.

Nanny drew near to him and tried to cheer him up.

"Boy! You're not going to die on me now and let the white devils win, are you?"

Quao looked up and gasped, looking like he had seen a ghost.

"Shhh!" Nanny said, putting her finger to her lips. "Don't worry, I'm here now," she whispered with a broad smile.

"Shhhh!" Nanny put her finger to her lips to Johnny and Cuffy and the other men nearby, in chains. She hugged Quao and they both started to sob quietly. Then she went over to Johnny and cried with him, and then with Cuffy, she did the same. Next, it was Cudjoe's turn. They hugged and cried for a long time. "I'm here now brother; don't talk now, we will talk later." Finally it was Accompong's turn. They laughed and they cried for some time.

"I told that girl not to go over there and burden them down with crying and what is the first thing that she did? Cry, even more than the boys," Mada Kuzo laughed. But she had to admit that the girl loved her brothers so much that she couldn't help it; plus it was a good remedy for the boys to see that they were not abandoned and that someone out there really cared about them.

For the next hour, Nanny went over to each brother again and again; hugging and kissing them and telling them how much she loved them and would take good care of them on the voyage. She asked them what they needed and their first request was, as was expected, to jokingly ask to be set free. Nanny just wished that she could have granted them their requests, but she knew that she had to stick to the plan.

Suddenly the ship began to rock.

"I think we're moving!" a big strong broad shouldered man shouted,

"We're moving! The boat is moving! We're all going to die!"

"Stop saying that!" another man shouted. People began weeping and wailing loudly.

A short, slightly balding man with a scraggly beard banged his head against the wall until it bled as he attempted to kill himself.

Nanny became worried for the men. They were obviously troubled by their hopeless predicament. She had to do something fast, anything to refocus their attention. She remembered her grandmother blowing a cool breeze over the badly injured warriors back home to calm them down.

Nanny slowly blew a cool breeze over the men, which eventually lowered the high temperature in the hold. Then she whistled a soothing tune to quiet them down. Soon the men began to relax, some mumbling their prayers to themselves while others just closed their eyes and tried to think of more pleasant times.

Cudjoe and his brothers were very happy to see their sister but they had so many questions for her. They knew that she was special and followed their grandmother everywhere she went. But they were puzzled as to how she got on board without the guards seeing her, and although they loved her, they wondered why she wanted to leave Mada Puko. And most importantly, how she would avoid being discovered throughout the voyage.

Nanny, sensing their questions and concerns strolled over to Cudjoe and whispered that she would explain everything later in the night when everyone was asleep. Then she noticed an open wound on his knee dripping with blood. She slowly rubbed her hands together and gently covered the wound. Instantly the bleeding stopped and the healing began.

"Thanks Sis, I always knew that you were special; from you were a little girl," Cudjoe joked. "But now I know without a doubt that you're for real." Nanny smiled and patted his head.

For the next couple of hours, Nanny went around the hold healing the sick and the wounded and encouraging others. As she stopped by some of the men, they thanked her immensely and told her how wonderful she was. Some asked her if she was a God, to which she lovingly replied that she was not. Others asked for her name but she would not tell them for fear that she would put her brothers in danger. Nanny always reminded them not to tell anyone of her presence.

Late during the night, a short stocky guard with a small lantern came down to the hold to check on the men. They all kept quiet and some even pretended to be asleep. He looked around the room thoroughly then checked the chains on some of the men. Seemingly satisfied, he turned and went back upstairs.

Cudjoe and the men were very worried for Nanny. They wondered where she was hiding. The guard had searched the place thoroughly without finding her. They didn't want to imagine what would have happened to her if she was caught. After the guard left they all looked around desperately for her. Cudjoe called out to her in a low nervous voice.

"Mada! Mada! are you there?"
Nanny suddenly stepped from behind a column at the far end of the hold, smiling broadly.

"We were worried for you," Cudjoe said.

"Yes Mada, we were all worried for you," the men declared. But no one asked her where she went.

"Is everybody ok?" Nanny asked.

"Yes," they affirmed.

"Thanks for your concern, but I'm fine, don't worry too much about me because I can take care of myself," she reassured them.
"By the way men, I'm going over to check on the women now. I'll be back in a short while."

"Thank you, that's a good idea," a broad shouldered man said. "My wife is over there, and she is pregnant."

"What's your name?" Nanny asked.

"Brugio," replied the man.

"Don't worry Brugio, I'll check upon her," she promised.

Nanny casually walked out the door and up the stairs towards the deck. She lifted the trap door and quietly came out. She stealthily walked past the lone guard on duty at that time of the night and went over to the stairs leading down to the women's quarters. She stopped at the top of the stairs and looked back to see if anyone was watching. With no one there, she quietly lifted the trap door leading down to the hold. Nanny slowly closed it behind her and walked downstairs to meet the women.

The hot thick murky air intermingled with the strong, foul smell of stale urine and feces were just as nauseating as over at the men quarters.
The hold was just as cramped. The women slept peacefully on the floor, some with their babies close beside them while others slept on the second level shelves. Like the men, they only had a cloth tied around their waist leaving their breasts exposed. However, unlike the men's quarters, there were no chains or shackles in sight. Nanny felt troubled at the sight of the women. They seemed so helpless.

'What will happen to these children?' she thought.
Then she saw some women from her village and her heart sank even further.

She quietly strolled over and sat beside a dear old friend of her mother's, busy breast-feeding her baby.

"Is how that baby eats so much, Miss Birdey?" Nanny joked, with a broad smile.

"Nanny is that you girl?" Miss Birdey asked, opening her eyes wide in amazement.

"Yes Miss Birdey, it's me Nanny. How are they treating you?" Instantly the woman began crying her eyes out.

"Shhhh! Miss Birdey," Nanny cautioned, putting her finger to her lips. "Do you want to bring the whole of them down here?"

"What is going to happen to us Nanny?" she asked. Suddenly she stopped crying, looked intently at Nanny and asked, "Nanny what are you doing here? And why are you dressed like that?" Nanny looked Miss Birdey squarely into her face and replied, "I'm here to help you ladies. Nobody will hurt anyone of you as long as I'm here."

"I think you're too late," Miss Birdey said. "Look over there on the floor is Miss Chunny's granddaughter. They just brought her back."

"Back from where?" Nanny asked, looking down at the young girl curled up in a fetal position, holding her stomach and weeping quietly. Miss Birdey had tears rolling down her face. She wiped her eyes with the back of her hand and blew her nose. Looking away from Nanny, she shook her head over and over again in disgust. After hesitating for some time, she began to speak in a trembling voice, "They come here for the little young girls in the night and take them away and rape them. What are we going to do Nanny? So every night they're going to come and take away our young girls and rape them? Massa God help us! These white devils are never satisfied. They want everything that we Africans have."

"Don't worry Miss Birdey," Nanny said. "I will deal with them, mark my words. After tonight they will dare not come down here and touch one of these girls."

"And how do you plan to stop them when they have weapons?" Miss Birdey asked.

"I will deal with them Miss Birdey, don't you worry about that. They're going to wish that they never set eyes on these young girls."

The next day, the men and women were kept in their respective holds, with the men in irons all the while. The captain wanted to reach open seas before bringing them up on deck to get some fresh air. Many of the men had sores on their ankles where the iron had chafed their skin. They were fed only once and their stomachs were rumbling, but none of the crew seemed to care. Some guards came down to the hold to look around a few times during the day and to check the irons; that's it. When they came down, Nanny noticed that they always covered their noses and couldn't wait to leave.

Nanny devoted most of the day in the hold to her brothers and the men. They told her over and over how hungry they were and she promised that she would bring them food and water that night. She worked non-stop taking care of the sick, healing wounds and relieving those in pain.

As the evening turned to night, Nanny hinted to her brothers that something big was happening over at the women's quarters that she had to take care of; promising to tell them the details later. She quietly crept past the guards on deck and walked slowly down the stairs to the women's quarters to find all the women visibly upset and worried. Some were crying and wringing their hands in panic while one middle aged woman in a corner had a huge gash on her forehead caused by banging her head against the wall.

When they saw Nanny they rushed towards her; everyone talking at the same time. Nanny put her finger to her lips, instructing them to be quiet so that the guards would not hear the commotion and come down to investigate.

"Ladies, ladies! One at a time; what's wrong?" she inquired.

"They took a little young girl already! What're we going to do?" a little lady holding her baby in her arms, asked loudly.

"Don't worry, I will find her and bring her back safely, then I will teach these white devils a lesson," Nanny said between clenched teeth, then quickly disappeared.

Nanny moved speedily around the ship to find the girl, without making the crew any wiser. She knew that time was against her. The more time elapsed the more danger the girl was in. Eventually she walked into a room and heard a little girl crying in a corner. She hurried towards the sound and found a big bald burly man with a whip in his hand whipping a nude little girl, no more than twelve years old, and telling her to be quiet.

An extreme anger came over Nanny when she saw the little child in so much pain that she instantly transformed into a large two hundred pounds leopard.

The beast fixed its eyes on the man and let out a low deep throaty growl showing off its strong powerful teeth. The man nervously dropped his whip and his soaked pants fell down around his ankles. Large beads of sweat quickly formed on his forehead. The leopard continued its deep growl as it slowly walked towards the man. He froze, not knowing what to do next and wondering if he was dreaming. He moved very slowly away from the girl and walked backwards towards the door. The leopard continued to growl while slowly walking towards him. The man slowly reached down to grab up his pants from his ankles but toppled over on the ground. The beast pounced towards him with a vicious growl, showing her sharp teeth, and then stopped abruptly, a few inches from his crotch. The man cried out in panic and quickly scrambled to get away. He tried several times to get up from the floor but fell down repeatedly.

He staggered around clumsily, at the same time backing away from the gruesome beast. As the leopard advanced he timidly backed away. He kept walking backwards slowly up onto the deck and towards the rails, trying desperately to keep his distance. Eventually the petrified man reached the rail. He stopped and looked below at the dark cold waters of the ocean. He contemplated for a few seconds then gingerly climbed the rail as the enormous beast skinned its teeth and growled threateningly at him. When he reached the top of the rail he paused and as he was about to jump overboard the leopard suddenly disappeared! He blinked his eyes and wiped the sweat from his forehead with the back of his hand. He slowly climbed down from the rail and sat shaking uncontrollably on the floor wondering what had just happened.

He looked around anxiously but no one was in sight. The deck was deserted except for a tiny light in a window away off. He realized then and there that if he had jumped overboard no one would have missed him until in the morning, and by then the ship would have been miles away. He wondered if the beast was there to protect the little girl. 'Could these miserable Africans have a guardian angel?' he wondered. Should he tell the others? Would he be ridiculed by everyone?' It was no secret that he was a heavy drinker and could be violent when he was drunk. Would they think that he was hallucinating?

After much thought, he decided to keep it a secret from the other crew members and hoped that this was only an isolated incidence. He slowly rose from the floor and cautiously walked towards his quarters where he dropped to his knees and searched under his bed for the half bottle of rum he had hidden from his roommate. After much effort, he eventually found the bottle. He raised it to his parched lips and didn't stop until it was empty. Moments later he dropped on his bed and was out like a light, with his boots on.

Nanny quickly returned to the room to find the girl in shock. She comforted her and assisted her back to the hold. When the women saw them together they rejoiced and thanked Nanny, but wondered if this was the end of the matter.

The little girl quickly regained her composure and began telling her story. She spoke about the cruel rapist and how terrified he was when the leopard showed up. Nanny looked on with admiration as the women laughed until they cried.

"He wet himself," the girl said giggling.

"Serve him right," said one mother, breast feeding her baby.

"So what do you think happened to the rapist?" another woman asked.

"I don't know," the girl replied. "All I know is that the beast fixed his business for good."

All the women suspected that Nanny was the one who had changed into the leopard but no one was brave enough to ask.

Nanny was happy that she was able to save the little girl.

'Tonight was a good night for the women,' she thought. They had won a small victory. This was the first time that she had seen them in such a high spirit. The little girl spoke eloquently and was a good storyteller. Nanny wondered what great contribution this little girl would have made to her people if she had remained with her tribe.

'What a waste of humanity,' she thought. This made her even more determined to save these young girls from the monsters upstairs.

After leaving the women Nanny remembered that the men were hungry and she had promised to bring them some food. She hurried down into the belly of the ship and started searching around for the storeroom.

Eventually she opened a door to reveal a large supply of food. The shelves were stacked from floor to ceiling.

"Wow! They have enough food here to feed a whole army," she said to herself.

"So why are they not feeding the people? What are they saving it for? This is wickedness. The people need to be fed and I'm going to make sure of that." So for the next few hours she collected food from the storeroom and took it to both the men and the women. After eating, everyone was in a jovial mood; quietly laughing, singing and telling stories, just like they would back home in the village.

For the next couple of nights, Nanny transformed into the beast and sat at the bottom of the stairs leading down to the ladies quarters. She let out her deep ferocious growl displaying her vicious teeth whenever any man tried to enter. Like the good shepherd protecting her sheep from the hungry wolves, Nanny would protect these women from those wretched perverts.

One night, five guards with muskets in hand went down into the hold looking for the leopard. They searched everywhere from top to bottom, but the animal was nowhere to be found.

They tried to question the women if they had seen the animal, but they pretended not to understand. After the men left the women all had a haughty laugh. So the nights became peaceful and the women slept well knowing that the leopard was at the bottom of the stairs protecting them.

Over the next few days the weather was great; there was not a cloud in the sky. All around, as far as the eyes could see was water. The captain finally decided that the captives should be brought up on deck to get some fresh air and exercise. When the men and women heard this, they became very excited. At last they would be able to see the outside world and breathe some fresh clean air for a change.

The men's shackles were checked carefully before they were led upstairs on deck. They shuddered in pain as the bright light hit their tender pupils. The warmth of the sun on their bodies and the salty smell of the ocean felt refreshing. After the men were settled in, the women and children were led up on deck. They all sat quietly on the floor and enjoyed the sunshine and the fresh air blowing off the ocean. Mothers called out sternly after their children to stop them from wondering around; for fear that they might be whipped by the guards.

Nanny sat quietly with the women and listened while they talked to avoid drawing attention to herself. She had warned the ladies not to draw too much attention to her as this could be dangerous. The men and women spent the entire day on deck enjoying the wonderful weather.

The guards initiated an exercise program for the captives by persuading them to standing up and dance. To get them started, the guards began clapping their hands and stomping their feet to a lively beat, while some banged on pots and pans.

At first only the very young kids took part. Then the teenagers began shaking their feet to the beat. Before long they were all jumping up and down and rocking to the rhythm. Next, the parents joined their children. Finally the adults got involved and broad smiles and laughter could be heard all around the deck.

For those men and women who refused to dance, the guards threatened them with the whip. That was all that was needed to get everybody, including Nanny, dancing to the strange beat of the ship crew.

Dancing became a regular routine whenever the captives were on deck. After a few days, the men and women took over, singing their own tribal songs and knocking their shackles to their own beat.

The young people looked forward to these times because it relieved the boredom of the trip, plus it allowed them the opportunity to create their very own music for the enjoyment of everyone, including the crew.

The crew liked when they danced because the whole lot was not as grumpy when they went back into the hold in the evening. The adults also enjoyed the exercise too because they slept better in the night.

However, Nanny found that she had to guard the girls more closely on the nights following their dancing on deck. The white devils would be out in force to take away the girls that they had seen that day and had tagged for later conquest. But they abandoned the idea very quickly when they saw the blood thirsty beast blocking the entrance to the hold.

The worse days were the ones when the weather was bad or the sea was rough. The men and women all stayed below the entire time.

In the last three weeks of the voyage conditions in the holds became unbearable. The seas became very choppy as the waves climbed higher and higher. Everyone realized that they were now in new seas because conditions were changing so rapidly. Some days the guards would take the captives on deck for only a few hours before they would have to be taken back to the hold because so many of them were sea sick and weak from the continuous retching and puking. Many of them did not want to dance on deck anymore and the guards did not insist. At least they were not starving because Nanny made it her duty to visit the storeroom every other night.

One night while she was in the store room, Mada Kuzo appeared to her and told her that a major storm was heading their way but the Captain of the ship didn't know about it. She informed Nanny that the waves were gigantic and would cover the ship.

"Get extra food tonight for the people Nanny, because most of it will be destroyed and there might not be much left. Tell them to make sure that they eat up the food," Mada Kuzo advised.

"But Gramma, if they eat too much food now, won't they get sick?" Nanny asked.

"Maybe, but they're going to need some kind of nourishment in their bodies anyway. Now listen carefully Nanny!" Mada Kuzo said, quickly changing the subject. "The next problem is that the hold might be filled up with water. If you don't release the men they will all drown because the ship will start taking on water and the hold will be the first place to be filled up. The difficulty you have on your hand is; if you release the men, will they try to take over the ship and pay back the white devils for what they have done to them? I can't tell you what to do pet, but you don't have much time, because the ship is sailing straight into the storm."

"Mada Kuzo, tell me, how much time do we have?" Nanny asked anxiously.

"The good news is that the storm will hit you in the morning. If it was during the night then I would be more worried. The bad news is that you can't even imagine what is coming your way, and some people might die."

"Mada Kuzo, will any of my people die? Tell me! Tell me!" Nanny begged, but Mada Kuzo was gone.

Nanny sat on one of the food barrels in the store room and contemplated what to do. She couldn't allow any of her people to die. She wondered what the men would do if they were set free. Would she be able to control them? She thought long and hard then decided to talk with Cudjoe and her other brothers to get their advice.

The brothers assured her that they would keep the men under control.

"Yes Sis, you go and warn the women," Cudjoe instructed. "Leave the men to us."

After Nanny left Cudjoe spoke to the men.

"Gentlemen listen! I have some very important news. I just spoke with Mada and I have some good news and some bad news. The bad news is that a terrible storm is coming our way and we're sailing straight into it because the Captain does not know that it is out there. It will strike us hard for many hours, and, and...," he paused.

"What! What are you saying?" one man demanded.

"Well," Cudjoe paused. "The waves will be very, very high, sometimes coming over the deck of the ship."

Some of the men began to murmur while others swore quietly to themselves. "We're all going to die!" one man down at the far end yelled.

"Have we come all this way to die?" another cried out loudly. "I wish they had killed me from the beginning."

"Shhhhh, shush!" the other men scolded him. "Do you want the guards to come down here? Let the man finish speaking."

"Gentlemen, down here might be flooded," Cudjoe informed them.

"I'm telling you, we're dead! dead! dead!" shouted the same man at the end.

"Shut up your damn mouth; let me hear what the man is saying," came a strong rebuke from a tall, thick, muscular gentleman five spaces from him.

"The only way that we can survive this storm is if we're out of these chains," Cudjoe continued.

"True, true," they all agreed.

"But this is the problem; Mada is worried that if she frees us all, some of you might start a riot on the ship and many people could get hurt. And she does not want to lose anyone of us. So, you all have to promise me that there will be no riot on board. We will finish this trip with dignity and hold our heads high. We will not act like those selfish white devils upstairs. We will show them that we don't have to resort to savagery like them. So gentlemen, do we have a deal?"

There was a moment of silence in the room. Some of the men cried when they reflectedon what they had been through. From their own people beating and selling them to the white devils who in turn continued the punishment. They had the scars to prove it. They wondered if they could ever forgive them. Cudjoe waited patiently while the men pondered over their options.

"By the way gentlemen," Cudjoe interjected. "We only have a couple more days left of this journey. Even if we killed all the white devils upstairs and took over the ship, we could not turn back now. We have to finish this journey. Mada has promised to take care of us over there. She has already proven herself in so many ways, hasn't she?" he asked.

"Yes, yes, she has been good to us, and we trust her," they all chimed in, as they reflected on how she had healed their wounds, and risked her life to steal extra food to give them so that they would not go hungry. The men trusted her. She was their provider and they would never forget her.

"Well, what is your answer?" Cudjoe demanded, interrupting their thoughts.

"Yes! Yes! We agree," they all declared. "We will not fight the white devils, at least not yet. We will listen to you and Mada." Cudjoe was elated. He couldn't wait to tell Nanny.

Nanny arrived at the women's quarters to find the ladies relaxing. Some sat around talking while others played with their children. The women looked so peaceful. She wished that she did not have to tell them the bad news. She thanked Massa God for Mada Kuzo because without her warning these women would surely not make it out of the hold safely. Nanny thought of all those other slave ships that ran into storms like this one approaching and how many captives came out alive. She knew that the crew would never go out of their way to save any of them. So if anybody was going to help these ladies it would have to be her.

Nanny gathered them together in the centre of the room and told them about the upcoming storm and the possibility of flooding in their quarters. The women became terrified because they realized that they were trapped. Many of them began to cry.

"What will happen to our children?" one mother lamented. "Will they all drown?"

"Is there anywhere else on the ship that we can stay if the hold is flooded?" another woman asked.

"Can we trust these white devils to get all of us out of here if it starts to fill up?" another young lady inquired.

"I can't answer most of your questions right now ladies," Nanny began. "But what I can promise you is that we will not lose anyone to the storm. That's my promise to you ladies. Don't worry."

"Mada we trust you with our lives," one mother, breast feeding her baby said. "You promised to protect us from the white devils them and you've never failed us, so I believe you." The other ladies all shook their heads in agreement.

"Ok ladies," Nanny said. "I have to go over and see how the men are preparing for the storm. I'll be back soon." And with that she slipped away. As Nanny left, the women felt like sitting ducks in a pond.

"I miss Mada so much when she's not here," one woman commented.

"Who else can we trust?" a short lady with a piece of cloth tied around her head, asked openly. "Mada is the only person who has never let us down. Everything that she promises, she does."

"She must be sent from Massa God to save us," another woman suggested.

"I love that woman more than cook food," a little lady with pretty white teeth said, flashing a broad smile.

"I would give my life for Mada," a tall strapping woman with her hair in braids, declared.

"I wonder what's going to happen to us when we reach land?" a young girl pondered. "I wish I could go with Mada."

"Me too! Me too!" they all agreed.

As dawn approached, the clouds began rolling in. The winds increased in speed and the ship started rocking wildly. Nanny slowly descended the stairs to the men's quarters. The men looked restless. Cudjoe cautioned everyone to be silent and to listen for instructions.

"Gentlemen, could I have your attention please?" Nanny called out. "Thank you," when they settled down.

"The storm will be here soon, so we must get you men out of these irons. Please don't provoke the white devils upstairs. We don't want any bloodshed on board. We know that you are the best warriors in the world and you could take those idiots upstairs any day; but you don't want to win the battle and lose the war, right?" she asked, not expecting an answer. "We're here to win the war. Are you all with me gentlemen?"

"Yes Mada, we're with you!" they hollered.

Nanny skillfully removed the shackles from Cudjoe and Accompong's legs and they in turn began freeing the others. In a short while all the men were free. Tears flowed down the faces of some of the men when they tasted freedom for the first time. For some, they felt the compelling urge to battle; to avenge those who had wronged them. Their Ashanti military tradition was flowing through their veins again and was now coming to the fore.

Bodeiwei, one of the most experienced warriors of the tribe, a man who had fought many battles, was asked by some of the young men to lead them into battle against the ship crew, in spite of their promise to Nanny. After much discussion he was finally able to convince them not to renege on their promise, but instead to focus on helping each other to ride out the storm. Cudjoe and Nanny thanked Bodeiwei for his quick response and invited him into the inner circle to develop strategies to keep everyone safe during the tempest.

The winds grew stronger and the waves climbed higher. The ship dipped and lurched forward and upward as the tide became more ferocious. Like a gigantic washing machine the ocean churned, removing all traces of dirt from the hull.

Everyone on board, including the crew, was being tossed around like miniature toys. As the ship climbed the mountains of waves, water burst frighteningly over the deck and washed quickly down into the hold showering the men and women with frigid salty sea water. The men screamed out loudly in desperation.

Many of them became very sick; retching and vomiting all over the floor. Mothers tenderly clutched their young ones, consoling them as they puked nonstop.

The sea continued to rant and rage with unlimited energy. Men and women called out to their gods to spare their lives, believing that they would be going down with the ship at any moment.

But with an experienced captain at the helm barking orders, and a tireless crew working frantically to keep the ship afloat, the fight was not yet over.

As the water washed over the deck and down the hold, the men searched around desperately for containers to scoop out the water. When they found one in a corner they quickly formed a human chain to remove the water.

The guards were in shock when they saw the men resolutely bailing out the water as if they were a part of the crew. They quickly drew their muskets in fear, but lowered it to focus on the tumultuous storm raging in the ocean. Some of the men marched over to the women's quarters, without interference from the guards, to help them scoop out the water. The men worked under difficult conditions for hours, removing water from below deck and looking out for each other.

The storm raged for the next few hours with added intensity. Everyone including the crew became exhausted and wondered how much more they could take.

As the evening approached, the storm began to lose its power. Everybody knew that the end was in sight and gave thanks to God. The men spent the next few hours removing all the water from both holds and making sure that everyone was safe.

Finally, as the storm faded away the men sat around in groups and reflected. They had so many questions for Nanny but were afraid to ask for fear of offending her. What if she had not released them, would they have made it? Who was this woman? Why was she here helping them? Was she sent here to save them? But who would send her? Was it God? It must be God, because nobody else seemed to care about their predicament. They were just simple village folks trying to take care of their families yet here was this mysterious woman risking her life to keep them safe. The men became aware that they were in the presence of greatness and they never wanted to be separated from her.

Suddenly, several fully armed guards marched down the stairs towards them. The atmosphere became tense. No one moved.

"Don't tell me that after all that we've done here today these white devils want to put us back in chains?" Cudjoe mumbled to himself. "How can I prevent a bloodbath here today? After the men have tasted freedom, will they willingly go back in chains? It looks like these white devils have cold water, not warm red blood running through their veins."

Cudjoe looked across at the men. The men glanced back at him from the corners of their eyes for a response; but not wanting to reveal himself, he nodded slightly for them to stand down.

All of a sudden, out from behind the guards stepped the captain, in the same white suit and colorful broad hat that he was wearing when they came on board. The two sides stared at each other. The captain looked closely around the room, taking note of the shackles and wondering how the men got free. He then looked at the guards, nodded his head and turned and left. The men all breathed a welcomed sigh of relief and started cheering. However they noted that the number of guards was doubled and the trap door leading down to the hold was now chained and locked at all times.

For the few remaining days of the trip the men were kept below deck, only allowing a small group at a time to come up on deck to get exercise.

Early one morning everyone below in the hold was suddenly awakened by a big explosion upstairs that rocked the ship. Everybody wanted to know what was taking place. The explosions became louder and heavier, rocking the ship to its core. The men began to panic and started crying out in despair. With the trap door locked the men realized that they were trapped and at the mercy of whatever was happening on deck.

"Is the ship under attack?" one man asked.

"I believe so," Cudjoe replied. "But what can we do? We're trapped down here like caged animals. I wish Mada was here," he said, never calling Nanny by her real name in front of the men.

"Yes, she would know what was happening," another man said.

Over at the women's quarters Nanny and the women too were awakened by the explosions. Mothers held their babies tightly, as they began to cry. Without saying a word, Nanny stealthily crept upon deck to see what was happening. The sun was just coming up when she gazed towards the source of the explosions. She was in for the shock of her life.

Coming towards them speeding rapidly was a gigantic vessel decorated with giant, colorful sails with a skull and cross insignia; discharging its enormous cannons at their ship. Nanny realized immediately that they were pirates bent on capturing their ship and stealing the cargo.

The vessel's fire power was enormous and terrifying. It was not a fair fight. It was like a lion toying with a mouse.

Nanny watched in amazement as her little ship tried to out-run this powerhouse of floating war machine, without success. The great pirate ship sailed confidently towards the slave ship; like a huge beast stalking its tiny prey.

The captain, in his wisdom, eventually decided to break off running away and instead stood his ground to fight, or so she thought. Nanny held her breath as the ship stood like a lamb to the slaughter, waiting on the beast to pounce.

The pirate ship finally stopped a few hundred yards out with its mighty cannons pointed directly at the tiny vessel.

The crew on the deck of the pirate ship became very busy as the two ships stood glaring at each other. On the other hand, Nanny noticed that the crew on her ship had gathered on the deck and was waving a white flag in surrender.

'They're going to give over my people to the wicked pirates without a fight!' Nanny thought, in disbelief.

'They will take them and sell them to God knows who, to take them to God knows where. I won't let them take my people; not now, not ever,' she decided boldly.

A few minutes went by without any incidence. Suddenly four small landing crafts were lowered, filled with armed men, rowing briskly towards the small ship.

Nanny felt a giant knot in her stomach. "This is for real!" she panted. "We don't have much time. I must prepare the men to fight for their lives because the crew has given up."

Nanny quietly unlocked the trap door and went down to the hold to warn the men.

The men listened attentively as she outlined the approaching calamity.

"And why should we help those wicked white devils upstairs?" a tall, heavy build man asked boldly.

"At this point," Nanny replied. "We're not in this for the white devils. We're fighting for our own survival. These men are pirates! Murderers! Criminals! They're ruthless! The only thing that they're interested in is gold. Yes gold!" she said, opening her eyes widely at them. "Life means nothing to them. If they capture you today, this morning, we don't know what will happen to you all. To them you're just cargo to be sold to the highest bidder. So gentlemen the choice is yours. You can lay down here like slugs and wait for them to come and enslave you again; whipping you mercilessly like dogs, and then putting you back in chains and selling you like goats or you can act like great Ashanti warriors and fight like hell for your lives! I'm here to help you to win this battle if you will let me. We don't have much time gentlemen, so those who are with me, raise your hands!"

Every hand was raised. "We're ready Mada!" they shouted.

Nanny placed her fingers on her lips. "Shhhhhhhh! Ok look around and pick up all the chains and irons that you can find, and also break down whatever you can find to make weapons. What we have on our side is surprise. The pirates don't know that we're not in chains. They're in for a big shock. Listen, wait for my signal. We will attack them when all of them have come on board. Plus, I don't think that they will fire their big cannons on us for fear of killing everybody including their own people. When you attack men, I want you to use your greatest Ashanti, blood-curdling war cry; crying out to your ancestors to favor us in battle." The battle was long and hard. The men fought like true warriors. With blood curdling war cries, they ran up onto the deck swinging their chains and pipes; taking the pirates by complete surprise. While the powerful cannons sat silently on board the pirate's ship, the pirates fought gallantly to recover from the surprise attack, but to no avail; the die had been cast. Eventually they scrambled back into their boats and hastily rowed back to their mother ship and sailed away.

Everyone laughed as they sailed away.

"Did you see the pirates' faces when we rushed up out of the hold and onto the deck?" a short stubby man said smiling.

"They looked like they saw duppy [ghost]! They screamed like trapped chimpanzees." Everyone laughed, some holding their bellies and getting very hysterical.

"I believe that the pirates were more afraid of the big roaring sounds coming up from out of the hold than our battle cries," another man noted.

"To me it sounded like a cage full of female lions with young cubs, getting ready to eat somebody," a bald head man joked.

"Then who was making all that racket?" one man asked.

"I know who but I'm not telling," a short, middle aged man said.

"Then Plunkie, I didn't know that you could kick like a mule?" another man joked. "The way you jumped into that pirate's chest and knocked him out cold, it sure wasn't a fair fight!"

"I personally don't think that they should call themselves pirates," another man said jokingly. "The way they ran away today, they should be called Pi'race." They all laughed joyfully. The laughing and celebration continued for some time with the men telling many tall tales and their version of the battle.

"This is one battle that I will never forget. I will tell my children and grandchildren," one tall gentleman said, with a smile. Everyone agreed.

The captain showed his appreciation by giving everyone an extra ration of food that day.

Chapter 7

It was down to the last three days before landing on shore, after spending ten long weeks on the ocean. Last minute preparations were in high gear. The men and women were led upstairs on the deck, in small groups, where they were washed and oiled, like cattle being groomed for the local fair. The stronger men and women were identified and placed into special groups. These people would be sent to designated farms while the weaker ones would be sold on auction in the marketplace. This was very troubling for Nanny because she didn't want to part with anyone. Food and water were no longer rationed and dancing for exercise was encouraged every day.

On the night before the ship docked, Nanny visited both the men and women's quarters to talk with them for the last time before they disembarked.

Talking with the women first, she gathered them around in the center of the room and told them how proud she was of them. Tears welled up in her eyes as she informed them that this was the last time that they would be together as a group. Then she related how she had visited the island earlier to explore the surroundings, in preparation for docking. The one question on everyone's mind was how she was able to get over there? But no one asked for fear of offending her. However, a little girl who was sobbing quietly, because of the thought of losing some of her best friends, asked the question boldly.

"Mada, I have many questions," she began, wiping her tears with the back of her hand. "Tell me something, how did you get over there? And is there a way that we can avoid splitting up because I don't want to lose my best friend Weigi?" tenderly hugging her friend. "We're friends for life and I don't see how we can live apart." By now both of them were crying and hugging each other.

"It's not fair Mada," they both protested. "We're not animals for them to treat us like this. Mada, I hate the white devils them so much. I wish that they were all dead. When I grow up I want to be just like you Mada, and fight them too."

Everyone in the room began weeping.

"What is your name chile?" Nanny asked.

"Pudewzi," replied the girl, with a smile.

"That is a pretty name," Nanny said. "Just pretty like you. Why do you say that I'm fighting them?" Nanny asked.

"Me and Weigi have seen how you protect us from the evil white devils every night and how you guard us like a shepherd taking care of his goats. We love you so much Mada and I want to be just like you when I grow up, so that I can protect our people from those wicked white devils. I'm not afraid of them Mada, I will fight them to death."

Nanny looked down at the little girl with so much love and admiration. Here was a child who understood the struggle at this tender age, and was ready to confront the enemy head on.

Nanny chose her words carefully when she addressed the girl, knowing full well that everyone was hanging on to every word that she said.

"My chile, for such a young age, you have shown such courage in the heart of this struggle. You represent the face of the resistance that the white devils don't anticipate. However, in your eagerness to confront the enemy, you have to be cautious. I cannot tell you how I got over to the island, but what I can tell you is that it is gorgeous! The land is just as beautiful as our land back home. It is mountainous just like ours and everything is green and beautiful. The bad news is that the white devils are brutal. They work our people very hard. They have a tight hold on power and our people are suffering badly. I'm not here to frighten you all, but I only want to prepare you for the worst. Some of you might be wondering if I will be going with you, and my answer is," she paused for a moment as she watched their eager eyes glued to her like a hawk in hot pursuit of its prey. "Is yes!" The ladies clapped and cheered and hugged each other with joy.

"Thank you ladies," she continued. "I promised to protect you when we left our shores and I will continue to do the same over there."

"But how are you going to protect us if they scatter us all over the place like chaff in the wind?" one older woman asked wisely.

"Good question, Mada Glewkz. We will eventually be together, just like now, but the difference is that we will be our own masters," Nanny predicted.

"I can't wait for that day to come," a little woman shouted.

"But don't tell anyone," Nanny cautioned. "Keep it to yourself. You don't know who to trust over there. Don't believe for a moment that just because you and somebody have the same skin color that you are friends. Absolutely not! I noticed that over there, there were many different tribes. I saw the Coromantee, Fanti, Akyem, Mandingo and Yoruba. I know that there are many more but I didn't see them. So what I'm saying ladies, is don't be fooled by the color of a person's skin. I dream of the day when we will be in charge of our own destiny and not dependent on somebody else to determine how we live. Listen to me ladies and listen carefully," Nanny said sternly. "We're here for good, so we have to make the most of it. It makes no sense for us to keep pining over the past. Our land, as beautiful and wonderful as it is, is in the past. It is up to us Ashanti women, just like in the past, to make the best of what this land has to offer, and to get our men to do the same. We will win this struggle when we as a people begin to take charge of our own lives. And ladies, remember, we have to support our men. They will bear the brunt of this struggle. They will be called insulting names for generations. Their manhood will be challenged every day. They will feel like failures. They will look for love in sex and having many babies. They will appear tough and have a, 'I don't care' attitude; but don't abandon them, that's when they've reached rock bottom and will need your support the most. The white devils brutalize our men every single day as a strategy to weaken our people so that they can remain our masters. I'm telling you all this ladies because the very survival of our people will depend upon how we treat our men from now on. We have to let them feel important. Let them feel like Chiefs in their homes, because outside in the real world, the white devils treat them lower than dogs. If you don't treat your men with care, they will sleep around with lots of different women and have many babies. Ladies we have our work cut out for us, and as long as we stay focused, we will be fine," Nanny emphasized.

"One more thing ladies, don't forget to teach our wonderful culture to our children. Teach them our songs and dances. Cook our food every day and celebrate our festivals. Nothing should change. They can force us to do some things but they cannot prevent us from practicing our culture. And that ladies, was my little speech. May Massa God be with all of us."

Everyone clapped and cheered at the end of Nanny's speech.

Then a little woman tenderly cradling her baby raised her hand timidly to get Nanny's attention. Nanny saw her from the corner of her eyes and seeing the seriousness in her eyes calmed everyone down and acknowledged the woman.

"What's on your mind young lady?" Nanny inquired. The woman looked up nervously at Nanny then down at the floor, avoiding eye contact. "What would you like to ask me?" Nanny urged lovingly.

"I hope you won't get mad with me Mada, but I just have to ask you this question," the lady began.

"Why are you really here? As far as I know, you were never captured and brought here in chains. You were never whipped. You were not even abused. So why did you come here? You did not have to come. Unlike us, you chose to be here, why?"

The whole room suddenly became silent; you could hear a pin drop. All eyes were now focused on Nanny. Many of the women had thought of the same questions but no one ventured to ask, for fear of offending her, especially after she had done so much for them.

Nanny thought for a moment before replying. She knew that this day would come and that she would have to be transparent with her explanation if she ever wanted to lead these people.

"I agree with you that I was never in danger and I was never captured," Nanny began. "As a matter of fact, it all started when I gave a speech to a group of Chiefs at a Confederation conference, about stopping the practice of capturing and selling our people. Some of the Chiefs did not like what I had to say. Some were blatantly rude and offensive during my speech.

Apparently they showed their displeasure with me by attacking and plundering my village and killing many of my people including both my parents. The murderers took all the strong young people including my brothers into captivity and sold them to the slavers. Oh my poor mother and father, what did they do to deserve this?" Nanny broke down crying and holding her belly.

"They were just simple farmers trying to make a living and taking care of their family. They would never hurt a fly, yet these monsters murdered them and burned down their home along with all the others in the village. And why? Greed! Pure greed! Greed by the white devils and more greed by our own people. And the worst part is that I was not there to protect them. I was not there! I was not there," she cried out loudly. "I was not even there to bury them; my poor mother and father," she moaned, shaking her head and wringing her hands.

There was a long pause, as Nanny struggled with her thoughts, tears running down her face. A lady nearby handed her a piece of rag which she used to wipe her face and blow her nose.

"I left as quickly as I realized that they had captured my five brothers. I refused to lose them too, to those criminals."

Nanny looked like a broken woman; a far cry from the larger than life, hard-core leader they were used to, who protected and encouraged them.

"Although I had planned to come on one of these trips to find out where the white devils were taking our people," Nanny continued, grinning slightly and wiping her tears and blowing her nose. "When this thing happened I decided to kill two birds with one stone. So here I am."

By now all the ladies in the room were weeping uncontrollably. Everyone was evidently moved by the story. The women rushed over to Nanny and consoled her.

"We didn't know," they lamented.

"We didn't know. We're so sorry," one woman cried.

"Here we are, focusing only on ourselves and not realizing that you were hurting just like us," another woman said. "We're so sorry for our selfishness. We're all in this struggle together."

"I'm so glad that you're here with us," a young girl with two missing front teeth said. "I mean, I'm not glad that your parents were killed, but

74

your presence here has been the best thing that could've happened to us."
Everyone grinned nervously.

"Thank you. It was nice of you to say that," Nanny said, giving her a
hug. She now realized how much she loved these people and would protect
them with her life.

Nanny was happy that she had opened up her heart to these ladies. She
didn't get a chance to grieve before because she was too busy taking care of
everyone. This helped her to mask the pain and kick it down the road.
However she knew that the day was coming when she would have to deal
with it and this was as good a time as ever to start the healing. She also
knew that she and her brothers would have to plan a proper memorial
ceremony for their parents someday.

After saying goodbye to the ladies, Nanny got back her composure and
went over to give her 'little speech' to the men. She reminded them of their
past glories during the storm and repulsing the attack by the pirates. She
challenged them to remain positive and to focus on gaining their freedom.
She also implored them to take good care of their families.

"Be a husband to your wife and a father to your children," she
encouraged. "They will love you and be grateful for it."
The men applauded when she ended her speech and all gathered around to
thank her for her leadership.

As the night progressed, the crew continued to scrub the ship clean
from top to bottom while the folks in the holds said their goodbyes,
knowing full well that this might be the last time that they would be seeing
one another.

Part Two

The New World

Chapter 8

The ship docked at the crack of dawn. The sailors lowered the gigantic sails and roped the ship to the dock. The dock buzzed with activity. Many people gathered around to greet the ship. Soon the gangplank was lowered and the captain and his crew walked briskly down to meet a small group of well-dressed men. They spoke for a shortwhile then the captives began to disembark; men, women and children. They walked slowly down the gangplank and onto horse drawn wagons waiting nearby.

Nanny learned that all the captives on board were purchased by four big plantations on the island. She was thrilled because she now knew where everyone was. Although there were so many plantations on the island, Nanny knew that she would eventually find them when the time was right.

It was midday when the convoy of five open wagons left the dock with Nanny and a number of men, women and the children destined for a plantation in the Parish of St Thomas. The wagons were filled to capacity and some people had to take turns getting off and walking.

Nanny was overjoyed that her five brothers were in the wagon train albeit on separate wagons. That was her prayer when the planters started selecting their slaves. She was happy to have them with her because now she was able to keep an eye on them.

The unpaved road was in a deplorable condition with mini craters all about making the ride bumpy and very uncomfortable. The convoy travelled all afternoon, along the narrow roads, over small rickety bridges and up steep hills. Several times the folks had to alight from the wagons and push them over the steep hills.

Suddenly a violent cloudburst appeared which caused everyone to scamper for shelter under nearby trees to wait it out. The rain brought a little reprieve from the punishing heat but it filled all the craters in the road and turned them into little mud pools, making the journey even more exhausting.

"Are we there yet?" a little girl asked, walking with her mother beside the wagon.

"I hope so my child," is all she said, trying to conserve the little energy that she had left.

Nobody spoke. Nobody made eye contact. Everyone was in his or her own little world wondering what the future would bring.

As the sun dipped below the horizon, the wagons finally arrived at a huge white arched gate. The wagons slowly rolled through and continued for sometime, passing acres and acres of cane fields in various stages of growth. No one said a word; they were all busy viewing the landscape and hoping for the best. As they continued further inland, they passed many workers in the fields. The workers kept their heads down and at no time acknowledge their presence.

Nanny felt a deep void inside her soul for the first time. She was just beginning to miss all the other men and women. This was the first night that she would not have them all with her. Luckily she had all her five brothers. It would have been devastating if they were taken away from her too.

As they passed through another set of enormous columns; standing in front of them was this big white Great House in all its splendor. Not far away in a little enclave was a row of smaller beautifully painted houses for the staff. The convoy travelled for another half a mile, passing acres and acres of sugarcane fields before arriving at rows and rows of unattractive housing barracks. The crudely built barracks were made of wattle and daub, with a little window and a door for each unit. Inside, the room was very small, shabby and unappealing.

Tucked away in opposite corners of the room were two small rickety beds. Nanny sighed quietly, wondering how two grown adults could live in such a cramped space. She didn't have long to ponder as immediately, a tall, slim young lady opened the door and timidly entered the room.

'Apparently this is my new roommate,' Nanny thought to herself. 'Oh! she has beautiful teeth!'

They greeted each other, exchanged pleasantries and shared stories with each other. The woman's name was Gylziia and she was from the same tribe. Nanny soon realized how much they had in common. Her mother was a spiritual healer and people came to her from all around to be healed with herbs or to ward off evil spirits. She admitted that she did not have the gift of healing, but used to assist her mother in performing the various rituals.

Nanny concealed her gifts for fear that she might be exposed before her time, but she liked Gylziia and hoped that they could be friends.

The noise in the barracks was constant, being situated so close to the nerve centre of the plantation. The departments included: the sugar mill, the distillery, the boiling and curing houses, the carpenter's shop and the blacksmith's shop, with its nonstop banging.

The following morning the new recruits were presented to the Busha [foreman] on the farm. He spoke very briefly before handing them over to their mentors. An experienced mentor was assigned to each new arrival. The mentor's job was to teach the new people the culture of the plantation; especially ways to avoid upsetting Bakra [owner/overseer], the Busha and most importantly, the head drivers [head slave].

Nanny's mentor was a big strapping woman called Putus. She was very jovial and made Nanny laugh. A member of the Mandingo tribe, she arrived at the plantation five years earlier. Putus worked in the cane fields with the men most days but sometimes when Bakra had those lavish functions at the Great House they called on her to work there.

For the rest of the day Nanny and Gylziia followed Putus around to learn the ropes.

Early the next morning, Putus came by Nanny's room and invited them down to the field before the other workers and the Busha arrived. Nanny was an early riser and couldn't wait to leave her tiny room and be outside. Putus presented them with a bag filled with mangoes, oranges and bananas which they greatly appreciated

"The head driver [head slave] gets very angry if you're late, and you don't want to be the first one to taste the wrath of his whip," Putus warned. "The key thing to remember ladies is not to get the Busha angry in the morning because it will follow you throughout the whole day," Putus continued. "And the more he gets angry, the more the whip will 'talk'," she smiled, demonstrating with her hand.

Putus led them down a narrow path, beside a glistening stream teaming with many colorful fish swimming near to the surface. The water sparkled like diamonds as the early morning sunlight bounced off the surface. The landscape was so beautiful that Nanny was forced to stop for a moment and enjoy the scenery.

"Apart from the white people them, this island is so beautiful," Putus said, matter-of-factly. "I wish that we could get a chance to enjoy it all."

"You will Putus, you will," Nanny blurted out without thinking.

Putus looked across at Nanny and something stirred inside her. 'Something about this girl,' she said to herself when she studied Nanny's face. She seemed so different from any other 'freshie' [new slave] she had known. She showed a depth of steel and focus and Putus wondered if Busha and the lot would be able to break her; or the bigger question was, would she make a run for it and join the Maroons in the mountains? Putus decided at that moment to hitch her canoe onto this girl's boat because 'a rising tide raises all boats.' She just felt that there was more to this new girl than what she was seeing.

It was soon time for the morning work to begin. The Busha gathered all the new workers together and divided them into three gangs. The first gang was for individuals from sixteen to fifty years old, who looked strong and energetic. They would be doing the heavy field work. Nanny was happy to be placed in this group because she got to work alongside Putus. People over fifty were placed into the second gang along with teenagers up to sixteen years old. The last gang was made up of old people and young kids.

After everyone was placed into their respective groups they were led off to a section of the field by a head slave called a head driver. He was the most feared and hated person on the plantation. Although he was from their same tribe, he was always ready to use his whip to enforce his authority and get the workers to work harder.

In Nanny's work gang the head driver was a tall, bald, muscular man with well chiseled shoulders; full of confidence and obviously loved his job. When he shouted with his deep baritone voice, people shuddered in fear.

"Do you see this!" he said, holding up his long, black, horrifying looking whip. "It is called Doctor Brukup, because it will show you no mercy. Work hard every day and do what I tell you and you won't get to meet Doctor Brukup. Ah! Ah! Ah! Ah!" he roared with laughter.
"I'm not your brother, or your father, or your friend. The only thing that I care about is getting Bakra's work done. Nothing else means anything to me. And if you don't do Bakra's work then your backside will pay for it. Now get to work!" he shouted. And with that he cracked his giant whip, making a very loud noise which frightened Nanny and the others; causing them to jump with fright and scamper off to find their work station.
"Ah! Ah! Ah! Ah!" he roared with an intimidating laughter in his deep baritone voice.
"Welcome to paradise! Ah! Ah! Ah! Ah!" he bellowed as he cracked his whip again and again.

'This man acts like a big idiot!' Nanny said to herself, in disgust.
'I think he loves his job too much. He seems to love punishing his own people. I hope I don't have to clash with him.'

A sudden rage came over Nanny as she remembered her poor parents who were brutally murdered at the hands of those murderers. This guy reminded her of them.

'I don't know how I will manage if he hurts any of my five brothers,' she thought to herself.
'I will just have to warn them to keep out of his way because I really don't want to hurt him.'

It was the harvest season on the plantation and the sugarcane had to be cut, put into wagons and taken to the sugar mill for manufacturing into sugar, rum and molasses. Time was of the essence. Speed was paramount. First, the over ten feet tall plants had to be cut at ground level. After, the leaves were removed and the tops trimmed by cutting off the last mature joint. Next, they were thrown into a large pile. Finally, the canes had to be picked up, tied and placed into wagons to be transported to the factory.

Nanny was provided with a machete and placed with a small group of women whose job was to pick up the canes from the large pile, put into smaller bundles, and load the wagons. She worked all day in the boiling tropical sun stopping only for a short time for lunch. At the end of the work day, although she was tired and aching all over, she collected pieces of dried wood and cow dung to make a fire to cook her supper. She then dragged herself into bed and off to sleep.

In the weeks that followed, Nanny worked alongside Putus, improving her skills and learning more about the plantation. After work they would collect dried cow dung together and cook their supper. Nanny liked cooking with her because they got more time to talk, plus Putus always brought many different kinds of strange foods for Nanny to sample.

Putus knew everyone of importance on the plantation; how long they were working there, and other details like how many women they were sleeping with. Everywhere she went she introduced Nanny to her friends. People were always calling out to her. She was a social butterfly and Nanny could not have asked for a better mentor.

Putus talked constantly, from morning until night. She liked Nanny a lot and treated her like a little sister, always trying to give her the necessary information to protect her from danger.

Nanny realized very early that Putus could be an asset in her future plans because everyone knew her and she knew everything that was happening on the plantation. But she had to be cautious. She wondered if Putus could be trusted. Was she an 'informer' for Bakra to gain favors? She suspected that some of these mentors might be 'informers' working undercover for the Bakra; to build relationships with the new recruits so that they could know what was happening inside the barracks. She made a point not to divulge too much but rather to ask questions and listen.

On the weekends, Putus took Nanny around to her little kitchen garden at the back of the barracks where she planted little plots of yams, okras, bananas, plantains and susumbers. She helped Putus in her garden, all the while learning about the new crops on the island.

This was a very exciting time for Nanny because there was so much to learn and Putus did not disappoint. She was a great teacher and storyteller with a wealth of knowledge. Nanny wondered what contributions Putus would have made to her tribe if she had remained back home. She just knew that Putus would have been great because she was bright, knowledgeable, with a great personality, and liked to help people. 'Maybe she would have been a Chief, yet here she was, building up other people's land and making others rich. What a waste.'

One night, while in bed about to fall asleep, she heard a familiar drumming sound in the distance. She sat up quickly and strained her ears to listen. The drums sounded familiar although they were not as authentic as the real Ashanti talking drums. She listened carefully and tried hard to decode the messages that were being broadcasted. 'Yes they are inviting people to join them in the fight against the white devils,' she contemplated. Nanny wondered who these people were and how they were able to live up in the mountains. As she drifted off to sleep she dreamed about freedom and wondered if these people might be her ticket to liberty. She made a mental note to ask Putus the following day about the talking drums.

"Those mountain people are dangerous!" Putus said, when asked about the talking drums.

"It's forbidden for anyone to make or own a talking drum here," Putus warned. "If Bakra catches you with it, you will get 21 lashes with the Cat-o-nine whip."

"That sounds all doom and gloom, but what do you Putus feel in your gut? Forget about Bakra for a moment," Nanny asked, peering straight at her.

"Old people have it to say that they are free African people because the Spanish people ran off and left them up there when the British came with their big weapons and took over the island. They call themselves Maroons and they refuse to be ruled by the British. The British have tried over and over again to capture them but they're good fighters, the best on the island."

"So why are they trying to recruit people like us Putus? Nanny asked.

"The Maroons are always trying to recruit young men and women from the plantations to join their warriors to fight the British. They would like to build a bigger fighting force so that they can take on the British, instead of running and hiding in the bush. Some people say that right now they are only a small group with very little weapons, and so they have to run and hide from the British. Many young men from the plantation run off to join the Maroons in the mountain, but not all of them reach the meeting point before Bakra's dogs catch them. And when they are caught they are mauled by the dogs and beaten to within an inch of their lives. The boys are tied up and the head driver whips them until they pass blood. Then Bakra leaves them tied up for days outside; the sun burns them and the rain wets them, and nobody can help them without Bakra's permission. Most times Bakra will sell them to other plantations after they get well, for fear that they will corrupt the other young men. Trust me Nanny, I've thought about it many, many times, but I'm afraid of the dogs. I heard that they don't take the dogs off you when they catch you. They let the dogs maul you while they just stand around and laugh," Putus explained.

"I shouldn't be saying this to you Nanny, but some how I trust you. Nanny you wouldn't believe how I hate these white people," Putus said with anger in her voice. "I hate them for what they're doing to our people. I hate them for removing all of us from our homeland, leaving it impoverished and ruined. You might see me looking cheerful and friendly, but it is all an act. I'm used to it. I was the Queen of my tribe along with my husband, who was the king, until we were viciously attacked by a twin tribe's alliance. My husband and most of the older people were killed and the entire village was burnt to the ground. Me and many of my young people were taken away and sold to the white devils," she continued, with tears flowing down her face, as she reminisced about her homeland.

"We used to entertain Chiefs, Kings and Queens and dignitaries from visiting tribes all the time. We were a proud, rich and powerful tribe. I had servants who catered to my every need. When I came here it was very difficult at first, but I'm a survivor Nanny, yes survivor! I refused to give up. I refused to let them get the last laugh. I miss my husband so much Nanny and I miss my country, and I know that I might never see it again." Tears flowed freely down Nanny's face as both women lamented over their past. They both knew that they had to be free, just like the Maroons. Free to control their destiny. Free to live in this new land without fear of oppression.

"I don't know anything about you Nanny. Tell me a little about yourself," Putus implored.

"There is not much to tell other than they raided my village, killed my parents, captured us and sold us to the white devils; and here we are on this beautiful island living in fear and being beaten every day by our own people. Something is wrong with this story, don't you agree?" Nanny asked, peering at Putus with steel like focus.

"Yes I agree Nanny," Putus replied, awkwardly.

"Well we have two choices, don't we?" Nanny continued. "We can stay here and cry our eyes out like this for the rest of our lives or we can use our brains," Nanny said, pointing to her head.
"Massa God did not give us this," pointing again at her head. "To sit on. Massa God gave us this brain to think and find solutions to difficult problems. And another thing Putus, Massa God did not give us a spirit of fear, it is all our doing. He gave us a spirit of courage, strength and perseverance. Everything is right here inside of us to overcome any obstacles; we just have to tap into it."
Nanny stopped talking and looked at Putus. She looked uncomfortable and nervously chewed on her finger nails.

"This is the first time that anyone has ever spoken to me like that. From the first time I saw you I knew that you were special. I knew that you were no ordinary slave like us. I believed you when you said that we had to use our heads because the white devils would not just say, 'here African people, here is your freedom, take it,'" she joked. "Just know that I believe in you Nanny, and I will follow you to the ends of the earth. You are the real thing, no questions asked."

"Thanks," Nanny said smiling. "I believe you. Anyway, let's get some sleep because tomorrow is a long day and our lovely head driver is resting comfortably in his bed right now, gathering up all his strength to work Doctor Brukup on our backside."
They both laughed and turned in for the night.

Chapter 9

The whips cracked from morning until night.

"Why do these monsters use their whips so much?" Nanny asked Putus one day. "The people get a whipping for the flimsiest of reasons around here."

"That's true, no one is safe from it," Putus said.

"Take Bertie over there. He was whipped to an inch of his life because he didn't dig the holes deep enough to plant the cane tops. That is the reason why he is limping like that. He will never be the same again. We both came here the same time, and I liked him at first because he looked so strong and handsome. Now look at him. From the day they whipped him, he was never the same again. Oh poor man. I tell you Nanny, the way I feel right now, if I catch that head driver alone one dark night, he would feel my wrath. That wretch is a wicked man and he will pay for it one day," she continued.

"Look over there at that lady. Her name is Feonwna. She got a proper whipping a few months ago that caused her to lose her baby, because the head driver said that she stopped too often to urinate. Can you imagine that Nanny? What should the poor girl do? I'm telling you Nanny, they're so cruel. The only thing that they care about is the Bakra's work. Old people have a saying that the white people are so terrified of us that they get the head drivers to beat us into pulp, to keep us so scared and submissive that we won't try to kill them," Putus laughed sarcastically.

"But the opposite is also true. We hate them so much that the more they whip us, the more we want to kill them, or better yet, burn down their plantation. I tell you Nanny, the way the white people treat us Africans, every one of them should be afraid. Every one of them should sleep with one eye open and their hands on their musket. They don't seem to understand that the more they beat us, the more attractive the Maroons in the mountains appear to us. When we hear that a plantation has been burnt we rejoice, because we know that it was cruelty to the people that caused it. When I was a little girl back home, my mother always said that, 'Nobody ran away from good,'" she continued. "Try not to get a whipping from those goons my friend, because whenever they start, they take a set on you, like 'Pitcharie bird on a cow's back.'"

'Boy, this woman can talk,' Nanny said to herself. 'But I could listen to her all day because she has so much knowledge of this place and I need to know it inside out.'

Nanny couldn't wait for the night to come. Although she was very tired from the long, hard day's work, she looked forward to the talking drums. A warm feeling engulfed her as she listened to the sweet sounds coming from the drums in the hills. It made her feel whole again. It soothed her aching heart and soul. The drums reminded her of the wonderful life she had back home; her mother and father, her wonderful grandmother, all the elders and family members of her tribe, the laughter, the tears, the celebrations and festivals. A feeling of nostalgia filled her body and a rage soared inside her belly.

"These people need to be back home with their families; not here in this far off land being overworked, underfed and brutalized," she said quietly under her breath, not wishing to wake her roommate. "I must find these drummers sooner rather than later."

For weeks the drums kept her awake at nights and after tantalizing and massaging her emotions, she would finally fall off to a sound sleep; dreaming about the good times in her homeland and a new life with the Maroons.

Nanny secretly told her brothers about the talking drums. They too had heard the drums and were happy when Nanny brought it to their attention. She informed them of her plan to visit the Maroons the next time she heard them drumming. Cudjoe warned her to be careful, and then they all broke out laughing, knowing what they knew about her.

Nanny stayed up late every night, listening for the talking drums to shatter the silence of the dark quiet night and lull her to sleep, but it was not there!

"I wonder when they will be back?" she said to herself.

Nanny's roommate Gylziia, like everyone else on the plantation, had heard the talking drums.

"Those drummers are really good," she commented to Nanny one night. "Do you know what they are trying to say on the drums?" she asked.

Nanny nodded slowly, "Yes, partially, not the whole thing. Those drummers don't sound too bad, but they left the Motherland a long time ago." They both laughed.

"I used to be a talking drummer in my village," Gylziia volunteered. "My father was one of the greatest talking drummers in our tribe and he trained all of us brothers and sisters to play the drums."

Then she came out and boldly asked Nanny, "Do you suppose that people here run away from the plantation and join them?

"I've heard that some people run away to join them, but not all of them make it, "Nanny began.

"People say that Bakra has some vicious tracking dogs that anyhow they pick up your scent, they never stop until they find you. And when they find you, they maul you near to death, while the trackers just stand around and laugh off their heads."

All of a sudden Gylziia dropped the bombshell.

"If I leave here they would never track me down," she said, with a steadfast determination.

Nanny quickly changed the subject for fear of revealing too much. She did not know if she could trust this girl. Later they went to bed without mentioning it again.

A few days later, Nanny was shocked when she arrived home after work to find Gylziia curled up on the floor in a fetal position.

Nanny rushed over to her side and asked her what was wrong.

"That wicked man, that head driver. He whipped me for no apparent reason!" Gylziia cried.

"Tell me what happened," Nanny pleaded.

"The wicked man told me to load up the wagons with the cane, and I was working as fast as I could," Gylziia began. "Remember I told you this morning Nanny that I was seeing my woman cycle and my belly was hurting me? Well, I was doing my best, but that evil man thought that I was not moving fast enough and so he hit me in my back with the big black whip. So I asked him why he hit me, and do you know Nanny, the spiteful man started beating me; saying that I was feisty in talking back to him. I believe that he was just showing off because Bakra was watching him," Gylziia said in disgust.

"Look at my back Nanny! Look at my arms! Look at my legs!" she cried. "I didn't deserve this, I didn't deserve this. That wicked man will pay for this," Gylziia said, with rage in her eyes.

"Nanny I don't know about you, but none of these heartless people will ever hit me again, I'm getting out of here."

Nanny didn't know what to say, so she kept quiet.

"Nanny, I swear, the next time I hear the drums, I will take off and join them. I don't think that they will treat me worse than this," she continued in anger. Then she looked Nanny squarely in the face and said, "Nanny, I'm begging you, don't tell anybody about this, because I don't want anyone to know my plans. I will go by myself if you're not coming."

Nanny got a clean rag, dipped it in a little basin of water and gently cleaned Gylziia's wounds. Gylziia winced in pain as the rag touched her tender skin. Nanny felt so sorry for her roommate that she could not hold back the tears.

"Don't worry Gylziia, everything will be alright," she said as she deftly passed her healing hands over Gylziia's body and the wounds began to heal.

"Thanks Nanny."

Then she looked at Nanny with a surprised look on her face.

"What did you do?" she inquired. "I'm feeling better already. I felt something warm just passed through mybody. Are you a spiritual healer?" she asked Nanny straight up.

"Yes I'm, but don't tell anybody," Nanny begged, putting her finger to her lips. "Bush has ears. You know that Bakra don't like people like us. We make them nervous," she said, showing her white teeth in a slight grin.

"I would never betray you Nanny," Gylziia said. "I just wish that you would come with me."

"We will see my friend, we will see," Nanny replied. "Remember, don't be in a rush. As Putus said, sometimes Bakra sends his goons out there to trick the people. They play the talking drums and direct you where to meet them and when you get there, they surprise you. Then they beat you with the whips until you wet yourself. After that, they won't keep you here for long. The first trader that comes by, they will sell you. So be very careful. Don't do anything before you talk with me, ok?"

"I won't," Gylziia promised.

A few nights later Nanny was lying in bed, on the verge of falling off to sleep when she heard the talking drums starting up from a distance. Gylziia jumped out of bed and began to get dressed without saying a word.

"Where are you going?" Nanny demanded.

"I'm going to get my freedom tonight!" Gylziia replied. "I'm not spending one more night under Bakra's roof."

"Don't be foolish," Nanny scolded. "What you're doing is risky. You promised me that you wouldn't do anything without checking with me."

"Well, I'm telling you now," Gylziia said. "I'm leaving. I can't stand this place any longer."

Nanny jumped out of bed and rushed over to Gylziia's little crude bed.

"Ok! I know that you're ready to leave, and I can't stop you because you're a big woman. But do me a favor, don't leave yet. Let me go and check it out to make sure it is safe," Nanny pleaded.

Gylziia stopped dead in her tracks and gave Nanny a funny look.

"What do you mean that you're going to check it out? So, you're saying that you Nanny, the woman I've been living with here all this while, is going to leave here and go up into the mountain and check on these people?"

"Yes, I'm telling you not to throw away your life by making any hasty decisions," Nanny said, ignoring her question.

"What kind of powers do you have that could take you up there?" Gylziia continued to pry, but Nanny would not budge for fear that Gylziia would be able to use it against her.

"Alright, I'll not go tonight, but if I hear it again tomorrow night and we're still here then I'm gone, and you cannot stop me," Gylziia said defiantly.

"Fair enough," Nanny said meekly.

"Now I would like you to do me a favor. Stay right here and go to bed, and if Bakra or anybody comes here looking for me just tell them that I'm tired and gone to bed. Don't worry I'll make up the bed to look like I'm sleeping."

Nanny skillfully propped up her bed like she was sleeping in it, then headed towards the door, only stopping briefly to tell Gylziia not to wait up for her. She quietly slipped out the door, crept quietly behind the barracks and quickly morphed into an owl and flew off towards the drumming sounds in the distance. As she shot up higher and higher in the sky, she looked back to see the diminishing lights of the plantation far below. She could still recognize some of the major buildings like the boiler house, the store houses and the Great House. As she flew farther away from the plantation the drumming sounds grew louder and louder.

Suddenly, looking over to the right, she saw shadows moving towards the sounds. They were moving erratically and looking behind as they ran forward. Nanny recognized them as some young men from the plantation who were trying to escape. She looked in all directions around them as they hurried along but it did not appear that anyone was tracking them. She felt excited for the men and was secretly cheering them on for their bravery. She quickly flew a wide circle around the men and continued on her way towards the drumming.

As Nanny approached the rendezvous point, she suddenly felt cold as the hairs on the back of her neck stood erect. The pulsating sounds of the talking drums became louder and louder, but something did not feel right. There was something in the music that was phony. The message was becoming garbled and unintelligible. It lacked soul and emotion. Then it struck her that this might be a trap.

"Putus was right," she said to herself. "This looks like a trap, set up by Bakra to catch runaways."

As she descended through the darkness she could see a group of men holding dogs, hiding in the bushes, while four men vigorously pounded on drums in the clearing.

Suddenly Nanny felt sick. The men back there were walking straight into a trap and there was nothing that she could do to help them without blowing her cover. She felt sorry for the men as she watched them move closer and closer to their fate. The men looked very fit and strong as they advanced nearer and nearer to the meeting place.

"I will stop these ambushes by Bakra," Nanny promised. "I will attack them with my people, and discourage them from coming out here at night. I will make things right. Right now nothing is fair. Bakra has weapons, dogs, the false drumming, everything! And what do these poor people have? Only their hopes and dreams of a better life. The poor people are doing nothing wrong; they only want their freedom. Freedom to live out their dreams as normal human beings. What's wrong with that?" Her mind flashed back to Gylziia and she felt sick. She could have been one of those young people down there advancing towards danger.

Nanny perched on a tree branch a few feet above the men with the dogs hiding in the bush. She counted, one, two, three, four white men and, three, six, nine, twelve head drivers. The head drivers held the dogs firmly and kept them silent. Some continuously fanned away the annoying mosquitoes that were buzzing around their faces. They looked tense and spoke in hushed tones. Nanny listened intently to their conversation.

"I hope that we catch a few tonight, because these bloody mosquitoes are eating us alive," a tall lanky white man said, jokingly.

"Yes, I hope so too," another replied. "These savages don't appreciate anything at all. They are like children; we have to protect them from danger."

"They don't realize how good they have it here. Why do they want to leave?" another one asked. "Do they believe that those Maroon criminals can take better care of them? Can they give them food and shelter like we can? Will they take care of them when they're sick? Why are these bloody bastards so stupid? Then again, as you said earlier, they are like children, never thinking things through. My little six years old daughter Mary is smarter than all of them put together," another one boasted.

"Look at those ones over there with the dogs," a tall lanky one said, pointing over at the head drivers. "They know where their meal ticket is and they will fight to protect it. I just like when a slave realizes his station in life. It makes life so much easier for all of us."

Nanny felt like puking when she heard the ignorant conversation taking place among the white men. She quietly flew over to another tree to keep from hearing any more of their blasphemy.

"Garbage! Utter garbage! These disgusting buffoons! Who do these white devils think that they are?" she said to herself. "They've wrapped themselves into this cloak of superiority that they fail to see the brilliance of our people. What a waste. It will take them centuries before they realize the extra ordinary abilities of our people. They say that we act like children, but I wonder who is acting like children, we or them. They act like spoiled chimpanzees that get into a fit when they don't get what they want. We on the other hand, don't take captivity too well. We will always try to find a way out."

From where she sat in the tree, the men looked like little children with toys, playing hide and seek. Nanny thought hard how she could prevent the coming confrontation between these ruthless men and the eager young men seeking their freedom, but nothing came to mind that would not jeopardize her cover. So she waited and waited for the inevitable clash.

In a short while the six young men, none older than nineteen, entered the clearing. When they saw the drummers they started dancing and hugging each other with joy. Nanny felt sick to her stomach because she knew that this celebration was short lived.

Suddenly the young men stopped celebrating and stood frozen like they had seen a ghost. Nanny felt sorry for them. They were like her babies being sacrificed on the altar of oppression. Tears flowed freely down her face as she saw the boys being beaten with the whips and mauled by the vicious dogs. The white men just stood around laughing as the vicious dogs attacked the helpless boys over and over again. The screams echoed in the distance disturbing the tranquility of the valley, as the young men cried out in agony. They curled up into tiny balls trying to protect themselves from the unending attacks as they continued their cries for mercy.

Nanny felt helpless. What could she do to help these poor, innocent young men? Then an idea popped into her head. Instantly she began making wild hooting sounds in the dark. The men froze in their tracks, looked all around and up in the trees, not sure of what to make of the strange sound. They quickly abandon the beatings, tied up the men and dragged them back to the safety of the plantation. Nanny smiled as she saw how scared they were.

"Imagine that, these men all have their big weapons and dogs, and yet they're afraid of a few birds. And they say that we act like children."

It was well past midnight when Nanny eventually dropped into her bed. Gylziia was fast asleep clutching her little bag; the same bag that she would take with her to freedom.

The next morning the plantation was all abuzz with the news of the six young men. The head driver gathered all the workers in the wagon yard, outside the boiler house for a quick meeting before the start of the work day. In the centre of the yard, tied to tall wooden poles were the six young men from the night before; swollen all over and blooded. One of them had his right eye so swollen that he could not see out of it. They were covered in bite marks and scratches. Standing on a tree stump above everyone was the head driver ready to address the gathering.

"Bakra has done so much for you," he began in a quiet voice. "From the day that you got here he has been taking care of you. Who gives you food to eat and clothes to wear?" Nobody in the crowd replied. "Who gives you somewhere to live and a bed to sleep on?" Again nobody said a word. "Who takes care of you when you're sick?" Nobody answered. "You people," he said, pointing his finger at them. "You're all so ungrateful, worthless, and good for nothing. Bakra is like a father to you. He looks out for you everyday of your lives and what does he ask in return? What does he ask in return?" he repeated in a loud voice.

"The only thing that he asks you to do is to cut his cane and get it to the factory on time. Is that too much to ask after he has done so much for you?" he asked. "What more do you want from Bakra?" he shouted at the top of his voice. "What more can he do for you? Tell me! Tell me right now!" he called out, raising his hands in the air in frustration. "Look at me," hitting his chest. "I came from the same place, just like you. And I came here the same way, just like you. But what you all want to do is run off and join those good for nothing criminals up in the mountain. But I'm warning you, those criminals will get you all killed. It might sound exciting to be up there in the mountain running up and down like wild hogs; but the truth is that you really live like wild animals in the bush. Why do you think that they come down here to raid the plantations? Because they're starving!

Do you hear me! They're starving!" he emphasized.

"Plus they're nearly naked because they don't have any clothes to wear. Do you want to give up all this for that kind of life?" he asked, extending his hands. "Many of them wish that they could come back down here and get back to their three square meals a day and a nice bed to sleep on at night. I know that you're smarter than that; after all, you're my people," he said, softening his tone. "My people, I love you to death." He smiled and looked around the crowd for a moment, then he switched back to his caustic demeanor and said, "But if anyone of you ever foolish enough to try it, this is what will happen to you," pointing to the six young men, all bloodied up and a few looking delirious. "They made a big mistake last night, and now they're paying for it. Remember this! Bakra has the best team of trackers in Jamaica. We make tracking down our people our top priority, and we lose only a few lucky ones every year. Many plantation owners send their trackers here to be trained. So know this; we will hunt you down, like the low life you are, and find you if it is the last thing we do.

Now one more thing, I know that some of you knew that these boys were going to try something last night. Some of you might say that it is not your business and you're not an informer for Bakra; but Bakra pays well for information like this. Bakra takes good care of anybody who takes care of his business. You don't have to give us any names, just tell us when and we will track them down. Remember!" he said, wagging his long bony finger at them. "Don't bite the hand that feeds you. Now get out there and do Bakra's work!" he shouted.

"And don't get into my way today or you won't like it."

He then cracked his mighty whip and everyone scrambled away and hurried to their work station.

That evening when Nanny arrived home, she found Gylziia sitting on the doorstep. When she saw Nanny she ran and gave her a big hug and told her thanks.

"What's that for?" Nanny asked, pretending that she didn't know.

"Let's go inside and talk," Gylziia said. As they walked inside and closed the door Gylziia grabbed her and hugged her again and again.

"Nanny I will never question you again," she exclaimed. "Look how you saved my life last night," she said. "How did you know that it was a trap?

Suppose I did not listen to you last night and dashed out there like a blinking fool; look what would've happened to me! Nanny I respect the very ground that you walk on. I will never doubt you again," she kept talking, on and on.

"It was nothing," Nanny replied, trying to make light of the incident.

"Nothing Nanny? What're you saying?" Gylziia asked, seemingly perplexed.

"I believe that you're the greatest woman on this island right now, today! You're very special! There is nobody like you. I shall follow you wherever you go."

Nanny began to blush. No one had ever said this to her. No one had ever made so much fuss over her.

"Alright Gylziia, calm down," Nanny urged. "I hope that you were not talking about me today out in the field. You know how the stupid head drivers get nervous when they hear about people like me."

"No! No! Nanny," Gylziia said, shaking her head. "After I'm not a fool. But tell me something Nanny, where were you when they caught the young boys?" Gylziia asked.

Nanny hesitated. "You know that 'bush has ears and eyes' (someone is always listening and watching). I will tell you everything one day. Yes, everything will be revealed to you one day; just be patient my friend."

Gylziia did not know what to make of it. Nanny was so calm, and confident. It was as if she had everything under control. She did not understand all of what Nanny was saying but she knew that she was in the presence of greatness. This was the first time that she had seen so much power in the hands of a woman. And the puzzling thing was that she did not flaunt it. She displayed such humility and grace.

'Who was this woman,' Gylziia wondered. 'Why was she here? What did she want? When she spoke, she spoke with such authority and confidence.' Gylziia quietly fell asleep that night thinking about Nanny and being happy that she was her roommate.

Chapter 10

The sugarcane harvesting season was at its peak. The slaves worked around the clock, day and night; cutting the cane, loading it onto wagons, and getting it to the factory.

As the long, hot tropical sun pummelled the countryside, the whipping became even more frequent and brutal. Everywhere you went around the factory-yard, people could be seen nursing their wounds and walking with varied degrees of limp. The slaves looked ragged and beaten up. Some walked around like they were in a stupor, awakened only by the crack of the whip on their backs.

Nanny came very close to tasting the whip one day. She was standing around under a large Guango tree after lunch, laughing and talking with other co-workers while they waited on their head driver to arrive and to give them their instructions for the afternoon. Suddenly another head driver, passing by on his way to work in another field, and thinking that they were goofing off, took out his whip. Out of the corner of her eyes Nanny saw the head driver hurrying towards them with the whip in his hand. She was just in time to call out to the other ladies to run, while she herself ran as fast as she could to get away from this violent man. But not all of the women were as fortunate. The older, larger women took the brunt of the whipping. Some cried out in pain, while others cursed under their breaths.

"The damn boy could be my son and he's using that blastid whip on me," one angry, elderly woman swore in disgust. "I know that if he was back in the Motherland he would've had more respect for the elderly. But the white people have trained him not to honor his parents or old people for that matter. What kind of world are we living in today when young people don't respect old people?"

"The white people them don't think about those things," another woman said. "All they think about is money. They don't give one damn about us. We could be dead for all they care."

One lady, while trying to get away, tripped and fell and broke her leg. Despite writhing in pain on the ground and crying out in agony, the head driver kept whipping her without mercy. Nanny was so angry to see the barbaric treatment of the woman that she was tempted to snuff out the head driver on the spot, but held back for fear of exposing herself.

When the head driver eventually left, obviously pleased with himself that he had helped Bakra to 'fix' the lazy women, Nanny and the other women rushed over to the woman on the ground, bawling out in pain and holding her leg.

"Look what that stupid man did to my leg," she cried, showing the open cuts caused by the whip and her leg obviously broken. "And with my leg like this, how am I going to manage?"

Nanny placed her hands on the woman's broken leg and felt the separated bones. The woman winced in pain as Nanny touched her leg. Nanny gingerly put both hands on the part of the leg that was broken and the bone suddenly snapped back in place. The woman looked up at Nanny with a puzzled look on her face. She had suddenly felt this swift warm electrical current travelling up and down her leg. And when it stopped, the pain was gone and she could move her leg freely again.

"Shhh! Shhh!" Nanny cautioned, putting her finger to her lips and giving her a wink. The appreciative woman smiled back at Nanny and then slowly rose to her feet with the help of the other women.

"Is what happened?" a loud mouth woman inquired. "I could swear that you said that her leg was broken. But now she is able to walk." Nobody responded. Everyone fell silent in thought. They all knew what they saw, but no one said a word for fear of words getting back to Bakra.

The next morning, as Nanny opened her front door to leave for work she was stunned to see a big pumpkin sitting on her step. She looked around but there was no one in sight. She eagerly called inside to Gylziia who was busy trying to find her slippers under the bed, to tell her the good news. They were amazed at the size of the pumpkin and puzzled as to who could have left it there.

"Maybe it was the lady who fell down yesterday and you healed," Gylziia said with a giggle. "She was in a very high spirit the entire afternoon."

"It was no big thing; but if it is her, then I'm thankful," Nanny said smiling.

The next morning, the same thing happened. This time the person left a big portion of Yellow yam on the doorstep. Nanny and Gylziia both wondered who was donating the food, as they placed the yam on the table, closed the door and hurried to work.

At work Nanny observed the lady whom she had healed looking quite busy and hard at work. She wondered if she was the person leaving all that food at their doorstep. She glanced over at her a few times throughout the day, but by the end of the day she was nowhere nearer to solving the problem.

That evening, while eating the pumpkin and the yam in a pot of soup, Nanny and Gylziia devised a plan to find out who was leaving this food on their doorstep.

As night fell they took turns staying up, looking to see who would be coming by to leave the package. They waited and waited all night long, but no one came.

"Maybe they've stopped coming," Gylziia said looking disappointed.

"I hope so," Nanny commented. "Because I was beginning to feel a little uncomfortable about it. I wish we could find out who it is, so that we can thank them."

A few nights later the two ladies were sitting up in bed talking and laughing and reminiscing about their past lives back in the Motherland when suddenly they heard a little shuffling outside. They fell silent immediately and quietly crept over to the little window to peek outside. They stood on either side of the window and slightly pulled the curtain back to peek outside. Outside, walking away from their door was the same woman whom Nanny had healed. She stopped momentarily and looked back to see if anyone was watching. When she was certain that she was alone she turned and hurried on her way. Nanny and Gylziia looked at each other and smiled.

"She is a good woman Nanny. She can't thank you enough for what you did for her," Gylziia said.

"I agree," Nanny responded. "I will talk with her tomorrow at the market. Let's go outside and see what she has left us this time."
Nanny quietly opened the door to find a small bag on the doorstep. She quickly picked it up, returned inside and placed it on their little table. She opened the package and was in for a surprise. A dozen mangoes! Nanny's favorite.

"A woman after my own heart!" Nanny exclaimed. "I like her, yes I like her a lot!"

The following day was Sunday, and that was the only day that Bakra gave everyone some time for themselves. A visit down to the market in the village square was a must for everyone. Some people went down there to sell their surplus produce from their little garden, but most people went down there to shop and to socialize with their families and friends.

Nanny got up very early, before the roosters and hurried over to meet Putus in her garden. She had ripe tomatoes, lettuce, peppers and callaloo to sell at the market. Nanny liked going to the market with Putus because she got a chance to sit with her and while selling, meet and talk to a lot of people; something that was hard to do during the week. It was also a good time for her to spend quality time with her brothers without drawing attention, although by now many people saw the resemblance.

In the early morning fog, Putus moved quickly around the garden cutting the mature callaloo and lettuce, and handing it to Nanny to tie and place inside a large crocus bag. She then skillfully picked the tomatoes and peppers and then carefully packed them into bags. The Sun was slowly rising when everything was finally packed and they were ready to go.
The two women made katas [a round wrap placed on the head to cushion the load] and placed them on their heads to balance the load.

The marketplace was slowly coming to life in the early morning hours with higglers [sellers], searching diligently to find a 'good' spot to put down their wares. Putus searched around for awhile to find her special spot. She swore by it. According to her that was the only spot where she had good luck and was able to selloff everything that she brought.

When she finally found the spot, the ladies gently took the loads off their heads and placed them on the ground. First, Putus took out her brightly colored blanket and placed it on the ground. After, they carefully laid out the produce as they anxiously waited for the shopping to begin. By six o'clock the marketplace was bustling with activity as early morning shoppers arrived and more higglers displayed their wares. The air soon became saturated with the sweet smells of tropical fruits, beautifully displayed everywhere: mangoes, ripe bananas, plantains, paw paws, sour sops, sweet sops, apples, pineapples, June plums, you name it; on stalls, after stalls, after stalls. Vegetables were in abundance too, and higglers could be seen sprinkling water on them to keep them fresh.

Next to them were the ground provisions: yams of all varieties, green banana, dasheens, coco, cassava, sweet potato, and on and on. Further down were the 'dry goods' higglers unpacking used clothes for men, women and children. Others were selling pots and pans, tools, muskets and ammunitions, swords and other items.

By eight o'clock the marketplace was packed with patrons, some trying to buy quickly and head back home to get as much work done as possible, while others were just out to browse the market and enjoy the day.

As the morning progressed, more people arrived. Mothers brought their children and allowed them to run around and play freely while they shopped. The atmosphere in the market was so different from on the plantation; like night and day. Here, it was stress-free and people acted more civil towards each other. The air was filled with laughter as folks met each other, sometimes for the first time. People talked about their lives and their families and reminisced about their past lives. Everyone was very careful not to talk too much or too loudly about conditions on the plantation, for fear of informers. No one spoke about the Maroons or about the talking drums at nights, although everyone secretly wanted to know who had ran off to join them that past week.

It was about nine o'clock when Nanny saw the woman. She was well dressed with a beautiful floral hat in the shape of a bird. She approached Putus' stall, greeted them with a broad smile and looked at the provisions on the blanket.

"How much a bundle for your callaloo?" she asked boldly. Putus told her. Then she asked about the peppers, lettuces and tomatoes. Putus told her the prices and waited for her to place an order. The lady finally ordered a bundle of callaloo and some peppers. As she paid her bill and was about to leave, Nanny walked over to her and asked if she could speak with her.

"Sure," the woman replied pleasantly.

Nanny hesitated, and then told the lady that she had seen her the night before at her door.

"I know that you're the person leaving all those nice foods at my door," she began.

"Is something wrong?" the lady asked, looking concerned.

"No! No! Everything is fine," Nanny replied.

"Don't get me wrong; I love them, they're some of my favorite foods, but I'm begging you to stop."

"But I don't mind doing it," the woman protested, with a broad smile on her face.

"Nobody has ever done anything like that for me. I'm indebted to you for life."

"No, no, you don't," Nanny insisted.

The woman looked very disappointed.

"Listen," Nanny said, looking her straight in the face. "I appreciate what you've been doing, but the fact of the matter is that I would have done it for anybody, even for the worthless head drivers, whom I hate like poison."

They both laughed.

"What is your name?" the woman asked.

"Nanny."

"Well Miss Nanny, Massa God bless you for what you did for me and I will always be grateful. I'm here if you need me for anything. And by the way, did you know that from that day I have not felt any sort of pain in my whole body? No lady, my whole body feels like a young gal again. Praise be to Massa God!" she said, raising her hands in the air. They both had a good laugh.

Nanny put her finger to her lips and begged her not to mention it to anyone, and she readily agreed.

When the lady left, Putus came over to join Nanny, with her hands on her hips.

"What happened to you and that lady?" she asked inquisitively.

"Nothing much," Nanny said. "I will tell you about it later."

Just then Nanny's five brothers, Cudjoe, Accompong, Cuffy, Johnny and Quao arrived. Nanny had told them earlier in the week that she would be there with Putus. She greeted each of them with a hug and a kiss. She introduced them to Putus and it left her speechless. As the boys shook her hand she smiled and blushed like a teenage girl meeting some young hunks for the first time.

"Nanny, why didn't you tell me that you had all these handsome brothers?" Putus asked.

"What other secrets are you hiding from me? Backside [wow]! This one is the 'dead stamp' [identical] of you," pointing to Quao, the baby of the bunch.

Nanny and the boys laughed and talked about everything under the sun, except what was happening on the plantation. She accompanied them to the other stalls to buy yams, dasheens, and other provision that Putus did not sell.

"This island is really fruitful," Nanny said while walking and looking at the various stalls. It reminds me so much of the Motherland. Everything grows here; you just have to stick it in the ground."

"This is truly paradise!" Quao, the youngest brother exclaimed.

"It would be paradise if we were free people to enjoy it," Cudjoe said with a frown on his face.

"Why do we have to live like this on the plantation? Why? Why?" he asked under his breath, between clenched teeth.

Nanny, sensing a tension brewing in the air at the wrong time, and definitely the wrong place, quickly changed the subject to something more pleasant.

"Have you boys heard about the big celebration coming up?" she asked pleasantly.

"No," the brothers replied.

"Well, it seems that they have this big celebration on the island every year at this time, Putus was telling me. It sounds like a big thing around here, because even Bakra takes part in it."

"That lady Putus is so smart," Cudjoe said, smiling. "It looks like she knows everything that is happening around here."

"Big brother is in love!" young Quao chided, pointing a friendly finger at his big brother.

"Watch your mouth little one," Cudjoe rebuked him lovingly. Then everyone burst out laughing.

It was now noon and the sun blazed overhead forcing many people to find shade or take out their umbrellas. Many people were still arriving at the market, although many of the early morning higglers, including Putus, were packing up to go home.

Putus was very pleased with herself. She had sold off all that she had and had the money to prove it.

Cudjoe and the other brothers picked up their bags said their goodbyes to Putus and each gave Nanny a big hug.

As she rolled up the blanket, Putus turned to Nanny and said,

"Thanks for coming today Nanny. I really like when you come to the market with me," she continued with a broad smile. "You always bring me good luck. You gave me a big shocker today with your brothers. They looked so handsome, especially the oldest one; what's his name again?"

"Cudjoe," Nanny replied, with a smile.

"Yes, Cudjoe. He is the best looking one out of all of them," she said smiling.

"But why is he so serious? Is he always that serious?" she asked.

"Yes, Cudjoe is the most serious one of the bunch, but he's very funny too when you get to know him," Nanny added.

"If I was looking for a husband, it is somebody like him that I would want; the strong, handsome and serious type."

"Be careful, old people have a saying that, 'silent river runs deep,'" Nanny said smiling.

"Why do you say that?" Putus asked.

"Nothing," Nanny replied. "Just that you should check out the inside of the package too." They both laughed.

"Everyday you surprise me more and more, Nanny. I'm so happy that we're friends. And now that I've met all of your handsome brothers, maybe

I might be in your family one day, who knows. This is really my lucky day! When we get home please come with me to the garden so that I can cut some fresh callaloo and things for you and Gylziia."

Nanny smiled, not saying a word, but in her heart she was thankful for the opportunity to spend the day down at the market with her.

While they were walking home, Nanny asked Putus about the holiday coming up.

"The holiday is called Christmas. That is the best time we have around here," Putus explained. "Work stop braps [entirely], and Bakra gives you some new clothes and shoes. Some years Bakra leaves the plantation and goes off with his family to visit friends far away, so the whole place is quiet and peaceful. Even the wicked head drivers are nice to us for a change," she laughed.

"Lawd missis, it is the best time of the year!" she exclaimed. "It's sweet! It's sweet! I can't tell you!" she shouted with a bright glow on her face. "We always look forward to this season, more than any other time of the year, my friend. Then on December 26th we all go down to the market square to watch the Jonkonnu parade. Boy that is sweet! The men dress up into brightly colored costumes and then march through the streets. They wear masks like horse head and cow head. The devil costumes are the scariest! Sometimes some people will dress up like kings and queens or a house to look like the Great House; that always makes Bakra happy. I'm telling you Nanny, when the horse heads come out, all the little kids start crying. Then they have the little band of musicians playing gumbay drums, fife, fiddle, grater and any kind of old pots and pans that can make lots of noise; coming up behind the dancers. It is a whole lot of fun! fun, fun, fun! You will love it girl!"

"Then Putus," Nanny asked innocently. "Why is this holiday so special?"

"Well, I'm not so sure, but old people say that it was brought here from Britain by Bakra. They celebrate it with their own type of funny music, dancing, and masquerades. But we have taken it and put our own sweet African style into it to give it some life."

"Then suppose I don't want to celebrate it, what will happen?" Nanny asked.

"Nothing will happen," Putus replied, looking at her strangely. "You will still get everything like everybody else, but you will miss out on some fun times. My little advice to you friend is; you'd better enjoy Christmas because that's it for the year. Come January morning, everything is back to normal. It's like the devil took a holiday during the Christmas season, but returned with a vengeance in January. So you might as well enjoy the short break."

"Thanks for telling me. It sounds like fun! I'm looking forward to it," Nanny remarked.

"One more thing I need to tell you Nanny; during the Christmas break many people use it as a time to run away. Everything is so relaxed around here during the season that some people just take off. In most cases Bakra won't miss you for days and by then you're far away." Nanny kept walking up the hill, looking straight ahead in silence, not wishing to see the expression on Putus' face.

As they continued walking towards the plantation Putus eventually broke the silence. "Tell me something Nanny, I notice that sometimes you talk like Bakra them, in their speakie, spookie [foreign] voice. Where did you get that talking from?"

"I don't know," Nanny said, relieved that they had switched the subject. "I think that I pick up languages pretty easily."

"All I know is that it sounds funny coming from you," Putus laughed. "It's like the voice don't match the person."

"So, are you saying that I could not be a Bakra's wife?" Nanny asked jokingly, in a heavy British accent.

Putus looked at her in amazement, not believing what she had just heard. Then she broke out laughing.

"Lawd girl, you could've fooled me." And they both burst out laughing.

As she prepared for bed that night Nanny reflected on all that Putus had said that day, especially the part about people running away during the Christmas holidays when everything was relaxed. Bakra would be in high spirit and most of all, no one was watching you. There would certainly not be a fake drumming team out in the bush to catch anyone.

"This could be a good time to escape," Nanny said under her breath. But on second thought, was the timing right? This kept her awake long into the night.

A few days later Putus invited Nanny to go with her to visit an old friend. Putus warned her that her friend was a very nice gentleman but was a great talker.

"Yes Putus, very talkative," she said laughing, knowing full well that nobody could talk more than Putus.

"What are you laughing about?" Putus insisted, and then joined in the laughter because she knew what Nanny was thinking.

They walked down to a small shed at the back of the blacksmith's shop where they found this little old man with a long scrappy white beard working quietly in a corner on a 'Horse head' costume. Littered on the floor were scraps of rags, wires, and paper.

"How di [How do you do?] Mass Benji!" Putus greeted the old man.

"How di my chile!" came a warm and friendly reply.

"I brought you a new girlfriend," Putus joked.

"You're always bringing me pretty girls," the old man joked, looking at Nanny and giving her a wink.

"And what is your name lovely lady?"

"My name is Nanny."

"What a beautiful name, Nanny, for a fine-looking lady," he said, smiling. "For a pretty little lady, you look so strong and spiritual; a born leader. Don't let these bastards turn you into a sheep, you're a lioness! Queen of the jungle," he smiled, giving her some fatherly advice.

"You are the generation that's going to shake up this place. I'm too old, and sometimes when I think back to my youth, I believe that I was too scared to fight these white people. But your generation, you especially, I can see it in those sharp eyes of yours, that you're not going to put up with this foolishness for too long. You see my daughters, when I was your age, because I came to this country as a little boy, but that's a long story, many of us young people at the time really believed that if we worked very hard, Bakra would eventually give us our freedom. So I worked very hard, day after day, but nothing changed. The only thing that changed around here was the Bakra. When the new Bakra arrived, everything started all over again. So I worked hard for this new Bakra and he stayed for a little while and then he moved on and a new one arrived, and on and on it goes. I can't forget when this one Bakra came and he didn't like a bone in my body. Nothing I did pleased him. He was even planning to sell me to another plantation. But Massa God was not sleeping. So before he could sell me he came down with a bad sickness and 'kicked the bucket' [died]. Yes, died! I've never rejoiced when a man goes to meet his Maker, but this one time I was happy. He's buried in the burial plot over yonder," pointing in the direction.

"So you see ladies, I realized then and there that Bakra only cared about one thing, money!" he said raising his voice. "And as long as he's making money he doesn't care one damn, if we live or die," Mass Benji said, with a sad look on his face.

"Sometimes I feel like kicking myself for not running away long ago and joining the Maroons. But I was really scared or maybe I was just a coward. I was afraid to go up against Bakra. I didn't believe that life could be better under the Maroons. We used to say that it was only worthless people who ran away and lived like wild animals in the mountains. But over the years we got to realize that they were the smart, ambitious ones. The ones who choose life, to live as they pleased. How I wish I could go back to those days," he lamented, looking down on the dirt floor.

"Ok, let's talk about something more pleasant," he said, with a shy smile on his face and more energy in his voice. "What can I do for you lovely ladies?"

"What did I tell you about this man Nanny?" Putus said, with a broad smile. "Do you believe me now?" she joked. They both laughed.

"Mass Benji, please tell Nanny how you got to use this shed to build your costumes," Putus begged.

"Alright, let me tell you this one quickly," the old man began. "The blacksmith department uses this place as a store house for their scrap metals and junk, but loans it out to the costume builders once a year to build their costumes. Many years ago, when I was a boy, they used to have to build the costumes under that big Guango trees over there. But some years the rain would fall and ruin the costumes. So seeing that I was working in the blacksmith's shop at the time, I asked the Busha if we could build the costumes under the shed, out of the rain. At first he refused because, as he put it, 'Bakra wouldn't want that.' So I decided to build the prettiest king and queen costume and a big colorful Great House to impress the Bakra. The Bakra was so pleased with my work that he said that we could use the shed whenever we wanted to. So we've been using it ever since. But I remember years later when the same wicked Bakra who wanted to sell me, wanted to take it away from us, all because he didn't like me. That man was a brute [bad man]," he said with disgust. "But I promised not to talk anything that was unpleasant, so I'm sorry," he apologized again.

"You see," he continued. "Some Bakras loved the masquerade, especially when we built the king and queen and the Great House costumes. Some of them however did not care one way or the other about it, as long as it did not interfere with their work. But there were some who absolutely hated it, for one reason or the other. I remember one Bakra saying that the masquerade was used as an excuse to avoid work. He said that from the first day he came to this plantation he noticed that we were all a lazy bunch, and he was going to change all that. Ha! Ha! he didn't last more than a year. They had to send him back to England, because he was sick so often. Everybody was so happy when he left. Some people said that it was Mada B [spiritual leader] who had cast a spell on him, but who knows if that is true."

For the next couple of hours Nanny and Putus sat around with the old man, helping him with the costumes, and listening to his fascinating stories with joy and laughter. As they said their goodbyes, Nanny felt a deep love for the old man. She loved his stories and would listen to him all day.

'There must be a better way for Mass Benji to live out his final days in dignity,' she thought to herself.

Chapter 11

Nanny could hardly sleep the night before she was to return to work after the Christmas holidays.

"Where did the time go?" she asked Gylziia, her roommate, but not expecting an answer.

"That's what happens when you're having fun," Gylziia giggled. "I could get use to this life of freedom," she joked. "But our 'free paper burn' today; it is back to Bakra's work. By the way Nanny, have you made any decision about what we were talking about before Christmas? I'm still serious about it."

"Just be patient," Nanny reminded her. "When the time is right I will tell you," she continued, as she quickly grabbed her hat and lunch container and ran out the door, followed closely behind by Gylziia.

The moon was full in the early morning sky as all workers rushed to their work station before the big Karchy horn blew signaling the start of the work day.

It was as if Christmas never happened. The hardship of life on the plantation returned with a vengeance. The whipping began immediately after the Karchy blew on all those who were late. The big burly head driver looked very annoyed and mean. He was on the war path. No one was safe that morning. The word was out; do your work and keep as far away as you can from the head driver.

"Nanny, it looks like the head driver's undergarment is too tight this morning," Putus whispered to Nanny while they worked.

"It really seems that way," Nanny said smiling. "Would you like to see something funny this morning? Let's loosen him up and have some fun," Nanny suggested with a mischievous look on her face.

"Ah, awe!" Putus uttered. "What are you up to this time chile? You'd better be careful because we don't want any trouble with that man this morning," Putus cautioned. She remembered the last time when the head driver was acting horrible, just like now, Nanny promised that she would fix him.

She watched him out of the corner of her eyes all day until she found the perfect opportunity. The head driver went into the bush to relieve himself and all of a sudden the workers saw him running out of the bush, crying out, with his trousers around his ankles. No one dared to laugh for fear of offending him; but it was really a sight to behold. After work Nanny couldn't wait to tell her what had happened.

"The driver was busy doing his business when he turned around to see a big snake a few inches from his bare bottom. You should've seen his face when he saw the snake. It was like he was about to pass out. He didn't care who saw his nakedness, he just wanted to get away from that snake," Nanny laughed, until tears came to her eyes.

"No Putus my friend, this one will be classic, my best performance to date," she laughed.

Suddenly the sounds of a barrage of musket fire could be heard all around. Everyone immediately fell flat on the ground. Not long after, the explosions ceased. Then a voice from the bushes shouted, "Driver! Where is the driver? Stand up driver," the voice commanded.

Slowly the head driver stood up timidly facing the voice in the bushes. "My beloved African people told me that you've been beating them mercilessly for no reason at all, is that true?"

The head driver hung his head and did not respond.

"So you've refused to answer my question? I would bet if it was Bakra talking to you, you would be glad to answer him," the voice continued.

"Now I would like you to step forward so that all the workers can see you clearly."

The head driver nervously stepped forward, holding his head down; refusing to make eye contact.

"Next I want you to strut like a chicken and then give us the biggest rooster crow that you can muster up. So work your arms up and down and strut around and give us your loudest crow; remembering that my men here have their muskets pointed straight at your big, fat head, and all they're waiting for is my order to shoot."

The head driver strutted around slowly, crowing like a rooster; but the sound was very weak.

"Is that the best you can do driver? If you were a rooster crowing like that in the early morning, your master would take up his musket and blow off your head," the voice said, sounding very annoyed.

"That is not a champion rooster; that is a scared iddy biddy [little] rooster ready for the cooking pot. Come again driver, let me hear the biggest, baddest rooster crow around here."

The head driver did as he was instructed, strutting around flapping his arms and crowing at the top of his lungs.

"That's good son," the voice said. "You did well. Give him a clap everybody! Now driver, I'm a very busy man, don't let me have to come back down here again about you whipping my people. Now my beautiful African people just send and tell me if he's not treating you well. Alright I'm leaving, until next time. Warriors move out!"

Everyone went back to work, most people trying hard not to make eye contact with the embarrassed head driver.

After work Putus asked Nanny how she had done it.

"Easy," she said with a smile. "I just project my voice and let it sound like a lot of explosions all around," Nanny explained.

"But how come I didn't see your mouth moving?" Putus asked, completely baffled.

"That's the trick; you have to do it without moving your lips. Watch my face, 'I can talk like this without moving my lips'"

"You're good chile! Who taught you how to do that?" Putus asked.

"Nobody, I just figured it out by myself."

"Remind me never to get you angry," Putus commented, smiling.

That night Nanny had just fallen into a deep sleep when she was suddenly awakened by a series of explosions outside. Muskets were going off in all directions. Gylziia also jumped up out of bed. They looked at each other and without saying a word both rushed to the window to peek outside to find out what was causing the commotion.

"I wonder if the Maroons have come to attack the plantation," Gylziia whispered.

"I'm not sure," Nanny replied.

"Then suppose they are the Maroons, what are we going to do?"

"I would have to find my brothers and tell them. We can't leave without them," Nanny insisted.

"What brothers?" Gylziia asked, looking rather puzzled at Nanny. "Do you mean to tell me that you have brothers here on the plantation and you didn't tell me, your roommate, about them?" she asked, looking somewhat disappointed.

"I'm sorry, but I never tell anybody about them because I don't want Bakra to know."

"Then how many of them are there?" Gylziia asked.

"Five," Nanny replied quietly.

"Five! So how are you going to find them now?" she inquired. The explosions were now coming closer to the barracks.

"Look Nanny!" Gylziia whispered with excitement in her voice; pointing towards the buildings to the north of their barracks. "They're breaking into the storeroom and taking out the tools and materials. And look way over there, Nanny!" she exclaimed. "It looks like they're setting fire to the cane fields! The whole place is burning down!"

"Yes I see it," Nanny replied, trying to be calm and not wanting to show her excitement.

"Nanny! please! please! Let us go now, in this commotion," Gylziia pleaded. "Nobody will notice that we're gone until tomorrow morning, and by then we will be miles away."

"Ok, but before we leave, we have to find my brothers. I know that they're wondering about me right now."

"Alright," Gylziia agreed. "We will find them first and then we will leave, ok? I don't want to spend one more night in this evil place."

"Take it easy Gylziia," Nanny cautioned. "Calm down. We don't want to make any unnecessary mistakes. First of all, let's pick up a few things to take with us."

They quickly packed their little bags, grabbed their sweaters and headed towards the door. As they were about to open the door they heard a loud knock on the door. Both women looked at each other with a sickening feeling in their stomachs. Nanny slowly opened the door and was shocked to see Putus standing in the doorway with a little bag in her hand and a broad smile on her face.

"Come in quickly," Nanny said, beckoning with her hand. "What are you doing here Putus?"

"I knew that you'd be going with the Maroons tonight and I didn't want you to leave without me," Putus said smiling. "See, I'm packed and ready," she said, holding up her little bag.

"You've come just in time," Nanny said. "Me and Gylziia were just getting ready to go and find my brothers before we leave."

After looking through the windows for a few moments Nanny announced, "I think the time is right for us to go ladies, so let's go." Suddenly the emergency Karchy alarm began blaring loudly, waking up everyone. Everybody was expected to rush to their assigned emergency station.

The three women looked at each other with defiance in their eyes and without a word Gylziia quietly closed the door behind them and they blended into the night. Nanny led the way as they moved carefully; hiding behind buildings, trying desperately to avoid being seen by Bakra or his men as they walked towards the male barracks. Men and women could be seen hurrying to find their emergency stations.

Along with the blaring of the Karchy horns, the three women could hear the fire crackling and raging in the cane fields in the distance as more and more laborers were rushed over to contain it.

As Nanny and the ladies turned the final corner to the men's barracks they came face to face with some strangely dressed men coming out of the blacksmith's shop with an assortment of materials and tools in their hands. The three women stopped in their tracks and held their collective breaths for a brief moment. Both parties froze, and for what seemed like hours, no one spoke; everyone just stood there staring at each other like they were from a different planet.

The men, all wet and sweaty looked shiny like black pearls in the moonlight. They reminded Nanny of some of the young warriors back home.

"Are you the men who beat the talking drums?" she asked.

"Yes ma'm [Miss]," a tall muscular young man replied.

"Leave all this and come with us," another one said, his hands filled with tools. "You will never regret it. Don't waste your young lives in this wicked place."

"Yes, this place will only bring you hardship and misery," a tall skinny man with scrappy beard remarked.

"Yes we're coming," Nanny said, smiling as she looked over at Gylziia and Putus for approval.

Just then they saw a group of young men coming over towards them. Nanny quickly recognized them as her brothers, led by Cudjoe and some friends. Nanny hugged them and everyone greeted each other.

"We were just coming to get you Nanny," Cudjoe said. "The time is here."

"I know," she replied smiling.

"We have to leave now," interjected one of the Maroons. "They're waiting for us."

No one asked who the, 'they' were, neither did they care. The only thing that was important was that they were on their way to a new life.

Everyone helped to carry the tools, machetes, food stuff and anything else that they could carry off with them from the plantation.

"Take anything that you can get your hands on," one short, stocky Maroon said. "It is payment for all the free labor Bakra got out of you and not to talk about the brutal beatings. Tonight you get back your life, and nobody will ever put you back in bondage again," he said proudly.

"Ladies and gentlemen, it's time to go," a tall muscular man with big broad shoulders interrupted with a broad smile, his white teeth shining in the moonlight. Then in the next instant he became serious and barked orders at his men.

"Warriors, stay alert! Keep your eyes open, I don't want to lose anybody tonight. Prangah, you're the youngest one, so come up front with me." He was referring of course to a tall lanky boy not more than sixteen years old, most likely going on his first raid.

There was excitement in the air as the group hurried away from the plantation in the opposite direction of the raging fires.

Gylziia couldn't believe that she was actually leaving the plantation. And to top it off, she was leaving the past behind with her hero, Nanny. She had to pinch herself constantly and bounce her shoulder against Nanny's to reassure herself that she was not dreaming.

"Sorry Nanny, but I had to do that because I never believed that this day would ever come." She felt buckets of sweat running down her face and back, in spite of the coolness of the early morning air, and she loved it.

Chapter 12

The Maroons led Nanny and the rest of escapees quickly away from the plantation. They walked briskly in a long line, keeping their eyes open for Bakra's men. After a few miles away from the plantation, the air became suddenly quiet. Only the sounds of insects could be heard. The march up the hill was hushed, stifling the excitement that was dying to come to the surface.

Eventually they came upon a clearing in the forest where a few dozen other men and women were sitting around in the shadows, waiting for the other raiding parties to arrive. This was the Maroons' rendezvous point, a place reserved for them to take stock of the warriors' condition and the booty collected.

Piled to one side was a mound of provisions, supplies and weapons they had carried away from the plantation. Nanny and the group put down their load and greeted the others with smiles and quiet chatter for awhile until the same former group leader from down at the plantation said in a rather stern but friendly voice, "Ladies and gentlemen, let's get going, we have a long way to go, and we don't want Bakra to catch up to us."

Everyone picked up their loads and started the trek back into the forest to begin the steep climb up into the Blue Mountains.

As daylight forced its way through the cool morning mist, everyone on the trail was drenched in dew and sweat from head to toe. Nanny could barely see the plantation they had left far below in the distance. The air was fresh and clean like a new world had just opened up. The smell of burning

117

cane and the noise of the factory, of the day before, had suddenly evaporated. It was as if the world had stood still. This was a strange new sensation for Nanny. It felt rather unusual, as if she was losing her hearing. However whenever someone spoke, even in a whisper, you could hear the echo way in the ravines below.

'This is odd,' Nanny thought to herself. 'How could such a beautiful place like this exist and people are forced to coop up like chickens in a cage on the plantations; with those wicked white people making their lives a living hell?'

Nanny thought back on all the misery that she had left behind and felt sorry for those people still there. She remembered how she felt when she was leaving the plantation. That was a feeling that she would always cherish. She wished that all the other men and women trapped on the plantations would experience that feeling before they died.

The more Nanny thought about it, the more goose bumps covered her sopping wet body.

"Wow! This is awesome," is all that she could say.

"What did you say?" Gylziia asked, huffing and puffing up the hill, behind her.

"I'm just saying that life is great!" Nanny said smiling, her voice echoing in the distance.

"I wish more folks had come. I feel sorry for them. When I think about it; right now they're under the whips of the head drivers. Poor thing them."

Nanny's mind flashed back to the evening she and Putus had spent with the old man, at his costume work shop. She remembered the look of hopelessness in his eyes. She wished that he could have been with them, if nothing more than to fulfill some of his latent dreams. Nanny looked at Gylziia and Putus and the twenty other brave young men and women who had come away to join the Maroons. They were the future of the new Jamaica; a country where everyone would be free to pursue their dreams and aspirations without fear of Bakra.

Nanny was happy to be part of this future. She now realized that she had been preparing for this role all her life. She was not in Jamaica by accident. Her ancestors had chosen her to lead her people to freedom. They had given her all this power to challenge an unjust system. To bring balance in a world that was tipped in favor of the white devils. Now she knew why she was chosen.

Growing up she wondered why her grandmother kept her so close to her; sometimes even over the protests of her own mother.

All her mother wanted was a healthy child, a boy preferably, but what she got was this special girl. Nanny laughed to herself when she remembered hearing her mother talking one day to one of her friends, telling her that she had prayed so hard to Massa God for a son to give to her husband, 'But from the day that baby was born all thoughts of a son disappeared.'

She smiled when she thought about the many times that she had won arguments at home because her mother could not follow her reasoning.

"I don't know who you're or why they send you here to provoke me," her mother would say, in frustration.

Nanny recalled when she was quite young, her grandmother holding her up in the air and telling her, "You will make a difference in this world, do you hear me my baby? You will make a difference."

Nanny wondered what that meant at the time, but now things were becoming clearer. This was bigger than her mother, grandmother, or the Ashanti tribe.

Gylziia felt the excitement building up in her stomach as she thought about the journey to her new life. It seemed like ages that she had some measure of control over her life. Tears came to her eyes when she remembered the day she was captured from her village. She and four of her girl friends were coming from the river with containers full of water on their heads, laughing and talking, when they were suddenly pounced upon and captured by men, laying in wait in the bush. She remembered how she fought hard and struggled with them. She sunk her teeth into the arm of one of them and bit off the ear of another, until one of them came up behind her and hit her over the head with a rock. She remembered feeling this splitting pain at the back of her head, then when she woke up after several hours, she was tied up, and had a coffle around her neck, attached to other women. All the women were without a stitch of clothes. Gylziia felt so embarrassed that she was exposed in this way with so many men standing around, and there was nothing that she could do about it with her hands tied. She noticed some of the men laughing and pointing at her.

"That one there acts like a little cheetah," one of them said, to laughter. "She bucked like a bull and bit off poor Afghi's ears."

"If she had bitten off my ears, she would be dead by now," a bald head man with two big ears remarked.

Gylziia remembered feeling so thirsty when she woke up. As she cried out for water, a tall fierce looking man with a big scar on the right side of his face came over and gave her some water from a little pouch. She felt like she was in a dream. This was like an out of body experience. But she knew that it was real because of the splitting headache.

"Are you ok Gylziia?" Putus inquired. "You seem awfully quiet."

"I was just thinking about the misery that I passed through. Only Massa God knows what I've been through," she continued. "Putus did you know that I thought of suicide many, many times, but I didn't have the guts to go through with it? The lowest point in my life was when the white devils took me and raped me over and over again on the ship. I was a virgin Putus; never been with a man before, and the nasty white devils them took me and raped me. After it happened I just wanted to jump over the side of the ship into the sea and drown myself. I told Nanny over and over, that if she was not coming to join the Maroons, then I would go by myself."

"I know what you mean," Putus agreed. "I also passed through a similar situation like you on the ship, but I was determined not to give them the satisfaction of thinking that they had conquered me. They might hurt my body but I will never let them control my mind," she said defiantly. "I will join the raiding parties and attack the plantations and let them pay for all the hurt that they've caused me. I will show them no mercy; just like they did to me.

"I'm with you girl," Gylziia said. "They will surely pay." The ladies both burst out laughing, their laughter echoing way in the deep ravines below.

Nanny came up from behind, picking up the pace and caught up to them.

"Tell me what's so funny?" she asked Putus and Gylziia, playfully.

"We were just saying that those white devils are going to 'pay for roast and boil,'" [get what's coming to them] Gylziia said, smiling.

"They're going to feel the full wrath of the African women," she continued.

"Yes, they're going to get a taste of their own medicine," Putus said. "And you Nanny, you're going to lead us into battle against those brutes," she predicted.

They waited for a response from Nanny but none was forthcoming.

"Did you hear what we said Nanny? You will be our leader. I know you will do a much better job than any man," Putus pointed out.

Nanny did not say a word, but only smiled to herself.

The group continued the steep climb up the mountain as the sun rose high in the sky. Then just as they reached the top of a steep hill, they looked down to a startling sight.

Down in the valley below was the most beautiful waterfall that Nanny had ever seen. The glistening water gushing over the rocks was too beautiful and tempting to resist. Nanny and all the new runaways became very excited. But just as they were about to rush towards it the Maroon leader cautioned everyone to be quiet.

"This is a very dangerous part of the journey because the British soldiers always set up camp near to the falls to catch runaways and return them to the plantation. So everybody be quiet. Don't make a sound. I will send a few of my scouts to look around down there and make sure that everything is safe."

He quickly turned to a young man nearby and said in low firm voice, "Kofi, take a couple men and go down and look around. The rest of you remain quiet until they return."

In a flash the men disappeared down the hill towards the falls without making a sound. Nanny followed the men down as far as she could see.

The journey was becoming more intriguing by the minute. This was the first time that she had heard of the British soldiers. Who were they? What were they like? Where did they come from? All these questions flashed into her brain and no answers were forthcoming. She remembered on the ship hearing one or two of the white devils talking about England, but she did not pay it any attention. Was it the same place? Are these soldiers from there?

The Maroon scouts crept up very close to the enemy without being seen. They noted the number of guards on duty and where they were stationed.

They observed other soldiers busy cleaning their weapons. The men quietly withdrew and hurried back to the Maroon leader. The Maroon leader subsequently made the decision to make a detour around the waterfall to avoid any confrontation with the soldiers.

"It's a good thing that we didn't come into these mountains by ourselves or we would be caught," Gylziia commented.

"It looks like these Maroons really know these mountains," she continued. "I'm getting to like them more and more."

For the next few hours the group trekked quietly in a north easterly direction, making a wide circle to avoid the soldiers before turning north again on the way towards their camp. The trail was becoming steeper and more difficult to climb for the new runaways.

"Wow! These Maroons run up and down the mountain trails like mountain goats," Gylziia observed. I wonder when I'll be able to do that."

"You're young, you will get use to it in no time," Putus reassured her. They continued walking until they came upon a small stream fed by an abundance of clear, clean water gushing out of the rocks. The Maroon leader indicated that the spot was safe and they could rest there for a moment or two. While there, they could drink the water, fill their containers and take a dip in the stream.

With the Maroons on guard, Nanny and the others enjoyed the cool clean mountain stream.

"This place is nice, such beauty!" Putus exclaimed, splashing around in the stream. "I love this place so much. I wish we could stay here forever!"

"Yes missis [girl friend]!" Gylziia squealed with delight as she splashed in the water.

Not long after the leader came over and told them that it was time to leave.

"We have to keep moving if we're going to reach home before brown dust [night fall]."

Nanny felt her pulse racing when she heard the word home. She had not heard that word for such a long time. Nobody ever believed that they were at home on the plantation. The word home brought back so many memories; good and bad. Tears came to her eyes. 'Home sweet home. Wow!' She could not believe that the word could have such a profound emotional effect on her. The more she thought about it the more ideas flashed into her consciousness.

Home was where the heart was. Home was where the family lived. Home was where you felt safe and secured. Home was where you learned to build trust.

But trust was one of the biggest problems that new runaways would have, thanks to the legacy of Bakra's system; a system where you were taught to distrust your fellow man. 'The white devils sowed the seeds of mistrust from the beginning,' Nanny thought to herself.

Home, mmmm! The word sounded like music to her ears. Nanny wondered if these people were now her new family. So far they had treated them with respect, shared their food and guarded over them like mother hens keeping their chicks safe from danger. Was that enough though to classify them as family? Nanny kept all these thoughts in her heart.

As the evening sun began to set, the Maroon leader picked up the pace on the trail. He spoke quickly in low tones to his troops and they all became more alert.

Nanny wondered if they were near the camp and the team was making sure that they were not being followed. She did not have to wait long for her answer. As they rounded a corner they suddenly came face to face with two perfectly camouflaged Maroon warriors dressed in leaves and war paint, with muskets in hand, directing them quickly towards a small opening in the rock. The urgency in their hushed tones was enough to get everyone hurrying to get off the trail, and through the narrow opening. The passage way was so narrow that only one person could go through at a time, and only sideways.

Everyone waited patiently in line for their turn to enter the passage way. The guards, sensing the nervousness of the new people, reassured them that they had nothing to fear. Although many of them were not fully convinced, they did not utter a word. When it was Nanny's turn, she skillfully slid her small wiry frame sideways through the opening.

On the other side she was surprised to discover a beautiful countryside decorated with rolling hills and valleys intersected by a clear bubbling mountain stream snaking its way through giant floras.

"This is gorgeous!" Putus shouted, as she hurried towards the stream. "Who would believe that such a beautiful place could be in these mountains? I wonder how many more spots like this one is around here."

"I agree," Gylziia concurred. "You would never believe that all this beauty was just off the trail. I would bet that the British soldiers pass here every day and they don't know that it is right under their noses," she grinned.

Everyone rushed towards the gently rolling stream and jumped in to cool off. The smiles, laughter and frolicking could be heard throughout the valley.

"I just love this place!" Gylziia cried out with delight.

"This is paradise!" another woman exclaimed, tears running down her face. "Why did I stay so long on Bakra's plantation?" she lamented. "It is five years, come this June that I've been working on that plantation. I should've left there a long time ago. Look how nice this place is!" she continued. "But if truth be told, I was afraid. Afraid of what Bakra would do to me if I was caught. I was especially afraid of those tracking dogs and what I heard that they did to you if you were caught. But Lawd, I'm so sorry that my friend Bubbles didn't come too. We came here the same time off the ship and we have been best friends ever since. She's more of a coward, so when I told her to come with me, she hesitated, but I had to take care of my future, so I left her." She paused for a moment, wiped her eyes with the back of her hand and said, "But I miss her so much, it hurts me down to my belly bottom. She was the best friend I ever had."

"Don't worry," Nanny said to her gently. "You will see your friend again."

"And what makes you so sure lady?" the woman asked, turning towards Nanny.

"Lady, if this woman says that you will see your friend again, then you will see her again!" Putus interjected.

"And what's so special about this woman?" the lady continued.

"You will soon find out, just mark my words," Putus said.

'That's the problem right there,' Nanny thought to herself. 'Good woman but don't trust anybody, especially somebody with her same skin color.'

"Let's get going folks, the camp is just over the hill," the leader said finally. "Mass Willie, our great leader, is anxiously waiting for us."

The last mile took them up a very steep, narrow path which ended in a roughly hewed out plateau. At this elevation the view of the surrounding landscape was breathtaking.

'This place was chosen with care,' Nanny noted. She was becoming even more impressed with these Maroons.

Contrary to what Bakra had told them, these people were not wild and disorganized. They were skilled warriors and it would be a big mistake for the British soldiers to take them for some misfit group, just trying to survive.

As the weary group entered the village, all the men, women and children came out of their huts to greet them. A few men who were building some new huts in one corner of the property and some women working out in the field ran over to greet them. Everyone seemed so warm and friendly like they were long lost relatives.

Finally a little old man with grey hair and a slight limp came towards them with outstretched arms and a broad, friendly smile.

"Welcome my children! My name is William Ransford, but everybody here calls me Mass Willie. We're so happy that you've left that miserable plantation to be here with us. We're the Maroons, and we're a free people who will never be ruled by the British or any other people on this island again. I heard that you bumped into some British soldiers on your way up here. Don't worry about them. They are walking duppy [ghosts] and they don't even know it."

"Putus, what does he mean by duppy?" Gylziia asked in a whisper.

"Ghost!" Putus replied. "Ghost, don't you know ghost?"

"Oh!" Gylziia started saying.

"Shee! Shee! Be quiet! Let the man speak," Putus cautioned.

"Don't worry, we will never stop fighting for our right to live as free people," Mass Willie told them. "We will never give up. And if you would like to know, we know everything about them. We have men watching them all the time. We know every move that they make, so don't you worry about them," he reassured them.

"By coming up here today you're also saying that you wish to live as free men and women, and I congratulate you for your courage," he continued.

"No more beatings!" he emphasized and all the people cheered.

"No more being treated like a nobody!" Everyone cheered, including the new runaways.

"No more working for nothing! Those days are over. This is a brand new day!" he announced, with pride.

"By coming up here today ladies and gentlemen, you're telling everybody that you would like to contribute to the building of a free society for your children and grandchildren; and we applaud you for that. We hope that you will give us your skills and knowledge and your promise to help us build this beautiful country that will make all our ancestors and future generations proud. I believe in you," he said, wiping back tears. "We all believe in you," he continued, extending his hand. "And we promise you! Yes we promise you, that you will never be alone again. We're all here for you. I know that you're tired right now, so get some sleep and tomorrow we will talk some more."

Chapter 13

Nanny had barely set her head on the make shift pillow, curled up on the floor, sandwiched between Putus and Gylziia when she fell fast asleep. She slept for only a few hours when she was suddenly awakened by a familiar visitor.

"Nanny my chile, you took your sweet time getting up here," Mada Kuzo, Nanny's spiritual great-grandmother said, with a broad smile.

"Sorry Gramma," Nanny whispered, not wishing to wake up Putus and the other ladies sleeping beside her on the floor. She rubbed her eyes vigorously to remove the sleep and to give her a clearer sight of her great-grandmother.

"I was being very careful with the folks," Nanny continued nonchalantly.

"I know my chile, 'haste makes waste,'" Mada Kuzo said smiling.

"I'm so proud of you my chile. You've made all of us over here so happy. You never lost a single soul on that ship, and they looked so healthy when they came off. You've done a wonderful job my pet."

"I did my best Gramma," Nanny said feeling self-conscious.

"Now Nanny," Mada Kuzo said. "There's a lot of work to be done here, and there's very little time. You see Mass Willie, the Chief? Well, he won't be with you all for too long. He will be coming to join us over here soon."

"What's wrong with him Gramma?" Nanny asked anxiously.

"He has a very bad sickness and there is no cure," Mada Kuzo replied.

"But he looks fine to me."

"I agree with you my chile, I agree," Mada Kuzo said, shaking her head.

"So who is going to replace him?" Nanny inquired.

"Well, that is where you come in my pet," Mada Kuzo said, looking straight into Nanny's eyes.

"But, but...," Nanny began. As if in anticipation, Mada Kuzo quickly cut her off by saying, "He won't be leaving you until you're ready. Plus, I'm always here if you need me."

"But I just got here Gramma," Nanny protested.
"The people don't even know me. Do you think that they will trust me?" Nanny asked, showing some concern.

"Don't worry, you will be fine. All you have to do is love them and take care of their basic needs."

"And how do I do that Gramma?" Nanny inquired rather childlike.

"You will know what to do my chile, you will know," Mada Kuzo replied.
"Caring for the body will be much easier than caring for the mind," Mada Kuzo said. "People don't know who to trust now-a-days pet. The only person who they really trust right now is Mass Willie. But after he's gone we could have problems if we're not careful. You will have to build back that trust in the people if you want to lead them. The advantage that you have is that, as a woman people will trust you more than a man because most of the troubles of the people; from our homeland to over here on the island were caused by man, not woman. Do you understand?"
"Yes Gramma."
Nanny gently stroked her chin then asked, "So Gramma, do you really believe that I can lead the charge against the British soldiers?"

"You will not only challenge the British pet, you will help to drive them off the island eventually," Mada Kuzo said. "They will be forced to make deals with you my chile, but be careful; white devils talk through the two sides of their mouth, as I told you before," Mada Kuzo warned.
"My chile, I'm depending on you. Your ancestors over here are depending on you. The people are depending on you, and above all, the future of Jamaica depends on you." And with that she was gone.

"Who were you talking to?" Putus asked, leaning up on her elbow.

"Nobody," Nanny fibbed, not wanting to talk about her spiritual great-

128

grandmother.

Putus twisted her head to the side, raised her eyebrow and gave her a questionable look.

"Ok, ok! I will tell you about it one day," Nanny promised. "Let's get back to sleep."

The following morning the entire community was up at the crack of dawn, busily preparing for the day. The smoke around the huts rose stubbornly in spite of the thick misty morning air. The strong distinct smell of peppermint tea permeated the air. Men and women with hoes, forks and machetes on their shoulders walked briskly to their fields to begin their day. Young warriors trained up and down the hillside until their bodies sparkled with perspiration. In one corner, some men skillfully built new huts while others repaired older ones for the new arrivals. Women with baskets on their heads, walked carefully down the hill to the gentle flowing river below, to wash their clothes.

Nanny and the other new arrivals were invited to a grand welcome breakfast feast at the Chief's palace. This was a tradition started long ago by the Chief.

Over breakfast, he again welcomed them to the village.

"My wish for you all is that you will take this opportunity to better yourself and build up this community. Please enjoy your time here with us, but never, ever forget those that are left behind on the plantations. Just like you, they don't deserve to be there. And we will never leave them there. If they want to be rescued then we will be there to assist them, and I hope that you will join us. Our job is never done until all our people are free from the oppression of Bakra."

The Chief also challenged them to be good, productive citizens, looking out for each other and caring for each other as brothers and sisters from the Motherland.

All throughout breakfast Nanny kept thinking about what Mada Kuzo had said about the Chief. She could not say if he was sick or not. He spoke with confidence and moved about with little effort, even though he had the slight limp.

At the end of the meal, Nanny thanked the Chief and his staff for the sumptuous breakfast, on behalf of the group.

The Chief took a second look at Nanny and liked her immediately.

Later Nanny and the group were invited outside by a team of elderly folks to receive further instructions.

"Ladies and gentlemen we have many work programs here," one elderly woman addressed the group. "Feel free to join any of these programs that you like; however everyone is expected to attend military training in order to defend the village if we're ever attacked. As I call out the programs, please go with one of these elders to the job site. Construction!" the speaker shouted out. A few men, including Nanny's five brothers got up and followed a tall elderly gentleman down the road to their work site.
"Field work!" she shouted. A group men and women went with an elderly woman towards the field.
"Clinic!" she continued. Nanny and a few women, including Putus and Gylziia, got up and followed another elderly woman towards a huge hut with a wide entrance. As they walked away, Nanny could still hear the woman calling out more programs.
"Hunting! Security!

At the entrance to the hut, the elderly woman stopped and turned to address them.

"Here is our clinic where we house all our sick people in the village. I'm so happy that you will all be working here with us because we're so short of help."
As Nanny entered the hut, she noticed a foul stench permeating the entire place.

"The place smells stink like something died in here," Gylziia whispered to Nanny while covering her nose with her hand.

"Shhh!" Putus said. "Be careful what you're saying because they might hear you."
The patients on make shift beds looked feeble and neglected. Nanny felt a deep compassion for the suffering patients, some of whom were moaning and groaning in pain.

For the next few hours Nanny and the group went from bed to bed taking care of the sick and disabled. They cleaned their wounds, changed their bandages, changed the blankets on the beds, gave many baths and fed them their meals. Putus and Gylziia went down on their knees scrubbing the floors and wiping down the few furnishings in the room, while Nanny and others packed up all the soiled clothing and placed them outside for the washer women to take down to the river to wash. Other ladies combed and braided their hair and took care of their nails.

At the end of a demanding day, Nanny and the ladies felt exhausted, but very satisfied. The clinic was clean and the patients seemed more comfortable.

The following morning Nanny, with permission from the Chief, took a group of ladies from the clinic, and a guide, into the forest to search for medicinal herbs.

The night before she had spoken with Mada Kuzo about the condition of the patients in the clinic.

"Most of the medicine that you need to heal these people is in the forest," Mada Kuzo told her.

"The medicine is in the herbs chile; you know that already. Take what you've learned from your grandmother, Mada Puko, and go into the forest and find them. The forest on this little island of Jamaica is full of herbs, you just have to go in there and pick them," she continued.

"Give the patients lots of herbal baths and steam baths. Let them drink lots of bush tea, to cleanout their bodies and then build them up again. And for the future my chile, try to change what the people eat. Get them to eat more fruits and vegetables instead of the whole lot of salted fish, salted pork, and salted pig tail. All that salted meat that Bakra has been feeding to the slaves on the plantation is very bad for them, very bad. That large amount of salt is what is causing all these problems. Get them to eat less of that slave food, or if they have to eat it, only sometimes. Get them to grow more fruits and vegetables. Get them to raise more chickens, pigs, goats and cows. They need to be eating mainly fresh foods instead of all that dreadful salted food. Milk the cows and drink the milk. My chile, if the people eat healthy they will be in good physical shape and live for a long time. Bakra don't care if slaves live or die, so all that salt is not his problem. For him, all that salt is a way to keep his meat from spoiling. Maybe even he doesn't know that too much of that salt is what is killing off the people. When the people get sick because of all that salted food, Bakra just sends them to pasture [retire], and buys himself some more young slaves; because his work has to be done. But now that they are free people, it is their responsibility to take proper care of their own health. They can't blame Bakra or anybody else for their health problems."

"Thanks Gramma, I understand," Nanny said.
"I see my work 'is cut out for me here'. I will begin first thing in the morning."

Out in the forest Nanny was surprised at the wide variety of herbs that was available and the ease with which she found them.

"I have never seen anything like this Nanny!" Putus exclaimed. "This place is like the Garden of Eden," she continued.

"It looks like every herb is here! It seems like anything will grow in this place. You don't even have to stick it in the ground. As long as it falls to the ground it will grow. What a land!" Gylziia remarked.
Nanny picked the different herbs and showed them to the women. Then she gave the ladies a quick lesson on how to recognize the plants and how to use them. "This one here is good for joint pain. Just get a few leaves of it and tie it onto the affected area and it will draw out the pain. This one is good for belly ache, and this one over here is good for bed sores. Oh yes! And this one here is good for wash out. One good dose of it and it will clean you out thoroughly. This one over here is good for the men them sex drive," to which Gylziia giggled.

"Look at this one over here Nanny," Gylziia beckoned. "The leaves look so pretty, but it smells funny," she said, picking off some leaves and giving a few to Putus and Nanny.

"Ah! Ah! So this one is here too!" Nanny remarked.

"You know it Nanny?" Gylziia asked.

"Oh yes! We used it back home to treat all different kinds of sicknesses. This herb my friends, is the most versatile of all herbs. It is the most confusing of all the herbs too because it has so many uses. Just name it and it cures it. I will tell you more about it later; right now let's hurry up and collect these herbs before the rain comes down."

Under Nanny's guidance they collected and placed the various herbs in bags, making sure that each bag was properly labeled. This continued all morning until the sun stood overhead.

On their return to camp Nanny and the ladies began preparing special herbal baths for the patients. When they removed their clothes, Nanny noticed that many of them had bed sores, blisters and swellings.

"Ahhhhh! This is good! Massa God bless you, young lady!" exclaimed an old lady when she was lowered in the bath pan, steeped in herbs.

"I agree, I agree," another woman uttered.

"Ohhhhh! Yes! Yes! Thank you! Thank you!" another woman shouted, as the water soothed her aching body.

"This is the best I have felt for a long, long time," another said.
The elation continued as the patients enjoyed the pampering. Smiles and laughter were now replacing frowns and pain.

Early every morning, Nanny and the ladies arrived at the clinic to care for the sick. They gave them their baths and herbal medicine, prepared their meals, combed their hair and changed their garments and the blankets on the beds.
Many of the patients, who were now feeling better, wanted to talk with Nanny and the other workers. Although she was busy, Nanny made the time to sit with them and talk for a while.
They recounted all the cruelty that they had experienced on the plantation and on the ship coming over to the island. The women spoke about being raped, being beaten and being branded on their bodies. They showed the sickening scars on their backs, arms and legs. One lady even showed her blind eye which she said happened when one of Bakra's thugs whipped her mercilessly because she refused to have sex with him. They wept most of all when they spoke about the loss of their families and friends. Nanny cradled their hands, hugged them tenderly and wept with them.

After a few days some patients became healthy enough to be discharged. Before they left, Nanny prepared small packages of herbal medicine for them to take on their way.
As the days turned into weeks more and more patients left the clinic. Eventually words started spreading about Nanny's healing herbs. Folks began arriving at the clinic from very early in the morning and they waited all day to be treated.
Nanny found herself going to the forest frequently to collect herbs. Sometimes she had to send Putus and Gylziia because she had so many waiting clients. Everyone wanted to see Nanny, even the Chief. Nanny

remembered Mada Kuzo's words about the Chief's health. Although she did not let on, she convinced him to change his eating habits.

In the coming days, Nanny and the Chief became rather good friends. He began consulting her on many issues besides his health. He trusted Nanny so much that he invited her to be part of his inner circle of advisors.

One day at a meeting the Chief announced to the committee that they were planning a raid on a small plantation in the east. Nanny listened attentively as the Chief outlined his plans, including the date of the raid. However when he was finished, she was not convinced that the men were adequately prepared for the mission in such a short time, and she voiced her concerns strongly. The Chief was taken aback by Nanny's queries.

"What do we know about this plantation?" she asked boldly. "In fact the big question is; what measure do you use when choosing which plantations to raid? What type of security do they have? What exactly do we want from this plantation? Is it food, weapons or what else? Do you know if any slaves will be coming back with us? How will we gauge the success of this mission?"

Everyone on the committee, including the Chief was surprised by the questions that Nanny was asking. No one had ever questioned the Chief in this way. Where did she get all this knowledge? Some wondered if she was a spy planted by Bakra to disrupt their plans. Others thought that she was just trying to impress the Chief, while still some wondered if she was trying to upstage the Chief.

Sitting directly across from Nanny was this tall, skinny, bald head man who took an instant dislike to her, because he thought that she was a threat to him becoming the next Chief. He had been waiting patiently for the last three years to take over from the Chief when he retired, and now here was this little brash, hurry come up [immature] slave girl trying to upstage him.

"I think that everything will be fine Chief," the man stood up and addressed the Chief.

"We will continue to do what we've always done. I think young Nanny here is over reacting, Chief. She is new around here and doesn't know how we do our business."

"What does being new here have to do with answering the questions?" Nanny interjected.

"The mission must be able to stand up to scrutiny; otherwise it is a hit and a miss. And when you have a hit and a miss, people could get hurt or worse, Massa God forbid, people could lose their lives."

There was complete silence in the room. Everyone looked at the Chief for his response. This had never happened before in these meetings. Usually when a raid was planned the Chief would announce it and that was that. No one questioned the decision. It became routine for everybody, and that was what Nanny was afraid of. She knew that when people took their enemies for granted, they became careless, and mistakes followed.

The Chief thought long and hard before he spoke.

"Ladies and gentlemen, let us all calm down. We're all on the same side."

Then turning to the tall, skinny, bald man he ordered, "Garugah, report back to me by the end of the week on our readiness for this mission. Thank you young lady for your thought provoking questions. Ladies and gentlemen," he said abruptly. "This meeting is adjourned."

The raid was a complete success with only a few minor cuts and bruises. Thirty new runaways returned with the team, with half of them being women. The booty collected was priceless. They broke into the armory and confiscated many prized weapons and ammunition; something that they needed badly. The troops raided the warehouses and brought back many bags of foods, farm tools and implements. They also brought back large quantities of clothing; something that was in very short supply in the camp.

"I'm sorry that I was so hard on you the other day in the meeting," Garugah said to Nanny the afternoon after the raid, as she was taking a break from work. "But you were right, we were not prepared at the time and maybe things would've turned out differently if we had gone ahead with our plans. You see Nanny; our plan had always been to inflict as much pain as possible on Bakra for all the misery that he has caused us. But because of you, we made a good study of the plantation and identified what we needed, and that is why everything ran so smoothly. It never occurred to me that a woman like you would know anything about this business. But I was wrong and I'm man enough to ask for your forgiveness. Good day!" as he tipped his hat and went on his way.

"What does Baldy want now?" Putus inquired, as Garugah was leaving.

"Oh nothing," Nanny replied. "He was just telling me about the raid on the plantation last night."

"I heard that he will be the new Chief when Chief Willie 'goes out to pasture' [retire], but nobody likes him," Putus volunteered. "He thinks that he is Massa God's gift to all of us. He doesn't take kindly to people telling him what to do, especially women. He believes that women are only here for one thing; to have kids and take care of babies, but he has something else coming if he thinks that he's going to treat us like that."

"And how do you know all this Miss Putus?" Nanny asks with a sly smile.

"Research my friend, research," Putus responded, with a smile. "I talk to the people and they just tell me what is going on around here." They both laughed as their break ended and they returned to work.

A week later the Chief summoned Nanny to his quarters. She wondered what was so important that his senior assistant had to come herself.

"Come quickly, the Chief needs you!" is all she said.

Nanny rushed over to find the Chief in bed, writhing in pain. She ran quickly to his bedside and placed her hand on his forehead. He was burning up and sweating profusely all over his body. 'I have to get this fever down or he won't make it,' she thought to herself.

Nanny rushed back to the clinic and made a mug of hot herbal tea and brought it over and gave it to the Chief. She held it to his lips as he sipped it sluggishly. She then carefully wrapped him in a thick blanket, which caused him to sweat even more. She gave him the tea three more times during the day, and the fever slowly began to wane.

Nanny stayed by his bedside all night keeping a close watch over him like a lioness taking care of her young cub. By morning the fever was gone and the Chief was able to sit up in bed.

"Welcome back Chief," Nanny said, when he opened his eyes.

"Thanks Nanny," he said, flashing a weak smile.

"You were the only person that I could think of when the pain hit me."

"I'm glad that you called me Chief," Nanny said.

"But we need to look more closely at your health to find out what brought it on."

"I place my life in your hands, Nanny," the Chief said, smiling. Then suddenly the smile vanished and he became serious. "But don't hide anything from me," he reiterated, pointing his bony finger at her. "Tell me everything that you've found out. I'm a big boy and I can take it."

"I promise," Nanny told him. She knew that the time was coming when she would have to tell him the truth, but until then she would prolong the inevitable.

Chapter 14

The Chief became very sick and was fighting for his life. Garugah the acting Chief began acting more like a Chief; bossing everyone around and implementing new programs. Chief Willie became worried at the thought of Garugah replacing him when he was gone, and mentioned it to Nanny on one of her visits.

"Nanny I'm worried about Garugah," he began.
"He doesn't have any love in his heart for the people. He's an opportunist. What can we do?"
The Chief looked worried in his weakened state. Nanny felt elated at being confided in by the Chief, however she knew that worrying was detrimental to his frail health.

"Don't worry Chief," Nanny said, trying to console him. "We will put our heads together and find a good solution."

"I believe that you would make a good Chief, Nanny," the Chief said suddenly.

"Me Chief?" Nanny asked, hitting her chest lightly with her right hand.

"Yes you Nanny!" he said, pointing his finger at her.
"You would make a brilliant Chief. You have so much love in your heart for the people and the people love you a lot. You're the type of person that the people need if they're to be truly free."

"But I'm new here Chief; you have so many people here with more experience than me," Nanny protested.

"I agree with you Nanny," the Chief concurred.

"But true leadership is not based on age, but on action. You've proven yourself so many times here in such a short while, more than anybody else I know. I wish you would consider it, Nanny. You would make this old man happy," he smiled.

"But what about Garugah, Chief? You know that he has been waiting in the wings all this while to take over from you."

"Don't worry about Garugah," the Chief reassured her. "I have a plan for him if you decide to take the job."

"I will think about it Chief, and let you know as soon as possible," Nanny said cautiously.

On leaving the Chief's house, she hurried over to her brothers' house to tell them the news.

"That's good news!" Cudjoe said, hugging her, followed by Accompong, Johnny, Cuffy, and Quao.

"We're so proud of you Sis," Quao said. "You make us proud every time."

"I know that you will make a great Chief Sis," Accompong said.

"Do you believe that the people around the Chief will allow this Sis?" Cuffy asked.

"Well, the Chief told me that I should not worry about that. He would take care of them," Nanny explained.

"Nanny, you are our big sister and we're here for you," Cudjoe reminded her. "We will do whatever we can to help you."

That night Nanny could hardly sleep. She thought long and hard, not on whether she would take the job, but rather on how she would rule. She decided to tell Putus and Gylziia the following day before talking with the Chief.

The next morning while they were out in the forest reaping herbs Nanny told them about the proposal.

"You know that the Chief is very sick and they're trying to find a successor for him," she began.

"Don't tell me that they're thinking of offering you the job?" Gylziia blurted out.

"Why don't you be quiet girl, and let Nanny speak," Putus rebuked her.

"Well, the Chief personally offered me the job and he wants an answer soon."

"So what are you going to do?" Gylziia asked, interrupting Nanny again.

"I think I'm going to take it," Nanny began.

"Yes! Yes!" Gylziia shouted. "I know that you will make the best Chief ever!"

"That's great news Nanny!" Putus remarked. "I agree with Gylziia, you will make a wonderful Chief. And guess what? We will call you Queen Nanny instead of Chief. Chief is more for a man, than a woman."

"So when you're Queen, will we have to bow down to you?" Gylziia asked bowing gracefully.

"As I was saying, when I take up the job, I will need both of you in my corner. You two are my closest friends. You're like the sisters that I never had. I would like both of you to be my sounding board. But remember, anything that we talk about you have to keep it a secret. And most importantly, I expect you to watch my back. Don't be afraid to tell me what you think; I won't be offended. So what do you say ladies?" Nanny asked.

"Of course we will!" Putus and Gylziia shouted in unison.
"Nanny we love you so much, you would never know. If it wasn't for you, maybe we would not be here. We will do whatever you wish," Gylziia expressed.

"So it is all settled then. I will give the Chief my answer this afternoon," Nanny said. "Let's get back to the village."

"Yes my Queen," laughed Gylziia, taking a bow. They all broke out laughing as they headed down the hill.

That evening Nanny went over to visit with the Chief and told him of her decision.

"Today you have made this old man happy. Now my heart is at peace," he said, with a broad smile on his face.

"And what about Garugah, Chief?" Nanny inquired.

"Oh, I spoke to a Chief friend of mine in the west end of the island and he will be inviting him down there soon, so don't you worry."

"Ok Chief," Nanny replied.

"Now, as a new Chief we have some very confidential things I need to tell you which you have to keep in your heart. The only person that you can tell is the other Chief who will be coming after you. Understand?"

"Yes Chief, I understand," she said nervously.

"Tomorrow I will call a meeting of all the tribal Elders and announce my decision. Until then keep it a secret."

"Yes Chief," Nanny assure him, as she prepared to leave.

After leaving the Chief's quarters, Nanny leisurely walked around the entire length and breadth of the village by herself until it was dark. She was surprised at the little things that she was now noticing that she had one time overlooked. For example, the garbage was blowing around in the wind making a mess. The idea came to her to make garbage collection a part of the skills program, and offering it to new arrivals. As she walked around, an uneasy feeling came over her about the site. She began having doubts about the location of the village.

"Our village is too close to the soldiers' camp," she heard herself say. "We need more distance between us. We have to close this village and move further up into the Blue Mountain where we will be more protected." Nanny realized that this idea, although it made sense, would not be an easy sell. This was the only place that most of the people knew. They had put their blood, sweat and tears into this place; and now they would have to abandon it? Would they be willing to trust her judgment? Nanny thought long and hard of all the reasons why they should stay and compared them with the opportunities that awaited them if they moved further north, up into the mountains. She was convinced that the latter was the more prudent action. She made a mental note to discuss this with Mass Willie and her new advisors when she took over as the new Chief.

When Nanny arrived home, Putus and Gylziia were furious.

"Where have you been?" Putus demanded.

"Yes! Where were you?" Gylziia inquired. "Why are you so selfish? You had us worried, wondering if duppy [ghost] or something took you away."

"Calm down ladies, calm down; I only went for a walk around the village, to see it for myself," Nanny tried to explain.

"Then you didn't know how the village looked before?" Gylziia asked, looking rather puzzled. "What is there to see?"

"I agree with you Gylziia," Nanny said. "But now I'm looking at the village through the eyes of the Chief."

"Not Chief," Putus quickly corrected. "Queen."

"Alright Queen," Nanny conceded.

"Yes I have to look at everything here now through the Queen's eyes," she continued, winking at Putus.

"Do you ladies understand? And that is why I need you two so much. I liked the way you reprimanded me. Never stop doing that, although, not in front of the people. It will keep me grounded. I don't want you to be intimidated by my power and authority. In other words, I don't want you to be yes men or women, like all the rest. I need to know that when you say something to me you're talking from your own belief and not from what you think I would like to hear. I love you two so much and I need your honest opinions. Never be afraid to take me aside and tell me that I'm messing up. I promise you, although I might not like what you're saying, I will give it serious consideration."

"You sound like a Queen already and you haven't even been crowned yet," Gylziia laughed, and they all joined in.

"I'm serious ladies, this is important business," Nanny reiterated. "People's lives are at stake here. Our future is in the balance here, and we don't want to fail."

"Can you imagine that I've spent all this while cooking our dinner and we're going to let it go to waste?" Putus asked jokingly to change the subject.

"Gylziia, you go and get the plates. Nanny, you set the table and let me bring in the food."

"Ahhhh! Fantastic! Excellent!" yelled Nanny, as the aroma hit her nostrils and the food walloped her hungry palate.

"This food is delicious Putus, the best I've tasted. Tell me something Putus; have you been holding out on me and Gylziia all this while?" she asked jokingly.

"Nothing is too good for my Queen," Putus replied, seemingly embarrassed.

"I agree! I agree!" affirmed Gylziia, with her mouth full.

At the end of the meal all three ladies sat around the table and chatted until the wee hours of the morning.

"I tell you ladies, this is the life," Putus said. "Here we are, three free

African women sitting around doing what we want to do and nobody to rule over us."

"I know what you mean," Gylziia said. "If we were down on the plantation now, we would soon be waking up to go out and do Bakra's dirty work. The people who I hated the most were the head drivers. How could they be so cruel as to whip their own people for the slightest things, I will never know."

"If you ask me, I believe that they enjoy whipping the poor people because it makes them feel important," Putus added.

"Nanny, what do you think?" Gylziia asked.

"I believe that the whole system is bad," Nanny said flatly.
"We have a lot of mistrust and blame to go around," she continued, shaking her head. "Mistrust is why we have people like the head drivers beating our people to death. Mistrust is why people will do anything to get into Bakra's good books, even if it means beating his own people to death. The white devils have sown the seeds of mistrust from way back in Africa when villages raided other villages to sell people into slavery. It was a 'dog-eat-dog' system, where I had better sell you before you sell me," she explained. "Your own family or friends or neighbors could sell you into slavery. So, if your own family cannot be trusted, why do you think that they would care if somebody who only happens to have the same skin color live or die? I'm telling you ladies, the whole situation is a big mess, which won't be fixed anytime soon. In fact I would predict that three hundred years from now people will still be talking about this."

"Three hundred years?" Gylziia asked, looking puzzled.

"Yes Gylziia, three hundred years, and guess what? They will be just as puzzled as we are right now. They will study it to death and write hundreds of books on the topic and still won't know everything."

"And why is that?" Putus asked.

"Because everyone reacts differently to slavery," Nanny explained. "But the one thing that links all this misery is mistrust, yes mistrust!"
Nanny thought hard for a moment and then said, "Let me try to explain mistrust a different way. Mistrust is like you're riding this giant beast, and you're holding on for dear life, afraid to jump off for fear of being eaten by the same beast. So you keep holding on, hoping, just hoping that the beast

would fall over one day and drop dead; so that you could walk away. Does that make sense?"

"Kinda," Gylziia replied. "But that was heavy stuff Nanny, very difficult to understand."

"I know chile; there are no easy answers, and that is why we have to work at it one day at a time," Nanny concurred.

"Then Nanny, does mistrust affect the white devils too?" Putus asked.

"Oh yes, for sure. Because of slavery, they have this false sense of superiority. Some of them truly believe that they are smarter than us and so they treat us like children. They want to protect us from what; I don't know. On the other hand, there are some of them who believe that we're like elephants, and will never forget or forgive them for what they are doing to us. As long as they think that way and not use our skills and talents, their society will not grow as it should; and they will have this massive brain power going to waste. They have to realize that their future is now tied up closely with ours. To think otherwise is foolish. But we will see," she said.

"So what are you going to do about it as Queen?" Gylziia asked.

"As I said before, with all of us working together, we can start building back the trust that was lost, one day at a time," Nanny reiterated.

"I'm all for that," Putus agreed.

"Then tell me something Nanny, how do you know all this?" Putus asked, sarcastically. "Are you keeping a secret from us?"

"Secret, what secret?" Nanny retorted. "I just think a lot and make up my mind about things," she said, trying hard not to appear offended.

"Oh, because I wouldn't want to know that you're not one of us, and you only came here to fool us," Putus said calmly.

"And there goes the mistrust I was talking about," Nanny laughed, then everyone joined in.

"Yes ladies, mistrust affects every part of our daily lives. It's like disease with many, many strong roots. And as you chop one off, another one grows back."

"I'm sorry I doubted you Nanny, it won't happen again," Putus apologized.

"Don't worry about it. You're not much different from the people that you live with. Let's get some shut eye ladies because tomorrow is the big day when everything will be revealed." And with that they all went into their separate bedrooms.

The following day the Chief called an emergency meeting of all the executives and Elders at his quarters. The air was charged with excitement. Everyone wanted to know who the Chief would pick to replace him. Various names were thrown around, but Garugah was the name most mentioned.

At the beginning of the meeting the Chief thanked everyone for coming and then delved into the business at hand. After spending a considerable amount of time outlining the reasons for his choice, the Chief announced that Nanny would be the new Chief. There was a sudden uneasy hush in the room as everyone contemplated the decision. Then, slowly, a few people rose and started to clap. More people joined in until eventually the entire room stood up and applauded.

"I trust the Chief," one elderly gentleman whispered.

"He must know something that we don't," another man was heard saying.

"I believe that the Chief is dead wrong this time. What can a little woman with no experience and just coming off the plantation do for us here?" a big elderly gentleman remarked.

"This is madness," another one said. "She's too young and green. I wonder if the sickness has gone to the Chief's head."

"Shhhhh!" a short, heavy set man with a deep base voice said. "Let me hear what the young lady has to say."

"Chief, members of the advisory body, ladies and gentlemen, good day," Nanny began. "I would like to thank you Chief for having the courage to choose me to take on this important job of Chief of the Maroons. I'm humbled by your faith in me Chief, knowing full well that I have a giant sandal to fill and a hard act to follow; but I will do my best," to which the audience laughed.

"I've never ran away from a challenge before and I'm not about to do so now," she continued. "I will work hard and smart, day and night, and with all of your help, be the best Chief that I can be; always remembering that it is not about me, it is all about the people's business, your business. Thanks again Chief, I will not let you down. Thanks again everybody," then she took her seat. The applause was deafening and continued for some time.

"She sounds alright to me," one man said to his friend beside him.

"I think we have to give her a chance," said another.

"I think we're in for some very exciting times," remarked a large elderly woman in a bright floral dress.

"I like her," said a tall man with a bald spot at the top of his head.

"She has guts! We will be fine!" a tall strapping man with a broad smile from ear to ear commented.

At the end of the meeting the Chief invited everyone to join him at the feast prepared to formally welcome Nanny and to allow her to meet and socialize with the past and present leaders.

As Nanny mingled in the crowd shaking hands, hugging and kissing, the response was very encouraging.

"Congratulations!"

"I'm so proud of you."

"Young lady, I have faith in you, don't let us old people down."

"I'm available if you need my help."

"I wish I was thirty years younger, young lady, because I would've taken up the cause with you. Don't be afraid to try new things, I will back you all the way."

Nanny heard herself saying, 'thank you, thank you,' over and over again and making a mental note of the people she could call upon in the future.

"Congratulations young lady!" a familiar voice from behind her said.

Nanny turned around to stand face to face with Garugah, all smiling and friendly. She extended her arms weakly but he lovingly grabbed her and gave her a big hug, nearly cutting off her breath.

"So what is going to happen to you now?" Nanny asked nervously.

"Oh the Chief, I mean the old Chief, convinced me to go out west and help to develop the region. He said that there were tons of opportunities for development out there. I'm very excited about it and I can't wait to start. Sorry love, I won't be here to bug you, and teach you a thing or two, you're on your own. But me and a lot of the folks here think that you will make a great Chief."

Nanny felt relieved at the way he took her appointment and most of all, the fact that he would be leaving. She smiled and looked across the room to see the Chief smiling back at her.

"Chief, you're the best," she mumbled to herself.

The next evening the Chief called all the citizens of the village to a special meeting. Everyone stopped working early and gathered in the village square.

"Ladies and gentlemen, boys and girls, I have some great news today," the Chief began. "As you all know, because of my health we have been looking for a new Chief for some time now. Well, the time has come for me to tell you all that we have chosen a new Chief for our village." There was an instant buzz in the crowd.

"I wonder who it is?" one heavy busted woman asked.

"It is that big mouth man who thinks that he knows everything," another woman said, shaking her head in disgust.

"I hope it is not him or things will be hard around here," whispered a man with a short scrappy beard.

"Everybody quiet down!" a tall burly man shouted above the crowd. "Let the Chief speak!" Within a few moments the crowd was dead silent.

"After much thought and discussions we've selected Nanny as our new Chief."
The crowd suddenly irrupted into shouts of jubilation. Drummers came out and started drumming excitedly as the people began dancing and gyrating in the square. Some people banged on pots, pans and anything they could put their hands on that could make noise. One man blew the Abeng skillfully to everyone's delight.

"Thank you Massa God!" one woman shouted. "Now I know that I made the right decision to run away from Bakra's plantation."

"Long live the new Chief!" shouted another woman.

"It is time that we got a woman to lead us," a shaky old lady, rocking on her walking stick remarked. "The men are no good."
Nanny smiled and hugged and thanked everyone as she mingled in the crowd.

"Chief Nanny we love you!" shouted a young girl jumping up and down and gyrating to the rhythmic beat of the drums.

Then the people began bringing out big pots, building a fire and organizing foods for a feast. When the Chief saw what was happening, tears came to his eyes. He had doubted the character of the people. He was not sure how the people would take the news so he decided to have a low key affair. And what a big mistake that turned out to be. There was love all around for Nanny. Everyone knew her, adored her and trusted her. He had no doubt that he had made the right decision.

For the next couple of weeks the Chief and Nanny sat down together in his quarters to go over the transfer of power. The Chief had so much to tell her, and Nanny had so many questions to ask, that she wondered if there was enough time.

At one session Nanny asked the Chief about the Maroon's history.

"We have a great history, Nanny!" Chief Willie began, with a sparkle in his eyes. "Our people were brought here as slaves by the Spanish many, many years ago. My great-great-grand father was one of those people who were brought here by the Spanish. My father used to tell me stories that his father told him about the Spanish. They were nice people, not like these arrogant, feisty, British people, who believe that they are God's gift to mankind. My father used to tell me so many good stories about the Spanish that we could be here talking for days. Good people! Good people!" Chief Willie declared, nodding his head. "Why I say that Nanny is because they cared more about us as human beings. Not like these brutes, the British, who only want us for one purpose; labor to work in their cane fields cutting their dirty sugarcane. They don't care much if we live or die. If we live great! more labor to work their fields. If we die, so what! run down to the slave market and buy some more slaves to replace them. It's just like replacing your mules. The Spanish were not like that," he emphasized. "So when the British marched into the island, our great-great-grandfather, and many of the other slaves, ran away with the Spanish up into the mountains to make a last ditch effort to fight them. My father told me of his great-great-grandfather and the other slaves on the run for days, without sleep, with the British, with their heavy artillery, chasing them. They hid in caves and slept in trees, anywhere to escape the British.

The Spanish were finally beaten by the British and eventually they gave up and escaped from the island in boats leaving behind my great-great-grandfather and the other slaves with a bunch of weapons.

148

After the Spanish left my great-great-grandfather and the others decided not to surrender to the British but to keep on fighting. They built settlements in the mountain and married the pretty Arawak women who were also fighting alongside them. As time went on they ran out of food and were nearly naked, so they used their weapons and raided the nearby plantations. They set fire to the plantations and then collected foods, clothing and weapons. They also encouraged many of the slaves on the plantations to run away and join them in the hills. The maroons went back to their Ashanti roots of living off the land and using guerrilla tactics to battle the British. The British were at a lost as to how to capture them. The plantation owners also lived in constant fear of attack; even up to today. My great-great-grandfather, my great-grandfather, my grandfather, my father and now me have been fighting those British devils a long, long time and I hope that you will continue to fight them until they leave this island for good," the Chief said, opening his eyes wide. "We didn't ask them to bring us here, but now that we're here, it is only right that we should control our own destiny."

Nanny was at a loss for words at the end of the story.

'Look what these people have been through,' she thought to herself. 'We can't stop now! The fight must continue but with more intensity.'

"What are you thinking about Nanny?" Chief asked, noting how focused she was.

"I was thinking Chief that the only thing that will break the British is force. But the force I'm thinking about is to attack them from numerous points at once on the island: East, west, north, and south! Spread them out so thin that they become overworked!"

"That's my girl!" the Chief said with a gleam in his eyes. Nanny smiled. "Anyways young lady, this old man is getting tired; we will talk again tomorrow."

Nanny left the Chief with an added respect for the Maroons and a resolve to keep up the pressure on the British; using the plantations as a cash cow. She was very excited about what she had learned that day and couldn't wait for her next visit with the Chief.

But that was not to be. Early the following morning, Nanny and her household were awakened by an urgent knock at the door.

"Who could be calling at this hour of the morning?" Nanny asked, still half asleep.

"Chief Nanny! Chief Nanny! Come quickly; Chief Willie is not breathing well!" pleaded the Chief's Aid. Nanny did not need to hear another word. She dressed quickly and ran with the Aid back to the Chief's quarters.

As she entered the house, she knew that it was too late; the Chief was gone. Tears slowly flowed down her face as she entered his bedroom. She slowly walked over to his bed and gently closed his eyes with her hand. She stood by his bedside for some time, looking down at his frail frame with a deep sense of grief.

"Why did you leave so soon?" she asked under her breath, shaking her head with both sadness and disappointment. "There were so many more things that I needed to know. I was about to ask you about moving the village further up into the mountain, but now I have to make the decision all by myself. Mada Kuzo knew what she was saying. He stayed just long enough to teach me some things. I will always be grateful."

Nanny asked for a clean sheet to wrap the body. The Aid took out the abeng and began to blow it loudly to announce to the village that the Chief had passed away. In a short while, the square in front of the Chief's quarters was filled with people, some crying openly in a rather raucous manner, while others wept quietly as they became enwrapped in their grief.

"He was a great Chief, the best one we've ever had," said an old lady leaning carefully on her cane.

"I knew him from he was a little boy," she continued, not caring who was listening, but just wanting to talk and show her respect. "He never had a mean bone in his body. He took after his father who was also the Chief before him. I will miss him," she said, wiping back tears from her eyes.

"That's true," another old woman said. "He never played favorite. He always called it as he saw it; and that was why people loved him so much. I remember in those early days when food was very scarce around here because the British soldiers were raiding us constantly; so we couldn't go out to hunt or find food. Chief made sure that nobody went without food. He personally shared the little that we had to make sure that nobody was left out. Sometimes he would even go without so that all of us could eat.

And that is why we old people loved him so much."

"Do you know why he never got married again after his wife died?" one elderly woman asked, but did not wait for an answer. "Because he dedicated his life to help us, and that is why I will never forget him." Standing across from the women was a group of elderly men reminiscing about the Chief.

"Me and Willie, I mean Chief Willie, grew up together," one short, stocky grey haired man said. "As a boy, he was the best swimmer in the river and the fastest runner in the village. That boy could run faster than a Cheetah. And when we went into the bush to hunt, no wild hog was safe. He could just smell them, and when he found one he wouldn't stop until he killed it. As youths, we used to feel sorry for the poor wild hogs." They all laughed.

"He was also good at catching crabs. At the beginning of the crab season, he was the first person to say, 'Let's go to crab bush.' And when we got there he would fill up his bags in no time. He used to love catching the left hand crabs, the one we call 'Left hand Pampee.' They were the most challenging; but when you cooked them, ah! sweet! delicious."

"Did you know that Willie could jerk wild hog?" another elderly man asked. "Yes man, he would go up into the bush, pick his own herbs, season up the meat and then jerk it. Ahh! delicious! It was so good that you licked all of your fingers." Everyone laughed.

"What I remember most about Willie is that he was very kind," said a tall bald head man with a heavy grey moustache. "He would take the shirt off his back and give it to you, if you needed it. What a man! He was just like his father."

Nanny quietly left the men talking among themselves. She was so happy that she was able to hear about the Chief from the people who knew him best.

Chapter 15

The Chief's funeral was a grand affair. Maroons and other village leaders came from miles around to pay their last respect. The ceremony lasted for hours, with speech after speech from several leaders and the people who knew him well.

As Nanny sat quietly and listened to the various speakers, she got even more insight into the type of person the Chief was; his character, the love he had for his people, his leadership style, and the way he conducted his business. The quality that Nanny heard over and over again was that the Chief was loyal and always kept his word.

When it was her turn to speak, Nanny rose slowly from her seat, wiped away her tears with a handkerchief, and spoke about the man she came to know, to respect and to love.

"He was like a father to me," she emphasized. "He saw something in me even before I realized it myself. I will truly miss him."

As the simple wooden casket was lowered into the grave, the congregation sang a series of songs that the Chief loved. The singing continued non- stop while the men worked feverishly until the casket was seen no more.

The day after the funeral, Nanny invited the visiting Chiefs and their delegation to visit with her for a few more days. She wanted to know more about them, and more importantly, what was happening with the resistance movement in the other parts of the island. While the delegations were being chaperoned around the village by young men and women, Nanny met separately with each leader.

On the final day, all the Chiefs met together and each leader gave a brief report on what was happening in their community and what their needs were.

The Chiefs spoke of the difficulties they were having recruiting young people and especially women to their communities. Some spoke about the need to fortify their village against attacks by the local militia and British soldiers, while others talked about the lack of training for their warriors.

"What we need right now Chief Nanny, are leaders," one Chief from the west said. "We have many good, loyal foot soldiers, but what we're lacking is good leadership."

Nanny thought long and hard about the plight of these leaders. Thanks to Chief Willie, she had a handle on those problems. Chief had spent his entire life trying to make this village safe and sustainable. Now it was her turn to provide assistance and leadership for these new settlements. She thought about the many emerging junior leaders she had in the village, including her brothers, and wondered if they would be interested in going to help out these new communities. She made a mental note to talk with her two brothers, Cudjoe and Accompong, and also Garugah, the former assistant Chief; to see if they would be interested in going out west to help these communities.

At the end of the morning session, Nanny sent an urgent message to her brothers. When they arrived she told them about the problems that the leaders were facing in their communities and asked if they would be interested in going to help them.

"So Sis, you would like us to go out west and help these Chiefs in their communities?" Cudjoe asked.

"Yes guys, that is what I am asking," Nanny replied, hopefully.

"But do you really believe that we can help these people?" he asked.

"Yes, I have no doubt that you guys can help them," Nanny replied confidently. "They're desperate for help. If we don't help them now, they will not survive as a community because the British will crush them."

"So how long will we have to be down there?" Accompong asked.

"It's up to you guys. Whenever you want to come back, you can come back," Nanny replied.

After much discussion the brothers agreed to go.

"Although I will miss you boys a lot," Nanny said. "I'm so happy that you've decided to go. Accompong, you can go with the St. Elizabeth delegation, and Cudjoe, you can go with the St. James delegation."

"So when do we leave Sis?" Cudjoe asked.

"The day after tomorrow," Nanny replied with a smile.

"Well, that means that we don't have much time!" Cudjoe exclaimed. "Come Accompong, let's go and get our things together. Sis, we will see you later."

"Just a moment before you leave boys. I will arrange a meeting with the two leaders tomorrow, so that you can get acquainted."

After her two brothers left Nanny summoned Garugah to her quarters. She carefully outlined the problems facing the visiting leaders.

"When I heard their stories this morning I thought about our conversation the other day," Nanny told him. "Are you still interested in going down the country to help to develop these communities?" she asked him directly.

"Yes Chief, I'm more than ready," Garugah replied, with a broad smile. "I think it is my destiny."

Nanny was very pleased with the news.

"They're leaving the day after tomorrow; do you think that you could be ready?"

"Oh yes Chief!" he said excitedly.

During the evening session, Nanny proudly announced that she would be sending three of her best leaders to help them in their communities. There were cheers of joy all around. When it was announced that Cudjoe would be going with the delegation from St. James there were shouts of joy from that group. Then the cheers got louder when she announced that Accompong would be going with the St. Elizabeth delegation. Finally, Nanny announced that Garugah would be going with the Clarendon delegation and that brought the loudest cheer from the back of the room. At the end of the conference everyone left in high spirits.

That night, Nanny hosted a lavish banquet for the visitors and the entire village. It was designated as a grand send off for the visitors, but most importantly for Cudjoe, Accompong and Garugah.

Everyone arrived well dressed and full of anticipation. The musicians played beautiful music throughout the night to everyone's delight. The young men and women danced to the music while the elderly sat around and conversed among themselves between bouts of dancing. The lavish meal was prepared under the supervision of Putus who pulled out all the stops for this grand occasion. Everyone went away feeling totally filled and satisfied.

In her speech to the audience, Nanny thanked the visitors for coming and wished them a safe trip home. She then presented each of the leaders with a hand-crafted gift. She implored them to make the development of their communities their top priorities and to make good use of the leaders she was sending them.

"We here in the east are depending on you to create chaos for Bakra and the British soldiers in the west. We want to attack them from the east, the west, the north and the south. Let them feel the might of the Ashanti warriors!"

Then she instructed, "Everybody, repeat after me, 'we will never stop fighting until all African are free on this island!'" The audience complied.

"Again!" Nanny shouted to the group.

"We will never stop fighting until all Africans are free on this island!"

"Again!"

"Remember these words when things are not going your way and you feel like giving up," she encouraged them.

"Nobody said that this journey would be easy; but one thing I know and Massa God knows it too; that the worst thing that can happen to us now is ten times better than life under Bakra. Don't you ever forget that."

Everyone left the banquet in a high spirit and a new determination to challenge the status quo.

Early the following morning, as they were about to leave, Nanny hugged Cudjoe and Accompong tightly with tears in her eyes.

"Don't start the crying again Sis," Accompong said. "We will be alright. You know that we can take care of ourselves, so don't you worry. It's not like we will be down there forever; we will be back here in a short while.

We'll keep you informed on what's going on down there."

"I agree Sis," Cudjoe smiled. "And it is not like we're going back on the boat." They all laughed as Nanny wiped away her tears.

Chapter 16

It was a month now since Cudjoe and Accompong left to settle in the western part of the island. Nanny anxiously awaited some news. In the meanwhile there was so much work to be done. Her plans to move to a new settlement were in progress. She had authorized her younger brother Quao to lead an expedition to explore areas further north in the Blue Mountains where they could build a more secure and permanent settlement. They had left over a week ago and had still not returned.

Nanny and her leaders were also planning a raid on a big plantation to the south. She instructed Putus to select some women and to go down to the marketplace on the weekend to seek out women from that plantation who could give them some valuable information. Nanny instructed Putus to get a physical layout of the plantation including: where Bakra stored his weapons, the store houses, the male and female barracks, and most importantly, what the security arrangements were like. She was leaving nothing to chance. Her plan was to get the warriors in and out of the plantation as quickly as possible without exposing them to unnecessary danger.

On Sunday Putus gathered Gylziia and a few women and headed down to the marketplace along with the usual group who were going there to sell their goods. Some of the provisions were earmarked for the ladies who cooperated with them, and gave them valuable information.

At the market, Putus and the other women separated and began seeking information. It did not take Putus long to find a tall slim built lady buying yams at a vendor's stall. Putus skillfully attempted to strike up a conversation with the woman.

"What a pretty dress you're wearing!" Putus began, smiling. The woman smiled back at her showing some pearly white teeth.

"Did you make it?" Putus asked.

"Yes lady," the woman replied.

"Have you been sewing a long time?" Putus continued, smiling at the woman.

"Yes, ma'm," replied the woman, smiling back.
"I've been making my own clothes from I was back in my country."

"And what tribe are you from?" Putus asked.

"I'm from the Ashanti tribe," she said proudly.

"Good to know that," Putus remarked.
"I've been looking for a good dressmaker to make some dresses for me and my friends for a long time. Would you be interested?" she asked. "We will pay you well."
The woman looked across at Putus and gave her a big smile.
"And if you make them good for us," Putus continued, "We will give you lots of business."

"I can make the clothes for you and your friends," the woman responded excitedly.

"Good, what plantation are you from?" Putus asked, casually.
She told Putus which plantation she belonged to and that she worked in the cane field, loading the wagons. She also shared how the head driver had been wicked to her; beating her every day because she refused to have sex with him.

"I know what you mean," Putus said quietly, not wanting to attract attention. "I used to live in constant fear like that."

"What do you mean, used to lady?" the woman asked, with a puzzled look on her face.

"Come with me over here," Putus indicated. "We can't talk here, 'bush have ears.'" (People will hear us)
The woman obediently followed Putus under a big shade tree away from the crowd.

"I know what it is like to be beaten by those wicked head drivers. I was

158

just like you until one day I decided to do something about it."

"What did you do, kill him?" the woman asked inquisitively.

"No! No!" Putus exclaimed, smiling. "I thought about that many times but I didn't have the stomach to do it."

"So what did you do?" the woman asked, showing keen interest.
Putus looked around to see if anyone was listening.

"Have you ever heard about the Maroons?" Putus asked in hushed tones.
The woman's eyes popped wide open as she looked fearfully at Putus.

"Yes ma'm," the lady replied timidly.
"I heard that they were criminals and murderers. Bakra said that all of them were dying of hunger in the mountains and that is why they come down and steal food from the plantation. If word ever got back to Bakra that I was talking to a Maroon they would beat me to death," the woman said nervously.

"Do I look like a murderer?" Putus asked, looking disappointed.
"Look at me, do I look hungry? Do I look like I'm in need?" Putus questioned.

"No, no ma'm," the lady stammered.

"Call me Putus; what is your name?"

"Puncy," the lady replied, quickly looking around nervously.

"Don't worry, nothing will happen to you," Putus said reassuringly.

"Do you want a better life Puncy?" Putus asked.
The young lady nodded her head.

"Well, you can't spend all of your life on the plantation and give Bakra all of your labor for free."

"So what must I do?" Puncy asked eagerly.

"It is as easy as making the decision to stop serving Bakra and stop taking all that beating from the wicked head driver," Putus said gently.

"If it is only a decision I have to make, well, I've been thinking that there must be a better way to live. And do you know Miss Putus, it is up to yesterday that that wicked man whipped me. I'm just tired of this beating Miss Putus. Tell me what to do" she begged.
Putus smiled warmly and began telling her about the plan to raid their plantation in a few weeks.

"Guess what I would like you to do for me?"

"Just tell me what to do and I will do it," Puncy said excitedly.

"Find out where Bakra stores his weapons. Remember you have to be very secretive. You can't trust a soul."

Before they said goodbye, Puncy promised to meet Putus the following week and provide her with the information she needed. After concluding their conversation the two ladies walked leisurely over to the stall where Gylziia sat talking to a woman. Putus hoped that this woman was a potential client.

At the stall Putus asked Puncy, "Did you buy all your food stuff already to take home?"

"No ma'm, I was just about to pick up a few things when I met you."

"Would you like some yams, pumpkins and some vegetables to take back with you? Don't worry about the money; you're one of us," Putus offered.

"I would love that ma'm; thank you ma'm," she replied meekly.

"Call me Putus; that is my name, it is not ma'm."

"Yes ma'm, sorry, I mean Miss Putus," the woman said with a smile.
After gathering what food she needed, Puncy said goodbye and left.

"It looks like you have a good one there," Gylziia said quietly.

"Yes, she is a nice young lady," Putus replied.

"I'm so sorry for her. The spiteful head driver at the plantation beats her everyday because she doesn't want to have sex with him. Everyday is the same thing; cruelty and violence on the plantation. I wish all slaves were free like us to do as we please. How about your lady?" Putus asked.

"Sounds like a good lady too, but she is very scared of Bakra. She said that Bakra told them that Maroons were thieves and murderers and were never to be trusted. But when she saw me she realized that Bakra was just fooling them. She promised to tell me next week where Bakra stores his weapons and other things."

On their way home Putus and the ladies were in high spirits. They had sold some of the food provisions for cash, given some away to their new found friends and traded some for weapons. They had also recruited five other women from the plantation who were willing to spy for them. One wanted to leave right away with them but was gently told to return to the plantation and report back the following Sunday. All the ladies were

160

reminded not to discuss their conversation with anyone on the plantation; 'because you don't know who to trust.'

Nanny was quite pleased with the report and congratulated the women on a successful venture.

Over the next few days the troops trained hard for the upcoming raid. Nanny told the young men and women how proud she was of them and was looking forward to a successful foray. She reminded them of the importance of the mission to the future of the village. The troops looked excited and geared up for action. Many of them were going on a raid for the very first time and having Chief Nanny there made them feel special.

Later, Nanny visited the special lady's unit as they prepared for the mission. Their job was to find the women's barracks and to encourage as many women as possible to runaway with them.

This was one of the first units that Nanny initiated when she took over as Chief. She believed that women were the best recruiters for other women. When Nanny first discussed the idea with Putus and Gylziia they both loved it and Gylziia even volunteered to lead it.

Nanny thanked Gylziia and the women for volunteering for the mission. She reminded them of the importance of increasing the female population of the village, and getting as many women as possible to freedom.

Next, Nanny visited the clinic to find the women busy cleaning and taking care of the sick patients. Lately, because of her busy schedule, she was only able to visit the clinic occasionally. The building looked and smelled good; a far cry from her first visit. Nanny hugged all the women and thanked them for their hard work and dedication to the clinic. She then went around and visited with each of the patients. They all had high praises for the staff, especially Putus.

"She is a God send," some said.

"I didn't know that people like her still existed," others said.

Before she left, Nanny reminded the staff of the upcoming raid and the need to be prepared for casualties.

The next day, Nanny visited the building site for the new arrivals. The head man in charge gave Nanny a tour of the site and told her of the progress they were making in completing the units. After thanking everyone for their service she sat with them and had a quick lunch, before she was off again to meet with other leaders to plan strategies.

Later that evening Quao and his team returned from their expedition. The men looked exhausted and ragged, but otherwise healthy. Nanny gave them all a hug and thanked them for their service.

After dismissing the men, she sat with Quao over supper, to discuss the trip.

"Sis, we found this place way up in the mountain. It is gorgeous! It is like you're on top of the world looking down on Massa God's handy work. It is the most beautiful place I've ever seen. Everything is green and luscious; maybe because it rains every day, sometimes all day long," he said smiling.

"Sis, it is the perfect spot to build our new village. We only discovered it by accident. How it happened was like this; early one morning in the thick fog, as we were wading across the rushing stream and onto the river bank, we suddenly heard a rustling sound coming directly towards us. We quickly dropped to the ground, not knowing what to expect, but trying to remain alert. Then from the corner of our eyes we saw a wild hog coming out of the bushes and scurrying away in a flash. We all looked at each other and wondered what had just happened. We realized that there must be a secret passage in the area.

We searched the vicinity for a long, long time until finally we found this mysterious entrance. I'm telling you Sis, the entrance looks like any two ordinary trees standing in the forest, until you stand between them and baps! something strange happens. Sis, nobody can find that entrance unless they stand directly between the two trees. We spent a long time going over that place thoroughly and we couldn't find it. Don't ask me how it works Sis, because I couldn't tell you. Me and the men tried to find the entrance without going between the trees and we couldn't find it!" Quao said excitedly. "It is weird and I can't wait to go back up there!"

"So what did you see when you went inside?" Nanny asked excitedly.

"There was this long narrow ridge overlooking the river below," Quao said. "The ridge is so narrow that only one person can cross at a time. As you walk carefully up the path you can hear the rushing waters of the river below. At the top of the ridge it opens up into a vast tract of land with beautiful trees. To get there Sis is a bit tricky, but after you reach your destination, it is paradise!" he exclaimed.

"Nobody will be able to find us there, not even the British. We can make raids on any plantation and then go back up there, and just disappear!" he said with a sparkle in his eyes.

"Sis, you just have to see it to believe it! Oh, one more thing I forgot to mention; we saw a couple of old broken down sheds on the land. It looked like some groups of people used to live there long, long time ago, because we saw some things that they left behind."

"I believe that they belonged to the early Spanish people and the Maroon warriors during the war with the British," Nanny said, feeling happy that she got the opportunity to learn about these early people from Chief Willie. Before they turned in for the night, Nanny promised to visit the site with Quao when the opportunity presented itself.

For the next couple of weeks, Nanny became so preoccupied with the upcoming raid that the visit to the new settlement was placed on hold.

Chapter 17

Everything was in place for the raid. Nanny met for the final time with her unit leaders. The fire unit, responsible for setting fire to the sugarcane fields reported their readiness. The welcoming unit responsible for luring slaves away from the plantation reported their readiness. The armory and weapons unit reported their readiness. The warehouse unit responsible for gathering all the food, equipment and supplies reported their readiness. The Great House unit responsible for raiding Bakra's house reported their readiness. Finally the security squad, made up of physically fit young men and women and responsible for neutralizing the opposition and overall safety of the team, reported their readiness. Nanny was very pleased and thanked the leaders for their hard work in getting their units ready. Everyone became excited when Nanny announced that she would be going on the raid, although she would be waiting for their return at the rendezvous point with the standby unit.

The standby unit was made up of young men and women, usually in their teens that were in training for upcoming missions. Their role was to do the heavy lifting. Because they were well rested, their job was to relieve those who had been carrying the weapons, foods and supplies up from the plantation, and getting it home safely. They were also expected to carry any injured personnel back to the village.

Apart from providing moral support for the young men and women, Nanny also wanted to see how her new strategies were working. She strongly believed and had taught her leaders that 'focus on the mission and speed of execution would reduce casualties and ensure success.' This mission was her first real test and she was as nervous as a young mother hen looking over her chicks.

The night before the raid, Nanny had supper with the troops. After the meal she gave them a pep talk.

"Ladies and gentlemen," she began. "I'm so proud of you all. You have been preparing for weeks now for this mission and your leaders are confident that you will carry out this mission with competence." She continued by telling the gathering that she would be accompanying them on the mission, to which everyone broke out into spontaneous applause.

"This is good news," one young man said.
"As long as the Chief is with us, nothing can stop us."

"I'm glad that Chief Nanny is coming with us," a young girl, going on her first mission blurted out.

"True, true," another young lady agreed. "Just knowing that she is with us, gives me the confidence to take on Bakra and his men.

Nanny waited patiently at the rendezvous point with the standby team as the invading force advanced confidently towards the plantation. At the outer perimeter of the property, the troops filed into their respective units under their leaders, and waited for the signal to push ahead.

For the next hour, the Maroons commandeer the plantation, neutralizing the little resistance put up by Bakra's security. They proceeded to collect weapons, foods and supplies from the warehouses on the plantation. The information from the women at the market was very precise. The diagrams of the buildings were very accurate. The welcome unit invited numerous men and women to come away with them.

As they returned in triumph at the rendezvous point, Nanny was surprised at how quickly they had completed the mission, and with minimal injuries. The units were in high spirit and did not look overly exhausted. Nanny congratulated them as they came into the clearing and expressed her appreciation for their hard work. She politely introduced herself to the new runaways and welcomed them into the fold.

Putus brought over the ladies from the market that had provided the intelligence and introduced them to Nanny. She hugged and thanked them for their service and promised that she would never forget their sacrifice.

On the final leg home, everyone remained alert and walked at a brisk pace. They walked along the familiar trails all night with the help of the bright glow of the moon. At the top of one hill, as Nanny looked back, she watched the troops coming up the hill behind her with the items on their heads; looking more like a long giant serpent advancing menacingly towards its prey, than as recent victors over Bakra.

A feeling of satisfaction came over her. She had almost completed her first challenge. Her next challenge would not be so easy. She had to convince the citizens that moving from this location further up into the Blue Mountain was in everybody's best interest; not only hers. For most of these people, this was the only village that they had ever known, apart from the plantation. They had also made some rather good memories here too. The last Chief was buried here along with many of their families and friends. Nanny knew that she had to frame her arguments well in order to get the people to change their thinking.

From what Quao and his team had described, Nanny was sure that the new site was beautiful, but was that enough? She really had to visit the area herself to get a firsthand look. This was too big a decision to leave to chance. She had to know without a shadow of a doubt that this was the perfect spot for the new settlement.

As dawn broke through the haze of the mountain air, Nanny and the victorious brigade entered the village at last. Some looked a little ragged and weary due to the long trek over the hills and their lack of sleep, while some of the younger ones were still excited from the raid. The energetic roosters began to crow jubilantly, signaling the start of a brand new day; and for some, a brand new life.

The entire community was up and about, anxious to greet their heroes and welcome their newest residents.

The cooks worked frantically around the fireside to finish preparing the morning breakfast for the troops. As they put down their loads there was a collective sigh of relief. A few energetic young men took off for the river to take a swim and unwind before breakfast.

Nanny spent the entire morning celebrating with the troops and meeting with the newcomers.

In her address to them she said, "I'm so proud of you all today because you have chosen freedom over slavery. You've chosen life over death. You've chosen hope over despair. This is your home now. No more head drivers to whip you to work or do other things to your bodies that you don't want to. You're now the captain of your own boat and we're here to show you the way."

Then she instructed them, "All of you repeat after me, 'I am a man or woman, as the case might be,'" she smiled. "I am free! I will never be owned by another human being again! I love my hands! I love my feet! I love my hair! I love my mouth! I love my nose! I love my teeth! I love my body! My body belongs to me and me alone! I love me! I love me because I was made by Massa God."

Next she instructed, "Turn to the person on your right, and if it's a man, say to him, 'you're so handsome!' And if it's a woman, say to her, 'you're so pretty.'

I am in Jamaica, not by choice, but I will be the best citizen I can be; Massa God is my witness. Ok! Give yourselves a big clap with your hands!" she instructed them, clapping her hands to demonstrate.

There were shouts of joy, and laughter among the new arrivals. Some wept openly and hugged each other.

"Let the healing begin today, right here, right now!" Nanny emphasized, to loud applaud.

"No more listening to the lies of Bakra! No more accepting the limitations placed on you! No more! No more! Today we take back what is ours! We reclaim our dignity! We reclaim our destiny! We are the generation that will dismantle slavery on this island! We are the generation that will force the white devils to change their ways! Never ever underestimate the power of a determined African people!"

"Nobody ever talked to us like this," one woman said wiping away her tears.

"This is the first time that anybody ever told me that I was pretty," another woman said, tears flowing down her face.

"Yes, Bakra always made us feel like we're just here to work for him and be his sex slave, but no more!" a little lady remarked confidently.

"My life has just begun today," one lady with a big scar across her face said. "I never thought that this day would come."

The newcomers were introduced to the Orientation Committee who took them through the introductory process.

Later that day, Nanny met with her close advisors and top leaders. She told them of her vision to relocate the village to a more secure settlement further up in the mountain and away from the British soldiers. She followed up with the report by Quao and his team; describing this new site.

"When are you planning on telling the people Chief?" a senior advisor asked.

"As soon as I'm positive that this is the right place," Nanny explained. "And that will happen after we return from the trip."

"Suppose the people don't want to go Chief?" another senior leader asked.

"You leave that to me," Nanny said. "I will give them the speech of my life," she said laughing, followed by everyone in the room.
"But seriously," Nanny continued, bringing back order to the meeting. "My job as the leader is to provide the vision for the people; because if there is no vision, we will all eventually perish."

The day came for Quao and his team to lead the delegation up to the new site. Nanny couldn't wait to get started. They secured their supplies and left in the wee hours of the morning. The fog was so thick that you could cut it with a knife. As they climbed the rocky trails, dew water stubbornly covered the foliage, and gently washed their feet. The moon provided ample light to follow the winding trail up into the misty heavens. Nanny felt refreshed and energized during the march as it also gave her time to think.

Her mind drifted back to her childhood, growing up in her village back in Africa with her grandmother. She remembered the many times she was up at this hour of the morning following her grandmother to visit the sick and delivering newborn babies. Yes, she remembered her grandmother, Mada Puko, doing everything for everybody and expecting nothing in return.
Nanny smiled when she remembered Mada Puko shouting at her one day, "Pay attention Nanny, I won't be around all the time to tell you what to do," when she was trying to teach Nanny something and she was not focusing.

Nanny laughed and asked, "If you're not going to be here Gamma, where will you be?"

"My child," Mada Puko said. "When you become a leader of the people, you will need to know all these things. No one will tell you. They will all expect you to know it."

"But Gamma, I don't want to be no leader of anybody. I just want to be Nanny; living here in the village, helping people and working with you Gamma."

"Don't worry," Mada Puko told her. "You're only nine years old, a mere child. You have many years to think about it. Just remember that the future awaits you and you need to be ready. Do you hear me child?"

"Yes Gamma," Nanny replied, unsure of what she meant and what else to say.

Nanny also remembered the first speech she made at the Federation of Chiefs Conference. She remembered how nervous she was before she was called up to speak. It was just like yesterday. She recalled how furious some of the Chiefs were. She wished that some of them were here now to see the fruits of their misguided actions. Well, here she was, a leader of a new nation; with all these people looking to her for leadership. Many of them were like children; trusting unconditionally and confident in the fact that they would not be abused. Nanny felt both honored and humbled. However she also knew that failure was not an option. Everyone was depending on her.

"You were right Gamma, you were right," she heard herself say.

As the morning sun forced its way into the atmospheric mix, chomping up the dense fog, the mountain peaks began to appear; tall and majestic. The surrounding landscape looked green and lush. Fresh spring water gushed out of nearby rocks and cascaded down the rock face into the rocky streams below, creating a churning hum.

Quao and his team kept up a steady pace, venturing occasionally from the bright sunshine to the shadowy paths sheltered by overhanging trees. Brightly colored birds punctuated the still air with their sweet melodic tweets of welcome.

The group stopped a few times to drink the icy cold water gushing out of the rocks and admire the beautiful springs adorning the picturesque countryside. The more they trekked up the mountain the more Nanny fell in love with the island. On leaving a canopied stretch and going up a major hill, Nanny found herself on one of the highest peaks on the mountain. It took her breath away. For a few minutes she was transfixed, just looking at the surroundings and admiring the beauty of nature.

"This is beautiful Putus," she said. I've never seen anywhere as beautiful as this place."

"Quao!" she called out to him, with her voice echoing in the valley far below. "You were right, there was no way you could've fully described this place to me. Wonderful Quao! Just wonderful," she said over and over, as she gazed out across the vast carpet of vegetation stretching as far as the eyes could see.

"It feels like we're on top of the whole wide world," Gylziia said excitedly, her voice echoing in the distance.

Turning to Nanny she said, "Chief, I could stay here for the rest of my life. I love it with all my heart!"

Nanny just smiled and gave her a gentle hug. "I agree with you my chile, but we have to move on; Quao is ready and waiting for us up front."

The sun was now fully overhead blaring angrily down on their heads, but they didn't mind because the cool mountain breeze was fighting that battle for them and they were like satisfied spectators.

"If those poor slaves on the plantations could only see this place, there is no way under Massa God's Earth Bakra could hold them again," Gylziia commented. "This is paradise already and we don't reach our destination yet. I wonder what could top this place."

"Patience my girl, patience," Putus suggested. "Remember that 'patient man ride donkey.'"

"What does donkey have to do with this place? I don't see any donkey up here," Gylziia asked, not being able to comprehend the old African proverb.

"It's just something that old people say," Putus replied, a little impatient. "Massa God help me! This girl gives me a headache with her whole lot of questions. I don't know what is going on in that big head of hers. She thinks so deeply into everything. It is either that she will be a genius or a mad woman."

Nanny laughed. She always laughed when those two argued. She loved them both like the two chatty, chatty [talkative] sisters she never had. They made her days worthwhile and kept her focused on the more important things in life like: family, friendship and loyalty. Yes, they were her family, warts and all, and she would not trade them for anything in the world.

Looking ahead Nanny could see Quao and his team waiting for them at the bank of the river.

"We're nearly there Chief," Quao said. "Across the river is where we will find the pathway. Stay close or you will miss it."

"Putus, what does Quao mean by miss it, miss what?" Gylziia asked.

"Sheee gal!" Putus said, sounding annoyed.
"Are you hard of hearing? Quao said that we should stay close to each other and don't wonder off."

"Then what's so special about here?" Gylziia inquired, somewhat confused.

"How must I know that?" Putus responded. "Didn't both of us arrive here at the same time?"

"Ahem!" Quao cleared his throat to get everyone's attention. "As I was saying, stick close to one another and follow me across the river."

The freezing water was waist deep at some point as everyone held their little bundles high in the air. As they waded carefully across the river, hundreds of fish of all sizes and colors swam playfully below the crystal clear surface. On the other side, the group stopped and dried off in the sun.

"By the way Chief," Quao said, addressing his sister. "This is where I told you that I saw the wild hog coming out of the bush. Kofi here will tell you that we jumped up with fright and then got flat on our bellies when it happened. We believed that we were under attack." Everyone laughed. Quao soon picked up his bundle and told the group to get ready. He led them slowly towards a cluster of tall enormous trees which obscured the sun. As they approached the trees, he began looking around frantically for the entrance.

Suddenly he called out, "Over here! Here is the entrance!"
Nanny looked ahead and saw Quao standing between two giant trees. He pointed westward towards a tiny passage, shrouded by creeping vines.

"The passage is right over there!" he said excitedly. "Notice that if you're not standing right here, it is very difficult to see it."

Nanny finally realized why Quao said that you had to stand between the two huge trees to find the entrance. It had something to do with the way the sun shone through the trees and hit the spot. Without the sunlight, a creepy shadow fell over the entrance making it almost impossible to discern. Nanny smiled as she finally figured out the mystery.

As Quao had said, this was a near perfect entrance and the British soldiers would have a very difficult time finding it on their own. Plus she would be working with the security unit to develop interesting ways to confuse them.

Quao led the way through the narrow passage that allowed only one person at a time to enter. The entrance opened up to a long, narrow, rocky ridge, high above the roaring river below. The ridge was like 'walking the plank' with only one person going across at a time.

At the top of the ridge, the trail turned sharply to the right then opened up into an expansive rolling terrain interspersed with clumps of trees and many different kinds of indigenous, multicolored shrubberies.

"Wow! This place is gorgeous!" Putus exclaimed, surveying the surrounding landscape. Everyone agreed, smiling broadly as they stopped to admire the beauty of the property.

"Quao my brother, you've done well!" Nanny said, running over and hugging him. "This place is breathtaking."

Situated in one corner were a few weather-beaten, broken down old huts; the same ones that Quao had reported.

Suddenly the sky became overcast as Quao led the group towards the huts. No sooner had they reached inside the main hut when the sky opened up and rain began coming down in bucket loads. The hut leaked from every section like a giant sieve and the dirt floor became flooded in no time. The entire hut shook violently as the thunder rumbled and the place lit up when the lightning flashed. Putus and Gylziia looked nervously at each other and then glanced over at Nanny beside them. She appeared so calm as if she had no care in the world and had everything under control.

That was what Putus loved about Nanny; her calmness in the face of danger. Putus strongly believed that Nanny was a great Obeah woman who had received unlimited powers that she could unleash at will; and yet she was as gentle as a young kitten for those who needed help. Putus wondered how the British soldiers would fare in battle against her. She would not want to be in their boots when Nanny was mad.

As she looked directly in Nanny's face, in the brief flashes of lightening, she saw the steely gaze and the power in her demeanor. She heard herself say under her breath, "I don't think that those soldiers know what they're in for when they go up against this woman."

"What did you say Putus?" Gylziia asked.

"Nothing," she replied.

"That's not true; I know that you said something. What is it? Are you afraid of the lightening?"

"It's nothing gal, mind your own business," Putus snapped at her and hissed her teeth in disgust. "I will never know why you talk so much!"

"Ok ladies, knock it off," Nanny said sternly.

"We have a lot of work to do."

"Ladies and gentlemen," she said, turning and addressing the group. "From what I've seen so far, this is a very beautiful and strategic location. Tomorrow we will explore the area thoroughly before heading back home."

Chapter 18

The decision was made; the relocation narrative would be presented to the people. Nanny spent many hours preparing her speech. She knew that every word would be scrutinized thoroughly. This was one of the most important speeches she would ever have to make in her life, and she knew that how she framed her argument would determine the citizen's response.

As she stood before the crowd she looked out at the sea of faces anxiously waiting to hear the news.

She began by thanking the people for giving her the opportunity to lead them and telling them how grateful she was for all their help in keeping the village safe and healthy. She went on to talk about the accomplishments of the village and the many changes she had seen from the time she got there.

Nanny then spent some time explaining the need for continuous change if as a people they wanted to continue developing and maintaining their independence.

"If we are to continue living in freedom and prosperity then we must look at relocation as an option," she told the large audience.

When she said those words, there was complete silence. Everyone was now focused on every word that came out of her mouth.

"Don't get me wrong, I love this site. This site was where I got my first taste of freedom. I love this site," she emphasized.

"But although this site is great, with all its wonderful features, yet its greatest weakness is the fact that it is located too close to the British soldiers' camp and we could be invaded at any time.

Secondly, our position here is not adequately protected against attacks. And thirdly, our ability to grow is limited," she pointed out.

"If we are to double or triple our present population then we have to relocate to a larger more secure community."

The silence was deafening. The air was tense.

"Listen carefully to what I'm saying folks," Nanny pleaded. "If there was any other way to do this, I would; but these are the facts. I would never mislead you," she continued.

"We have found such a place, ladies and gentlemen. I have been there personally and I must tell you that I am very pleased.

The place has everything that we need. Good strategic location making it almost impossible for any surprise attacks by the soldiers. The land is very fertile and is great for growing crops and raising animals. It has everything we need to increase our population and live a safe and healthy life.

In closing, let me stress that if we don't make this move now ladies and gentlemen, we will first of all be limiting our growth potential and secondly, setting ourselves up for future clashes with the British soldiers. Time is the enemy here ladies and gentlemen. Now is the time to set our course onto a brighter future, not only for ourselves, but for our children and our children's children. The decision is yours, ladies and gentlemen. I'm here only as your humble servant."

"We trust you Chief Nanny!" a short stout woman with a baby in her hands shouted. "Do what you think is right for us."

"Well, if that is what it is then we accept it!" another woman shouted.

"Yes!" the people shouted. "We're ready!"

Then the people stood and started shouting, "We're ready! We're ready," for a long time.

Nanny looked on with pleasure at the jubilation of the crowd and smiled to herself.

"Now the real work begins."

The clock was ticking. The deadline for relocating to the new site was in six months. There were so many things to be done in such a short time. First, Quao took a group of loggers up to clear the land and some builders to begin construction on the clinic, the Chief's residence and other huts. Nanny insisted that the village be built like a typical Ashanti village.

Down in the village, Putus and Gylziia supervised the cataloging of items to be brought to the new site while Nanny made plans for an upcoming raid on a plantation down in the southwest.

The plan was simple, set fire to the cane fields and if necessary, the main buildings and the Great House and collect as many items as they can physically carry. At the same time, Putus and her team would lure as many slaves as possible back with them to the village.

In the weeks prior to the raid, Putus and her team travelled down to the market on Sundays to collect intelligence about the plantation in their cross hairs.

The raid on the plantation was a success. The intelligence was more than adequate and Bakra was taken by complete surprise. The security was so lax that the few white guards all ran away leaving the entire compound to Nanny's troops. Everything was theirs for the taking; and that is exactly what they did. Anything that was not nailed down and could be carried off was taken. Putus and Gylziia recruited over fifty young men and women from their barracks and led them away from the plantation. This was their biggest and most successful raid ever and everyone was in high spirit on their return home that morning.

Nanny greeted all the men and women who took part in the raid, and congratulated them on a job well done. Over breakfast she welcomed all the new citizens to the village and commended them on their courageous decision to control their own destiny. She later introduced them to the Orientation committee who patiently took them through the introductory and settling in process.

One last minute thing that Nanny had asked Putus to do on the raid was to collect lots of extra clothing for the people. She remembered clearly that the nights became extremely cold further up in the mountain, especially when the rain fell. Keeping the people warm and comfortable was a top priority for her, because if they were under stress due to the extreme cold, then they would not be productive citizens.

Putus did not disappoint. From accurate intelligence, she was able to locate the building where Bakra stored the workers clothes. She spent some time gathering as many as she and her crew could physically carry.

As the six month deadline approached, Nanny sent more and more skilled and unskilled workers to the new site along with tools, seeds, clothing and foodstuff. After clearing the land, many workers, spearheaded by the Cultivation team, prepared the land and planted ground provisions and vegetables. They hoped that by the time the entire population arrived, there would be enough food to feed everyone.

Construction on the new village was well on the way and every week more and more families packed up and moved up to the new town. Most of the foodstuff and other materials were also on its way to the newly constructed warehouses; some temporary ones, built outside the town, and the permanent ones on site. More and more people arrived and were settling in well. Everything was going according to plan and Nanny was confident that the relocation exercise would be completed before the deadline.

Chapter 19

Nanny felt relieved to receive news from Cudjoe and Accompong. They both said that they would not be returning to the east for some time.

Nanny smiled a sly smile. "I bet you those two have found girlfriends down in the west," Nanny said playfully to Putus.

"It is about time," Putus replied. "Those two boys are good catches. If I was a few years younger, I would get Cudjoe to marry me and then we would be family. Wouldn't that be something Nanny?"
Nanny laughed out loud. "That would be something Putus, that would be something," is all she said.

"Did you know Nanny that the one Gylziia liked Accompong, and it looked like he liked her too?" Putus informed Nanny. "But I suppose it was not meant to be. Poor gal."

"But here we're, talking like we know for certain that they've found girlfriends down in the west," Nanny remarked.

"But that would be the only reason why they would stay down there," Putus insisted.

"Well let's not tell Gylziia about this until we're absolutely certain," Nanny cautioned. "I don't want her to start worrying, maybe for nothing."

"Then tell me something Nanny, who would you prefer to have in your family, Gylziia or me?"
Again Nanny gave a haughty laugh, and said in jest, "I would love to have my two favorite ladies in my family." They both laughed.

"The true words of a politician," Putus remarked

Nanny felt relaxed in her new home, in the new village surrounded by her people. She instructed the men to continue clearing the land, to make room for more huts and for planting more crops. In some cases they set fire to the tree trunks and left it to burn until the trees collapsed.

The town was designed like an Ashanti village back in Africa. Nothing was left out. The artisans tried their best to capture the essence of life from the Motherland and to incorporate them into their designs. This proved to be very popular among the folks, who felt a deeper connection to Africa; with their plantation life a distant nightmare. However, unlike those back in Africa, the huts here were built on slopes with trenches dug around them to take away the heavy flood waters.

The people spent their days planting crops, hunting in the forests and taking care of their livestock.

Nanny looked on with pride at the progress that was being made.

Chapter 20

Cudjoe and Accompong arrived the day before the celebration. Nanny, Quao and the other brothers were all happy to greet them. Nanny could not hold back, and ran over and hugged them.

"It looks like the girls are taking good care of you boys down there," Nanny chided.

Cudjoe and Accompong smiled, showing a tinge of embarrassment.

"Sis, this place is great! Quao did a fantastic job finding it," Cudjoe said with delight. "I'm also very impressed with your security. The guards stood still like statues and looked just like the trees in the forest. They blended in so well with the bush that no army can invade this place without you knowing. Brilliant Sis! Simple brilliant! I will have to send some of our men over here to get some training."

"Thanks Cudjoe," Nanny acknowledged, before skillfully changing the subject. "So are you boys going back?" she asked casually.

Cudjoe and Accompong looked at each other and hesitated for a while then Cudjoe answered. "I think so Sis," he said, with a serious look on his face.

"Me too Sis," Accompong added. "After the celebration we need to talk."

"Alright boys," Nanny said, surrendering to their wishes. Although she would miss them yet she knew that it was the right thing for them.

"Let's get both of you settled in, and then we can talk about all this later."

"Sis, have you seen Gylziia?" Accompong asked, acting coy.

"She is over by the clinic," Nanny responded with a smile.

"I will head over there and surprise her," he said as he hurried away.

On the morning of the celebration the entire village was up very early. Several food stations were set up around the square with different types of food in various stages of preparation. They included: jerked wild boar, roasted pigeons, boiled land crabs, roasted fish, roasted and boiled yams, boiled pumpkins, run down, blue draws; and as treats for the kids, coconut drops and grater cakes.

As the time drew near, Quao, who was in charge of coordinating the celebration, consulted with Nanny over last minute details.

"Everything looks great Quao," Nanny said with a smile, after going over the plans.

"You've done a marvelous job. Come, let's get dressed for the function."

Later that evening, the villagers, all beautifully dressed in their finest attire, began arriving for the celebration. The rhythmic beat of the drums could be heard for miles around. The drummers in their brightly colored costumes, played with such intensity and skills that it was hard for anyone to resist the temptation to tap their feet. The thunder bass drummers maintained a steady beat while the fundeh drummers played skillfully with their hands keeping the rhythm alive. Next to them, the high pitched keteh drummers improvised as they delivered their infectious beat to the delight of the crowd. And then jumping in were the gumbeh drummers bringing their unique sound to the mix. Finally coming over the top were the Abeng players piercing the air with their distinctive sounds.

Accompanying the drummers were the singers and the energetic dancers decked out in their brightly colored costumes. The singers sang many of the popular songs they learned in Africa while the young dancers performed their Ashanti dances with grace and style. Nanny and the Elders looked on with pride. Everything was going according to plan. The food was lavish and everyone licked their fingers [enjoyed the meal] with pleasure. As part of the entertainment, young warriors gave a mock demonstration of their military expertise using different weapons and hand to hand combat. The crowd loved it and showed their appreciation with shouts and cheers.

Then it was Nanny's turn to address the people.

"When Massa God gives you many blessings, he expects a whole lot from you in return," Nanny told her audience. "Remember where you're coming from; remember those who are still back there in slavery. You're not here by accident. You're here for a reason, and that reason is to help to stop this wickedness called slavery. Our generation will see the end of slavery on this island, and I want you all to be a part of it. In closing, let me remind you..."

"What are you going to call the village, Chief Nanny?" a little old lady sitting up front shouted out, cutting Nanny off.

Nanny hesitated; she wasn't sure what to say because it had not crossed her mind. The crowd sat in silence waiting on her to respond. She was at a loss for words, something that was unheard of. She placed her hand over her mouth as she contemplated what to say, but nothing was forthcoming.

Just then Putus walked out before the crowd and proclaimed, "In honor of our great Chief who has brought us to this beautiful land; from this day forward, the name of this village will be called Nanny Town."

The crowd erupted with joy and celebration. The drummers started beating their skins rhythmically as the dancers gyrated to the pulsating beat. The people formed a circle around the dancers and clapped to the rhythm of the drums. The young people and children all joined in dancing to the mesmerizing beat. Nanny joined Putus, Gylziia and other elders in the ring and danced to the music with the older people. Later she walked around and greeted everyone, wishing them well.

The ceremony was a great success. The dancing and celebration continued until late into the night.

Chapter 21

Cudjoe and Accompong were up at the crack of dawn to begin their long journey back to the west. They had spent the last two weeks bonding as a family with Nanny, Cuffy, Johnny and Quao. There was constant laughter as they enjoyed each other's company; swapping stories about the fun times they had back in Africa when they were kids. At times they laughed so hard that tears came to their eyes when they reflected on the fun times they had with their parents.

"I remember the time we were playing in an open field just behind our village, when Cuffy shouted, 'lion cubs!'" Accompong recalled. "Instantly we realized that we were in terrible danger because that meant that the mother must be nearby. Everybody began to worry except you Nanny. She just stiffened her neck, opened up her big steely eyes and started looking around for the mother. Then, before we knew it the giant beast was right there in front of us; ready to pounce.

Nanny barked at us to freeze and then slowly walked towards the giant beast. Do you remember Sis?" he asked, looking over at Nanny.

"Oh yes I remember," she said humbly, nodding her head.

"You never once took your eyes off the huge beast. Then you slowly walked up to it and pat her on the head and mumbled something to her. I believed that you were this close to being eaten, but the giant beast never moved a muscle; it just stood there, this great beast! It kept looking at you like we were not even there," he continued. "I was so frightened that I wet my pants."

"Me too," confessed Cudjoe, looking slightly embarrassed.

"Me too," admitted Cuffy.

"I was more worried about what we would have to tell our parents if the lion had eaten you Sis!" Accompong continued.

"But the weirdest thing happened; the lion just looked down at the ground and gently turned and walked away towards her cubs, looking as tame as a baby kitten. I couldn't believe what I was seeing."

"That's true," all the brothers agreed.

"Tell me something Sis; for a long, long time now I've been dying to ask you, how did you do it?"

"My dear brother Accompong," Nanny began. "I love you with all my heart, but if I tell you, then I will have to kill you," she laughed. Everyone joined in as Cudjoe playfully grabbed him around the neck and rubbed his forehead with his knuckles.

After they had all settled down again Cudjoe addressed Nanny,

"But Sis you missed out on a lot of fun times when we were growing up because you spent most of your time over at Gamma's house. Sometimes I really wanted to come with you guys but mother wouldn't allow me. She used to say that Gamma was training you, and I wondered what she was training you for. At first I believed that you were just staying down at Gamma's house to escape the work at home, but now I know better."

He paused, then looked into Nanny's eyes and said, "I love you Sis, you are my hero." The tears in everyone's eyes were pretty obvious.

"Sis, I also didn't tell you thanks for all that you've done for us," Accompong joined in. "You didn't have to come, but you chose to come and take care of us, and I'm grateful. I don't know of anybody else in the world who would've chosen to become a slave in order to save their family. I don't know if I would've done it, but you did it for us, and that is why you're the greatest sister and I love you very much."

Between tears, Nanny said with a smile, "I came because I didn't want you boys to go off and have all this fun and leave me at home with those old folks." Everyone laughed, as she gave them a hug.

"On a more serious note, I must say that you guys are my heroes because you never gave up, even when times were hard and the going was rough. You kept up each other's spirit and the rest of the men around you. And

184

now we're all here entering a new chapter in our lives. I believe that the stars are lined up for us to take up our rightful place in creating a new society in this new land. We're not here by accident, you know. We're here to fulfill our destiny."

Everyone went completely silent for a moment, and then Quao said jokingly, "What did I tell all of you? She can talk! Sis will burst into a speech as fast as you can say the word Ashanti." Everyone laughed. "Listen everybody!" Quao continued, trying to get everyone's attention. Then looking at Nanny he said, "Sis, you are the best sister a brother could ever have. I have learned so much from you. I don't know what would've happened to us as a family if you did not come. One day I hope to be a leader just like you."

"Ahhhhhhhhhh!" the other brothers heckled as Accompong gave him a friendly slap on the back of his head.

On the day before they left, Nanny and her brothers were down by the river having a picnic when Cudjoe began talking about life in the west.

"The British soldiers keep attacking our villages over and over again. And when they attack us we have to run away and hide in the bushes. The soldiers show us no mercy when they attack. They kill everybody; men, women, and children, with their big muskets. They are wicked. But things will be different when I get back down there. I'm going to put into practice everything that I have learned here this week. I will also be sending some of our men over here to train with your troops Nanny."

"I agree with you Cudjoe," Accompong interjected. "We need to double our efforts to defend ourselves against the British. In our area, we have little groups of brash young white men who attack our villages in the early morning, before daylight. They shoot directly into the huts, sometimes killing everyone inside. To them it is all a big joke. They act as if we are wild animals to be hunted down and killed. We have to strike back with equal force to show them that we're not here for their enjoyment. They are just young men with weapons and I doubt if they have ever been in a real battle," he said, shaking his head in frustration. "Sis, that's why I must go back, because we didn't trouble them; in fact, we always tried to avoid any confrontation with them. But it is not working at all and they're becoming more daring every day. If we don't take a stand now then these young white men and the soldiers will eventually recapture us and put us back on the plantation; and I would prefer death than to return to that place."

When Nanny heard the lament of her brothers she felt compassion for the villagers and promised Cudjoe and Accompong to assist in training their troops.

Then an idea came to her. "Listen my brothers; it is clear that the British are in control of the situation now, not because they're better, but because we're not organized. The Ashanti tribe did not become great warriors by being disorganized. They became great because of their superior organizational skills. We have to adopt those same principles if we're going to defeat the British."

"And how do we do that, Sis?" Cudjoe asked.

"First, we have to divide the island into two regions; the east here, and the west over where you live. Our region in the east could be called the Windward Maroons, and your region in the west could be called; let me think."

"The Leeward Maroons," Cudjoe suggested.

"That's a great name brother, I like it a lot," Nanny affirmed.

"I agree," Accompong added. "That name really represents us in the west."

"Well, alright then, that is settled," Nanny said. "We will share all information that we receive and help each other to fight our common enemy, the British. You guys will attack them from the west and we will attack them from the east. We will stretch their troops so thin that they become useless, and then we will drive them off this island," Nanny said, with her steely piercing eyes looking across the river. No one said a word because they all knew their sister quite well.

Later that afternoon, Accompong took Nanny aside to talk privately.

"Sis, Gylziia is coming back with me. We spoke about it and she has decided to come back with me," Accompong revealed.

"And where is she going to stay when she goes down there? Do you have somewhere for her to live?" Nanny inquired sternly.

"Yes Sis," Accompong responded quickly.
"I built a big house down there with my own two hands. She will be fine; I will take good care of her."

"You had better take good care of her, because I love that girl like my own family," Nanny warned him.

"I know Sis, she told me all the things that you have done for her. She loves you more than roast yam," Accompong joked.

"Then what about the girlfriends that you have down there? I don't want them to fight Gylziia," Nanny cautioned.

"I wouldn't let that happen to her Sis," he reassured Nanny. "And moreover I don't have any girlfriend down there. I've loved Gylziia for a long time Sis."

"I didn't know that you were so serious about her brother?"

"Yes Sis, I love her more than jerk pork," which caused both of them to burst out laughing.

"Gylziia is so smart Sis. I've learned so much from her. I'm so glad that she decided to come back with me because I really don't want to return without her. I dream about her every night."

Nanny was happy with the news. She wished that Putus could have heard all this.

"Sis, did you know that I got mad when she told me about that idiot head driver who whipped her for foolishness. I still can't forgive that man, and if I ever meet him, I would certainly hurt him."

"Leave the past behind my brother; leave the past behind," Nanny advised. "It is not entirely his fault. He was just following Bakra's orders, although some of them love their job too much. He is just a mere cog in the wheel of oppression. Refocus your anger on the true evil of this world my brother, and forgive our people; because they have been given 'straw basket to carry water.' I believe deep down in the bottom of my heart that if that man knew better, he would have done better."

"I hear what you're saying Sis, but it's hard," Accompong acknowledged.

"I know," Nanny agreed. "But it is for the best."

Nanny arrived home late that evening to find Gylziia quietly packing in her room. Nanny stood at the door and inquired.

"Then you didn't plan to tell me chile?"

"Yes Chief," Gylziia stammered. "You know Chief; it's a long time now that I told A.C. to talk to you."

"Who is this A.C.?" Nanny inquired.

"That is what I call Accompong Chief," she said flashing a bright smile.

"So you know what you're in for down there chile?" Nanny asked, raising her eye brow.

"I'm prepared for anything Chief," she began. "I will travel to the end of the world, as long as I am with A.C., I mean Accompong, Chief. I love your brother so much that I would do anything for him. He told me that down there the people are very friendly, and he has a big house waiting for me. I really don't care how big it is, as long as I can make life with him, I will be fine Chief."

"So did you tell Putus?" Nanny asked.

"Yes, I spoke with her last night. Sorry Chief, but I was afraid to tell you, because I thought that you would be mad, seeing that he is your brother."

"But why would I get mad?" Nanny asked, looking puzzled. "You know that I love you like a sister. I'm very happy for you and Accompong. I know that you will take good care of him. And trust me, that boy needs all the help he can get." They both laughed.

"Chief, I'm very excited!" Gylziia exclaimed. "I never imagined myself leaving you Chief, but when A.C. told me that he didn't want to go back down there without me, my little heart grew so big that it nearly burst. It was the first time that I was ever needed by anybody, especially a man." As she kept jabbering about Accompong, Nanny just smiled and thought that her little brother was lucky to have a girl like Gylziia.

Just then Putus dropped by for a visit. As she walked into the room she blurted out. "Then Nanny, the little gal decided to go away with a man, down the country," she said jokingly. Everyone laughed.

"Yes my dear," Nanny responded. "I'm so happy for her, and also for my brother."

"Then what about Cudjoe, is he bringing back somebody too?" Putus inquired.

"I didn't hear him say anything like that," Nanny replied. "But Cudjoe is so secretive when it comes to his business."

"If I was ten years younger," Putus began. "He would have to take me back with him."

"We know Putus," Nanny said jokingly. "Remember, 'every hoe has its stick in the bush.'" [There is a soul mate out there for everyone]

"I think that Putus' stick is growing roots by now," Gylziia joked.

"Watch your mouth gal, before I send you down the country with a fat lip."

"Sorry Putus, but you opened the gate and I couldn't resist."
The three ladies talked and giggled way into the night, while they helped Gylziia pack her belongings.

The following morning, the folks in Nanny Town woke up early to bid farewell to Cudjoe, Accompong, Gylziia and their western friends. Nanny hugged Cudjoe and with tears in her eyes told him that she loved him and was going to miss him.

"Don't start the cow bawling [crying] Sis. I'm not too far away. Don't worry, I will be back by Christmas. And Sis, you have to promise me that you will come down there and visit us very soon."
Nanny gave her word and promised to make the trip when the time permitted. Then she hugged Accompong.

"I'm going to miss you and Gylziia. Take good care of yourself my brother and don't let anything happen to my girl Gylziia. I hope it works out for both of you."

"Thanks Sis," he said. "And when you come down to visit us in the west you could kill two birds with one stone. What I mean is that you could visit Cudjoe in St. James and then come down to visit us in St. Elizabeth, before you go back home."

"Sounds like a good idea," Nanny remarked.
Then Gylziia ran towards Nanny and hugged her tightly, shaking and crying uncontrollably.

"I love you Chief, I love you," she wailed, not caring who was watching her.

"I love you too," Nanny revealed, desperately trying to resist the temptation to cry.

"You're like a mother and a big sister to me, and I will never forget you," Gylziia avowed, wiping back the tears.

"But it sounds like the gal don't plan to come back," Putus said jokingly.
Everyone laughed.

"Putus you take everything for a big joke," Gylziia remarked sternly, and then just as quickly she broke out into a broad smile. "And that is why I love you very much Putus. You keep me laughing all day long. I'm really going to miss you." With that she grabbed Putus and gave her a big hug and planted a big kiss on her cheek.

After saying goodbye, the three and their entourage started on their long journey across the mountain over to the western end of the island, keeping in their hearts the wonderful time that they had spent in Nanny Town.

Chapter 22

Construction in Nanny Town was progressing fairly well. The clinic was now completed and many new homes were going up every day. More and more land was being cleared and put into production. The beautifully terraced hillsides made planting much more convenient for the women and prevented the washing away of the soil. As the women toiled away in the field, they sang lively African songs. Occasionally there was laughter from one section or the other, usually from someone telling jokes. The atmosphere was so different here in Nanny Town than on the plantation where there was always the threat of the head driver's whip.

Some days when Nanny was not busy she would walk out to the field to do some weeding, clearing of the land or whatever the ladies wanted her to do. The women appreciated the Chief's visit because they got a chance to know her and Nanny also got to know them too. Before she left, Nanny always thanked them for their hard work and dedication to the building of the town and invited them to bring forward suggestions on how to make the town better. She always reminded them that Nanny Town was for them and not about her.

"I'm your humble servant and I'm here to serve you," she would say. The women always felt better about themselves and had a greater appreciation for their Chief when Nanny left.

"That woman is a blessing from Massa God," one lady with a brightly colored head tie remarked.

"True word," another said. "Chief is a special woman of God. I feel so safe with her here."

"Yes I feel like nobody can harm us," a short stout woman affirmed.

"I agree," another woman uttered. "And if it comes down to it, I will be right by her side if and when we have to fight the British."

"We too," the others all piped in.

Occasionally the women informed her about things that were needed in the town. These ranged from the need for more warm clothes to a variety of tools for clearing and working the land. Nanny always made it her duty to pass on the information to her leaders when they were planning the next raid or making purchases at the local market.

Over at the military training field, Nanny observed the young men and women going through their training. She noted the level of professionalism that was displayed by everyone and made a note to mention it to Quao, who was the Commander-in-Chief. As she watched the men and women train, Nanny thought about all that Cudjoe and Accompong had said about the British soldiers and the young local militias attacking villages in the West. She knew that it was just a matter of time before they would start their attacks in the East. What she needed was a greater fighting force capable of defeating any army or militia. And where were all the potential fighters?" she pondered. She shook her head and smiled to herself. She knew what she had to do.

Over the next few days, Nanny met with Quao and his military leaders to plan attacks on plantations in the south and protecting Nanny Town from outside attacks. Nanny grew hungry for intelligence about the British. She felt vulnerable without information.

She realized that to stay ahead of the British she needed to have all the intelligence she could gather. There was so much to be done to close this wide gap. She also needed to keep her people fully informed, and mobilized to face adversities when they came. Every adult citizen was expected to serve in the local force in protecting the town if it was ever attacked, and thus time had to be allotted for training.

Nanny asked Quao to ensure that the troops knew every movement of the British soldiers at all times. The next step was developing a sophisticated spy support network to monitor enemy activities and provide meaningful information for the leaders. To carry out this elaborate program Nanny needed to increase the number of spies on the plantations and in the marketplace. She appointed Putus to head her spy unit and asked her to devise a comprehensive plan to gather information in the region. Putus was very excited about her new assignment and started organizing her team right away.

But the job was not yet completed. She needed to develop a more sophisticated warning system for the town, especially when they were under attack. For this job she appointed Cuffy, her younger brother. He was a talented musician and strategist. She asked him to devise a coded communication system using the talking drums and abeng. Nanny hoped that when the system was fully operational, every citizen would be able to respond appropriately in an emergency.

She was pleased with the plans so far and smiled when she envisioned the next few months.

"If Cudjoe was impressed with what he saw the other day, wait until he sees us in the next few months," she said to herself. "We will have the most sophisticated spy network in this part of the world. The British won't know what hit them. They will be sorry that they ever set foot in Jamaica."

Nanny's days started very early in the morning and ended late in the night. She was in constant communication with her leaders, getting updates and consulting on issues. At the weekly meetings, she was briefed by the leaders of each unit and plans of action were implemented.

After careful reconnaissance, plans were set in motion for a series of raids on certain plantations in striking distance. The main objective was to procure as many weapons and ammunitions, warm clothes, and most importantly; recruit as many young men and women as possible.

The first raid was a complete success. Everything went according to plan.

Over the next couple of weeks Quao led the troops on a series of raids on plantations in their cross hairs.

A few weeks into the raids, Putus received some important news that Bakra and the soldiers were planning something big. They could not tell when the operation would take place only that it was soon.

Nanny called an emergency meeting of her advisors. She thanked Putus for the information and outlined plans for tightening up the security of the town. She soon began deploying her military patrols further out from the town. They combed the countryside for any signs of the British soldiers or local militia. And when they were spotted, the patrols noted their position and sent back messages. The warriors were given strict instructions not to engage the enemy, but were to use their guerrilla training to camouflage and blend in with the vegetation. This was a course that Nanny taught personally to every new batch of recruits. She always started the training by giving the recruits the speech on the importance of camouflage in warfare. She would take the troops out into the forest and teach them how to blend in with the environment, and most importantly how to stand still and disguise themselves to look like the trees and shrubs.

Quao kept Nanny abreast of the patrols in the forest and reported on their movements. She was pleased with the progress of her troops. They were becoming highly skilled and disciplined fighters soon capable of making the British stop and take notice. Yes, they were on their way to becoming a formidable fighting force.

Chapter 23

Nanny had only a few hours sleep. She was out with Putus and the midwives the night before helping young mothers and delivering babies. It was near dawn when she finally fell into bed.

Despite protests from Nanny's personal aid, Quao insisted that the Chief be awakened.

"Chief! Chief!"

"Yes Qutie! What is it now?" Nanny asked, sleepily.

"Sorry to bother you Chief, but Mass Quao is here, and he says it is urgent!" Qutie blurted out.

"It's alright Qutie, send him in," she said, yawning unashamedly and wiping her eyes.

"Morning Sis!" Quao gave a greeting, as he hurried into the room. "Sorry to wake you up, but a short while ago the West Patrol returned and they brought with them a little abandoned boy. They said that they found him wandering around in the forest away from his village; hungry and with a few cuts and bruises. The boy is now over by the clinic sleeping. He looked a little tired and a little dehydrated, but otherwise fine. He said that his village was attacked a few days ago by a group of young white militia with muskets. They shot up his village early in the morning while they were asleep in their beds. They killed everybody in sight; men, women and children, including his parents. They killed even the dogs, the pigs and the fowls. He said that he's only alive because his father shielded him from the shooters and told him to run away into the forest and hide."

"Cowards! Cowards!" Nanny, now fully awake, yelled in anger. "Those people didn't deserve this. Like us, they were just trying to survive in this new land. Those poor innocent folks could have been us Quao. When the boy is awake, I would like to talk with him. And please get the full report from the patrol," she instructed.

Later that morning Nanny walked over to the clinic to visit the boy.

"Hi there young man!" Nanny greeted the boy.

"I'm the Chief here, Chief Nanny. What is your name?" she asked.

"Ahaji, Ma'm," the boy replied, sheepishly.

"And what happened to your mother and father?"

"They were shot to death by the wicked Bakra man them ma'm," the boy replied, looking quite sad.

"I'm so sorry for your loss," Nanny said hugging the lad as he wiped his tears with the back of his hand. "Don't cry my love, everything will be alright. They will never get to you now. You're safe here."

"Then why are you crying too ma' m; you don't know my mother or my father?"

"I'm crying Ahaji because I know how you feel. The same thing happened to my own parents too. Come, let us go back to my house and have breakfast. Are you hungry?"

"Yes ma'm!" the boy answered boldly.

Over breakfast the boy spoke about his family and his village. He told Nanny that his family had run away from the plantation six months earlier after some men from the hills had raided the plantation. He said that they were having the best time of their lives when they were attacked. Then he went into details of the massacre.

"They just laughed as they shot everybody," the boy disclosed. "I think they were drinking because I saw some of them with bottles. They just shot us down like wild hogs."

"And how did you last so long in the forest?" Nanny asked, skillfully switching the subject.

"Chief Nanny, it was only Massa God who helped me," he began. "I kept running as my father told me to do; just running, not looking back. In the nights I slept way up in the tree. I stayed up there even when the rain was falling and I was wet down to my skin. Sometimes I got so cold that I

196

could hear my teeth rattling. But I knew that I had to stay alive if I was going to seek revenge on those murderers for killing my mother and father," he continued, tears rolling down his shiny face. "Chief Nanny, I would like to join your warriors to fight the wicked British people them. I will make them pay for what they did to my family. I want my revenge now Chief Nanny! I won't rest until I've killed off all the British people them," he said, with a determined look in his eyes.

"Take it easy young man," Nanny cautioned.

"There is ample time for you to join our army and fight the British. In the meantime, stay here with us and learn as much as you can; and when the time is right, I will be the first person to recommend you to join our fighting men and women."

The lad looked disappointed.

"Ahaji look!" Nanny held him gently by the arm. "You're too young right now to fight these very bad men. When the time is right, you will be ready, I promise you."

"Alright Chief Nanny, I'm holding you to it," the boy remarked. "The spirit of my mother and my father will not rest until I let them pay."

Nanny looked at the boy with admiration for his courage and bravery.

"And how did you meet my team in the forest, Ahaji?" Nanny asked, shrewdly changing the subject.

He laughed playfully for the first time; looking embarrassed like a little boy caught with his hand in the cookie jar.

"It was like this Chief; I was tired after walking all morning and stopped to rest, and also to pee pee [urinate]. So I looked for a nearby tree to pee pee. I was in the middle of my pee pee when suddenly the tree grabbed me and covered my mouth! I was so frightened that I just 'peed' myself. He told me not to scream and he would take his hand off my mouth. So I shook my head to say that I would not scream. After he removed his hand he told me that he was a Maroon and that he would not hurt me. He then stepped out from behind the bushes and I was in for a shock!" he continued. "Sorry Chief Nanny, but I was surprise to see that it was not a man, but a woman! She made a funny signal and suddenly the whole place was packed with Maroons! I was so frightened that my head spun and I nearly fainted. Here I was in this peaceful forest, minding my own business, but not knowing that people were watching me all the time." Then he smiled a broad smile, showing his shiny white teeth. "Chief Nanny, they were so nice to me. They gave me lots of food to eat and water to drink. The women fussed over me like I was a baby. They made me feel so special, just like my mother. I'm so glad that they found me. I was beginning to wonder if I was the only person in the whole wide world."

Just then Putus entered the house and said with a bright smile, "What a nice little boy Chief! I heard that he was very brave out in the forest." Then she turned to the boy and asked, "What is your name?"

"My name is Ahaji," the boy replied. "And what is your name?"

"Putus, Miss Putus to you," she answered.

"I like you Miss Putus because you remind me so much of my mother," the boy interjected.

"And I like you too Ahaji. Would you like to come and live with me?" Putus asked casually, before looking over at Nanny and giving her a wink. Nanny knew that Putus badly wanted a little child to live with her, and to love, so this could be a good fit.

"Yes, yes, ma'm," the boy stammered, not sure of what to say.

"Are you sure Ahaji?" Nanny asked. "We don't want to force you into anything."

"Yes Chief," he replied boldly this time. "I would love to live with Miss Putus. She looks nice, just like my mother."

"Then it is settled, Ahaji," Nanny declared.
"You will go and live with Miss Putus."

"Yes Chief Nanny!" the boy said, looking quite happy like he had won a million dollars.

Then he turned to Putus and thanked her for taking him into her home and promised not to disappoint her. Putus smiled and thanked Nanny as she and the boy left. Nanny smiled as she saw how happy her good friend was. She obviously needed the boy just as much as he needed a guardian.

For a moment Nanny wondered how she would cope with a child at this stage in her life. She pictured herself cooking and feeding the child and tucking him in comfortably in bed at nights. She quickly shook her head and dismissed the thought, and brought her mind back to the challenges of Nanny Town. She was the mother of the town and the citizens were her children. She had high hopes and expectation for them and would, like a mother hen taking care of her chicks; fight anyone who tried to harm them.

The following afternoon Quao came by the clinic to seek out Nanny who was visiting with the sick and the elderly. She loved visiting her patients, especially the elderly, because they reminded her of the Motherland and were not afraid to tell her the truth. She always left there humbled and energized and anxiously looking forward to her next visit.

Nanny was deep in conversation with her old friend Mada Fufu, who was telling her about the good old days back in Africa when Quao approached them with a concerned look on his face.

"Sorry to bother you Chief," he whispered in her ears. "But one of our patrols did not return," he said, trying to hide his anxiety.

"Which team is it?" Nanny asked, getting worried.

"It's the East Team Chief. They were supposed to return from last night but we have not yet seen or heard from them."

"When was the last time that you heard from them?" Nanny inquired rather calmly.

"The last time we made contact with them was yesterday morning," Quao answered. "They reported that everything was alright and they would be returning by the evening. They reported seeing soldiers in the area but they did not engage them. I'm worried Sis; something might be wrong, and the Sun is going down fast."

"So what do you have in mind?" Nanny asked calmly.

"Well, me and my leaders were thinking of sending out a couple search parties to find them."

"That's a good idea brother, but before you do that, let me take a look," Nanny said confidently.

"Thanks Chief," Quao said. "We will wait until you return."

Quao always knew that his sister was special. She had proven herself time and time again. He had a deep love and respect for her and never doubted her motives. He never forgot how she had taken care of him and his brothers. In fact, she was the one who kept them strong, when all around, everything seemed so hopeless. That was one of the main reasons why he decided not to travel down to the western parishes with Cudjoe and Accompong. He felt the need to stay by her side and protect her back.

After Quao left, Nanny quickly said her goodbyes and quietly transformed into a black crow and circled the town before heading in the direction that the patrol had sent out their last report. The air was cool and fresh. Nanny had forgotten how much she enjoyed flying. With the air rushing over her body she felt energized. As she flew above the tree tops she could see the waterfalls, streams and rivers below. She continued for sometime along the mountain ranges until she noticed movements way out in the distance.

As she drew nearer, she recognized a small unit of heavily armed British soldiers, lying in ambush among the trees. Then looking over to the west her heart sank. Coming towards the British; right smack into the ambush was her lost patrol, looking tired and weary, unaware of the looming danger ahead.

Nanny knew that she had to act quickly to avoid the bloodbath. These soldiers were not about to forgo this action; something that they had been trained for and maybe had not seen for quite a while.

She had to make a decision whether to warn her troops or take on the soldiers by herself. She realized that even if she warned them there could still be a gun battle; and from her viewpoint, the men were outnumbered and outgunned and would suffer heavy casualties.

The black crow perched in a tall tree above the soldiers and peered down on them with interest. She scanned the surrounding landscape and could see all of them crouched in their concealed location, ready to strike. She silently flew down from the tree and positioned herself behind them, trying not to attract their attention. Switching to invisible mode she carefully reached into her pocket and took out a small pouch containing a white powder.

This powder was a secret herb that was passed down from generations; to put large animals to sleep. It was also used in smaller dosage in warfare to conquer the enemy. Nanny learned from a very early age how lethal this herb was and even as an adult kept the knowledge to herself for fear of it getting into the wrong hands. She was thrilled when she found the herb growing wild in the Blue Mountain along with all the other herbs; oblivious to everyone. She remembered the day Putus asked her why she was gathering so much of the plant and what it was used for. She smiled and told her that it was good for belly ache; which was the truth, because it had so many useful properties.

Nanny crept effortlessly towards the soldiers. She moved quickly from soldier to soldier dusting them with this unique powder. In a short while, all the soldiers were fast asleep, some still holding onto their muskets.

Meanwhile, the lost patrol kept advancing, unaware of the ambush. Suddenly, the scouts out in front crouched to the ground and gave the signal for everyone to freeze. The patrol froze and waited for further instructions. The scouts pointed to the threat ahead and instructed caution. Using signals, they beckoned everyone to creep forward cautiously and to keep their eyes focused.

The group was in for a shock when they came into the pathway. Lying on the ground fast asleep were the British soldiers; many with their muskets still in their hands. As the men carefully approached the sleeping soldiers; with their muskets fully drawn, and machetes ready, they suddenly froze. Walking out from behind a huge tree, with her arms outstretched was a smiling Chief Nanny.

"Hello my children!" she greeted them enthusiastically. "I missed you all so much that I came to look for you," she said, hugging some and slapping others on the back.

"Don't worry about these soldiers," she said, pointing to the soldiers all sprawled out on the ground. "I've put them all to sleep and they won't wake up for some time."

Everyone was curious as to how she did it, but no one asked for fear of offending the Chief.

"Quickly remove their uniforms, boots, muskets, food, water containers and anything else of value," Nanny instructed. "We will hide their uniforms along the way. Let them return to their camp and never ever forget this day when the might of the Ashanti warriors prevailed."

"But, but what about their water, Chief?" the patrol leader asked, somewhat merciful.

"They have plenty of water in the river. Don't worry about them. Let them live like us for a change. They have to learn that they don't own these mountains; we do!" Nanny said, with anger in her voice. "Look at them; they don't look so mighty now. They think that they're better than us because of the color of their skin. What fools! They're no different from us! If you cut them right now, don't they bleed the same red blood like us? If you poke them, don't they hurt just like us?" Nanny questioned disgustedly. "Hurry! Let's get out of here; we have a long way to get home," she urged. The patrol quickly removed the soldiers' uniforms and boots, leaving them only in their shorts. They took away their muskets and the stockpile of ammunition. Finally they packed up all their spoils and headed for home. "They're lucky that they're not in the desert right now," Nanny said with a bit of humor in her voice. "At least in these mountains they can readily find food and water," she continued, waving her hands. The group trekked for a mile before Nanny found a small underground cave where they rested for a while and hid the soldiers' uniforms among the rocks.

"Let them find their uniforms here," Nanny teased. "They think that they know every inch of this island. Well, let's see how good they are to find these." Everyone laughed.

As they continued their trek home, Nanny thought about the British soldiers just waking up from their slumber. They looked so young. Many of them didn't even have a little hair on their face yet. Their march back to camp without clothes would be hard, but they were soldiers; they were used to hardship and pain. And to be candid, if the shoe was on the other foot; she knew that they would have shown no mercy. At least she had allowed them to live.

'We're not murderers like them. We will not stoop to their level,' Nanny mulled over in her mind. 'We will kill them yes, but only in a fair fight, because, like our ancestors, we're a people of principle.'

Nanny acknowledged that the British would not forget this humiliation any time soon and would start looking for her settlement in earnest. But she was confident that they would not be able to find Nanny Town. And even if they did find the town, the citizens would fight them to the death. The people would not only be fighting for their lives, they would be fighting to preserve their African way of life.

Yes, the day was coming when her warriors would have to confront the British in fierce battles. This was inevitable, especially after what had happened today. By humiliating them in this manner, they had made their presence known. Soldiers from all over the island, and even back in

Britain, would hear about this unpleasant incident and would want their revenge. So, to prepare for the coming offensive Nanny decided to spend more time in training the troops. She planned to work more closely with Quao in developing strategies to outmaneuver the British.

Nanny's mind was going into overdrive. Ideas flowed in from everywhere as she led the trek home. In her mind, she was busy mapping out military strategies and covert operations. She visualized her army in battle, outwitting the British and claiming victory after victory. She didn't have a fiber of doubt in her being that her troops could defeat the British in strategy and in hand-to-hand combat. What they lacked in arms, they made up for in preparation and commitment.

The patrol winding its way behind her over the hills looked so happy and cheerful, a far cry from their days on Bakra's plantation. They were like a family to her and she was so proud to work with them.

As they walked into the village after midnight they were surprised to see so many people waiting up for them. The town's people had decided not to go to bed while the patrol was still out there. The coffee pot bubbled on the fire, and as the people sipped the delicious brew they sang good old African songs to pass the time.

There was jubilation in town as everyone hugged and kissed the returning men and women. Some mothers wept openly, hugging their sons and daughters tightly. Nanny looked on with pride. They were truly becoming citizens of Nanny Town; loving and caring for each other.

Chapter 24

The population of Nanny Town grew steadily. With Nanny's encouragement, many folks were becoming entrepreneurs. They reaped their crops and took it to the local markets to sell on Sundays. In return they bought: tools, clothing, pots and pans, weapons, and other items. Some people became so successful that they could now afford expensive garments and fineries at the market.

With the rapid growth in population, more and more lands had to be cleared to satisfy the demand. Nanny pondered the situation over and over in her heart. Could she satisfy the growing demand for land space without exposing her people to danger? What was the cut off number before she would have to say no more new arrivals? She wished that day would never come because the slaves on the plantations were hurting badly.

"Chief Nanny! Chief Nanny!" Qutie, her personal aid called out to her, interrupting her thoughts.

"What is it now Qutie?" Nanny asked.

"Miss Putus is here to see you ma'm. Should I send her in?"

"Oh yes Qutie, tell her to come in."

Putus entered the room holding a pot of food wrapped up in a clean white dish towel.

"What do you have there Putus?" Nanny asked jokingly.

"I have some nice cook food for you from a secret admirer," Putus replied, with a lighthearted laugh.

"I'm too old for that right now; just give me the food and you can keep the admirer," Nanny joked. "So who could that be anyway?" she inquired.

"Let's eat first. I would like to know what you think about this food," Putus said walking over to the dining table, setting the pot down, and carefully removing the cloth wrapper.

"Qutie my dear, please bring me two plates and some utensils," Putus shouted out to Qutie.

"Yes Miss Putus," Qutie responded as she hurried off to the kitchen to get the items.

Shortly after, Putus shared the food between them, and they sat down to eat.

"This food is delicious!" Nanny said excitedly after taking a few bites. "I have not tasted food like this since I left Africa. Who is this person?" she asked inquisitively.

"He is a nice man my chile, not to mention how handsome he looks. You would like him," Putus began.

"Then how did you meet him?" Nanny inquired.

"I met him at the market one Sunday when I was seeking information about a plantation," Putus revealed. "And if you would like to know, I didn't find him. Before I left the market to come home, I was buying a few things at this stall; minding my own business when he just came up to me and started talking. In our little chat he told me that he came from the nearby plantation and that he worked in the Great House as a junior cook. At first I thought he was joking, and was only telling me that to befriend me, but one day he brought me some food like this. I'm telling you Nanny; the food was so mouth-watering that I licked my fingers, and nearly ate it all off before I reached home. The man can cook chile! From that day Nanny, I've never doubted him."

"So how did he know about me, one; and two, why don't you take him for yourself, seeing that he found you first?" Nanny asked curiously.

"I can always depend upon you to give me a hard time," Putus responded. "You're not the Chief for nothing."

"Answer the question!" Nanny demanded.

"Well, first of all, he is not my type," Putus said casually.

"And why not?" Nanny asked, although she knew the answer already.

"I don't know how to explain it Nanny, but he's too smooth, too sure of himself. I like my men to be a bit rough, you know what I mean?" Nanny smiled, "You mean strong and strapping, with a whole lot of muscles, but shallow above the neck," to which both of them laughed.

"It's not so bad," Putus snickered.

"Then tell me; how did he know about me Putus?" Nanny asked, getting back to the argument.

"He told me that everyone on the plantation knows about you; how you help runaway slaves, and how you're nice and loving to everybody," Putus began. "They know a lot about you but they keep it a secret from Bakra and even the idiot head drivers, because you know that they're Bakra's hench men. Those head drivers would report their own mothers to Bakra. They're so wicked; I don't know how they sleep at night. I remembered this lady at the market telling me how the head driver whipped her mercilessly because he said that she was spreading rumors about Bakra. But it was not a rumor; it was the truth. Bakra got two slave women pregnant on the plantation and they both gave birth in the same month. The women were not telling any lies; they said that Bakra forced them to have sex with him and they got pregnant. So you see Nanny, nobody tells the head drivers anything. They are evil."

"So what does that have to do with me?" Nanny asked, seemingly impatient.

"Be patient and let me tell you the whole story."

"Alright I'm listening," Nanny said jokingly.

"As I said before, he was always curious as to what you looked like. And by the way, he was my main contact in the Great House. Because he cooked for Bakra, he was always there in the Great House listening to them talking about what was going on around the plantation. At first he said that he wasn't interested, it was all mumbling to him, but after he met me, he started taking notice of what they were saying and reporting it back to me. Because of him we got to know everything that was taking place on the plantation. From when Bakra was there and when he and his family left the plantation to visit other families, to when the local militia was planning raids on nearby villages. He also told me that the British General visited the Great House very often to have dinner. The General was a very good friend of Bakra and his family, and he even spent week-ends over there where they would go hunting for wild hogs and shooting birds in the forest.

Nanny, I really miss him in the Great House because when he was there nothing happened without our knowledge. He was our eyes and ears over there. He's right now trying to recruit someone else in there for me, but it is not easy because you don't know who to trust these days."

"So Putus, this gentleman has a name?" Nanny asked, trying to sound only slightly interested.

"I was wondering how long it was going to take for you to ask me that," Putus blurted out.

"His name is Adou, and he came from a village way up north, back home. He told me that his father was the Chief and that he was in line to take over when they captured him and put him on the ship. Back home he said that he was a professional tracker in the bush. Nanny, he could help to train our troops in tracking the soldiers. He also said that he knows how to mix different herbal medicines too; something like what you do."

"Then how long has he been here?" Nanny inquired calmly.

"Only about two months now," Putus replied quickly. "Nanny don't you remember that tall, stout, slightly balding man standing at the back of the room when you hosted the last welcome breakfast for the new arrivals?" Putus asked.

Nanny pondered for a while before replying. "I can't say that I remember him," she said, shaking her head and pouting up her lips.

"There were so many smiling faces there, plus I was having so much fun to take notice."

"Well don't you worry; he was watching you very closely. He never took his eyes off you for the entire time. I caught him looking at you several times and he just smiled. Nanny my chile, this one is hooked. He really likes you. Every day he asks me about you," Putus added.

"So why are you just telling me about him now?" Nanny asked, looking intently at Putus.

"That is a good question, my friend," Putus said with a broad mischievous grin.

"I know you like the back of my hand, my fearless Chief. I also know that for you the timing has to be right to approach you on some matters. So I've been biding my time, waiting for the right time to tell you."

"You make me sound like a monster," Nanny cut in. "Am I that bad?"

"Well not bad, but not good either," Putus laughed.

"You said that he knew everything that was happening at the plantation, right?" Nanny inquired, trying to be serious.

"Yes, he was the best; I'm sure of that," Putus reiterated.

"Let me be the judge of that," Nanny said, with a straight face. "Arrange a meeting for some time this week; I would like to hear what he has to say."

"And then are you going to see if you like him?" Putus inquired coyly.

"I don't know about that. I just want to get some information out of him," Nanny replied, in a professional manner.

"Can I come to the meeting too?" Putus asked, with a friendly smile. "Don't worry I will be on my best behavior."

"Yes you should be here," Nanny replied. "I will also invite Quao and a few of our senior leaders; so that we can all find out what information he has that we can use. Who knows, maybe we could learn a lot from him."

"That is what I love about you Chief. You have to mix a little business with a little pleasure," Putus teased.

"Putus, we have to be serious, lives are at stake here," Nanny rebuked her sternly.

"Sorry Chief, I was only joking. Can't you take a little joke?" Putus apologized.

"I know that you take this job seriously, and that is why the people love you so much. Because of you we can all get a good night's sleep and don't have to worry about a thing."

"Putus, I'm here to serve the people and I will not allow any man to come between me and the people, do you hear me?"

"You don't have to tell me Chief, I know that."

At the end of the meal, Putus said she that had an errand to run and left Nanny, but not before promising to arrange the meeting.

The meeting arranged for that Wednesday afternoon, was very productive. After the initial introductions, everyone got down to business. Adou explained that he had spent five years on the plantation, moving up from working in the cane field, cutting and loading the wagons, to being transferred to the kitchen in the Great House. This came about because his best friend who was working there recommended him to Bakra. His first job was washing up the dirty pots, pans, plates and utensils after each meal and taking care of the gardens and lawns around the Great House. In later years he learnt to prepare the food under the watchful eyes of the Master Chef of the Great House; an elderly gentleman who had spent over twenty years on the plantation. Before he ran away, he assumed more and more of the duties of the Master Chef who was getting up in age and would retire soon. When he was not in the kitchen cooking, he was serving the family and guests at the dining table. On special occasions, for example Christmas, he would pull out all the stops to impress Bakra and his guests. Because he was so good at his job Bakra trusted him and spoke openly around him. Maybe they thought that he would not be interested in or understood what they were talking about.

One day Adou recalled the General and his top officers attending a dinner at the plantation. At the end of the meal they all retired to the verander to relax over a drink and talk among themselves. Adou was assigned as the waiter to serve the tea and rum and cater to their needs. He listened carefully to what they were saying and tried to make sense of their conversation.

From the conversation, apparently the General was ordering more troops from England to deploy across the island; especially in the west. The General sounded extremely annoyed when he spoke about the problems plaguing the plantations, especially those communities in the west that were facing mounting troubles from the Maroons and the other escaped slaves.

"Those criminals are attacking and burning down the plantations for no apparent reason," the General remarked sternly. "They attack the plantations, burn the cane fields, steal everything that is not nailed down, murder anyone who tries to resist them and then scurry back into their scrubby little holes like rats."

"So why can't your soldiers just round them up and capture them?" Bakra asked innocently.

"It is not that easy my friend," the General replied. "These parasites have their own codes and methods of communicating that we have not yet been able to break. They constantly spy on our camps and observe our movements. I wrote a letter to the King some time ago, explaining the situation here on the island and requesting additional troops. Fortunately, last week I received a reply and they have promised to send me the reinforcements that I requested in the next couple of weeks."

"The sooner the better," one officer said.

"They promised to send us some of Britain's best fighters. Some of them are being transferred from the jungles of Africa here; so we will see," the General remarked, raising his glass. "Gentlemen we cannot afford to lose this island to a bunch of ignorant rebels. What would the French think about us?"

Adou informed the group that the General was especially annoyed with a group of Maroons in St. James. He called them 'a blood thirsty gang of marauding criminals.' "They constantly terrorize the plantations in that Parish; killing many of the plantation owners and their families and burning down many acres of canefield," he lamented. "We have not been able to subdue them for various reasons, the main one being our numbers. We just do not have the manpower to contain them," the General said with regret.

"I heard that there is also another group down in St. Elizabeth causing just as much trouble as that group in St. James," one of the top officers said.

"Yes and there are reports coming out of the Parish of Clarendon, of plantations being burnt and land owners being killed on a regular basis," another top brass added.

"Here in the east, the plantation owners are facing the same problems," another officer informed the group. "There are some ruthless groups of mavericks who operate from up in the Blue Mountains and are burning down the plantations and carrying away slaves. Rumor has it that it is being led by a woman; and that's all we know."

"London will soon want to know what we're doing about all this," a young lieutenant interjected.

"Yes, and this is an election year, so no politician wants this sort of thing on their plate," another said.

"Gentlemen, gentlemen; let's not get ahead of ourselves," the General said rather calmly. "We will have this thing under control just as soon as we get reinforcement. We are after all, the best trained army in the world. Do we doubt our own capabilities against a bunch of filthy criminals gentlemen? Remember, we did not become the greatest nation on earth by second guessing ourselves. This island will be governed by the law and order of His Majesty, The King of England, no more, no less!" he shouted. There was complete silence on the verander, with all eyes focused on the General.

"Does anyone here see it differently," he asked, lowering his voice to a near whisper. "Let him speak now."

No one responded.

The General then slowly rose to his feet and addressed his team. He looked intently at each of his men and spoke softly.

"Alright then, so we're all on the same page. Gentlemen we know that these imbeciles are mostly from the Ashanti and the Coromantee tribes in Africa. They make up a large portion of the workforce on the island. They are known for their hard work on the plantations, but they also account for most of the rebellions on the plantations. They are very difficult to control and they run away at the drop of a hat to join the other Maroon criminals in the hills."

Then the young Lieutenant rose to his feet to speak.

"General sir, seeing that the Ashanti and the Coromantee tribes are the main tribes causing most of the problems on the island; could it be time for us to recommend to the plantation owners that they buy slaves from other tribes?"

"That is a good suggestion Lieutenant, we will certainly look into that further," the General stated.

"Gentlemen," he continued. "This situation is like a football [soccer] match in which the rebels are in the lead at the end of the first half, but the second half is coming and we will be more prepared. We will smoke them out of their scrubby little holes and destroy them, so that the other slaves on the plantation won't get any bright ideas."

After he said that they all packed up, said their goodbyes and left.

"Chief Nanny, I got scared for all those Maroons and I never knew any of them," Adou continued. I was especially scared for you Chief. The General and his soldiers are out to capture and kill all Maroons to set an example."

"Thanks for your concern Adou," Nanny said appearing unperturbed. "But I think that we're well protected here."

After Adou left the meeting Nanny sat with the group and reflected on what they had just heard.

"I wonder if these fresh batches of soldiers are on the island already," Nanny thought aloud, slowly rubbing her chin.
"Quao have you noticed any extra movements from the soldiers over the last couple of weeks?"

"No Chief, everything is about the same," he replied.

"We need to send a message down to Cudjoe and Accompong to find out if the fresh soldiers have arrived down there as yet and warn them if they don't know that they're coming," Nanny said.
"Putus please arrange that and let me know what they say."

"Should we stop the raids Chief, or is it business as usual?" Quao asked.

"It is business as usual brother, but we have to be more careful. Try getting the troops in and out of the plantations quicker. Speed is what will make the difference between life and death. Every plantation knows by now that they will be hit; the only thing that they don't know is when. Putus, double your spying effort. Get as much information as you can on every plantation before we give the go ahead to raid it."

"Yes Chief," Putus responded.

After Quao left, Nanny invited Putus to have supper with her. During the meal the ladies talked about a variety of things that happened that day. Then the subject turned to Adou.

"That Adou is a very knowledgeable man," Putus said, trying to get a response from Nanny; but she did not take the bait immediately.

"Boy he has a memory like an elephant."

"Yes he is good," Nanny replied. Her tone was evasive and her face gave nothing away. "He makes a good witness," she continued, trying not to appear overtly excited.

"Is that all you have to say?" Putus asked, looking intently into Nanny's eyes.

"What? What? Why are you looking at me like that?" Nanny inquired seemingly puzzled.

"Is that all you have to say about Adou?" Putus asked again. "Oh, he makes a good witness!" she said in a mocking voice. "What about he's nice and sexy?" Putus said, sounding annoyed.

"Ok, I think he's handsome, as well as smart," Nanny eventually agreed. "Are you satisfied?"

"It is not about me," Putus reminded her. "I'm only looking out for your best interest, and when I see a man like Adou dying to talk to you I have to put my nose into it."

"Putus you're my best friend and I love you, but I don't think it's going to work."

"What do you mean, not going to work?" Putus asked, squinting her eyes and with a questionable look on her face.

"I mean this fellow, what's his name?"

"Adou!" Putus butted in angrily. "Have you forgotten his name already?" she asked, shaking her head in disbelief.

"So Miss Genius, you prefer to throw away the best fruits off the tree to the hogs before you sample them yourself?" Putus asked sarcastically. "That sounds like a great plan Nanny, a great plan!" she said, sounding rather annoyed.

"The truth of the matter Putus is that I have no time in my life right now for a man; even though he is handsome and sexy, I have to admit. I have to focus on running this town."

"That is all well and good my friend," Putus agreed. "But when you get old, the job will pass on to a younger person and you will need a loving companion to keep your company. This man worships the very ground that you walk on and will never abandon you."

"And how are you so sure of that?" Nanny asked flippantly.

"I just know a good man when I see one," Putus responded positively.

"And you're talking from a giant pool of man knowledge, I presume?" Nanny asked mockingly. They both laughed.

"Listen Nanny, he is cooking dinner and bringing it over to my place on Friday evening and I'm inviting you."

Nanny thought for a moment before agreeing to go.

"Alright, I'll be there on Friday."

"Don't eat anything before you come over because he's cooking up a storm," Putus advised.

"I'll keep that in mind," Nanny promised. And with that Putus said her goodbye and left.

Nanny had to admit that the man was fine. His tall, dark, solid frame topped off with a slightly balding head, made him look very handsome and much taller than he actually was. When he spoke, with his rich baritone voice, something deep inside her soul sprang to life. This was a feeling that she had not felt for a long time. In fact she never thought that she would ever have these feelings again, let alone in Nanny Town.

'But how would it work?' she pondered. Here she was the Chief; the one whom everyone looked to, to protect them and to build them a lasting community, and here she was having this major distraction. How effective could she be if she had to take care of a man? Would he be highly demanding on her time? Would he be jealous of her success? Would he play second fiddle to her on special occasions? He looked a lot younger than her. If she made this decision, would this man love her when she became old and he was still in his prime? Or would he leave her for a younger, more attractive woman? Nanny suddenly felt very funny. Why was she thinking so negatively when she hadn't even spoken to the man, one-on-one yet?

Friday night went quite well at Putus' place. The food was great. Adou, knowing that Nanny was coming, went out of his way to impress her. He began cooking from midday until well into the evening. The variety of dishes was beyond belief; from jerked pork to dukunu, and escovich fish to roast yams. Everything was hot, spicy and sumptuous. Later he brought out the rum cake and washed it down with Blue Mountain coffee.

"The food was delicious Adou, thank you," Nanny commented at the end of the meal. "When did you find the time to make all this food?"

"For you and Miss Putus Chief, this was nothing. If truth be known, I could've made many more dishes if I had more time," Adou replied.

"Thank you, but I think that this was just the right amount," Nanny said. "Anything more than this and Massa God would have sinned us." They all laughed and slowly sipped their hot black coffee.

"Then Adou, where did you learn to cook like this?" Putus asked between sips.

"It was my mother who taught me how to cook," Adou answered. "She always said that, 'woman can cook but if you really want to lick your finger [enjoy a good meal], then you must make a man cook.'"

"So could your father cook as well?" Nanny asked.

"I believe so, but he was so busy that I never saw him cook a regular meal. But I know that he made a great jerk pork!" he said with a broad grin on his face. "That is what you would call, 'eat off your finger Jerk pork.' When you start, you don't want to stop eating." This made them all laugh.

'He's not only handsome but he's funny too,' Nanny thought to herself.

'I hope that the one Nanny realize that she has a special man here. He cooks, he's caring, and on top of all that he's a natural comedian. What more could she want? I'm telling you, if he was my type I would've snatched him up faster than you could snap your fingers. I know what I will do. I will go and clean up the kitchen and leave them to talk.'

With that she politely excused herself from the table and started picking up the dirty dishes.

"Let me come and help you wash up Putus," Nanny volunteered. "If Adou can cook all this lovely food for us, then that's the least I can do," she said with a charming smile.

"It's alright Nanny, I'll be fine. You two sit and talk," she said as she quickly left the room before Nanny could insist.

"How did you meet Putus?" Nanny turned and asked Adou.

"It's a long story. How much time do you have?" he asked jokingly.

"I don't have any young ones at home, so I'm in no hurry," Nanny replied with a smile.

Adou then began telling Nanny how he was admiring this beautiful woman in the market and just knew that he had to talk to her. He watched her as she went about her business talking to people and occasionally buying food stuff. "She looked so, so; I can't find the English word for it," he said. "I meant to say that she looked and walked like an African queen with her head held high and her shoulders erect. I wanted to find out which tribe she was from and if she had a man. We talked for some time and she told me a little about herself. Then she started telling me about her best friend; how she was nice. So I said to myself, 'why is she telling me about her friend, when it is she that I'm interested in.'" Adou took a sip, leaned back and relaxed as he continued the story.

"Did you know that she didn't believe that I could cook? She thought that I was lying. So, I'm a man that if you say that I can't do something, then I'll work hard to prove you wrong. So I cooked a small dish for her; and the rest, as Bakra used to say, is history."

"What do you mean that the rest is history?" Nanny asked curiously.

"I'm not too sure, but it sounds good, and Bakra always used it. You know how these white people them talk funny."

"Yes I know," Nanny said, and they both laughed.

Putus decided not to rejoin them after she had finished washing up the dishes, when she saw how much fun they were having. This was the first time that she had ever seen her friend laugh so much and so hard. She looked like a teenage girl talking to a new boy for the first time; latching onto every word that was coming out of his mouth. She looked so happy and contented. She wished that she could find someone as fine as Adou. But as the saying goes, 'every hoe has its stick in the bush,' so Putus was certain that someone was out there for her; she only had to be patient.

Nanny wondered why Putus was taking so long to wash up the few plates.

'I bet that she's staying away so that me and Adou can talk. That is why I love her so much; she is always looking out for me.'

Chapter 25

It would be dark soon as Cudjoe and his warriors made last minute preparations before leaving on a raid of a little plantation down in the south west corner of the parish. They had spent weeks researching the plantation and were confident of success.

Before they left Cudjoe gave his warriors some last minute instructions.

"You all know what to do. We've practiced over and over for this mission. When we get there we will move in fast and hard. Our people on the inside will be there waiting for us. Stay close and look out for each other. Veterans take good care of the younger warriors and show them the ropes. Unit commanders, keep your units together and stick to the plan. No heroism, especially among you young ones. Listen to your commanders. Our spies have reported that Bakra and his family are gone to Montego Bay for the week-end and the young militia men are up into the hills hunting wild hogs. But that doesn't matter; we still have to be careful. And for those young men out there hunting, keep your eyes peeled; I don't need any trouble on the trail. One more thing men, anybody who tries to stop you, just kill them; even if it is a slave. I just hate those self-righteous slaves who believe that we are the enemy and would rather lose their lives for Bakra. Why they would want to defend Bakra's plantation when he treats them worse than his dogs I don't know."

The mission was a complete success. Cudjoe led his men onto the plantation with his customary shock effect. With abengs blaring the warriors rushed forward, enthusiastically roaring their blood curdling Ashanti war cries and wielding their machetes in the air. This was followed up with a barrage of explosions from their muskets filling the air with thick smoke. Cudjoe and his men had now seized the moment and were in total control. The little resistance by the few old white men soon melted into the shadows.

The intelligence was perfect. Cudjoe and his men set fire to the canefields and collected everything of value from the warehouses and the Great House then set them on fire too.

At the height of the action, Cudjoe was forced to kill a slave with his musket. The slave was quietly creeping up from behind on one of his young warriors busy packing up some farm tools near a shed. As the slave raised his machete in the air to chop off the young Maroon's head, Cudjoe calmly raised his musket and squeezed the trigger.

"Thanks Chief," the young man said, visibly trembling at such a close call, before walking off with the handful of tools. Cudjoe felt no remorse for killing the slave. In fact he felt more relieved than ever that he had not lost any of his men.

When the troops arrived at the barracks they found many of the slaves waiting, some with little bundles containing their personal belongings. The warriors persuaded as many men and women as possible to join them before they heard the familiar abeng sound; signaling that it was time to leave.

The men quickly withdrew from the plantation with all their spoils and disappeared into the night, leaving the cane fields, the Great House and the warehouses in flames.

The next morning, Cudjoe was quite pleased with the results of the night before. In his address to his people, he thanked the warriors and all those who had assisted in making the raid a success. He could not find enough words of praise for the spies on the plantation.

"Those people are the main reason why we've been so successful and did not lose anyone last night. We will make sure that they're never in want and when they're ready to come and join us, we will gladly bring them out."

He also welcomed the new men and women and congratulated them on their decision to take such a bold step. He promised them that they would never again suffer at the hands of Bakra and challenged them to begin dreaming again like they did back in Africa.

Later that day, Cudjoe received a message from Nanny. Whenever he heard from his big sister he always got nervous. Although she was older and he knew that she could take care of herself, yet he always worried about her and his other siblings, way over there in Nanny Town.

In the message she warned him that the British had requested reinforcement from England to defeat the Maroons, especially his group in the west.

"Be careful my brother, they want to crush you and use you as an example. Send me a message and let me know if you've seen them." Cudjoe called an emergency meeting of his top leaders to discuss the message that he received. No increase in troops was reported, however they noticed that the British were building new military forts not far from the settlements.

Cudjoe and his leaders affirmed that they would not be intimidated by the British. If the soldiers mounted unprovoked attacks against the Maroons, then they would have no choice but to retaliate.

"We will control these hills at night," Cudjoe declared. "During the day we will stay out of their way; we will avoid confrontation, but come night we will attack them hard and without mercy if they venture into these parts."

Cudjoe sent a message back to Nanny thanking her for the information and giving her an insight into his plans.

Early the following morning Cudjoe was awakened out of a deep sleep with a report that the local Militia was attacking a small settlement to the East. It was a settlement that Cudjoe knew quite well. He had many good friends living out there. They had a hot spring where people came from all around to take baths for its healing properties. Many stories have been told of how runaway slaves were healed when they took a bath in the stream. People swore by it; that the hot springs cured arthritis, joint pain, boils sores, belly ache, yaws, ring worm, Chigger, and many other ailments. Cudjoe and his men always visited the hot springs to recuperate after a long battle. Many wounded warriors have spent numerous days down there until they were restored to health.

Cudjoe quickly ordered up his troops. In a short while the warriors all assembled in front of his house in full camouflaged outfit, ready for battle.

"Gentlemen, this mission is crucial to the very survival of our friends and neighbors down at the village," Cudjoe began. "If the militia destroys that settlement, then we could be next. The white devils must not win this one gentleman. They must be defeated at all cost; to let them know that Maroons rule in this part of the country and no matter how many big weapons they may have, what we have is a big heart," as he hit his chest a couple of times for emphasis. "So when you fight today gentlemen, think about the reasons why you're doing it. You're fighting for your own survival. You're fighting to uphold truth and justice; something that the white devils don't have a clue about. As we prepare to go into battle, make our ancestors proud. Let us hold our heads high and do battle in true Ashanti fashion. Let's move out!" And with that they started the march towards their objective, moving quietly and cautiously to avoid detection.

As Cudjoe and the troops drew near and looked down into the valley, they saw smoke rising from the tops of the huts and heard exploding muskets. Looking closer, they observed the young militia men laughing and shooting into the huts of the people while they slept. As some of the folks ambled out of their huts, still obviously drowsy, they were met with a hail of bullets, mixed with drunken laugher.

When Cudjoe saw the massacre taking place, a sudden hatred welled up inside of him. He realized that he would have to act quickly or all the people would be killed.

As the troops moved into position among the trees, Cudjoe gave the signal to attack. The blast from the abeng was frightening, followed by the blood curdling cries of the warriors. The young militia men were caught by surprise. Cudjoe and his men attacked with fearless gusto, killing and maiming them without mercy. The Maroons did not give the militia a chance to recover. They intensified their attack until all the white men were killed.

After collecting all their weapons and ammunitions, Cudjoe instructed the men to check on the people in the huts and provide assistance to those who could be helped. As they went from hut to hut, the warriors wept openly when they saw the mutilated bodies of the men, women and children.

The troops quickly did what they could for the villagers, before Cudjoe gave the order to withdraw and head for home.

Chapter 26

Nanny was overjoyed when she heard from her brother Cudjoe. He was safe and was aggressively engaging the enemy. She worried constantly about her two brothers because they were so far away from home.

Over the next couple of days, Nanny received regular reports of British troops patrolling the forests in earnest, looking for runaway slaves, and returning them to the plantations. All this was happening under the watchful eyes of her elaborate spy network.

"It looks like the soldiers are preparing to stay here for a long time Chief," Quao said.

"It seems that way my brother," Nanny agreed. "This might be a permanent base that they're setting up in anticipation of the arrival of reinforcements."

The lookouts watched keenly as the soldiers brought in large quantities of materials and supplies to construct the fort. Even though the soldiers knew that they were being watched from the bushes they never let on. Every morning they diligently positioned guards on their perimeter as the others toiled in the boiling sun busily constructing the fort.

The soldiers couldn't wait for nightfall to arrive to finally rest after a hard day's work in the scorching tropical sun. Conversations and socializing was at a minimum as the soldiers retired to bed early for a well deserved rest.

But not tonight! They didn't know yet, but there would be no rest for them. In the middle of the night they were suddenly rocked out of their bunks by deafening explosions, continuous blasts from abeng horns and bloodcurdling war cries from the attacking Maroon warriors. Nanny's forces attacked the fort with ferocity, killing and maiming the soldiers and burning it down to the ground.

This set the soldiers back a number of weeks as they had to wait for new materials and supplies to arrive from Britain. But they were not deterred; they picked up the pieces and started all over again.

A few days later Nanny finally got the news that she had been dreading. The spies on the plantation sent a warning message that the reinforcement troops from England had arrived. The report also said that the British had imported expert trackers from Central and South America to comb the mountains and hunt down and capture the Maroons.

A hollow feeling seeped inside Nanny's stomach. The first thing that she thought about was her two brothers, Accompong and Cudjoe. Were they in danger? Did they know about these trackers? She had to send messages down to them fast, to warn them.

Nanny called an emergency meeting with Putus and Quao to brainstorm strategies to counter the new reality.

"Let's analyze this situation," she said. "What do we know?"

"Well, we know that they're well armed; much better armed than we will ever be," Quao suggested.

"Yes, what else?" Nanny asked seriously.

"They have brought in expert trackers from South America," Putus added.

"Yes, what else?" Nanny urged.

"They're building forts, which means that they're planning to stay for a long time," Quao speculated.

On and on Nanny probed, leaving no stone unturned; trying to get everything out on the table.

"Ok, what are our main challenges right now?" Nanny asked.

"Well we don't know the size of their army," Quao responded.

"Ok, what else?" Nanny continued to probe.

"We don't have enough weapons or ammunitions," Quao added.

"What else?" Nanny inquired.

"We don't have enough intelligence on these people?" Putus mentioned.

"Good, what else?" Nanny prodded.

"We don't have enough information on them in the western part of the island."

"Anything else?" Nanny asked, as she continued probing.

For the next few hours the three discussed and debated the situation. Sometimes the discussion became very heated and emotional, but in the end they all hugged because they loved each other and knew that it was never personal.

One thing that they all agreed on was that to win this battle without matching fire power they would have to use all their skills to outmaneuver the enemy. Nanny also realized that she would have to play a more active role in the battles; using her unique gifts to advance the fight and beat the British at their own game.

Over the next couple of weeks, hardly a day went by when British patrols were not spotted. They were increasing in numbers and becoming bolder during the days. The lookouts however tracked their every move, noting the time that they left the fort and their numbers, and the time that they returned after their patrol.

Another group shadowed them as they patrolled across the hills and valleys in search of runaways. Nanny's scouts were so well trained in camouflage that the British soldiers did not have a clue what they looked like.

One very hot afternoon, a small unit of soldiers, after marching up and down the mountain trails all morning without encountering any runaways, decided to rest under an enormous cotton tree; unaware that they were being observed closely.

The soldiers were all in a good mood laughing and having a good time when suddenly they heard,'Click! Click! Click! Click!' as the familiar sound of the locks on the muskets surrounded them. Some of the soldiers quickly raised their muskets to discharge in the direction of the bush but their commander, in his wisdom, ordered them to stand down. The soldiers waited and waited anxiously for what seemed like an eternity, but there was no movement coming from the bush. Suddenly from behind the trees and shrubberies stepped scores of fully armed Maroon warriors shrouded in their intimidating war paint.

With muskets trained on them, the warriors ordered the soldiers to lie on their bellies. They quickly tied them up with twine and then removed their boots, the whole time not uttering a single word. In a flash, the warriors withdrew and vanished back into the shadows of the forest with the soldiers' muskets, ammunitions, boots, water bottles and supplies.

The soldiers were surprised at how well trained, disciplined and efficient the Maroons were. They felt fortunate to be alive. Apart from being embarrassed, now they had to think about the long trek home without their boots and weapons.

Later, Nanny congratulated the unit leader and the men and women, on a job well done. The challenging training was paying off. Nanny was convinced that her fighters could take on any of the British soldiers and win.

A week later Quao reported to Nanny about a group of runaways they had found wandering in the forest.

"They had a very interesting story Chief," Quao said.

"How interesting?" Nanny inquired.

"It sounded like they're not from around here. They said that they came from a far away Parish and that they're running away from the militia there," Quao continued.

"Where are they now?" Nanny asked.

"They're holding up in a cave not far from here with our men," Quao replied. "We have given them plenty of food and water and a change of clothes, so they're safe and comfortable right now."

"I would like to talk with them tomorrow," Nanny suggested. "Get Putus to come with us too so that we can all hear what they have to say. Then before we can bring them into town, we have to call a town meeting and inform the people."

"But why do we need to tell the people?" Quao asked, looking perplexed.

"Our folks need to know about the people who are coming to live amongst us," Nanny explained.

The following day, Nanny and her delegation met the men in the cave outside of town. After formal introductions they all sat down to talk.

"So why are you here?" Nanny demanded.

"We've ran away from our plantation in the Parish of Clarendon,"one lanky, buck teeth youth nervously replied. "Over four hundred of us rioted on the plantation a few weeks ago because Bakra them was treating us very bad. They worked us from early morning until late night. Sometimes we had to work all through the night to cut the cane and bring it to the factory. They beat us for the slightest things. But the thing that really caused us to burn down the plantation, chop up and killed Bakra and his family and all the other white people them on the plantation was when our people started to disappear. Just like that Chief! If you're heard complaining about conditions on the plantation then baps! You're taken away, gone! They come and take you out of your bed in the middle of the night, like duppy [ghost]. Sometimes you can hear the poor people kicking and screaming, and then they're gone; and we never set eyes on them again. We all became scared when night came Chief because we didn't know who would be next. So what else could we've done Chief?" he pleaded. "What else?

If we stayed there we could be next. Everybody was like ducks in a pond, just waiting to be picked off, one by one. So a couple of us made the decision to take things into our own hands. We waited patiently and when the time was right we overpowered them, seized their firearms, and killed them, then ran away from the plantation. Shortly after, the other white people them in the area formed a militia and started rounding us up. It wasn't too hard because they had so many horses and dogs and weapons. We on the other hand were on foot and we didn't even know where we were going, so it wasn't too long before they rounded up many of our people. We were lucky because Bohpi here found a cave and we hid in there for days until the militia left.

I'm sorry for all those people who they recaptured and brought back to the plantation. I hope that they didn't capture Breda Bertie though, because he was the ring leader who planned this riot with us. If he is found then I'm sure that he will be hanged from the nearest tree to set an example and to frighten everybody. We were lucky to escape, thank Massa God! We hid during the days and traveled only at nights, following the moon and the stars. And here we are Chief, desperate to find some place, any place safe to stay."

At the end of the story, Nanny thought for a moment. She wondered if they were telling the truth. The reports confirmed that they were just wandering around in circles and appeared lost, confused and in need of help.

"And why should we believe you?" Nanny asked sternly, looking directly at them with her fiery piercing eyes.

"We're telling you the truth Chief!" Bohpi cried out with fear. "We're not here to trick you. As Massa God is our witness Chief; we're just looking for a place to start over. We will make good here Chief, if you will give us a chance. We will not disappoint you."

Nanny raised her hand and the men fell silent. "I will give you my answer tomorrow gentlemen," she said with a straight face. "Have a good day." And with that she turned and left with her entourage following closely behind her.

That night Nanny called a town meeting to discuss whether the men should be allowed in.

"No! No! No! They should not be allowed here," some said.

"They could be spies sent here by the militia to gather information and report back our location," others added.

"I don't trust the Coromantees them. They're always fighting; even when they were back in Africa. They're trouble," another elderly man remarked.

Then a little old lady stood up and said in a rather shaky voice, "I believe that we should allow these young men in. And do you know why I say that? Remember how we all got here; somebody had mercy on us and took us in. Then why should we deny this opportunity to these desperate men?" she asked.

"But this is totally different," a plump lady in a brightly colored hat said. "At least they knew which plantation we were coming from, but these men here; do we know where they came from?" the woman asked.

"We heard that they came from some village in the Clarendon Parish," a tall slightly balding man at the back of the room said. "People say that, that Parish is the biggest one on the island; so they must have come from far." The meeting was split down the middle between those who agreed and those who opposed. Finally Nanny stood up to address the people, after listening to what they had to say.

"Ladies and gentlemen, I'm really happy to see how you're talking to each other without fighting. I don't think that Bakra would believe this if he saw us now. You're truly becoming citizens of Nanny Town and I'm so proud of you all," she said, smiling like a proud parent.

"Hear this ladies and gentlemen; there is a risk in everything we do. If we leave them out there and do nothing, then the patrolling soldiers will find them and torture them to find out what they know. And if we take them in then we run the risk that they might turn out to be spies. Which is better, leave them out there for the soldiers to capture them or take them in and keep one eye on them until we're sure? The choice is yours; so we need to vote on the matter."

The vote was nearly evenly split down the middle, with the 'yes' side winning by a narrow margin.

The men were allowed into Nanny Town the following morning, but not before they were blindfolded as they approached the secret entrance that led inside the town.

Chapter 27

Putus strolled from vendor to vendor in the market shopping for outfits for Ahaji when a tall, dark and handsome young man came up to her and asked if she was Putus.

"Who wants to know?" she inquired abruptly, sounding slightly annoyed.

"Sorry ma'm," the man quickly apologized. Then he looked around before finally whispering, "I didn't mean to upset you ma'm, but I have a message for your Chief," opening his eyes wide when he said it like it was a heavy burden that he had just unloaded.

"And what is the name of the Chief that you're looking for?" she whispered back.

"I have a message for Chief Nanny, the greatest Maroon Chief that this island has ever known," the man said proudly, with a smile.

"And who is saying all that?" Putus asked with suspicion.

"A lot of slaves on the plantations in the west."

"Then how did they know about the Chief?" Putus inquired.

"Every single slave on the plantations down in the west has heard how she saved the people on the ship and never lost a soul on the passage over here from Africa. People talk about her like they talk about the good old African Proverb about the man long, long time ago who parted the Red Sea with his hand and allowed the slaves to go across on dry land to safety. And after all of them crossed over he stretched out his hand and the sea came back and killed off Bakra and all his soldiers who were pursuing them to put them back into slavery. Slaves talk ma'm, slaves talk," he continued.

"Everybody wants to meet her, because they say that she is the only person who can deliver us from the hands of the British oppressors."

"What do you want to talk to the Chief about?" Putus prodded.

"Sorry ma'm, but my Chief said that I must only talk to Chief Nanny," the man said, with a pitiful look on his face.

"So how did you find me?" Putus asked sternly.

"It wasn't easy ma'm, it wasn't easy," he began. "I've been here week after week talking to people about the Chief, but nobody wants to talk to me. Everyone tells me that they don't know who that is. My Chief sent me over here from Westmoreland Parish to find her. He told me never to come back until I found her; and my Chief is one stubborn man who never takes no for an answer."

"So what is your name and where are you staying?" Putus asked, showing more interest.

"Sorry for my bad manners ma'm; my name is Phooju and I'm a Coromantee. I sleep up in a cave not far from here. My Chief would like to arrange a meeting with your Chief," he said quickly. Putus thought long and hard about the young man standing before her. Could he be trusted?

"Who told you my name?" Putus demanded.

"It's a woman by the name of Joptah ma'm," the man replied. "At first she said that she didn't know any Chief, but by talking and talking we found out that we came from the same village back in Africa and we knew some of the same people. So she got to trust me and told me about you."

"Ok Mass Phooju from Westmoreland Parish," Putus said sarcastically, "If you're here next week this time I will give you my answer; good day!" as she picked up her little bundle and walked away, promising to find this woman called Joptah.

Later that evening through her spy network, Putus located Joptah who confirmed all that the stranger had said. Putus was relieved, because she prided herself on being a good judge of character and this stranger really looked honest. Now she felt more confident to tell Nanny about the stranger.

At the meeting Putus told the team about her meeting with Joptah and how she confirmed everything that the stranger had said. She also told them that she was awaiting reports from the scouts who had secretly followed him back to his cave.

"Putus, you're a good judge of character; tell me, what jumped out at you about this young man?" Nanny asked.

"Chief, I have a very good feeling about this young man," Putus said.

"Did you ask him why he came alone?" Quao asked.

"Sorry Quao, I didn't ask him that, but that is a good question. When I see him again, I will ask him."

"The next time you meet with him I would like Quao to be there," Nanny suggested.

"So where do you want to meet this man, Chief?" Quao asked.

"Let's surprise him one night in his hideaway," Nanny said, with a mischievous smile on her face and a twinkle in her eyes. "Yes, let's catch him when he least expects it."

The following Sunday Putus arrived early at the market along with Quao and a couple of his fully armed undercover scouts. They quickly scanned the area and positioned themselves strategically for the arrival of Phooju. Their orders were to provide protection for Putus at all cost. Most of them mingled with the bustling crowd pretending to be shopping but keeping their eyes peeled for any signs of trouble.

The meeting went quite well. Phooju was just as cordial as the week before. He joked with Putus like they were old friends. After the exchange of pleasantries Putus told him that Chief Nanny had agreed to meet with him in a few days.

"Thank you, thank you Miss Putus. My Chief will be happy," Phooju smiled with joy.

A few nights later Nanny and her entourage of security along with Quao and Putus invaded Phooju's cave while he was fast asleep. As he opened his eyes he found his crude bed surrounded by fully armed warriors with torches in hand. He felt terrified as his eyes scanned the hardened faces of the warriors. Suddenly the circle parted and stepping out of the shadows was a little wiry woman. At that moment there was no doubt who was in charge.

"Why do you want to talk to me?" Nanny demanded in a commanding voice.

Phooju rose quickly to his feet, towering over Nanny.

"My Chief, Chief Waputa would like a meeting with you Chief Nanny," Phooju stammered, trying to overcome his nervousness.

'Imagine me talking to the great Chief Nanny,' he said to himself with delight. Me, little knock knee Phooju, who people didn't think would come to nothing. Who is going to believe this back home? But she's so small,' he thought. 'I thought that she was much bigger than that. Her bodyguards look like born killers though,' he pondered. 'I love these people already; I hope that they and my Chief can do business.'

"And why does your Chief wish to meet with me?" Nanny asked, glaring at him with her deep steely eyes.

"He would like to talk with you about working together to fight the British soldiers and the militia across the island," Phooju replied. "You've the biggest village in the east and we've the biggest village in Westmoreland. So he wants our two villages to join forces and share strategies to fight the British; like we used to do back in Africa." Nanny looked Phooju up and down. She thought about Putus' assessment of the man and agreed with everything that she had said.

"Tell your Chief that I would be happy to meet with him," Nanny said. My team will work out the details with you; goodnight!" And with that Nanny melted into the shadows of her burly security, leaving Phooju alone again with his thoughts; wondering what had just happened. He smiled in the dark and had to pinch himself as he went back to sleep, dreaming of his first encounter with the great Chief Nanny. He would remember this day for the rest of his life.

The meeting between Nanny and the Chief from Westmoreland was planned for the first Tuesday of the following month. The rendezvous point was agreed upon and everything was set. The meeting place was a popular spot where Nanny and her people visited often; with its fresh, unspoiled, pristine river, teeming with fish and lots of Cray fish hiding under the rocks. This was the perfect spot to have a picnic, and best of all, it was unknown to the British. The running joke among Maroons was that,'Bakra was down on the plains fighting and dying over the flat lands when the beauty and splendor of the island was in the mountains.

On the morning of the meeting, Quao deployed a unit of attack warriors and positioned them strategically on both sides of the river. On the top of the ridge, others were positioned as lookouts for both the visitors and the British soldiers and given strict orders to move in and attack if things went south.

Suddenly the abeng horn sounded, signaling the arrival of the entourage from Westmoreland. Everyone got into position, hoping for the best, but preparing for the worst.

After the formalities in which Chief Waputa presented Nanny with numerous gifts, they sat down to talk.

"Thank you Chief Nanny for agreeing to meet with me," he began. "I've been looking forward to this meeting with you for a long time."

"And why is that?" Nanny asked curiously.

"Your reputation is widely known on the plantations in the west. People talk about you like they know you personally. Some people believe that you've come to overthrow the British and rule this country."

"And what do you believe Chief Waputa?" Nanny asked calmly. The Chief was taken aback by the boldness of the question and thought for a while before answering.

"That's a good question, Chief Nanny. To be honest, I don't know what to believe."

"I like your honesty," Nanny smiled. "Now what can I do for you?"

"We Coromantees in the west believe that the time is right for us to put an end to the British rule and establish an African kingdom here in Jamaica," Chief Waputa began. "We've put up with enough brutality from the British. They're getting from bad to worst. They're not only raping our women but they're sending soldiers out to attack and murder innocent people in their villages. The time is now Chief Nanny! Yes, the time is now."

"Tell me more Chief Waputa," Nanny urged.

"We're proposing that you Maroons control the mountain regions and we in turn will control the flat lands that the British people now occupy. Between you Chief Nanny and your people controlling the mountains and we in the west controlling the plains; together we could rule this entire country, and drive out the British."

"So, do you have the manpower, the weapons and the ammunition to defeat the British?" Nanny asked calmly.

"We will have the weapons and the manpower to bring the fight to them," he replied boldly.

"When do you think that you would be ready?" Nanny inquired.

"In the next few months," he replied boldly.

For the next two hours Nanny and the visiting Chief debated the plan with Nanny probing deeper and deeper to find answers. In the end she thanked the Chief for coming and promised that she would give him an answer after consulting with her advisors.

Neither Putus nor Quao liked the plan and told Nanny as such.

"I don't think that the time is right Chief," Quao said. "I don't know about those people; but we're just not ready to take on the British."

"I agree Chief," Putus added. "Maybe in a few years time, but not right now. We would need a lot more arms and many more trained warriors to defeat the British. We should never underestimate the might of the British," she affirmed. "People say that they have the most powerful army in the world."

"I believe that we will drive out the British one day, but it won't be quick or easy," Quao said. "It will take blood, sweat and tears. Contrary to what Chief Waputa said, this is not the time. Don't get me wrong Chief, the idea is good, but the timing is bad. I believe that we need to continue this struggle on our own."

Nanny listened attentively. Quao and Putus had given her a lot to think about. They were both dead set against the alliance with this Coromantee Chief, and for good reasons. For one thing, they needed more information about these people. The Coromantee were known for their great leadership and military skills; but they were also known for their aggressiveness and impatience. Nanny didn't like the idea that they wanted to take most of the best farm lands in Jamaica and relegate them to the mountainous regions, without any form of discussion.

"I'm in full agreement with you two," she said finally. "This is definitely not the right time for us to fight the British. We also need more information about these Coromantees. We could be making a deal with the devil."

Nanny had made her decision.

"Putus please set up a meeting with Phooju and relay our decision to him."

"What should I tell him Chief?" Putus asked with a slight smile.

"Tell him that after thinking long and hard about the offer, and although we think that it is a great plan, we do not wish to join with them at this time. However we might look at it again in a year or so when we're more prepared."

"You make it sound so good Chief," Putus said. "You let them down so gentle." Nanny smiled back at her.

Meanwhile, daily reports coming in indicated that the British were intensifying their attacks on innocent Maroons villages. Scarcely a day went by when a village was not burnt to the ground and the inhabitants killed.

When the villages were attacked by the local militia the conditions were even worse. These wannabe soldiers showed no mercy and killed the villagers without a thought. When Nanny's warriors entered these villages some of them cried when they saw the carnage; dead men, women and children, all shot to pieces, some at point blank range.

"What could possess these white people to treat another human being like this?" Putus asked Nanny.

"They don't see us as another human being capable of thinking, feeling and having dreams and desires like them," Nanny replied with tears in her eyes.

"Chief, we've got to do something for these poor people. We need to be left alone to live our lives," Putus pleaded.

"I was thinking the same thing Putus. I think that it's time for me to have a meeting with the British Chief," Nanny declared. "I think he needs to meet us face to face. As long as they only see us at the other end of their muskets, they will never respect us, or for that matter, take us seriously."

"And how do you plan to talk with this very important gentleman?" Putus asked. "For one thing he is well guarded."

"Then Putus, when has security ever stopped me?" Nanny asked jokingly.

"I see what you mean Chief," Putus responded, knowing full well what she was capable of doing. "So when do you plan to go?"

"Do me a favor Putus; let your lookouts report back to me whenever the British Chief is in a camp nearby. I would like to pay him a visit in his tent during the night."

Putus did not bother to ask how Nanny would enter such a fortified encampment. She was only sorry that she couldn't be like a fly on the wall. Nanny looked across at her friend and smiled; knowing in her heart exactly what she was thinking, but realizing that this was something that she had to take care of by herself.

A week later Nanny got the news that she had been waiting for. The General and a contingent of soldiers had set up camp nearby. Nanny was provided with a detailed layout of the camp and the exact tent where the General would be staying.

Nanny moved stealthily into the General's tent whipping pass the oblivious guards stationed at alert outside, with muskets in hand. Her eyes quickly swept the entire area. The tent was sparsely furnished with a few bags, a simple desk and a modest cot in the corner on which the General laid, fast asleep. Leaning beside his cot was his musket.

Nanny moved effortlessly towards the cot, quickly seized the musket and placed it gently in the corner across the room. She then quietly walked back and stood at the foot of the General's cot; looking down at his tall, pudgy frame for some time.

'He doesn't look so mighty to me,' she pondered to herself. 'But then again, looks is deceiving. He is the Chief here.'

Suddenly the General jumped up out of his sleep and quickly reached for his musket. A surprised look came over his face when he realized that it was not there.

"Looking for your musket, Mister Soldier Man, Sir?" Nanny asked nonchalantly. "It is over there in that corner," she continued with a devious smirk, pointing towards the corner.

"Don't bother calling out to your guards outside, I'm only here to talk to you."

"Who are you? Where are you from?" the General demanded.
'She speaks perfect English,' he said to himself.

"I come from the Motherland," Nanny replied abruptly.

"Why are you here?" the General asked, obviously upset at being disturbed.

"I'm not here to hurt you Mister Soldier Man, Sir," Nanny revealed. "If

233

I was here to hurt you, you would be dead from in your sleep. I am here to tell you to stop hunting down my people. They just want to be left alone to live out their lives in peace."

"I can't do that!" the General snapped back harshly. "I am only doing my job. I am following orders."

"Well, tell your superiors that what you and your men are doing is wrong. You are killing innocent people," Nanny informed him.

"And what business is it of yours?" he asked firmly.

"It is my business alright," Nanny fired back. "I've seen what you and your soldiers have been doing and I want to put you on notice. This is one fight that you will never win. You don't seem to realize that you're not dealing with children. We're not some wild stupid bush men that you captured and brought over here on your big ugly slave ships. You have brought to this country some of the brightest minds from the Motherland. We've come from one of the greatest civilization on earth; so it would be a grave mistake to take us for granted Mister Soldier Man, Sir. We have been conquerors in our land for centuries and now you want to keep us in chains. That is a big mistake you're making, Mister Soldier Man, Sir, and time will prove us right. Our children and our children's children will rule this country and also those great lands across the seas to the north; you mark my words," she said, pointing her finger to the north. "Statues will be erected in this land to honor our heroes who will continue to fight you until you leave this island for good. Bringing us here from the Motherland was short sighted on your part. You meant us evil and wickedness; but by God's help, we will find a way to determine our destiny. You see Mister Soldier Man, Sir, we are faster and stronger than you British in these mountains and we know every part of it. Nothing happens around here without our knowledge," she said with pride.

"We will beat you at your own games. We will influence your music, the food you eat and the clothes you wear. And this little Jamaica here; you will be tired to hear about us! The whole world will know about us. We will change your world forever; you mark my words!" she proclaimed confidently.

"When will you British people realize that you need us just as much as we need you? Our lives are forever linked from this time onward into the future. This was not of our choosing; but by God we will not lie down and let you all walk over us like door mats. You see Mister Soldier Man, Sir," she said, lowering her voice to a near whisper. "Between our great minds and your great minds, we can achieve much and make things better for both our people. But if you continue to deny us our rights, be certain that there will be no peace on this island," she emphasized, with her eyes blazing red like fire.

"Don't be fooled Mister Soldier Man, Sir, we are Ashanti warriors, some of the greatest warriors the Motherland has ever known, and we have adapted to this little island like ducks to water. So you and your men will suffer a great deal at the hands of our warriors until you come to your senses. The choice is yours."

"So what I am hearing," the General said with a sly smile on his face, slowly sitting up, swinging his feet over the side of the cot and sitting on the side.

"So what you are telling me woman, is that you and your little rag-tag bunch of warriors or whatever you call yourselves are superior to our Royal Majesty's Army? Ah! Ah! Ah! Ah!" he laughed heartily, waving his hand in the air. "You and your people will change the world? Ha! Ha! Ha! Ha! What a big joke!"

Then the General stopped abruptly and with a stone cold glare at Nanny said, "Now listen to me little woman, and you listen well! You little piece of maggot filth," he said, pointing his bony finger menacingly at her. "You and your people will always be our slaves, do you hear me?" he said, raising his voice. "Slaves! That's it! Nothing more, nothing less! We brought you here to serve us and that is the only thing that you will ever be; slaves for us! Slaves for our children and slaves for our children's children," he continued, waving his hand in the air with pride. "You savages!" the General carried on, in his baritone voice; pointing at Nanny, "Will not amount to anything more than that. Now, after we have crushed you and your miserable little bunch of misfits like cockroaches under our mighty boots, and hang you personally from the nearest tree, everything will go back to normal; and you wretched and ungrateful people will finally realize that it is futile to fight against the mighty British Empire. Do you understand what I am saying slave woman?"

Nanny paused for a moment, then with blazing fire in her eyes, replied, "So you think that I am joking?" somewhat disappointed at his stubbornness.

"Do you think that I came all this way down here to beat up my gum? I think you're making a very serious mistake Mister Soldier Man, Sir. No one needs to die. But mark my words; the next time we meet, I will not be so nice. At that appointed time, you and your soldiers will feel the full wrath of the Ashanti warriors!" And with that she vanished without a trace.

The General sat with his hand stroking his chin pondering what had just happened. He wondered if he was dreaming or if this was all real. He reckoned that he wasn't dreaming because his musket was way across the room. But how could this be? When he first arrived in Jamaica, he learned from the locals that there were a lot of ghosts or duppy, as the slaves called them, on the island; however he quickly dismissed them as rumors. But, could this be one of them? Was he visited by a duppy?

He called out to his guards and asked them if they had seen anyone; of which they all said no. He was too embarrassed to explain what had just happened when the guards asked him if something was wrong. But the more he thought about it the more annoyed he became. 'Who was this feisty little African woman? She spoke perfect English and with so much authority. She could pass for an aristocrat in the courts of London. And those narrow, steely, piercing eyes; they were really scary and deadly. She was well learned, talking about her people influencing our music, our games, our dress and our food. Who in London in their right mind, in this the 18th century, would want to dress like these pathetic people, listen to their silly music and eat their pitiful food? I think this slave woman is crazy!' he mused.

'But what is this world coming to?' he ruminated. As a respectable General, soon to be retired, no one dared to speak to him like that. Back in London when he spoke, everyone, including the politicians paid attention. No one lectured him; he always did the lecturing. His men had so much respect for him that they would never, ever address him in that manner. Furthermore, he was handpicked by the King of Britain to come down to this god forsaken island, infested with mosquitoes; to subdue these miserable, ungrateful slaves and crush the numerous uprisings across the island. But he was getting too old for this chaos and couldn't wait to get back to his life of luxury in London.

Numerous questions popped in his mind.

He wondered what she meant by, the next time they met she would not be so nice? What type of lady speaks like that to a gentleman; especially a man of his statue? Did she really know who he was? On the other hand, she certainly did not seem threatened by him or his platoon of soldiers. What type of person would think of breaking into an army camp; in particularly that of the greatest army on earth, and confront of all people, the General? That demonstrated a serious lack of respect for authority, primarily British authority; and that should never be allowed to happen.

Then again he wondered if she was some sort of a sorcerer or, as the slaves called them, Obeah woman. The slaves were usually very scared of these people. They were said to have supernatural powers and if you got them angry, they could turn your head behind your back. They were known to cast death spells on people. Everyone on the island knew that was one group of people that you never, ever got into a quarrel with.

If she was an Obeah woman he figured, at least she did not cast a spell on him. In fact, she was quite calm most of the time when she was there.

But then again this was ridiculous. He was the man in charge, representing the Crown and protecting its properties here on the island, and when he spoke everyone jumped; so no little Obeah woman, if that is what she was, would prevent him from doing his job, even if it cost him his life. His honor was at stake here. This was becoming personal.

As he finally went back to sleep, he had a nagging feeling that this would not be the last time that he would be meeting this little mysterious African woman; and that the next encounter would not be so pleasant.

Chapter 28

The conflict between the militia and the Maroons was heating up. The clashes were becoming more frequent and violent. The Maroons and free settlers were beginning to fight back with deadly consequences. This was now putting the British soldiers in the middle; protecting the white folks and their properties on one hand, and also going after the Maroons.

More and more slaves than ever were running off to join the Maroons. Nanny's lookouts and trackers were now finding them wandering around in the forest on a regular basis. Apparently word had spread that,'you only had to reach the forest and Chief Nanny would lead you to freedom.' Many of the young men immediately joined the warriors so that they could fight the militia, raid the plantations and liberate their relatives and friends. It was their way of giving back.

At the weekly meeting the leaders anxiously awaited Nanny's report on her meeting with the British General.

"He didn't think I was serious after all that I did to him," Nanny began. "Imagine this; I got into this man's tent, passing his fully armed security guards outside, took away his musket from beside his bed and he woke up to find me standing over him. I could've killed him then and there, but as I told him, I was only there to warn him to stop hunting down our people. Do you know what he did? He just laughed in my face and told me that we would never be free; that we would always be here to serve them and their children. I'm telling you, a rage boiled up inside my belly like a volcano, and I just felt like killing him on the spot; but what good would that do? All that would happen is that they would replace him with another idiot from Britain," Nanny said, shaking her head in disappointment.

The room was silent at the end of the report. Then Putus cleared her throat.

"So what are we going to do Chief?" she asked, knowing full well that Nanny always had something up her sleeve.

Nanny thought for a while then remarked in a low stern voice.

"We have to change our strategy from avoiding the enemy to taking them on," she began, before she was suddenly interrupted by a spontaneous round of applause. After clapping for some time Quao raised his hand for everyone to quiet down.

"I'm very happy with this decision Chief," Quao said. "We've been waiting a long time for this day to come, and we're ready," he said confidently.

"Yes," Nanny said. "We need to put some pressure on these British soldiers. Believe you me, I also knew that this day would come, but I wanted to make sure that we would be ready. I was not only concerned about our warriors being ready militarily, but also about we as a people being ready to govern ourselves; that's the harder part."

"What do you mean Chief?" Putus asked.

"When you are oppressed or when you are the underdog, you're usually quite humble, but the problem arises when you're free and in control. You could become conceited and bigheaded. And guess what? You might find yourself doing the exact things that your oppressors used to do to you or sometimes even worse. So what am I saying folks? I'm saying that governing ourselves take more effort. It takes more integrity, it takes more backbone to stand up and do the right thing; even in the face of corruption all around you.

Remember, the reason why they sold us as slaves was partly because good people saw what was happening and did nothing about it. They did nothing because they didn't have the spine to take a stand. But I'm not foolish to believe that what I'm saying will be easy or without sacrifice. What I'm saying ladies and gentlemen is that our people failed us badly in Africa, and here in Jamaica we have the opportunity to start over again and make it right this time. We cannot afford to mess this up; do you hear me? We cannot afford to get it wrong this time," she said with tears in her eyes.

"And that is also why I didn't join forces with the Coromantees, because I didn't think that we were ready yet to govern Jamaica. Our problem is not solely with the British, although they are our immediate focus. Our problem is mainly with ourselves. We are our biggest enemy; not Bakra, not the British soldiers, not the Militia; remember that."

Then Nanny had everyone repeat after her, "The biggest enemy that I have to conquer is me." Everyone felt humbled at the end.

For the remainder of the evening Nanny and the committee sat down and planned strategies to confront the militia and the British soldiers head on. They would utilize more ingenious decoys to ambush the soldiers and use more creative disguises and booby traps in the bushes. The British would not have a free run of the mountains any more. They would have to think before they took a step, or venture into any cave.

The following day, Nanny got an important intelligence report about a large shipment of supplies to be picked up at the docks at Port Royal in four days and transported to the main fort in the Blue Mountain. The contents were top secret, and the only thing that the informant knew was that it was very important.

At the emergency meeting with her top military advisors, Nanny informed them about the shipment and the decision to attack the convoy and confiscate the booty.

"The biggest advantage we have on our side is that they don't believe that we would be bold enough to attack them," Nanny said with a smile.

"But we can take them Chief," Quao exclaimed.

"You know that and we know that, but they don't, and that is why we will get away with it," she remarked. "But it won't be easy. No doubt they will be heavily armed so we have to pick the right spot for the ambush and be quick and deadly."

"I know the perfect spot," Quao said excitedly.

"And where is that?" Nanny asked.

"Right at Cotton Tree Pass. The place is perfect to set our trap. The pass is between two hills. We could post men on both sides of the hills and then attack the convoy from both sides. There would be nowhere for them to run or hide."

"Sounds like a good spot," Nanny said.

"Anybody else has any other great spots along the route?" she asked. When no other suggestions came forth, Nanny asked everyone to look more closely at Cotton Tree Pass.

"What are some of the negatives of this location," she asked the group. "And how will we make up for it?"

For the next few hours they brainstormed every aspect of the operation. Later that day, Quao took a small team of his best scouts down to Cotton Tree Pass to map out the area and report back to the group.

"Thanks Quao, you and your men did a fantastic job. I think we've covered all our bases and have left nothing to chance," Nanny said.

For the next few days the troops practiced very hard, going over the drills and working on the timing. Eventually the plan was set and everything was ready. The troops would be divided into two big groups, one for each hill. Each group would be subdivided into three sub-groups. The first sub-group would prevent the enemy from running away. The rear sub-group would prevent the enemy from retreating and the middle sub-group would strike them hard.

On the morning of the ambush Nanny spoke to the young men and women for a few minutes before they left. She told them how proud she was of them and that with God's help they would be successful and return safely to their families. She reminded them of the importance of the mission; to rid the country of those evil British people and eventually set up their own rule of law, and govern themselves. Next, Quao gave his usual pep talk before they were off in the cool foggy early morning air; fully prepared for battle. The troops marched quietly down the hill towards Cotton Tree Pass, always keeping their eyes peeled for any signs of the enemy.

When they arrived they quickly unloaded their gears and took up their positions on opposite sides of the hills, facing the pass.

The air was charged with excitement. This was all new to them. Normally when they raided a plantation they encountered little or no resistance. The plantation owners were usually too scared to fight back and would normally runaway or hide until they were gone. But this time was different. They were now going up against professional soldiers who were well trained in the art of war and who would fight back with equal or more force. Today the Maroons would be tested as never before.

So the waiting began. How long? No one knew. They would know only when the convoy started heading up into the Blue Mountains. Everyone looked forward to the first report.

As the bright morning sun struck the trees, it revealed the concealed warriors; fully dressed in their camouflage fatigues and covered in war paints, ready for action. They were as ready as they would ever be. From the top of the hills, Quao and his warriors had a clear view of the pass and could hit any targets down below.

It was noon before the first abeng message rang out. It stated that the convoy of two wagons had just started up the hill at 'Duppy Gully' and were heading north with a detachment of fifteen soldiers, fully armed.

"This must be a very important shipment for them to have so many guards," Quao remarked to one of his senior leaders.

"True thing Captain," the warrior replied. "I wonder if they have weapons in those wagons."

"That would be a bonanza for us," Quao replied, with a nervous smile. "Lawd knows that we need some new weapons for our growing force."

"So they have fifteen men; that's good to know, right Captain?" one of his young and upcoming leaders asked.

"Yes Buthy, it is good news," Quao answered.

"But I wish we knew more about them," the young warrior contemplated.

"What do you mean Buthy?" Quao asked.

"Well Captain we need to know a few things like: are the guards travelling beside the wagons or behind, are they travelling together or do they have scouts ahead checking the surrounding area for possible ambush."

"Those are great questions, Buthy," Quao said.
"Let's relay a message back to our lookouts and ask them."

As the British convoy moved nearer and nearer to Cotton Tree Pass the abeng reports became more frequent and more detailed. One report stated that the soldiers had stopped for over one hour to repair a broken axle on one of the covered wagons. The soldiers circled the wagons and guarded the shipment while a few did the repairs. If the soldiers suspected that they were being watched, they did not let on. They just did their jobs as they were trained.

Finally the message that they had been waiting on echoed throughout the canyon; the convoy was close by and would be arriving in a very short time. Quao directed his men to remain alert and to listen for his orders. Suddenly the convoy came into sight. The two wagons were surrounded by smartly dressed soldiers riding on both sides. The warriors watched and waited patiently for Quao to give the order to fire.

The convoy moved slowly towards the pass unaware of the impending danger. However the Captain was taking nothing for granted. He carefully scanned the surrounding hillsides with his telescope as they journeyed into the trap.

As the convoy entered Cotton Tree Pass the warriors on both hills calmly aimed their muskets and waited on the order to fire. There were seven soldiers riding on one side, six on the other side and two driving the wagons. Everything was going according to plan.

As the convoy reached the middle of the pass, Quao gave the order to fire. The specially trained warriors did not disappoint. The soldiers didn't stand a chance. As the men were hit with the barrage of bullets, they fell from their horses and died on the spot. In the end, no one was spared in the onslaught.

The firing stopped when Quao gave the order. He motioned them to move in cautiously and to make sure that they were all dead. The warriors quickly made their way down. As they drew nearer to the convoy they began to see the full extent of the carnage. The soldiers were all shot to pieces by the awesome firepower of the warriors.

The troops swiftly moved towards the two wagons and expeditiously removed the covering to reveal an assortment of brand new muskets, ammunition, military equipment, and tons of hardware and food supplies; destined for the fort.

Quao instructed everyone to strip the wagons quickly, collect all the spoils and remove the weapons and ammunition from the dead. The troops hastily completed the mission and in a very short while they were on their way home laden down with the loot; leaving behind death and destruction.

Chapter 29

Nanny was quite pleased with the results and made it known to Quao and the troops as they laid out the spoils in the square for all to see. The muskets were brand spanking new and still wrapped in their original packages.

"These muskets look like the newest kind!" Quao exclaimed. "They even feel lighter and handle much better," he said excitedly exercising the locks.

"True, true Captain," Bawthy, a young warrior agreed; holding up one of the new muskets in one hand and an older one in the other. "Not even the soldiers here have them, so we're in luck."

Bawthy just loved the feel of a musket in his hand. It made him feel powerful; like a man, a free man, a man of equal status as the white man. He took pride in his weapons and especially liked to clean them until he could see his face clearly in them. He had a steady hand and was well known for his accuracy. No wild hog stood a chance when he went hunting.

"When are we going to try them out Captain?" he asked Quao excitedly.

"Tomorrow we will clean them up and test them," Quao replied.

"Whoopee!" Bawthy hollered. "I can't wait." Everyone laughed, because they knew him so well.

Later that day when the military leaders met to reflect on the mission, Nanny thanked them for their bravery and efficiency in executing the program.

"Team, you did a fantastic job! The mission was a complete success. I'm so proud of you all," she said with delight.

"Well, that is the good news. The bad news is that we've just disturbed the giant ant's nest. So we have to be prepared for the backlash, because I know that it is coming. We're not foolish to believe that the great British Army will take this lying down. They have too much pride and weapons to let this ever pass. It reminds me of the old African proverb where this large menacing giant was terrorizing this village. Everyone in the village was afraid except a little boy who faced him and defeated him with a sling shot and some pebbles. We will defeat the British eventually, but it will take a lot of sacrifice from every one of us," she said with firm conviction.

"We never started this war, and we never wanted this war either; we just wanted them to leave us alone, right?" Nanny reminded them.

"But we will not back down now. We will continue to be a thorn in their side until they give us our freedom," she declared, raising her fist in the air. Then, just as quickly she lowered her voice to a mere whisper.

"So my team, we have to redouble our efforts, leaving no stone unturned. We need to get more intelligence reports. We need to fortify our town, and improve our communication. We have to do these things and more to win this battle," she emphasized.

Then raising her voice louder, she asked, "Are you all ready to pay the price for your freedom?"

"Yes Chief," they shouted.

"Will you commit yourselves to do whatever it takes to remove the British from this island?" she continued.

"Yes Chief," they shouted again.

"Will you commit to keep yourselves and your troops physically and mentally fit to meet these new challenges."

"Yes Chief," they declared.

At the end of the meeting, as everyone was leaving Nanny walked over to Putus and whispered in her ears that she wanted to talk to her.

'I wonder what Nanny wants to talk to me about,' she contemplated. Her mind began to race; thinking up different reasons why the Chief would want to see her. Was this an official meeting or mere girl talk? Lately they were finding it difficult to spend leisure time together because they were both so busy.

After everyone left the two ladies sat down to talk.

"What is it Nanny? What do you want to talk to me about?" Putus asked anxiously.

"Putus, do you remember the man that you introduced me to?" Nanny began.

"Yes Adou, what has he done now?" Putus asked nervously.

"No! No, he hasn't done anything bad."

"Then what?" Putus urged.

"You know that we've been seeing each other for some time now."

"Yes, so what?" Putus demanded.

"Well, he has put the question to me."

"What question? Tell me!" Putus demanded, unable to take the suspense any longer.

"He asked me to marry him," Nanny said with a smile.

"And what did you say?" Putus inquired. Nanny hesitated.

"You know Putus that I'm getting up in age. I'm no spring chicken any more, and I don't know if I will have the time to take care of any man with my busy schedule."

"What did you tell him?" Putus insisted. "I want to know now! The suspense is killing me."

"I told him that if he would have me then my answer was yes," she said with a broad smile.

"Thanks Massa God!" Putus exclaimed, hugging Nanny. "You know how I've prayed for this day chile? Massa God is good."

"So Putus, we have a wedding to plan," Nanny said with delight.

"What date were you and Adou planning to have the celebration?"

"The last Saturday in this month."

"But that will give us less than three weeks," Putus said.

"I know, we have to get busy."

For the next three weeks, Nanny juggled many balls in the air while planning the wedding with Putus and the other elderly women.

Intelligence came in that some young militia fighters were gearing up to attack a new settlement.

As Nanny addressed her military advisors on the matter she made her position known.

"We have to help these innocent people. They will be wiped out if we do nothing. They neither have the weapons nor manpower to defend themselves. They are new; just starting out as a free village, and they desperately need our help. It is the right thing to do because we have the resources and the manpower to fight the militia."

Nanny paused for a moment to get their response.

"But Chief, is it right for us to send our young men and women into arms way for a cause that don't concern us?" a middle aged woman asked.

Nanny contemplated for a moment then spoke.

"If we don't help these people, then who will? And if we don't help them now, then when? After they are massacred? We have been blessed with so much after escaping the cruelty of Bakra. I don't believe that all that we have achieved up until now was by accident. My grandmother used to tell me that the more you get is the more you have to give. We've been

246

given so much more than we ever expected and therefore we can't help but to give back."

The decision was made and plans were quickly drawn up by the team.

"To show you that I'm fully committed to this cause," Nanny said. "I'll be going with our young men and women to help these people fight the militia."

The lookouts tracked the militia as they headed north towards the newly established village.

Nanny and her troops travelled quickly throughout the night through a narrow gorge to head off the militia before morning. When they arrived, they quickly took up a defensive position in the thick forest surrounding the village and waited on the militia to arrive.

They did not have long to wait. As the sun came up over the horizon a rumbling sound could be heard coming over the ridge. Nanny and Quao looked across at each other.

"Are you sure that you don't need a musket, Sis?" Quao asked, showing genuine concern.

"No, I'll be alright," Nanny replied. "Go ahead and give your troops their instructions. I'll be just fine."

Quao instructed his troops to remain alert and wait for his signal. The fighters further camouflaged themselves among the trees blending in with the golden light as the sun's ray hit the dew drenched leaves.

The militia came slowly over the hill. Nanny could see through her telescope that most of them were mere young lads with weapons; 'wet behind the ears.' A feeling of grief came over her as she realize that they were about to be killed and they didn't have a clue. An idea came to her on how all this looming bloodshed could be avoided.

"Are you sure Sis?" Quao asked, when Nanny told him her plan.

"Yes Quao, this would give them a way out."

"Ok Sis, so let me get this straight; we will call out to them and tell them to turn around and go back home. Then suppose they refuse?" Quao asked.

"Then my conscience would be clear that I tried to save their lives," Nanny replied.

"Well Chief we have to make our move now; let's do it your way."

Quao gave the signal and the abeng players began blowing their horns with intensity, which took the young militia men by surprise. They froze in their tracks, looked all around; not sure where the sounds were coming from. Then Quao barked another order and the abengs fell silent.

"Go back home white men! Go back home and your lives will be spared!" Nanny shouted out to them. "Do not take another step forward!

Turn around and go back home! These people did not trouble you. They just want to be left in peace. Turn back before it is too late."

Quao gave the third signal and the drummers started a slow march beat, beseeching the militia to turn around and return home.

But the young militia would have none of that. They laughed out loudly and brandished their weapons in the air in defiance.

They filed in formation standing shoulder to shoulder, grasping their muskets attached with razor sharp bayonets.

As they advanced Quao gave the orders. "Steady! Steady! Aim! See the white of their eyes! Fire!" he shouted. And with that, the warriors opened fire. The explosion was deafening, intermingled with a thick white smoke bathed in sulphur. The militia's muskets were no match for the new and superior weapons of the Maroons.

The battle lasted for sometime before the militia was totally destroyed. After carefully observing the deadly scene, Quao gave the order to cease fire. With weapons drawn, the troops advanced to where the militia men were and turned them over with their feet to ensure that they were all dead. Quao instructed his troops to collect all the weapons and ammunition and anything else of value from the dead. They quickly packed up their gears and prepared to return to base.

Suddenly the people of the village emerged slowly from their huts to thank the troops. In their hands and on their heads were bundles of yams, plantains, melons, corn, and banana. The team stood still and watched in amazement. Leading the group was a short elderly man walking with a slight limp towards Nanny. As he approached her he bowed his head and said, "May Massa God bless you and your people forever. What you and your warriors have done here today will never be forgotten by our people. Here is a token of our appreciation." And with that he took a big basket of fruits from a little girl's head and handed it to Nanny. This was like a signal for the others to follow suit; handing over their gifts to the troops with big smiles.

Nanny thanked the Chief on behalf of the troops and after a short while they bid farewell and left for home.

Nanny felt a heavy burden on her heart as she left the scene.

Quao looked over at her and sensing what she was feeling said,

"You tried Chief; Massa God knows that you tried to save those young men, but their stubbornness is what got them killed."

She understood what he was trying to say, but it didn't make it any easier. When they finally reached home Nanny went straight over to Putus' house to visit.

"Nanny, you look like crushed cabbage [depressed]. What is the matter?" Putus inquired.

"Putus, why is it that some people are so fool, fool [stupid]?" Nanny asked, shaking her head and not expecting an answer. "Today, those young white men didn't have to die. I personally told them to stop and go back home, and leave those innocent people alone; but did they listen? No! They never listened, why? Because they think that as white people they don't have to take orders from nobody; they know everything! Their parents believed that and then passed it on to their children. They don't seem to realize that things are changing fast. Everything is not all about them and what they want. They also don't get it that it doesn't matter where you started in life; it is where you're going and where you end up. Yes, we started out as slaves, but that is not who we are, or where we're going to remain. I admire every single runaway slave today because what they're saying to the British is; 'yes you changed my destiny, but no one asked you to bring me over here. In fact I'm saying no thank you; I will create my own future from now on. I will be the captain of my ship. You have done enough damage already.'"

Putus listened without saying a word. She knew that Nanny only wanted someone to be a sounding board for her thoughts. While she spoke, Putus quickly made two mugs of hot coffee. Nanny thanked her as she cradled the mug of brew with both hands and continued to talk. When she sipped her last drop, she placed the mug gently on the table, thanked Putus for listening, and then said goodbye and left.

"Will you be alright?" Putus asked, calling after her.

"Oh sure," Nanny said, trying to appear positive. Then she stopped and turned to Putus. "I was just having a 'pity party' and I just wanted a friend to be there to listen, and that is what you did. I'm so thankful that I have you as a friend Putus. Not many leaders have a friend like you and I appreciate you more and more every day."

The following week Nanny received an intelligence report that a remote British outpost, stocked with weapons and supplies had only a few soldiers guarding it. The outpost was one of the earliest ones built to monitor Maroons activities in that region. However many of the villages were abandoned for various reasons and the people moved on to live in new areas.

Nanny called a meeting with Quao and her military advisors and discussed the pros and cons of this raid.

"Chief, this raid could serve two purposes," Quao began. "First, we could get all those good quality weapons and supplies, and secondly, we would get the British very angry by burning down their fort," he said, smiling broadly.

Everyone laughed and nodded their heads in agreement, because nothing they loved more, than to get the British upset.

So the plan was set, Quao would lead the attack on the fort in the next couple of days.

The evening before the raid the warriors were busy with preparation. They carefully cleaned their weapons, packed their ammunition and sharpened their machetes, while the leaders met with Quao and Nanny to get last minute briefings. Lights out came early so that everyone would get a good night's rest.

Early the next morning the troops, led by Quao, left camp under the cover of darkness. As they drew nearer to the outpost, perspiration flowed freely off their bodies as everyone got 'pumped' for the mission.

Suddenly Quao gave the signal for everyone to stop. Everyone remained quiet as he quietly outlined last minute instructions to his leaders; sketching a diagram on the ground.

"Shumbeh, you take your squad to the back of the fort and set it on fire. Watch out for snipers. While you're doing that we will be in front keeping them busy. Any questions?" Quao asked, to which everyone said no. "Look out for each other," Quao reminded them. "Wait for my signal; and may Massa God protect us all."

The Maroons took up their positions and advanced just as the sun came up. The men looked polished and shiny as their bodies glistened in the early morning light.

Suddenly, Quao raised his hands and gave the signal that everyone had been waiting for. Instantly, numerous earsplitting abeng horns sounded off, giving the false impression that there were far more troops present than were actually there.

The troops operated like clockwork. Each team executed the plan that they were assigned. In a short while, Quao and his men blasted their way inside the fort and killed the small squad of soldiers who were frightened out of their sleep.

Quao ordered everyone to search the fort thoroughly for any weapons, ammunition, supplies, tools and documents; anything that could be of value. The troops collected many brand new weapons and a large supply of ammunition, along with supplies of medicine, tools, clothing, boots, socks, mosquito nets and foodstuff. Quao instructed the troops to store some of the booty at their temporary storage warehouses hidden on the outskirts of Nanny town.

After all the valuables were removed from the fort, the men packed up and left for home, but not before setting fire to the buildings. As they walked across the mountain, they could see huge plumes of smoke slowly rising in the air.

"Somebody will be very angry Captain," a smiling young warrior said to Quao. "Very angry!"

"I guess so my son," Quao replied. "I guess so; but we will be ready."

Chapter 30

The reports kept coming in daily of the atrocities committed by the British. They burnt food crops in the fields and patrolled the countryside seeking out villages and destroying the temporary food storage warehouses. They stopped vendors on their way to the market, confiscated their goods and then ordered them back home. No merchandise was allowed to be transported to the market. The British also tightened the siege by barring slaves from going to the markets on Sundays to sell their food or buy goods. Bakra also limited the free movements of slaves between the various departments on the plantation and unescorted trips outside the plantation.

"The folks on the plantations are locked down tight like vice," Putus reported to Nanny. "No one is coming out to the markets on Sundays any more. I have not seen any of my inside people for weeks now. Business is really suffering badly in the towns and villages. Everything is so scarce. And to make matters worse, the soldiers are capturing and returning people to the plantation. What a condition," she lamented.

"I heard," Nanny said, shaking her head in agreement and looking concerned.

"Why do you think that the soldiers are doing it Chief?" Putus asked.

"I think that they're really angry with us for attacking and destroying the plantations and their forts, taking away their weapons and killing so many of their soldiers. So, because they can't catch us, they're bent on making all African people suffer."

"But that's not fair," Putus remarked. "What did the poor slaves do? They're in enough misery already!"

"There is an old African proverb that says, 'If you can't catch Quashie then you catch his shirt,'" Nanny affirmed.

"You always have all these good sayings from back home in Africa," Putus commented. "How do you remember them?"

"I grew up hearing my grandmother using them all the time," Nanny replied. "For every situation she would have one for you. Sometimes I believed that she made it up, but it always made sense and fit the situation."

"I try to remember them when you use them, but I always forget," Putus revealed with a smile.

"I believe that the soldiers are squeezing everybody until somebody can't take it any longer and begin to talk," Nanny suggested, getting back to the conversation.

"Talk about what?" Putus asked, looking puzzled.

"Well for one thing, tell them who keeps burning down their forts, stealing their weapons and killing their soldiers," Nanny suggested.

"I see what you mean," Putus said thoughtfully. "Oh, so they need traitors," Putus said.

"Something like that," Nanny agreed.

"So what will happen if nobody talks?" Putus inquired.

"Well the British believe, and that is where they get it wrong again, that African people ever believe a single word that they say. They always talk through the two sides of their mouth; you can't believe a single word that they say. So they believe that by squeezing the people like this, something will give. They believe that the people will begin to starve so badly that Bakra's plantation will look like 'the great garden up in the sky filled with milk and honey.' It won't work though; because once you've tasted the sweet fruits of freedom, there will be no turning back to the slops of the plantation. To tell you the truth Putus, I knew that the British would strike back, but I didn't know that they would go so far as to lock down the whole island so tightly," Nanny stressed.
"I wonder how Cudjoe and Accompong are doing. I have not heard from them for some time now," she pondered aloud.

"So Chief, what you're saying is that the mighty British Army is really angry with us because we're costing them so much money and soldiers and above all, the peace and safety of their precious white people on the plantations. They believe that by pressuring everybody they will be able to put us back into our place," Putus concluded.

"I believe that's their plan Putus. But remember, they came and provoked us and we're just giving them back a taste of their own medicine," Nanny reminded her.

"Chief, the people are asking questions; what should I tell them?"

"We have to explain to them what is happening, and try to reassure them that we've everything under control. Fortunately we're self-sufficient in food, so we won't feel the pressures that other villages are experiencing," Nanny affirmed.

"Let's hope that the soldiers never find us, so that we can live here for the rest of our lives," Putus said.

"I hope so too," Nanny concurred.

"Chief you've always said that, 'to everyone who is given a whole lot, even more is expected.' Well, we have a lot of food here, more than we need; so what are we going to do to help those other smaller villages that are suffering?" Putus asked.

Nanny thought for some time and then looked Putus squarely in her face and said, "That's a very good question Putus. I always knew that you had a big heart the first day I met you. Ok, here is what we will do; call a meeting of the team tomorrow and tell everybody to bring their ideas on how we can help those hurting people out in the villages," pointing her fingers to the east, west, north and south.

At the meeting the following day, there was an air of excitement in the room. Everyone came with ideas on how to help the suffering people in the surrounding villages.

"We could pack bags of food and have the troops deliver them to the villages during the night," one elderly, slightly balding gentleman said.

"But wouldn't that be dangerous seeing that the British soldiers are all around?" one short, stout woman asked.

"I don't think so," the same gentleman replied. "Because for one thing, they won't patrol in the night because they know that we control the nights in these mountains, and two, between our lookouts and our fine troops, we will be able to navigate these mountains without the soldiers seeing us."

"Well said!" Putus exclaimed and everyone agreed. At the end of the meeting everyone left in a high spirit of generosity and gratefulness.

The food program was set to start in a few days. Putus was appointed to spearhead the collection and packaging of the food while Quao led the troops.

Nanny called a meeting of all the citizens of Nanny Town for the following evening to explain what was happening and to inform them of their plans to deliver foodstuff to the nearby villages at night.

"Good evening ladies and gentlemen," she began. "Thank you so much for coming. I promise not to keep you too long, but I believe that you should know what has been happening around here and what our plans are to counter it. Lately the British have been burning down all the farmers' fields and preventing anybody from going to the market to buy or sell goods. Because of this many people out there in the villages are starving." Suddenly there was a quiet moaning sound coming from the back of the room. A few old ladies quietly sobbed at the news of the suffering.

"Hunger is worse than Obeah Chief," one of them cried. "We must do something for them."

"That's the same thing we were thinking!" Nanny said. "We're fortunate to have so much food in storage that we're planning on giving away some to those people in the villages who are in need."

"Good idea Chief," a tall man with a white moustache shouted. "We have more than enough."

"Massa God blessed us so that we can bless others," another woman called out. Everyone clapped and cheered their approval.

"So ladies and gentlemen, by a show of hands, who would like to volunteer to prepare and package the food?" Putus asked. The response was overwhelming. Everyone wanted to contribute in some way or other. For the next couple weeks the people of Nanny Town worked diligently to prepare the packages and the troops delivered them to the villages under the cover of darkness.

Meanwhile, out in the west Cudjoe and his men were preparing for a big showdown with the British soldiers later that day. They skillfully cleaned and packed their weapons and sharpened their machetes. A few days before, Cudjoe had one of his spies plant a tip with one of the British soldiers convincing him that he knew the hideout of Cudjoe and his men.

As the sun came up, a detachment of soldiers from the main fort began the long march to find this hiding place in the canyon; quickly crush this bunch of criminals, and return to camp before dusk for supper. All in a day's work; at least that was the plan.

The lookouts tracked their every move from the time they left the fort, relaying the information down the line to the troops in waiting. As the

255

soldiers drew nearer, the situation became tense. Everyone took up their position. Cudjoe was especially anxious because he was trying this maneuver on the British for the first time. He had thought about it for some time but did not get the opportunity to use it until now.

"How this works," he was explaining to his leaders a few hours earlier, while drawing a diagram in the dirt. "It's a four prong or box attack. The enemy will be fired upon from all sides. They will get caught in a crossfire, and boom! they're destroyed," marking a big X to demonstrate the effect. "Any questions my youths?" he asked.

"No Chief!" they replied.

"Alright then, Oswuhi, you take the north end with your team, Bahgah, you take the south end with your team, Sukyps, you and your team take the east end and Alwaizi, you take the west end with your team. For the rest of you, stay with me."

The British did not stand a chance. As they marched bravely into the valley of death; unaware of the approaching danger, they suddenly heard the orchestrated clicks of the locks on the muskets; click! Click! Click! Click, down the line going on and on. This was their first face-to-face encounter with the fearless leader Cudjoe and his mighty Maroon warriors; an experience that they would never ever forget.

The crossfire attack came as a complete surprise to the British. They were caught flat footed. They did not know whether to run or stand up and fight an invisible foe.

The Bullets found their targets with extreme accuracy. Only a few soldiers escaped, and only because Cudjoe gave the orders to let them live, so that they could tell the tale of this massacre at the hands of the Maroons.

As the soldiers retreated the warriors collected all their weapons, ammunition and supplies that were left behind.

Finally, Cudjoe gave the order to move out and head for home; quite satisfied with another great victory over the British.

Chapter 31

The intelligence reports coming out of the plantations highlighted Bakra's frustration with the frequent raids and the high percentage of runaway slaves. This was becoming a real problem over the entire island and was threatening the country's sugar production. One informant even spoke of Bakra's decision to return to England and leave the plantation to an overseer after his entire family was killed in the last Maroon raid. There were also reports of large sums of money being paid out for information on the location of Maroon settlements.

"The British are getting desperate if they're offering so much money," Putus suggested.

"That's true," Nanny said, sitting back, closing her eyes and mulling over the information in her mind.

Suddenly she opened up her eyes at Putus and said, "We need to keep up the pressure on the British. They have tried everything from bringing in more troops, burning our fields, preventing the lowly slaves from going to the market, to now offering large sums of money for information, and it is still not working. What else is there for them to do?" she asked aloud.
"By continuing our attacks on their facilities we will keep their soldiers tied up fighting for a long time. I wonder how that rude General is feeling now that they're losing the battle." Nanny gloated.
"Putus we can't stop now, the tide is turning; we must keep up the pressure!"

"Yes Chief, I agree," Putus concurred.

Later that day Quao came by Nanny's house to give her the news.

"Sis, I have some bad news. The British have posted a big bounty on your head," Quao blurted out suddenly. "My men told me that they have posted your name all over the market place. Don't worry, I don't think that anybody will talk to them," he said, trying to reassure her.

"I'm not surprised, they've been throwing money around lately like drunken sailors to get information," Nanny said smugly.

"So what are we going to do Sis?" Quao asked.

"Same thing that we've been doing all along," Nanny replied confidently. "We're not going to change our plans. No way! We will continue the struggle for freedom. If we stop now, then all our hard work would've been in vain and our children would never forgive us. My brother we have Ashanti blood running in our veins, and that only means one thing; we never, ever give up. We will keep nibbling away at them until we're free. How do you eat a big elephant my brother?" she asked, and not waiting for an answer. "One bite at a time; and that's just what we will do."

Just then Putus came by to remind Nanny of her appointment with the dress maker for her upcoming wedding. When she walked in she sensed the mood in the room.

"What is the matter, somebody ate your white fowl?" she joked.

"If that was the only problem then everything would be alright," Quao answered, with a serious look on his face.

"Then why the long faces?" she pried.

"It's not all that serious, but the British have put up posters in the marketplace giving out lots of money for information on Sis here. So we were just discussing it when you walked in."

"Sorry about that Nanny, but I agree with Quao; nothing will come of it," Putus reassured her.
"The British will try anything to take back control. Back home we used to say that they're throwing lots of dung [cow manure] on the side of the hut hoping that some will stick. But in this case, very little will stick because our people are not fools. They won't sell their souls for a couple of British money. And if somebody should even do it, then we would defend you to death," Putus continued.
"What you're doing right now for our people Chief is beyond words.

258

You've dedicated your life to these people. You not only talk the talk, but you walk the walk. You don't give us something to do that you're not willing to do yourself; and that is why the people love you so much. We all love you so much. So don't worry about the British Chief. They have no soul. They believe that money can buy everything. They don't care about loyalty, honesty, honor or truth. No sir, they display their arrogance, their overbearing pride and their big egos on their forehead. The British could learn a thing or two about humility and meekness from you Chief," she opined. "Don't let me start talking," she joked.

"I hope not," Nanny laughed and Quao joined in. "Otherwise we'll be here all night and I have to go and fit my wedding dress before it gets dark." That was apparently the signal for Quao to leave.

As Putus and Nanny walked over to the dressmaker, Nanny inquired about the progress of the wedding.

"Everything is going fine," Putus reassured her. "Don't worry about a thing. I have everything under control. We'll give you a wedding that you'll never forget."

"Ok! Miss Putus my love," Nanny remarked, "I'll leave everything up to you and just enjoy the 'ride on the camel's back.'"

"Good," Putus continued. "Your husband-to-be is doing just that; listen to him for once."

"Putus, can you believe that in five days I will be a married woman?" Nanny asked, flashing a broad smile.

"You sound just like a young teenager with her first boyfriend," Putus laughed.

"I would like it to come quickly and go because I have so much to do right now," Nanny disclosed.

"Take it one day at a time my chile. It's not everyday that someone like you gets married," Putus suggested.

The days leading up to the wedding were quite hectic for the citizens of Nanny Town. There were so many last minute things to be done. Everyone was happy for the Chief. She was always giving of herself and now they would get an opportunity to show their gratitude.

The night before the wedding, Nanny rushed around doing last minute preparations with Putus when, to her surprise, in walked Cudjoe with his fiancé, and Accompong and Gylziia.

Nanny screamed with delight when she saw them, then ran into Cudjoe's arms.

"I'm so happy that you could make it!" she exclaimed.

"I wouldn't miss it for the world," he replied, smiling from ear to ear.

"Then who is this beautiful young lady?" Nanny asked Cudjoe with a mischievous grin. He smiled a sheepish smile as he told Nanny that her name was Tyruphia and he intended to marry her someday.

Nanny extended her hand and the young lady held it firmly.

"Please to meet you Tyruphia," Nanny greeted her warmly.

"Please to finally meet you Chief Nanny," she stammered.

"Call me Nanny; Chief is when I'm on the job, now I'm plain Nanny."

"Yes Miss Nanny ma'm," she said between girlish giggles.

"Make yourself at home," Nanny insisted. Then she rushed over to Accompong and hugged him. "I'm so happy that you've made it!" she said with glee.

"Not even the mighty British Army could keep me away," he said with a haughty laugh. Everyone laughed. Then, turning to Gylziia, she hugged her tightly and they both began to cry.

"Why are you two ladies crying?" Accompong demanded.

"When I saw Nanny, all the sadness and pain that we went through together came rushing back like a flood, and I just couldn't hold it in," Gylziia revealed, blowing her nose with a rag and wiping her eyes.

"You look good my chile," Nanny remarked.

"Thanks, you look good yourself," Gylziia affirmed with a shy smile.

Turning to Accompong and then back at Gylziia, Nanny added;

"It looks like you're taking good care of my brother chile. He looks like he has even put on some weight."

Then turning to everyone she declared, "I'm so happy tonight," wiping back tears. "You guys have granted me my final wish. I wondered if you would make it with the siege on."

"Sis, do you think that the British soldiers make a difference to our operation? I don't know about up here, but down in the west it is business as usual," Cudjoe remarked with pride.

"But let's not talk business tonight; we have plenty of time for that. Let us talk about something more pleasant; after all it is our big sister's special day tomorrow. And speaking of special day, where is the lucky man who captured my sister's heart?" Cudjoe asked jokingly.

"Oh Adou? He just left here a while ago to run some last minute errands. He should be back any time now," Nanny explained.

"I heard that he is a good cook and that was the key," Accompong teased lovingly.

Nanny just smiled like a teenager in love.

"Sis, you look so happy and contented," Accompong observed. "This guy has really made an impression on you."

Just then Adou walked in with a broad smile on his face.

"So you are the gentleman who stole my sister's heart?" Cudjoe asked jokingly.

"Guilty as charged," Adou replied casually. "And I'll be chained to her for the rest of my life," he said, followed by a hearty laugh.

Everyone joined in and for a while the room was filled with laughter and hugs as everyone got acquainted. The socializing continued late into the night over rum from the plantation and strong coffee.

"We had better get some shut eye now so that we can stay awake tomorrow during the ceremony," Cudjoe suggested, cradling his umpteenth glass of rum.

"True, true bro," Quao echoed in a slurring voice as he hugged his big brother. "Tomorrow we will continue this party, after we've married off our one sister."

Daybreak came too soon for some people. But for the majority of people in the town, they were up before the rooster crowed; busy with preparations. This would be the biggest and most lavish wedding that Nanny Town had ever had. Putus and her crew were pulling out all the stops. Nothing was overlooked. The town was beautifully decorated with items gathered from the raids, along with local decorations. All the tree trunks and rocks around the huts were painted white and the gardens and lawns were neatly manicured. The smell of food was tantalizing. The jerk pork simmered while the plantains, roast yams, roast and boil corn, and boiled bananas were all in various stages of preparation. In another corner, a group of ladies skillfully carved water melons into artistic designs.

Unlike Nanny and the folks the night before, Putus, knowing the magnitude of work ahead, had excused herself early and retired to bed. Now she was in overdrive, moving everything along in a timely fashion.

The wedding was a glamorous affair, the likes of which Nanny Town had never seen before. The whole town came out all beautifully dressed for the occasion. The women wore their brightly colored dresses matched only by their even more elegantly designed hats. The little girls with bows in their hair wore colorful mini-sized dresses, resembling little versions of their mothers. The excitement reached fever pitch as the appointed time drew near. For many people this was the first wedding that they would actually be a part of. Many of them had seen weddings taking place at the Great House with all the pomp and glamour; but they could only watch from afar and wish that they could have been a part of it. But now the shoe was on the other foot and they were now all invited to the ball. During the ceremony, many of the old people wept.

"Look what I've lived to see?" one old lady cried, "A wedding like this at Nanny Town."

"Same so, same so," another woman in a brightly colored red dress with matching red and white hat concurred.

"This just goes to show that we can do anything we set our minds to, in spite of the British."

"British! Who is that?" another woman joked. "Today they should be the furthest thing from our minds. We're here to celebrate with one of the greatest leaders this world doesn't even know about yet; but they will. People will remember Chief for the way she rid this country of those ruthless British."

"Sheee!" another woman interrupted. "The wedding is about to start."

Chapter 32

The day after the wedding Putus organized a community picnic down by the river. The newlyweds, with all her brothers and their spouses arrived to find scores of children and their parents playing in the water.

Over on the east side, the smoke rose doggedly into the sky as several cooks skillfully jerked wild boar meat. The old folks all sat nearby on smooth rocks chatting, laughing and swapping old time stories while some young people sat and listened with interest.

"This is the life Sis," Accompong declared after a brief swim. "I can't remember the last time I had so much fun. We need to come back here more often to relax."

"I have begged him all the time to let us come back but he always said that he was busy," Gylziia complained.

"Well, from now on I'm going to listen to my woman," Accompong laughed. "She is the brains in the family."

"That's my girl!" Putus affirmed.

As the sun slowly disappeared below the horizon, everyone packed up and headed for home. It was an enjoyable day at the river.

At home, Nanny and Adou relaxed with her brothers and their spouses over freshly brewed coffee.

"Cudjoe you look very fit and muscular," Nanny complemented. "Are you doing a lot of training down in the west?"

"Thanks, but no," Cudjoe laughed. "Although lately we've been quite busy trying to avoid the oppressors. But look at Quao, he is so broad and muscular," he remarked, trying to take the focus off himself. "I remember when he was this scrawny little kid, but look at him now, all buff."

"Thanks bro," Quao said, smiling. "I always looked up to you and Accompong when I was growing up. I always wanted to look like you guys and to hear you say that means the world to me."

"Yes Quao, I'm so proud of you," Cudjoe said. "I heard that you've been creating major problems for the British up here. I hope they realize that you're the face of the new generation of fighters. I know that with young leaders like you out there our future is secure because you will continue the struggle until we have freedom throughout the entire island."

"When did your mouth get so sweet bro?" Accompong joked.

"I tell you Accompong, as you get older you have to do more talking to motivate the young people them to continue the fight."

"So Cudjoe, how are you and your people in the west living under the British siege?" Nanny asked.

"The situation is getting serious Sis," Cudjoe commented. "My people are doing fine, but many people in the surrounding villages are near starvation. With the soldiers patrolling the hills and preventing any movement between villages, the people are trapped inside their villages with little or no food. The British hope that by starving the people, they will choose to return to the plantation without them firing a single shot."

"So how are you managing personally?" Nanny asked.

"Well, we plant a little plantain, bananas and yams and hunt wild hogs and pigeons in the hills. We just have enough for ourselves and although we would like to help other people, unlike you guys, we just can't."

"What about you Accompong?" Nanny asked.

"About the same as Cudjoe; we're just getting by," Accompong replied.

"Something has got to give though," Cudjoe said disgustedly. "Things can't continue like this for much longer or many people will starve; because no one, I mean no one is going back to the plantation; they would rather die."

For the next hour Cudjoe and Accompong recalled the many clashes that they had with the British.

"We let the British rule the day, but when night comes, we take back control, "Cudjoe emphasized. "The soldiers know that and so they never patrol at nights because they know what would happen. We've also set some ingenious traps for them and had lots of fun," he joked. "The best part of all this is the look on their faces when they realize that they've been outwitted by a bunch of runaway slaves," he laughed until tears came to his eyes.

"Imagine this, the greatest army on earth, outfoxed by a group of African slaves, ah! Ah! Ah!" he laughed, as he wiped his eyes. "Sometimes the trap was used just to take away their weapons and intimidate them, but sometimes it was to inflict as much pain and suffering as we can on them; especially after they've slaughtered a village. We know that we're better fighters in the bush, so all the new troops and the new weapons that they're bringing down here from Britain will still not make them win this war. No way! I even noticed that they've brought down professional trackers from far away to find us, but they're still no match for us. We often find them and just tie them up and leave them in the bush, because we don't have any fight with them. Our fight is with our oppressors, the British," he emphasized.

"The other thing that these British have to fight against beside us is the mosquitoes. Yes, the mosquitoes are giving them everything that they're looking for," Accompong added, with a chuckle. "So, they have their work cut out for them down there in the west. They have to deal with us on a big scale and then they have to deal with the mosquitoes on an even bigger scale," he laughed.

"So what do you boys think will happen?" Quao asked innocently.

"Well, it depends on who has the most to lose," Cudjoe replied. "Right now we have the most to lose, because what alternative do we have if we give up?" he asked harshly, to everyone's surprise. "Back to the plantation and the whips of Bakra. And who wants that? No one who has ever tasted freedom. So who has to blink first?" he asked the group.

"The British!" Nanny and everyone shouted in unison.

"I hope you all remember that when the time comes," Cudjoe said, with a straight face.

The coffee pot boiled on the fire long into the night as the conversation continued, with no sign of sleep.

The time went by quickly for Cudjoe and everyone from the west. Soon it was time for them to depart.

"Sis, it is always so hard to leave," Cudjoe said as he hugged Nanny.

"I know what you mean. I feel the same way brother," Nanny said, with tears welling up in her eyes.

"You must come down to the west and visit us one day Sis; promise?" he pleaded.

"I promise," she said between tears.

The next day Nanny was back at work meeting with Quao, Putus and her other leaders and getting an update on what had happened while she was away.

"We have to do more for the people out in the villages," Nanny suggested.

"That's all well and good Chief; but our storehouses are going down, so we have to be careful how we give out the food," Putus countered.

"Sounds reasonable Putus," Nanny agreed. "Let's do an inventory of all our storehouses; both our temporary ones outside the town as well as our permanent ones here, so that we can make a more informed decision," she suggested. "I would love to have this information as soon as possible Putus. In the meanwhile, we will halt all donations until we know how much foodstuff we actually have."

"Yes Chief, we agree," Quao and the others concurred.

Suddenly a series of big explosions were heard coming from outside the town.

"Chief! Chief! We're under attack by the British," a guard rushed into the room shouting.

"How did they find us?" Quao asked.

"We'll deal with that later," Nanny responded. "For now, let's find out what's going on."

When Nanny and Quao looked down the mountain with their telescopes their hearts sank. Approaching the entrance was a large battalion of heavily armed British soldiers attempting to enter the town. Some bombard the entrance with heavy artillery, while others searched desperately for other ways to enter the town.

"So they've found us," Nanny said calmly. "We will find out who betrayed us after we've dealt with these soldiers," she said defiantly.

"Putus, order the abeng players to blow like they've never blown before. Tell them not to stop until I tell them to," she called after her.

"Quao, get everyone armed and in their position as we practiced, and wait for my orders. The British will surely die here today if they try to walk across that narrow ridge!" she said between clenched teeth.

"Tell the snipers to pick them off one by one if they try to come over that ridge."

"Yes Chief," Quao replied, trying very hard to contain his anxiety.

For the next few hours the battle raged on with both sides discharging their weapons with intensity. Explosions mixed with thick white smoke sounded throughout the valley, disturbing the peace and tranquility of the mountain. Dead and wounded soldiers lay all around. Cries of pain and persistent groaning could be heard echoing throughout the valley below. Eventually the British, after suffering heavy causalities, stopped shelling and began withdrawing their troops. As the soldiers withdrew, the people rejoiced. Quao ordered his men to remain alert while they assessed the damage.

Nanny was very concerned. "We have a traitor in our midst and we have to find that person quickly," she told the emergency meeting.

"What could've caused someone to betray us like this?" Putus wondered.

"We have to find that person before they do more damage," Nanny stressed.

"But where do we start?" Quao inquired.

"Putus leave no stone unturned in your investigation," Nanny instructed. "Everybody is a suspect until they're cleared. In the meantime, I will call a meeting for tomorrow and let the people know what is going on and ask for their help in finding the traitor. Any questions?" When no one responded she adjourned the meeting.

As everyone left the meeting Nanny sat alone with her thoughts.

The following morning everyone turned out for the meeting to hear what was happening.

"Ladies and gentlemen thank you for coming," Nanny began. "We have a serious problem here. The attack yesterday by the British was not an accident. There is no easy way to say this; but we have a traitor, a spy living amongst us."

"Nooooo!" the people cried out in a chorus of disapproval.

"Are you sure?" one woman shouted.

"How do you know that?" a man shouted.

"I trust Chief Nanny with my life and if she says so, then I believe her," a little woman stood up and declared.

"Shhh!" another woman begged. "Let us hear what Chief Nanny has to say."

"Thank you," Nanny continued. "We know that the spy is living here; maybe he or she is even here right now. But let me tell that person something; we will not stop until we find you. If it means that we have to call upon our ancestors to tell us who you are, we will! And anyone who knows something, anything, even the smallest detail, please come forward and let us know," she implored. "The longer this person is out there the more danger we will be in; so please help us to find this person. And that person, whoever you are; give yourself up now. Don't think only about yourself; think about the future of this town. Think about the future of the Maroons," Nanny begged.

"Ladies and gentlemen of Nanny Town, we've come a long way and we can't stop now, but we won't move forward if a spy is amongst us. We have to root out this traitor as soon as possible."

As the people left the meeting, Nanny met them at the door and shook their hands and thanked them for coming. She also wanted to look each person directly in the eye to get a response.

"I'm so sorry Chief," one lady said. "But we will find the person who did it," she promised.

"It must be one of those new ones who just came," another woman suggested.

"We mustn't jump to conclusions without knowing the facts," Nanny cautioned. "Let's hold all judgments."

After everyone left, Nanny met with Putus and Quao to share information.

"Did any of you notice anyone suspicious?" Putus asked

"No, as a matter of fact, everyone looked genuinely concerned," Nanny answered.

"What about you, anybody?"

"No, I didn't notice anybody looking suspicious either," Putus answered.

"What about you Quao, anyone looked suspicious?"

Quao slowly shook his head. "No, everybody seemed fine to me."

"Answer me this question you two; who and who were missing from the meeting?" Nanny asked. "Maybe, just maybe, the spy is in this group. Let's make a list of all those who were not here today and investigate every one of them thoroughly."

"Good idea Chief," Putus said.

That night Nanny went to bed early with a heavy heart. Near midnight she was awakened by someone standing at the foot of her bed. Nanny rubbed her eyes briskly then exclaimed, "Mada Kuzo, what are you doing here?"

"Then is this how you greet your family chile?" Nanny's spiritual great-grand mother said, with a smile.

"Sorry Mada Kuzo," Nanny responded.

"My pet, I'm so proud of you; in fact we're all proud of you," Mada Kuzo said.

"We like how you've been taking care of your people, and also helping those people in the other villages. But we see big troubles coming and that is why I'm here."

"What kind of trouble Mada Kuzo?" Nanny asked nervously.

"You know pet, the British. They now know where you live, and they will not stop until they've destroyed this place."

"We're fine Mada Kuzo," Nanny tried to reassure her. "Did you see how we defeated them yesterday?"

"Yes I saw that, but they will keep coming back. Those British people never give up. No sir, they're stubborn like a mule."

"Tell me Mada Kuzo, who betrayed us?" Nanny asked directly.

"If you really want to know, it was a young man by the name of Sambo. He never really wanted to run away from the plantation, but his roommates threatened to kill him if he didn't run away with them. They were afraid that he knew too much about them and would talk, so they forced him to go along with them. I don't know if you remember him, but from the time he got here he never really tried to fit in; he just stayed by himself."

"And how did he find the British to talk to them?" Nanny asked eagerly.

"Easy, he met with them in the market," Mada Kuzo replied.

"How much did they pay him?" Nanny asked.

"He told them that all he wanted as payment was to be returned to the plantation as a head driver."

"So where is he now?" Nanny asked anxiously.

"Where else? Back on the plantation of course," Mada Kuzo answered.

"I will get him when all this is over," Nanny promised.

"Leave the boy alone chile. Your fight is not with him," Mada Kuzo advised. "He is only a fly caught in this giant web of oppression. Slavery is the only thing that he knows and he is blinded to every other way of life. You see chile, even if slavery ended tomorrow, and all the British people disappeared, slavery would still be around. My pet, slavery of the mind is the worst type of slavery. It takes a lot of time and patience to go beyond it. Slavery leaves plenty of scars my chile, and that is where the real work is. People like Sambo should be pitied, not condemned, because they are brainwashed. They see you Maroons as the enemy, always causing trouble for Bakra. As far as they are concerned you Maroons are worthless, good for nothing takers, who are just lazy and don't like to work. They have believed the lies of Bakra; that the duty of Africans is to work hard and serve all white people. So they don't feel any way to betray you, because they believe that they're saving you from becoming worthless."

"So what is the answer Gramma?" Nanny asked meekly.

"The answer is to put an end to this evil system my chile, put an end to it; that's the only way, before you can free the mind."

"Ok Gramma, answer me this question; suppose we did all that, how long would it take to eliminate slavery of the mind?" Nanny asked.

"That will be a tall order my pet, a tall order," she said, shaking her head with sadness in her eyes.

"How do I put this plainly?" she said, searching for the right words to say. "It will take a long, long time; generations to get free from it. Some people will use it as a crutch to justify their lack of drive. Some men will use it as an excuse to have many children with different baby mothers. To some people, Bakra will always be the one holding them back, even when Bakra is long gone. It's like Bakra is around every corner and behind every bush. He can't seem to get Bakra out of his mind. And that's where the main problem lies. We have to find a way to free the mind from the shackles of slavery. Not easy my pet, not easy," she said shaking her head.

Chapter 33

The report on the surprise attack was in. The report listed only a few casualties and some minor injuries. The secret entrance was severely damaged but the British were not able to get far inside the town. The British on the other hand suffered heavy casualties along the ridge and Quao had to bury some bodies that were left behind in the local cemetery.

Nanny and the leadership team spent the entire day analyzing the data.

"Did anyone find the traitor who caused all this?" Nanny asked.

"No Chief," Putus replied. "We have spoken with everyone here and we've still not found out anything yet, but we're working on it."

"Anybody knows a man by the name of Sambo?" Nanny asked.

"Yes I know him," Putus said. "Very quiet, don't talk much, but a hard worker. He lives beside Miss Punsy."

"Yes I know him too," Quao added. "He came to the shooting range a few times to learn to shoot, but he was never really interested in joining."

"What about him Chief?" Putus asked. "Is he the traitor?"

"Yes he is," Nanny replied, nodding her head. "I found that out last night." No one asked her where she got the information, although everyone was dying to find out.

"Where is he now?" Quao asked.

"Come to think of it; I have not seen him around here for some time," Putus said. "But then again, he was so quiet that he could be missing for a while and you wouldn't know."

"So Chief, do you know where he is?" Putus asked.

"Yes, I heard that he went back to the plantation."

"But that doesn't make any sense Chief," Putus remarked. "Why would somebody run away from Bakra's plantation and then turn around and go right back there?"

"True, true," Quao agreed. "That doesn't make sense. I think we have to bring him back here Chief and, and..."

"We're not going after him right now," Nanny said abruptly, cutting off Quao.

"We will get him in time, but what we will not do right now is waste a lot of valuable time and energy trying to find him. Our main focus from now on is on strengthening our security and our surveillance. We will start setting up more booby traps in these parts to trap the British," Nanny informed them. "To win this battle we will have to do things differently. We have to evade them by moving faster and concealing ourselves better. We have to fight them in the small spaces where we have the advantage"

The team worked all day until they came up with a comprehensive plan.

"Good job team, I like it!" Nanny told them.

"When do we start Chief?" Putus asked excitedly.

"Tomorrow we will start," she said, looking over at Quao, who nodded his agreement. "In the meantime we will increase our surveillance."

Early the next morning Nanny woke up before everyone in Nanny town and transformed into a bird and flew off in search of the nearest soldiers' camp. As she soared above the treetops a thick blanket of fog covered the valley making it difficult to identify objects below. She flew around for sometime before finally spotting a camp way below, nestled in a rugged terrain. Nanny quickly flew down and quietly perched on a branch high up in a tree in the centre of the camp.

The camp was a hive of activity. Soldiers hustled about organizing their weapons and equipment in preparation for the day's activities. Nanny wondered where they were going. She quietly flew around until she found the main tent.

The tent was sparsely furnished with two large tables covered with maps, a couple chairs and a few small lamps. Surrounding one of the tables were the Captain and his officers, busy studying a crudely drawn map of the region; unaware that they were being watched. Nanny walked undetectably inside the tent to listen in on their meeting and look at their maps. Clearly marked in bold on the map were the Maroon villages! A nauseous feeling came over her when she noticed that Nanny Town was clearly marked in red.

"That traitor Sambo," she cursed under her breath. But then she remembered what Mada Kuzo had said about people like Sambo and she slowly released her anger.

Looking closer at the map, Nanny identified the location of the camp. Her pulse raced when she realized that Nanny Town was only about a half days trek from the camp. 'But on the other hand, we're only a half days trek from attacking this camp,' she thought to herself. Looking at it from that perspective made her satisfied.

The Captain pointed to a little village on the map over in the north-east, a little more than a half days trek away, and made the announcement that they would attack it that day and return by night fall. He advised everyone to get their teams ready to move out immediately after breakfast in full combat gear. The meeting wrapped up shortly after and the soldiers hurried away to prepare for the day's activity.

Nanny looked around the camp, noting where they stored their weapons, ammunition and food supply. The camp was not very big and they only had a limited number of soldiers. As they prepared to leave, Nanny noted that only a small detachment was left to protect the base. That gave her an idea as she flew home.

On arrival she found Quao by the shooting range with his men practicing. She quickly called him over and told him of her plan.

"I like the plan Chief, and the troops could do with the exercise."

"How quickly could you get the team ready?" Nanny asked.

"Bumble bee unit is the team that is on alert point this week so we can be ready in no time," Quao replied. "But come to think of it Chief; I know of a short cut to that area that would take us there in half the time. It will take us through those underground caves and drop us out pretty close to that camp. We could attack them, then disappear into the caves and return home."

"Do I need to come?" Nanny asked.

"No, we will be fine," Quao responded.

"Well, good luck and take care of the troops and I will see you when you get back," Nanny said as she hugged him.

In a short while Quao and his strike force was on the move to find the soldiers' camp. They kept up a blistering pace to get to the caves without being seen. As they journeyed some distance in the underground caves, they came upon a pristine flowing stream. It looked so inviting that Quao suggested that everyone take a short break. He didn't have to tell them twice. As some drank from the pure chilly stream others filled their water containers before taking a dip. Finally Quao gave the orders to resume the march. The troops made good progress in the cooler surroundings and out of sight of the British.

It was just after noon when they exited the caves and arrived on the outskirts of the soldier's camp. Quao carefully surveyed the entire compound through his telescope and counted the few guards stationed outside. The camp looked quiet and sleepy. He brought his team together and drew a plan in the dirt. He utilized all the information that he had received from Nanny and strategically assigned the troops to different positions within the camp. Quao ordered everyone to wait for his signal.

The attack was swift and went like clockwork. The first group moved quickly into position without been seen. They move up on the guards and quickly snuffed them out without a sound. They looked around and when they were satisfied that the coast was clear they signaled the others to follow. The warriors moved in quickly and searched the camp, going from tent to tent, looking for any remaining soldiers. When none was found, Quao gave the order to search for weapons, ammunition and supplies and to report back as soon as possible. He took a few men with him and went directly to the main tent where they quickly collected all the maps, compasses, telescopes and other supplies and rushed back to the rendezvous point. The other groups all returned with loads of weapons and supplies.

"Is everybody back?" Quao queried.

"Yes Captain," his next in command replied.

"Ok then, Bumble bee unit, set fire to all the tents," he ordered.

"The rest of you pick up everything and let's go!"

In a short while the camp was on fire and Quao and his troops were safely underground, on their way home.

Nanny anxiously awaited the return of Quao and his team. She especially wanted to study the maps to learn more about the settlements that had been identified. She knew that this attack would be a big blow to the British; both in terms of their facilities and the information that they had lost.

Meanwhile, down in the west Cudjoe was busy preparing an ambush for a small detachment of British soldiers from the nearby fort. The plan was to use a decoy to trick them into a surprise attack and seize their weapons and anything else they were carrying. First, Cudjoe and his men watched the path from a distance as the approaching soldiers marched along unaware of the danger. As they drew nearer, Cudjoe gave the signal for a young lad, in hiding across the road, to run directly across their path crying uncontrollably. Cudjoe and his men got ready as they watched the soldiers stop turn to the right and headed in the direction of the boy. The youngster ran just fast enough to lure the soldiers into the trap. Then just as the soldiers caught up to the boy, they suddenly found themselves surrounded by a group of fully armed, camouflaged, guerrilla fighters. The surprised soldiers surrendered without a shot being fired. The warriors quickly relieved them of their weapons, tied them to nearby trees before disappearing back into the hills.

Cudjoe liked using this method of attack because it was usually quick and fruitful, with minimum risks.

Back at home Cudjoe examined the weapons seized.

"Wow, these are new weapons!" Cudjoe's assistant exclaimed, fiddling with the locks. "We need more of these to level the ground with the British," he said, raising a musket in the air.

"I agree my son," Cudjoe said. "I agree."

Chapter 34

Nanny and Quao studied the maps thoroughly. They identified all the villages including Nanny Town that were attacked.

"They plan to attack every village on this map Sis," Quao surmised.

"It seems that way," Nanny replied, trying to find a pattern and eventually be able to predict which village would be hit next.

"I notice that they've attacked the villages in the south, and after they came north and hit us, and then they went out east," Nanny said, studying the map closely.

"I wonder if attacking us was just something that came up quickly when they got the information from that worthless man Sambo, or they're planning to attack the villages in our region."

"That is something to think about brother, but what I would really like to know is where they're planning to hit next," Nanny said, scratching her head. "Any troop movements reported in this area over the last few days?" Nanny asked, pointing on the map.

"None reported," Quao replied.

"Well, we have to be on alert for these attacks from now on," Nanny said, looking obviously concerned. "Get the lookouts to report on any troop movements in the area, regardless of the size."

Early Sunday morning, just as the sun was coming up, Nanny stood on the edge of the cliff enjoying her morning coffee when suddenly she heard the sharp, quick sounds of alarm from the abeng.

'This could mean only one thing,' she thought. 'Soldiers on the move.' She listened carefully to the message, "Enemy on the move north! Repeat, enemy on the move north! Many soldiers! Beware!"

Nanny thought for a moment then decided to fly out over the area to see for herself. As she flew down into the valley and whisked above the tree tops she could see smoke rising stubbornly in the air around huts in the

277

distance. The air was fresh and clean, a far cry from the muck down on the plains. But this was certainly not the time to admire the scenery; there was work to be done. From the corner of her eye, way down in the valley, she saw what she was looking for; a large contingent of soldiers in full battle dress, on the march in the direction of Nanny Town. Whether they were on their way to attack the town, Nanny could not tell. She estimated that at the rate they were travelling, they would reach Nanny Town by mid day. So that gave her troops only a few hours to prepare. She immediately turned around and quickly headed for home.

In the meantime Quao, who had been awakened by the abeng, went in search of Nanny but could not find her. Adou, his brother-in law, told him that she had gone for an early morning walk; something that she does every morning. He went by Putus' house but she was not there either. At the same time the abeng messages were getting louder and more frequent. Quao quickly mobilized his troops and placed the whole town on alert, while waiting for Nanny to appear. Then he smiled to himself.

"I bet that she heard the messages and went out there to investigate." He did not have to wait long for the answer as a cheerful voice behind him said, "Miss me?" He turned around to see his sister walking towards him smiling.

"A little, but I could manage."

"I know you could," she agreed. "Come let me show you on the map where they are," Nanny urged.

As they viewed the maps Nanny pointed out where she had last seen them.

"They could be heading here!" Quao said, pointing to Nanny Town on the map. "If they're coming here then we have to stop them somewhere in this area," he continued, tapping his finger on the map.

"I agree," Nanny said. "That is an ideal spot. Get your troops together and let's move out as soon as possible."

"Ok Sis, meet you at the gate," Quao said, dashing off to roundup his troops.

Within the hour, Nanny and her warriors arrived at the spot and quickly positioned themselves to await the enemy. To set the trap, Nanny had some of her troops covered over with leaves and branches while others in their camouflage outfits stood firm like trees, to confuse the enemy. Quao hid trip wires under piles of leaves to kill or maim the enemy. Everything was in place and all the troops were ready for battle.

The British made good progress towards their destination. Soon they were in view, coming up over the hill. Nanny and her warriors were concealed so well that there was no inkling that trouble was ahead.

The battle began with loud explosions as the gunners blasted the surprised soldiers. Then they were hit with the next wave of troops hidden beneath the leaves and branches. Although they were surrounded and outmaneuvered, the soldiers regrouped somewhat and mounted a valiant but weak counterattack. Those trying to find cover were killed when they stepped on the trip wires hidden under the leaves.

Nanny watched the battle crouched alongside Quao. Bullets flew all around as fierce hand-to-hand combat took place. The warriors fought daringly, sustaining the pressure and eventually causing the soldiers retreated.

Suddenly, Nanny saw a soldier aiming his musket directly at a young warrior who was reloading his musket. In a flash, she darted over and stood in front of the lad as the soldier fired. She moved her hands with lightning speed catching the bullet. The soldier's eyes popped wide open in disbelief. He looked as if he had seen a ghost when Nanny calmly showed him the bullet. He checked his musket then looked back at Nanny as if in disbelief. The young warrior turned, quickly leveled his musket and shot the soldier in the heart.

"Thanks Chief," the young warrior said almost breathless, and then dashed off to help his other buddies.

At the end of the battle, the warriors examined the bodies on the ground to make sure that they were dead. Finally they picked up all the weapons and ammunition that were left behind and headed for home.

"How did you do that back there?" Quao asked Nanny on the way home.

"Do what?" Nanny asked, acting innocently.

"That thing you did back there to save the young man's life," he insisted. "How did you do it?"

"It was nothing," Nanny said, trying to dismiss the whole matter. "Did you know that many of our people back in Africa had that skill long, long time ago, and would do it much better than me? The white people think that it is Obeah, but we don't make them any wiser."

"I didn't know that," Quao admitted.

"Yes brother, there are many things that you don't know about the Motherland," she said in jest.

"Sis, the white people think so differently from us, why is that?" he asked.

"That's a difficult question Quao. The Great One in the sky said that no one is better than the other; everybody is equal, but the white people ignore that and do things their way and that is why we're having all this cruelty."

"Then Sis, do you believe that things will change for the better?" Quao asked.

"Well, from I was a little girl, I have been hearing that the Great One in the sky will be coming back to rule everybody; and then everything will be better."

"I hope that he comes soon because we're getting tired of this fighting and the killing," Quao said.

"Me too," Nanny concurred.

"I'm so glad that you came today," Quao said, flashing a quick smile. "The troops love when you come too. You've proven to them that you won't tell them to do something that you're not prepared to do yourself. They now know that you would even take a bullet for anyone of them." They both laughed as they headed for home.

Chapter 35

The citizens of Nanny Town were in a festive mood. The annual celebration of the founding of the town was only a day away and everyone remained busy cleaning their houses and gathering food supplies in preparation for the huge feast.

The celebration was initiated by Nanny to remind the people of where they were coming from and keeping the African culture and traditions alive.

The following morning, the festivities kicked off with a Thanksgiving ceremony followed by a tree planting ceremony in which all the citizens gathered around while Nanny planted a tree in commemoration of freedom and remembering those slaves who were still suffering on the plantation. For the rest of the day the people enjoyed telling tribal stories, singing tribal songs, face painting and playing African games. The young men and women played a variety of games that tested their strength, agility and marksmanship. Down by the river youths competed in numerous water sports that tested their skills and endurance. As the sun slowly disappeared beneath the horizon everyone gathered in the town square for the big feast followed by singing and dancing to the pulsating beat of the African drums. This went on until late into the night.

Early the next morning, Nanny and the entire town were suddenly awakened by the frightening blasts of abeng horns; warning of an impending attack by the British. Nanny and Adou jumped out of bed in a flash to answer a loud knock on the door. As Adou opened the door, Quao rushed in.

"Morning Adou, morning Chief!" Quao greeted them.

"Morning Quao!" they returned the greeting.

"Chief, the British are coming to attack us!" Quao blurted out. "According to our lookouts, a lot of soldiers with heavy artillery are heading this way from three different directions."

"How much time do we have?" Nanny asked calmly.

"About two hours," Quao said excitedly. "I've already put all the troops on high alert."

"That's good my brother," Nanny said. "If they're coming from three directions, that mean that they are dispatching soldiers from their main forts as reinforcements," Nanny surmised. "We can't take them on like we usually do on the outskirt of the town, we have to hunker down here and defend the town. It looks like we're in for a great battle," she said calmly, with laser like focus in her eyes. "We have to shoot to kill anybody who tries to come across that ridge. Every bullet must count my brother, every bullet," she instructed. "Let's go outside and meet the troops and the folks."

Outside it was all business. The entire town was mobilized for battle. The troops rapidly prepared for combat. Some reinforced their posts while others moved weapons around into striking positions.

In a short while, all the town folks gathered in the square to learn what was happening. Nanny addressed them for a short while, telling them about the coming danger and reassuring them that the town was well secured and could survive the assault. She reminded them that every able bodied person must take up arms to defend the town. She instructed them on where to pick up their weapons and also where to position themselves to defend the town.

Nanny finally went over to address the troops, all the while praying in her mind to find the right words to say to these young men and women. She looked out at them with their war painted faces holding their muskets and sharpened machetes and felt proud of them. Her mind flashed back to the early beginnings of Nanny Town when they were just building the army. And look at them now; highly skilled and confident. Her heart was full and bubbling over with pride.

"Ladies and gentlemen, today is a special day for all of us," she began, in a very calm manner.

"Today we will be tested as we've never ever been tested before. Today, we call upon our Massa God, in whom we put our hopes, and the power and wisdom of our great ancestors to protect us and give us the strength to win this battle. Today, we call upon all the training that you've received to defend this town and defend our freedom. Today, we will show the British just what we're made of," she said, with a steadfast defiance in her eyes. "Today ladies and gentlemen, we want you to remain focused on the job at hand, seeing the white of their eyes and making every bullet count. This battle, ladies and gentlemen, could very much change the relationship between us and the British forever. Today is your day to make history. This battle will be talked about for generations to come and your fight for freedom will never be forgotten. May Massa God watch over us all and keep us safe to fight another day. Dismissed."

The British began the onslaught with heavy shelling. The nonstop pounding continued all day long. With no answer for the heavy artillery, Nanny and her troops hunkered down and waited for the ground assault. The cannons struck some houses in the town, causing the people to scurry away in a panic looking for somewhere safe.

All throughout the day the cannons blasted the town. Nanny became very worried for her people.

'How long can this go on?' she contemplated. 'What are we dealing with out there? It looks like they have come to wipe us off the face of the earth; but I will never give them that satisfaction,' she clenched her teeth and muttered to herself defiantly. 'I know what I'll do.'

"Quao I'll soon be back, take over until I return. I have something to look into." And with that she was gone.

Nanny flew high above the trees, taking a bird's-eye view of the entire landscape. Suddenly an unpleasant feeling came over her at the sight below. The British were amassing in great numbers from three different directions with heavy artillery and battering rams.

'It looks like the great white devil means business today,' she joked to herself.

'I think that we've finally awakened the sleeping giant and he's not very happy,' she smiled.

'Wait, what's happening on that side?' she pondered, looking over to her right. 'It looks like they're setting up camp here. They're here to stay!' she exclaimed in disbelief.

'Unfortunately, this is one battle that we will not be able to win,' she said regrettably. 'We have to retreat from Nanny Town tonight before they launch their all out assault in the morning; because nobody can stop all these soldiers with their heavy artillery. The British soldiers have won this round,' she acknowledged, shaking her head in disappointment.

"We will live to fight them another day," she promised herself.

As she travelled home she mulled over where they would go. She remembered when looking at the map the vast expanse of virgin territory to the north east. She made a note to take another look at the maps with Quao when she returned.

On arrival, Nanny called Quao and Putus to a meeting and told them what she had seen.

"I can't believe that we have to leave this beautiful place," Putus cried.

"Me neither, but we have no other choice. By morning this whole place will be overrun with so many soldiers that your head would pain you," Nanny maintained.

"But what about all those old people; they can't walk!" Putus remarked.

"We will deal with them when the time comes," Nanny reassured her.

"The troops will be disappointed," Quao suggested. "They really wanted to take on the British."

"I hear what you're saying brother, but there is an old African saying that, 'young bird don't know storm.'"

"What does that mean?" Quao inquired.

"It means that they don't see what we've seen or know what we know, so don't worry about that right now. There will be many more opportunities to fight the British; trust me on that one," she said defiantly.

Pointing to the map she said, "If we travel North East we wouldn't have any forts or soldiers to contend with. Then all we have to do is lie low for awhile and regroup."

"How much are we allowed to carry Chief?" Putus inquired.

"Tell the people to bring only what they need and only what they can personally carry. We don't want to be weighted down with unnecessary loads on the trail. By morning we need to be very, very far away; so we have to make good time when we leave here."

"Again Chief, what are we going to do with the old people them?" Putus insisted.

"Yes I heard you Putus. Don't worry, I will deal with that," Nanny repeated.

"So what's the plan?" Putus asked seemingly impatient.

"I'll tell you about it when I get back," Nanny answered, trying to get everyone refocused. "Ok, let's spread out and round up the people; we have to be out of here within the hour. In the meantime, I'll go over to the clinic and break the news to the old folks," Nanny promised, as she rushed out the door.

At the clinic Nanny gathered everyone together in the centre of the room.

"Folks, thank you for seeing me. I have some good news and some bad news. Let me start with the good news. The good news is that we will get through all this. The bad news is that we have to make some tough choices. The British soldiers are building up in great numbers just outside the town, waiting to invade us and destroy this place. We have to get as far away from here as possible by tomorrow morning because that is when they're going to launch their attack."

"So what are you saying Chief?" a little old lady asked, cutting off Nanny's little speech.
"Are you saying that if you take us along that we would hold you back?" Nanny looked down to the floor, not wishing to make eye contact.

"Don't worry Chief," another woman said, "We understand. You and the young people them should go and leave us. What can they do but take us back to the plantation; and at the plantation we're too old to do much work. I think we will be fine Chief; you take the others and get as far away from here as possible."

"We all agree Chief," everyone said.
"You and the young people them will be able to come back and rebuild Nanny Town one day," another woman said.

"Thank you all for your courage and kind hearts," Nanny said as she hugged and kissed and cried with them.

"Continue to make us proud Chief. I don't think that we could've asked for a better leader," a tall, slim, elderly woman remarked.

Then a short stout lady came over and took a pouch out of her pocket and carefully placed it into Nanny's hand.

"Don't open it now Chief, but you might need it someday on your journey," she said with a motherly smile.

Nanny gingerly placed the pouch into her pocket without taking a peek. She made a mental note to look at it later. Before she left, Nanny and the old people hugged and kissed and wept openly, because they knew that this was the last time that they would be seeing each other again.

"Walk good Chief! Walk good!" they called out.

"You walk good too!" Nanny said, between tears. "Walk good." And before long she was off again to meet up with Putus and Quao.

The shelling suddenly stopped leaving an uneasy calm.

"Do you think that they will start the ground assault now, seeing that it is so dark?" Putus asked.

"I doubt it Putus," Nanny replied confidently. "I know that the British are brave and have lots of soldiers and weapons, but they're not stupid. They know full well that they only rule the day, but we rule the night. So I wouldn't worry about them coming tonight."

As they continued talking Quao came over to report that everyone was packed and ready to leave.

"Do you wish to say anything to them before we leave, Chief?"

"Of course my brother," Nanny said walking over to the group, with Putus and Adou following behind with their loads.

"My fellow citizens of Nanny Town, the time has come for us to abandon our homes and start over. We did good here, didn't we? And we gave the British them 'a run for their money,'" she smiled uneasily. "I know how hard it must be for all of you, but we have no other option. Change is never easy and freedom is not free. Nobody said that this journey would be easy. Folks, we have a few hours head start on the British and we have to make good use of it. I know that you're tempted to carry a lot of things but try not to 'bite off more than you can chew.' In other words, just bring as much as you can carry. I know that it means a lot to you; but remember, it is just stuff which can be replaced. Finally ladies and gentlemen, I can't leave here this evening without saying a big thank you to our seniors. They're making a great sacrifice for all of us."

Then addressing the seniors she said, "We would like to tell you how grateful we're for what you're doing and that we will never forget you. People like Mada Fufu, Miss Bhuttie, Mada Elkim, Miss Gerbie, Mass Zeik, and all you other men and women, too numerous to mention. You're our heroes and we will make sure that when this story is told, people will not forget your sacrifice. So ladies and gentlemen, get in your last hugs and kisses before we hit the trail."

Part Three

New Beginning

Chapter 36

The Maroons walked non-stop throughout the night; their bodies gleaming in the early morning light. Nanny kept pushing them to keep up the pace, promising them that well earned rest when the Sun came up; and by then they would be a safe distance away. The people walked in silence, keeping their ears alert, just listening for those magical words from Nanny.

As the Sun came up over the horizon, Nanny pointed back to the heavy black smoke rising far below. No one said a word. They all knew what that meant. A few sniffling sounds and moaning came from the back of the pack as people thought about those who were left behind.

"We've got to keep moving ladies and gentlemen; we're not yet out of danger! Please keep going; we only have a little more to go," Nanny pleaded.

By mid morning the Sun took charge of the day, burning away the stubborn overnight fog. Everyone became excited, anxiously awaiting the word.

They didn't have to wait long. As they came up to a gentle flowing stream, Quao sounded the abeng, signaling that the time had arrived. The people shouted with glee, dropping their loads and dashing towards the water. They splashed around laughing and singing and hugging each other for some time.

However not everyone was happy; some folks just sat by themselves meditating and reflecting on the folks left behind.

The trek resumed after everyone was refreshed, filled their water containers and had a bite to eat.

The last leg of the journey into the Rio Grande mountain range was very relaxed, with everyone in a cheerful mood and thoughts of the British only a distant memory.

The Sun was slowly going down when Nanny and her people arrived at their final destination. The land was cleared of trees as if it was carved out of the forest.

"Well here we are ladies and gentlemen, our new home," Nanny said excitedly.

"Look around and get familiar with the area. Tonight we need to find a place to rest until tomorrow when we will start building this community, just like Nanny Town."

Everyone dropped their bundles and began searching the surrounding area. Suddenly a small voice called out from inside a cave, "Chief! Chief! Over here! We have enough room inside here for everybody," he shouted excitedly.

He was right. The cave, although it had a narrow entrance, opened up into a deep cavern capable of holding many people. The walls had numerous crude drawings from the roof to the floor. Nanny made a mental note to study them further in the coming days. The floor was littered with garbage and bits and pieces of items.

"It looks like a lot of people used to live here and they left in a hurry," Putus observed.

"We have to clean up this place if we're going to live in here until our houses are built."

"I agree, let's do a little cleaning now," Nanny said, picking up the garbage and putting them outside the cave.

All of a sudden the inside of the cave became a bevy of activity as men and women cleaned up the area and marked out their spots for the night. After awhile, everyone settled in; but hardly anyone was interested in socializing after such a long day, instead most preferred to bed down for the night.

For the next few days everyone worked hard to find food and building materials to start their new homes. The men went out day after day hunting for wild hogs and any other animals in the forests, but they came back empty handed most times. On their lucky days they returned with only a couple pigeons, but hardly any wild hogs.

"I can't believe this," one frustrated hunter said, on his way back from hunting all day, "No wild hogs! It's like this place is cursed. I wonder why Chief brought us to this wicked place," he lamented. "It would've been better if we had stayed in Nanny Town and surrendered to the British. At least we would've gotten some good food to eat. Look, the place is so wicked that hardly any fruit trees are around here, and the ones that are here are not bearing one damn thing."
The other men listened to the man's rant all the way home with no one saying a word, because, although some of what he was saying was true, they realized that he was more interested in complaining rather than trying to find a solution.

"This area is not very fruitful Sis," Quao said to Nanny on the sixth day. "I wonder if that is the reason why nobody settled here. But look how nice the place is Sis! It is beautiful, just beautiful!"

"I agree with you brother," Nanny said. "I love it too, but I also spent an entire day with Putus searching the forest for herbs, but we didn't find much in there either."

"Then what are we going to do Sis?" Quao asked. "The people are getting restless and depressed. They really miss Nanny Town and all the food that was there."

"But Nanny Town is dead!" Nanny insisted.
"We have to stop thinking about that place. We have to move on. It was great while it lasted but now we're living here and we have to get used to it."

"I know what you mean," Putus said, coming by and joining the conversation. "The people are saying that this place is cursed."

"What else are they saying?" Nanny asked.

"They say that the land is barren; the fruit trees produce no fruits and if they stay here too long they will all die of starvation. So what're we going to do Chief? I'm worried. And you know that I've never been worried from the day that we left the plantation."

"Me too," Quao agreed. "This place is a real challenge Sis, and the people are not wrong."

"I've heard the murmuring too," Nanny said. "And I'm working hard to try and solve the problem. I truly believe deep down in my stomach that this is a good place to live, but if we can't feed ourselves here, then we have to find another site."

That night Nanny was visited by Mada Kuzo, her spiritual great-grandmother, in her sleep.

"Hello my chile!" she greeted Nanny, smiling from ear to ear.

"Mada Kuzo! Mada Kuzo! You're here! I knew you would come! I just knew you would come! You've never, ever let me down!" Nanny exclaimed, like a little girl who had not seen her great-grandmother for a while.

"I see you've been having some problems with your people my chile and you might have a mutiny on your hands," she chuckled. "Don't give in my chile, you're doing the right thing," she said, swiftly switching to a straight face. "Never give up the fight; remember freedom is not free."
Nanny smiled when she heard those words because she remembered telling her folks that same thing a few days earlier.

"Because of the work that people like you, Cudjoe, Accompong and others are doing, the British are now realizing that it is not business as usual. They believed that they would just come down here to the island, use up all this free labor, make a lot of money and take it back to England and live happily ever after with no care about we Africans. But they were not aware of the power of the human spirit. Not because you don't understand somebody, it doesn't mean that they're stupid! That is what they're coming to realize; that African people are not stupid. They know what they want and they won't stop until they get it."

"Mada Kuzo I need to feed my people!" Nanny blurted out, cutting her off. "The land is barren Mada Kuzo! So what should I do?" she begged.

"Calm down my pet," Mada Kuzo said kindly. "There is always a solution to every problem; you just have to open your mind. Knowledge is all around us; you only have to tune in to it. Take this place for example my pet, it has a bunch of potential, maybe not like Nanny Town, yet a lot of things can be accomplished here; if you only open your mind."
Nanny wasn't sure what Mada Kuzo was getting at.

"What do you mean, Mada Kuzo?" she asked anxiously.

"My chile, you have with you the answer to your problem," Mada Kuzo suggested.

"How is that possible Mada Kuzo?" Nanny asked, her interest now at its maximum.

"Reach inside your pocket my pet and show us what you have there." Nanny obediently reached inside her pocket and felt a small pouch which she took out and showed to Mada Kuzo.

"Open it my pet and let's see what is in there," she instructed. Nanny gingerly reached inside the pouch, took out a handful of seeds and showed it to Mada Kuzo.

"Do you know those seeds chile?" Mada Kuzo asked.

"Yes Mada Kuzo, they are pumpkin seeds. I love pumpkins," she added.

"Well my pet, I'm glad that you like it. I want you to quickly plant out all of these seeds on the hillside and I can guarantee that you and your people will never be hungry again. In the meantime, tell your people to be patient. Take care of the pumpkins my chile, and the pumpkins will take care of you." And with that she was gone.

"Mada Kuzo! Mada Kuzo!" Nanny shouted.

"Nanny! Nanny! Wake up," Adou, her husband shook her awake.

"What! What!" Nanny jumped up.

"You were talking in your sleep. Who is Mada Kuzo?" he asked.

"Long story," she said, trying to hide her embarrassment and dismissing the whole thing. Then suddenly she remembered the dream and quickly dug into her pocket and felt the pouch. She took it out of her pocket, carefully untied the string, reached in and took out some pumpkin seeds.

"What's that?" Adou inquired.

"Light the lamp so that we can see it better," Nanny said excitedly. "They are pumpkin seeds. I got them from a little old lady back at Nanny Town and I forgot all about them until now."

"So what's the plan?" Adou asked curiously.

"We're going to plant these pumpkin seeds on the hillside and take good care of them until they grow."

"And how do you know that pumpkins will grow in this area?" Adou asked.

"I just know that these seeds will grow a lot here to satisfy our need," Nanny replied.

"Sounds good my sweets! You know I will support you in anything you do," he said smiling.

"I know," Nanny acknowledged. "And that is why I love you so much," she said, smiling back at him.

"In the morning I will talk to Putus and Quao about these seeds," she said as they put out the lamp and went back to sleep.

"Where did you say that you got these pumpkin seeds again?" Putus asked, not believing what she was hearing.

"As I said," Nanny repeated for the umpteenth time, sounding slightly annoyed. "Do you remember on the last day at Nanny Town when I went over to talk with the old people? Well, before I left, a little old lady gave me this pouch and told me that it might come in handy one day. It turns out to be pumpkin seeds and we're going to plant them on that hill over there and take good care of them."

"How do you know that they will grow around here?" Putus asked.

"That was exactly what Adou asked me last night," Nanny said.

"Great minds think alike," Putus laughed.

"I just know that pumpkins will grow well up here," Nanny asserted. "So get some women and let's go out and plant these seeds."

Nanny and the women came together and prepared the land on the hillside and carefully planted the pumpkin seeds. Days went by as the people watched anxiously for the seeds to germinate.

"Do you still believe that those seeds are good Chief?" Putus teased.

"Have faith my friend, have faith," Nanny chuckled. "The plants will be here at the appointed time."

Early the next morning, as Nanny was doing her morning walk, with a mug of hot coffee in her hand, she wandered over to the hill where the seeds were planted and was in for a big surprise. She couldn't believe her eyes. All the seeds had germinated, and were looking very strong. Nanny ran to call Putus with the good news. "It is here Putus! It is here! Glory be to Massa God!" The people became very excited.

"I just knew that they would grow!" one man commented.

"Thank you Massa God! I knew that you wouldn't let us starve," a short stout woman cried out, raising her hands in the air.

"I will never doubt Chief Nanny again," a tall bald head man said.

"I don't know how she does it, but she always finds a way to save us," an elderly woman declared.

In the coming weeks, the entire hill became covered with pumpkins and they kept growing and thriving at an alarming rate. Everyone became excited about the pumpkins and took a keen interest in the way they were growing. No more talk of the land being barren and cursed.

"I take back everything bad that I ever said about your pumpkins Chief," Putus apologized. "As usual you were right. This place should be called Pumpkin Hill in memory of the first crop that we ever grew here," she proposed.

"I wonder where that old lady got those seeds."

"My question would be, why didn't she give us the seeds to plant at Nanny Town?" Quao asked.

"These seeds could have helped all those starving villages back there. Why didn't she give it to us then?"

"I don't have an answer to that question," Nanny responded. "But what I do know is that she saved the best for last and I'm so thankful. And Putus, I love that name Pumpkin Hill. It sounds so natural and it will remind us that we should never be discouraged or worse yet, give up, because something as lowly as a few pumpkin seeds can give us hope."

At harvest time there was a bumper crop of pumpkins. Nanny encouraged the ladies to bring the surplus down to the nearby market and sell them.

The pumpkins sold off very quickly. The people at the market loved them so much that they begged for more. In the evening the ladies returned home laden down with lots of foodstuffs and supplies, and eagerly looked forward to the next market day.

Chapter 37

The community of Pumpkin Hill grew rapidly. Pumpkin sales were going so well that the people had enough money to buy more food materials and supplies for their homes and tools to till the soil.
Nanny spent most of her days in the pumpkin fields, or out in the forest searching for herbs to make medicine.

"Look at this place," Putus pointed out to Nanny one day in the middle of the field. "Who would have ever believed a couple months ago that this place would look like this and the people would be so happy? Nanny I can't thank you enough for your vision and leadership. Without you, I don't know what would've happen to us."

"I didn't do it alone Putus. You and Quao have been the driving force behind me. You two are the sounding board for my ideas. You challenge me and you give me your honest opinions without fear, and that's what gets us through. You two are the real heroes; I'm only the cheer leader."

Over the next few weeks, Nanny kept thinking about Cudjoe in the west end. She wondered how he was coping with the British and if he had heard about Nanny Town. She wanted to surprise him; but how?

"That's a long trek across the island Chief," Putus remarked, when Nanny made the suggestion one day. "And with all these people, how could you think of doing such a thing?"

"My brother NEEDS me!" Nanny emphasized.

"Did he invite you and the whole town down there?" Putus asked directly. "Did you hear him say, 'My dear sister, please come and visit me,

296

and by the way, bring all your people with you because we're desperate for your company?'" She paused for a response. "I didn't think so; so why are we going Chief? What is the real reason?"

Nanny hesitated for a moment, and then with a stern look on her face replied, "To be perfectly honest Putus, I think that it's time that we united the Leeward and the Windward Maroons. With a united force fighting the British, we would be unstoppable. We would be able to crush them and drive them out of Jamaica for good," she added. "Putus, now is the time to reclaim our dignity and live as truly free men and women in this country."

"So do you think that Cudjoe will go for it Chief?" Putus asked candidly.

"Well, the most he can say is no," Nanny responded honestly.

"What you're saying makes sense Chief," Putus said. "I'm with you. We can call this the Great Trek!" she said jokingly.

"Now we have to try and convince Quao," Nanny said smiling.

The date was set; Nanny and her people would be taking the long trek over to the parish of St James a week from Sunday. Nanny instructed everyone to travel lightly because this trip was even further than their trek from Nanny Town. They would travel during the nights and rest during the days to avoid confrontation with the British.

For the first two days, the people made good progress; travelling during the night and resting during the day. The following day while resting, the lookouts signaled that a British patrol was coming in their direction. Nanny ordered everyone to remain alert and take up their positions. Everyone blended seamlessly into the surrounding bushes. Some stood still like trees while others covered themselves with branches and leaves; with weapons drawn and ready.

Everyone held their collective breaths as the soldiers walked right passed them without an inkling that so many people were in their midst. After they passed the people breathed a sigh of relief and relaxed again.

"I hate the days," Putus expressed, "It is too stressful on my poor heart. I'm getting too old for this Chief. I don't know how much more of this I can take."

"I hear what you're saying Putus, and believe you me, I understand; but what we're doing here is for our children," Nanny reiterated. "We don't want them to grow up in a world like this. We want them to grow up in a world in which they have no barriers placed on them. They should be the masters of their fate, not some white man from across the sea. Yes Putus I'm getting tired too but the job is not yet finished, and I won't rest until our people are free."

Putus looked intently at Nanny as she spoke and knew that she meant every word. Her love for her friend was so great that even if she wanted to quit, she couldn't because her friend needed her.

As darkness came, the order was given to move out. No one said a word; instead they conserved their energy for the long, difficult march.

They were only a few hours into the journey when the advance party signaled that there was a military camp up ahead. Nanny gathered everyone together and told them the news. She instructed them on creeping quietly pass the camp without making a sound. The camp was fairly quiet except for a smoldering fire in the centre around which two soldiers sat talking in low tones. The folks crept quietly pass the camp in single files, keeping their eyes focused on the person in front and not stopping until they were out of danger. After what seemed like eternity, everyone eventually past the camp safely, with the soldiers none the wiser.

The silent walk continued throughout the night with only a short stop at a little stream to rest and refill their water containers.

As dawn approached, the lookouts alerted the group that a small village was up ahead. Nanny decided to remain on the outskirts until daylight before approaching the village to try and buy some food and a place to rest. As the Sun came up, Quao and Putus cautiously entered the little village and asked to speak with the Chief. The people gathered around as they told their story to the Chief. He smiled broadly as he directed them to go and bring everybody.

"Welcome to our humble village," he said, showing his shiny white teeth. "My name is Chief Doohdi. Come! Come! Put your loads down and make yourselves at home. Breakfast will be ready in a short while. Chief Nanny! Please! Please! Come with me."

He led her over to his home and gave her a seat.

"Chief Nanny, we're so happy to have you here. We have heard a lot of great things about you; how you've destroyed the British forts and killed their soldiers; good for you! All our little girls here want to be just like you," he said with a broad smile.

"So you're going to St. James to visit your brother Cudjoe? Good man, good man! He is a very good friend of mine," he said, flashing his customary smile.

"Wow! You two look so much alike! And from what we've heard, both of you have the same fire in your bellies to drive out the British," he laughed heartily.

"You and your people can stay here as long as you wish. Here, I have a basin with water; freshen up and let's have breakfast, and then you can rest."

The breakfast of ackee and corned pork, roast breadfruit, roast yam, hot coffee and chocolate tea, was so tasty that it had everyone licking their fingers. Nanny and her people remained in the village eating and drinking and resting for two days before they had to leave.

As the evening approached and they were about to leave Chief Doohdi gave them extra food to take on their way.

"I told some Chiefs along the way to look out for you, so if you stop at any of those villages, they will take good care of you. One thing about us in the west; we take good care of our friends, especially you Chief Nanny," he said, with his signature broad smile.

Nanny thanked the Chief and his people for their hospitality before she set off. For the remainder of the trip Nanny stopped at numerous villages along the way, and everywhere they stopped, they were welcomed with open arms.

"The folks in the west are really nice," Putus said to Nanny. "I will never take strangers for granted again," she laughed.

Finally, they reached St. James and headed up to Cudjoe Town. They were making good progress and hoped to arrive there by morning.

An hour before sunrise they walked excitedly into Cudjoe Town to find the whole village, including Cudjoe, waiting patiently to welcome them. Nanny dropped her bags and rushed into the wide opened arms of her brother.

"Welcome Sis, I'm so glad that you could come," he said with a broad smile.

"Thank you for having us brother," she remarked.

"Wow! You still look good, even though you've just walked so many miles," he joked.

"We come from good stock my brother," she replied with a smile. Then Cudjoe held on to Quao and gave him a big hug.

"Welcome my brother! I'm so glad to see you," he said.

"Me too big brother, I'm happy to be here," Quao replied with a smile. Cudjoe then went around and shook hands with Adou, Putus and all the others. He welcomed everyone to Cudjoe Town and instructed his people to show them their quarters. Nanny and her staff were invited to stay in Cudjoe's quarters.

For breakfast a mouth-watering feast was provided including giant mugs of coffee and chocolate tea. For the rest of the day everyone relaxed and got more acquainted.

The following morning Nanny and Cudjoe woke up very early before everyone, and took a walk in the hills with their hot coffee.

"Sorry about Nanny Town Sis," Cudjoe said, shaking his head in sorrow. "You know how much I loved that place. The British would never have found that place if it wasn't for that damn traitor. I don't believe that he realizes what he has done."

"I just try to put it at the back of my mind," Nanny said, shaking her head and biting her lips, "Because if I think about it too hard then I would hate him. But you can't even hate him because he has been brainwashed by Bakra."

"So what's your plan now Sis?" Cudjoe asked, looking squarely at his sister.

For a moment Nanny looked way over in the ravines below, then turned to Cudjoe and said, "Brother I think that if we're ever going to defeat the British and drive them out of Jamaica, then we have to unite the Leeward and the Windward Maroons." Then she dropped the bombshell. We've come to join forces with you and your men to bring the fight to the British."

Cudjoe looked way out into the distance, then gently picked up a rock and threw it as far as he could, before turning back to her.

"Sis, I love you more than you will ever know, but I'm getting tired of this fighting. My men are also getting tired of this fighting too. Look at me Sis; I'm getting too old for this. I'm feeling aches and pains all over my body. In the mornings I can hardly get out of bed and I feel pain and stiffness in all of my joints," he said, rubbing his hands together and blowing on them for additional circulation. "Sis, I don't know how much more fighting I can do and I don't want to leave my people without a leader."

"But that's the beauty of this my brother; if we unite then we could share leadership," Nanny said with delight.

"I don't think that you're hearing what I'm saying Sis," he said, choosing his words carefully. "I believe that we should make some kind of a peace arrangement with the British. Yes Sis, the white devils!" he emphasized. "I would like to end this war with them."
Nanny could not believe her ears.

"My brother, am I hearing you correctly? Are you saying that you Cudjoe want to crawl on your belly like a lowly snake to the white devils and make peace?"

"That is not what I'm saying Sis. Listen to me carefully. I said that we would like to seek some kind of peace agreement with the British. But the difference my sister is that we will be negotiating from a position of strength, not weakness. The British soldiers know full well what we're capable of doing. They've tried everything; from bringing down their most advanced weapons from Britain to importing some of the best trackers in the world to capture us and yet they've failed. I believe that they're ripe for the picking Sis; so all we have to do is bide our time and they will come to us. It's like catching chickens with corn."

"And how long will that take?" Nanny asked sarcastically.

"Who knows? But we will wait until the time is right. What I don't want Sis, is an all-out war with the British because for one thing, you can't bluff a man forever; even if they're the British. The soldiers don't know that we're running low on everything, yes I mean everything: weapons, ammunition, food, and above all, young warriors. We've given them the impression that we're a large army; but Nanny, the truth is, we're only a small force, and we aim to keep it that way."

"I never want to make any peace with the British, no sir! Not now, not ever!" Nanny said sternly.

"Well that is where we disagree Sis," he said meekly. "The quicker we can make peace with them, the quicker we can put down permanent roots.

Our people need that Sis, they really need that. Come, come! Let's go and have some breakfast; we will talk more about this later," Cudjoe suggested.

For the next ten days Nanny and her people enjoyed the kind hospitality of the people of Cudjoe Town. Many friendships were developed, some resulting in permanent relationships. Nanny and Cudjoe talked regularly about how they could help each other, but they were unable to make any progress on joining forces to fight the British.

"Sis I'm sorry, but I have to turn down your offer to join forces," Cudjoe told her one day.

"As I said before, I believe that making peace with the British will be good for us and for them too. Right now nobody is winning this battle; we're not winning, and they're definitely not winning. All we have now is death and sadness. Sis, we have to find a different way to get along with the white devils. Don't get me wrong, I will still continue to attack their camps and pressure them into coming to the table to negotiate peace."

"I'm sorry you feel that way brother, but I can't stop fighting them right now; and as far as making peace with them, that is definitely not in the cards," Nanny declared. "I see no point in making any deal with those white devils because I don't believe that they can ever be trusted."

"I don't trust them either," Cudjoe said calmly. "But I believe that if we can get them to sign an agreement out in the open, then they will be forced to stick to it."

"I think that you've placed too much faith in these evil people my brother," Nanny said firmly. "They will never keep their word because they take us for fools."

"Sorry Sis, but I have to take my chances. I don't want to be fighting these people when I'm old and weak. I want our young men and women to grow up without fear, without war and with the understanding that they can achieve anything that they set their minds to. I want peace for them Sis, not for me alone," he emphasized. "And I hope that you too will come to that understanding one day."

"My brother I respect your point-of-view and I won't try to convince you otherwise because I see that you have made up your mind. I will leave tomorrow and travel back to Pumpkin Hill and continue the fight," Nanny said.

"But Sis, you don't have to leave so soon, after all, you just got here," Cudjoe pleaded.

"Thanks my brother but duty calls; I need to get back to the east. I will round up everybody and we will leave tomorrow evening," Nanny stated.

Later that evening Nanny spoke to Quao and Putus and told them of her decision.

"Well Chief, you can take comfort in the fact that you did your best," Putus said.

"But I really wanted to work with Cudjoe," Nanny lamented.

"Me too," Quao echoed. "It would've been dangerous! Nothing could've stopped us. We would be invincible!" he proclaimed, flexing his muscles and raising his fists in the air. They all laughed, but deep down they all wished that things could have been different.

The following evening as everyone gathered on the village square to say their good-byes, there were no dry eyes. Young couples cried openly as they hugged each other. A few young men and women asked Nanny for permission to stay in Cudjoe Town, while others got permission from Cudjoe to travel back with Nanny to Pumpkin Hill.

The folks brought out lots of foods for Nanny and her people to take back with them on their long journey.

"It's so hard to leave here," one young girl cried to her mother. "It's not fair!"

"Life is not fair!" the mother shot back, looking annoyed. "You're giving me a headache. How many times must I tell you that there is nothing I can do?"

On the side, two little girls played pita-pat with their hands.

"We're best friends for life," they both wept openly. Then they hugged so long that their mothers had to pull them apart.

Cudjoe and Nanny held hands in silence while watching their people say their tearful good-byes.

"The people are really going to miss one another Sis," Cudjoe said quietly.

"That's true my brother," Nanny replied, trying desperately to hold back the tears.

As they had their final hug; with tears in his eyes he said, "I'm going to miss you Sis. Walk good!"

"I'm going to miss you too," she replied, with tears in her eyes.

Chapter 38

Cudjoe fell into a deep depression after Nanny and her people left. He wondered over and over again if he had made the right decision. Here was the opportunity of a life time to fight the British with the greatest leader this country had ever seen, and he had turned her away.

He assessed the situation over and over again in his mind: his army was falling apart rapidly, weapons and ammunition were in short supply, his men were getting weary, it was becoming more difficult to recruit new members, and most importantly, the population was barely able to feed itself. Faced with all these major problems, did he have a choice? Would joining forces with Nanny have helped in the long run?

One night in a dream he was visited by Mada Kuzo.

"Hi Cudjoe," she greeted him with a broad smile.

"Do you know me?"

"No ma'm, I don't know who you are," Cudjoe replied nervously.

"Boy! I'm your great-grandmother," she said jokingly.

"Relax; I'm only here to talk with you. I noticed that you're second guessing yourself whether you made the right decision. Lawd knows, I love that girl so much, and she is wonderful, but I think that you made the right decision for you and your people at this time. If it was a different time, when you were much younger and had more energy, I know that you would've made a different decision. But this is now my son," she said, moving around the room.

"So you made the decision to make peace with the white devils my son;

that's good!" she flashed that broad smile again. "But what good is it with you lying around here every day feeling sorry for yourself while your people are suffering. Get up and prove to yourself that you made the right decision. Get up, go down to the river before daylight and wash yourself from head to toe and begin to lead your people again. Be the strong, cunning, fearless leader that your people have come to know; and eventually my son, you'll get the British where you want them. Don't spend one more day like this my son," she advised. "Your destiny awaits you; grab it by the neck and ride it to victory! I believe in you my son," she said, lowering her voice. We all believe in you, and we're rooting for you." And with that she was gone.

Cudjoe woke up suddenly with giant beads of sweat washing his body. He wondered what had just happened. 'The dream was as clear as daylight,' he thought to himself.

Now he knew what Nanny was saying when she spoke about her spiritual guides. Although he was still shaking, surprisingly he was not afraid. He smiled to himself before going back to sleep because he now knew that he had somebody, or a bunch of people watching over him and protecting him. Now he knew what he had to do.

Early the following morning, before the sun came up, Cudjoe hurried down to the river to take his bath. The cool water flowing over his weary, aging body was like therapy, rejuvenating his mind and his soul. Now, in his mind everything was clearer and more defined. Suddenly he felt hungry, something that he hadn't felt for a long time.

He dressed quickly and had a big breakfast of porridge, roast yam with salted fish, and a big mug of chocolate tea to wash it down. After breakfast he summoned his leaders and instructed them to do a complete inventory of the resources of the village and to report back by the end of the day. Next, he got together his top military leaders and spent the rest of the day plotting strategies to raid the nearby plantations and resume attacks on the British soldiers.

Everyone was amazed at the sudden transformation of Cudjoe. He had become so stern and distant; some said even rude. In the past, although he was tough, he would often joke around on their down time. But now he was all businesslike. This was the new Cudjoe and they just had to get use to him. To prepare for the upcoming raids, the men trained harder to get back in shape.

A few days later, intelligence came in that the Bakra at a nearby plantation was taking his family and some of his top people to Montego Bay for the weekend and there would hardly be anyone there to guard the plantation. Cudjoe made plans to carry out the raid with the aim of securing weapons, ammunition and food supplies. Clear orders were given to kill any slave who resisted or tried to protect Bakra's property.

The raid was a complete success with no one getting hurt and Cudjoe and his men capturing a large cache of weapons, ammunition, gold coins and food provisions.

Over the next six months Cudjoe and his troops raided many plantations; however they always avoided skirmishes with the British soldiers. Instead they hunted down the local militia and attacked them without mercy because of their cruelty towards the defenseless villagers.

One day an intelligence report came in to Cudjoe that the British were planning an elaborate attack against the Maroons. The British were recruiting every able-bodied white man they could find to fight the Maroons, the report stated. Cudjoe thought long and hard about the information and discussed his concerns with his leaders.
On closer examination, one of his leaders suggested that there was a serious flaw in the British strategy.

"Chief, but if they're recruiting all of their men to fight the Maroons, then who is going to protect their families when they're off fighting? They're leaving their backside wide open," he laughed.

"That's right!" Cudjoe agreed. "And that means that if they attack us, then they would leave their families at risk."

"And Chief, if the battle lasts a long time then that would make it even worse on their families," another leader added.

"From what you're saying gentlemen I doubt if this big attack will ever take place," Cudjoe surmised. "The British are not stupid. They have too much at stake here. But then again, we have to be fully prepared gentlemen; we can't be too sure because the British are known to take some unusual risks. They didn't become the greatest army in the world by accident."

"True, true Chief," another leader said.

Cudjoe and the men waited anxiously for weeks for the attack but it never materialized. Intelligence reports coming in said nothing about any attacks.

"Chief, I think that you're right; I don't think that they will be coming," a young leader said to Cudjoe.

"We still have to be cautious and remain on alert," Cudjoe reminded everyone.

A few weeks later, Cudjoe was surprised to receive a message from a Colonel Guthrie of the British Military proposing a meeting to discuss 'peace and other matters' with the Maroons.

Cudjoe immediately summoned his team of advisors to an emergency meeting to discuss the message. After reading the message to the group, nearly all of them were skeptical.

"Don't trust them Chief," one said. "They never ever keep their word!"

"I agree," a senior member added. "You have to be very careful Chief. I believe that they want to draw you out into the open and capture you."

"Think about it Chief," a tall elderly gentleman leaning on his well-polished cherry wood cane said. "Why would the greatest military in the world want to make peace with the likes of a simple bunch of Africans living up in the hills?" he questioned. "It just doesn't make any sense. There must be something that we're not seeing. That country would never choose peace unless it is to their benefit. They're conquerors, remember? Look what they did to the Spanish here in Jamaica."

Cudjoe listened to all that the men had to say, and then he addressed them slowly.

"One reason why I might be interested in meeting with these people is to hear what they have to say, and two, I want to look them straight in the eye to see their soul."

"They have no soul Chief," one man quipped, interrupting Cudjoe and causing everyone to laugh.

"Ok gentlemen, let's continue," Cudjoe announced after a few minutes of fun. "I've never been close to these people before apart from when we were not free; but now that we're free, I would like to argue with them man-to-man. If they think that they're coming down here to talk down to us, then they've made a big mistake. We will negotiate as equals, no Bakra over slave, white man over African. No way! It is big man to big man or no deal!"

"True word Chief! True word!" they shouted.

"And another thing, we will never agree to anything that will be bad for us or our children. It must be a deal that will benefit us and allow us to be better off than we are right now," Cudjoe emphasized.

"Same so Chief, same so!" they all agreed.

"Chief, they want us to pick the place for the meeting, preferably somewhere in our area," Cudjoe's assistant announced.

"Any suggestions?" Cudjoe inquired.

"What about Chuchuia Pass Chief," a senior member suggested. "With that big secret cave covered up right there, it is well suited for an ambush," he said, to laughter all around.

"We would be able to control the situation if we met them there in that little old hut near to the big Guango tree."

"Yes, I like that place!" Cudjoe said, nodding his head in agreement. "That's a good idea Shumbeh. Let's go down there tomorrow and inspect the area thoroughly before we make the final decision."

The discussions continued for hours with the main concerns being security and how to deal with this dangerous foe.

"So we secure the area; we lock it down tighter than a barrel of molasses, but what else could go wrong?" Cudjoe probed his team.

In the end they left the meeting feeling confident that they had covered all their bases.

The day finally arrived for the meeting between Colonel Guthrie and Cudjoe. Everything was set for noon. By midmorning Cudjoe had his warriors strategically positioned on the hill overlooking the little weather-beaten hut that would serve as the meeting place. Along with his many lookouts, Cudjoe surveyed the surrounding hills using his telescope for any signs of the British. They were known to be punctual and didn't like to wait.

As noon approached, several abeng horns suddenly began sounding off, announcing the arrival of the British. The messages all warned that the British were approaching with a large battalion of fully armed soldiers.

"Why do you think that they're coming with so many soldiers Chief?" Prekeh, Cudjoe's young assistant, asked.

"Intimidation my boy, intimidation," Cudjoe replied with a sly look on his face. "They think that they can scare us with their military might but that doesn't scare me one bit."

The abengs sounded louder and louder, echoing throughout the entire valley like the horn section of an orchestra at a London concert. But this was no ordinary orchestra. Interspersed between the mesmerizing melodies were messages relaying vital information about the movements of the troops.

Sometime later, the soldiers appeared into full view with their pomp and British pride, ready to take charge. Suddenly they stopped about one hundred yards from the hut. Cudjoe and his men watched as a tall, muscular, broad shouldered soldier turned around, saluted, and then slowly walked towards the hut, raising his hands in the air, to indicate that he was unarmed.

"What're they doing Chief?" Prekeh asked nervously.

"They want to talk to one of us to set the ground rules for the meeting," Cudjoe replied.

The soldier continued walking until he reached midway then he stopped and shouted, "We come in peace! We only wish to speak with you. Send someone so that we can have a word!"

Minutes went by without any response. Finally, Cudjoe instructed Prekeh to go out and meet the soldier.

"Don't let him bully you. Don't take any foolishness from him my youth."

"No Chief, I won't do that," he said, as he slowly walked out from his hiding place.

This felt like the longest journey that young Prekeh had ever taken in his life. His feet became heavier and heavier with every step he took. He remembered Chief telling him to count to ten and breathe deeply when he felt nervous. At that moment he was feeling extremely nervous, so he started his breathing exercises as he walked. The counting and the breathing was 'just what the doctor ordered.' By the time he reached the middle of the field his mind was clear and he had his nerves under control.

"Where is your leader? We need to speak with him," the soldier demanded rudely.

"So, is that how you're going to talk to me? Then I'm gone. I'm not one of your little slave boys that you can whip and spit on. We didn't call you to talk remember? It was you who called us. So when you've found some manners then you can call us."

The soldier was dumbfounded. 'Who are these savages? Nobody talks to us like that, especially a little runaway, illiterate slave. Obviously they are so dumb that they haven't heard of our military might,' he thought. 'I personally don't agree with making any deals with these criminals. I know that we can wipe them out, but the big wigs in England never listen. Then again, what will I tell the Colonel if this meeting falls apart because of me? There goes my promotion to Captain and getting out of this god forsaken hell hole.'

He took a long deep breath, and showing his teeth said meekly,

"Ok mate, I'm sorry, you win."

"Win what?" Prekeh snapped back.

"Don't worry about that, let's talk," he said.

So the arrangements were finalized. Firstly, the British were not there to trick the Maroons or attack them. Secondly, the two men would meet in the hut unarmed, with only one advisor each. And thirdly, the British Colonel would arrive at the hut first and then Cudjoe would join him. Both sides agreed and they both went back to their respective corners.

The Colonel arrived in the hut shortly after and sat and waited for Cudjoe. Minutes turned into hours, and still he did not show up. Cudjoe meanwhile was observing the Colonel through his telescope getting up every few minutes and walking around the hut looking utterly disgusted like a caged beast.

"He's ripe for the picking. I think it is time," he said, smiling at Prekeh and handing him his telescope.

The Colonel stood with his back to Cudjoe as he walked in.

"I'm here, what do you want to talk to me about?" Cudjoe asked casually.

"You! You people!" pointing his finger at Cudjoe. "What do you take this thing for?" he yelled at Cudjoe.

311

"What thing?" Cudjoe asked, acting innocently.

"This meeting!" he shouted, while in his mind he was screaming the words 'dummy! idiot!'

"You people have no respect for other people's time. Here you have me and His Majesty's Army waiting on you for two bloody hours! What's wrong with you people?" he yelled.

"So you've come here to quarrel with me?" Cudjoe asked, taking offence.

"I thought that you came here to talk peace. But if we're not here to talk peace then we're both wasting each others time, so I'm leaving," he said, making a slow walk towards the door.

'I can't let this fool leave!' the Colonel thought to himself. 'The Governor would not be happy if I let this opportunity pass-by to make some sort of a deal with these morons. Let me think. What can I do to stop him? These bloody Africans are so unpredictable, utterly shameful.' Then an idea flashed into his mind.

He boldly raised his hand and said, "Ok! Ok don't leave, I'm sorry," he apologized sheepishly. "But I hate when people don't keep appointments."

"But we didn't put any time on when I would join you, did we?" Cudjoe rebutted.

"You believed that it was right away, but I don't work like that." They both laughed nervously, followed by Prekeh and the Colonel's advisor.

"Well, let's start over again," the Colonel suggested, extending his hand. "I am Colonel Guthrie of the British Military, in charge of security for all of Jamaica.

"And I'm Chief Cudjoe of the Maroons," he said, taking a hold of the Colonel's hand.

"I have been in Jamaica for the last two years. But before that I was in the jungles of Africa," the Colonel volunteered. Then he looked Cudjoe directly in his eyes as he continued, "Do you know something Cudjoe? Can I call you Cudjoe?"

Cudjoe nodded in agreement.

"Cudjoe, I love this island of Jamaica very much. It reminds me so much of some parts of Africa. Tell me Cudjoe, do you love this country? What does Jamaica mean to you?"

Cudjoe was taken aback by the questions. He was not expecting a direct question like that from the Colonel and he wasn't sure how to answer it. He had heard rumors about how good the British were with words, but this was his first experience and he now knew that the rumors were true.

"I love this country," he stammered, "A lot."

"You know Cudjoe," the Colonel began. "Jamaica has so much going for it. We produce the most sugarcane in this part of the world. We are a very rich country, the envy of the world! Can I let you in on a little secret of mine Cudjoe? I'll be retiring in two years and I'm not planning on going back to England, no way! I want to stay right here," he said smiling, and pointing his finger to the ground.

"And that is where you come in Cudjoe, my friend."

Cudjoe's mind worked excessively hard while the Colonel spoke.

'He's very smooth,' he thought to himself, 'Too smooth. Imagine he's calling me his friend and I don't know this man at all. I don't trust him one bit; his mouth is too sweet.'

"Are you listening?" the Colonel asked, looking directly at Cudjoe.

"Oh yes," Cudjoe responded.

"I thought I was losing you," he smiled. "Let's continue. As I was saying, here is where you come in Cudjoe."

"What do you mean by that?" Cudjoe inquired.

"This country is going through some very serious financial problems because of the horrible violence on the island. No one from England wants to come down here anymore. Sugar production is at its lowest level because plantations are constantly being set on fire, many innocent people are being killed and many slaves are running away," the Colonel said, with a worried look on his face.

"So Cudjoe, the Government in England, yes Cudjoe, the very Government in England is not very happy, which in turn means that the Governor of Jamaica is not happy, which in turn means that I am definitely not happy, which is why I am here."

Then he said something that really shocked Cudjoe.

"The fingers are pointing squarely at you Cudjoe and your Maroons old chap, as the main cause of the trouble."

"But we didn't start the violence," Cudjoe protested. "If you really want to know, it was the local militia that started it. Those murderers attacked defenseless villages and slaughtered everybody: men, women and children. They show no mercy. They treat us like dogs. So what do you expect us to do? We can't just sit around and wait for them to come and kill us, can we? We have to defend ourselves."

"It really doesn't matter now who started it," the Colonel began when he was abruptly interrupted.

"But it does matter Colonel! If you don't know what happened in the past then how are you going to fix it?" Cudjoe asked.

The Colonel thought long and hard before he spoke in a quiet voice, choosing his words carefully.

"We acknowledge the problems in the past and we take full responsibility for our part in it, and I hope that you will do the same. But it is not only my problem Cudjoe; it is in fact our problem. Now what would you do if you were in my shoes?"

"But I'm not in your shoes," Cudjoe replied defensively.

"I know that my friend," the Colonel said smiling, and without skipping a beat he added, "What we both know Cudjoe, is that this situation cannot continue for much longer. We need to find a way to solve this."

"Keep talking, I'm listening," Cudjoe urged.

"We are committed to making peace with you and the Maroons, Cudjoe. We would go as far as to discuss a Peace Treaty with you and the Maroons, as long as it will stop this terrible violence."

Cudjoe couldn't believe what he was hearing.

'Did the Colonel just say that the British actually wanted peace? And he would go as far as discussing a Peace Treaty?' He wished that his sister was here now. Who could see this coming?

Ok! Ok, he had to be calm. He didn't want to appear too anxious, although inside he was exploding with joy.

"I hear that you want the violence to stop Colonel, but what are we going to get out of all this?" Cudjoe asked directly.

"Good question my friend," the Colonel smiled, sensing that he was making progress.

"Well Cudjoe, in exchange for giving up the violence, we are willing to give you large acres of lands," the Colonel promised.

"Ah! Ah! Ah!" Cudjoe laughed haughtily. "Land! But we don't need land; we have our own lands," Cudjoe reminded him. "Plus we have many more serious problems than land to worry about."

"Like what?" the Colonel asked, taking a keen interest.

"Like, we would like the Maroons to be recognized as an independent nation, capable of taking care of our own business," Cudjoe expressed.

"That's fine," the Colonel agreed, with a friendly smile. "I'll even sweeten the deal by giving you 2,500 acres of land," he started saying when Cudjoe interjected.

"Are you going back to this land thing again? How many times must I tell you that we don't need any land," Cudjoe maintained.

"You might not want land now my friend, but listen to what I am proposing. You would not have to pay any taxes on that land forever."

"But we're not paying any taxes right now," Cudjoe laughed. "Why do you think that we would ever pay any taxes? Ah! Ah! Ah!" he laughed. "You British people like to make jokes. Pay taxes! Ah! Ah! Ah! You would have to catch us first to collect it and that will be the day."

"Times are changing my friend. Change is coming whether we like it or not," the Colonel emphasized with a straight face. "But let me get back to what I was saying. We will recognize you Maroons as an independent nation, and you will not have to pay any taxes, not now, yah! yah! yah," seeing the smirk on Cudjoe's face. "Not ever! From hence forth, no Maroon or their children will be required to pay taxes. No taxes! Zero! You might not see the importance of this right now Cudjoe my friend, but your children and children's children will thank you for it."

"Ok, so what else do you have to offer?" Cudjoe asked, finally showing some interest.

"Before we move on, there is only one condition on the land deal," the Colonel said.

"What's that now?" Cudjoe inquired.

"The only condition is that the Maroons have to remain in only those towns that are recognized by the British," the Colonel said.

"Fair enough, we can work out the details," Cudjoe agreed, looking over at Prekeh and nodding his head.

For the next few hours the Colonel, Cudjoe and the two advisors hammered out some agreements that would benefit both camps. In the end Colonel Guthrie and his advisor provided Cudjoe and Prekeh with a first draft of the agreements.

In the draft proposal, among other things, Cudjoe and the Maroons would agree: to submit to British supervision; live under their own Chief but with a British supervisor, promise not to harbor any new runaway slaves, but instead, help the British to catch and return them to the plantation. The Maroons would be adequately compensated for their service. And the Maroons would fight for the British in case of an attack by the French or the Spanish.

As the meeting came to an end Cudjoe and Colonel Guthrie shook hands and Cudjoe promised to discuss the document with his people before signing the Peace Treaty with Governor Sir Edward Trelawney. In the meanwhile both sides agreed to suspend all hostilities towards each other.

Chapter 39

The town of Pumpkin Hill was fast developing the reputation as the town to buy the best pumpkins in the Parish. The town's people planted pumpkins everywhere. People came from far away to buy pumpkins. On market days there was the constant hustle and bustle in the streets as locals and visitors rubbed shoulder to shoulder. Some residents seized the opportunity to go into business selling hot meals, making clothes, and sharpening tools. The higglers [sellers] sold clothes, tools, utensils, weapons and ground provisions. Yes, Pumpkin Hill's market was becoming famous; a far cry from what it was when they returned from the great trek across the island. Now the people were happy making a living either as farmers growing and selling pumpkins and other crops, or as merchants selling goods and providing various services in the marketplace.

"Look how we used to walk many miles to the market Chief, and now we have our own market," Putus said to Nanny one day with pride.

"Massa God bless that woman who gave me those pumpkin seeds," Nanny said, raising her hands in the air in gratitude. "She is the one who made all this possible."

"But don't forget that it was your spiritual ancestor who reminded you about them," Putus acknowledged.

"I agree!" Nanny smiled.

"It must be a good feeling to have someone watching over you all the time and dreaming you when you're in trouble. I wish I had someone like that," Putus stated.

"Don't worry Putus, you have your own blessings too."

"Nanny, you're cut from a different cloth from all of us. You don't have a mean bone in your body and you would take the clothes off your back to give to somebody in need. I don't know how you do it."

"Thanks for saying that Putus, but it's not that hard. What I do every morning when I wake up is to ask Massa God to let me think more about other people and less about myself. As long as I do that I will always find someone who needs my help."

Meanwhile, down in the west Cudjoe had just finished signing the Peace Treaty with Governor Sir Edward Trelawney in the little hut. It was a gala occasion, with the Governor dressed in his regal attire surrounded by his smartly dressed officers.

Cudjoe and his entourage arrived on time in their colorful Ashanti ceremonial regalia. After some brief introductions and instructions it was time for the signing of the documents, sitting conspicuously on a little table between two simple folding chairs that had seen better days. Standing closely behind Cudjoe was Prekeh, his assistant, making sure that he understood all the instructions.

After the formal signing of the documents, Cudjoe shook hands with Governor Trelawney, Colonel Guthrie and his officers. The Governor then went over and shook hands with the Maroon Elders, laughing and sharing pleasant conversations. He graciously accepted various handmade gifts from the Elders and promised to cherish them.

"This is a great day for everyone," Cudjoe said to himself. "All we wanted was for them to recognize that we are people just like them. I wish that this day would never end. Look at that; people of different cultures respecting one another's differences."

Then his mind flashed back to his older sister in the east and a sinking feeling suddenly carved out a giant hole in his stomach. How would he be able to convince her that what he had done was not a 'sellout' to the British but was good for the Maroons too, in the grand scheme of things? He loved his sister dearly, but sometimes she was like an old relic from the past who was still bent on fighting old battles. She was so set in her ways that she would rather die than make any kind of compromise with the enemy.

'I wish that she was here right now, and then maybe she would see things from a whole different perspective,' he thought. 'Anyway, what is done is done; there is no turning back. I will just have to try and convince her that the war is over and it is time to enter this new phase of collaboration; where we work with each other, the British and the Africans, rather than against each other.'

Nanny was furious when she learned what Cudjoe had done.

"The boy has gone damn, blasted, crazy Putus!" she shrieked. "How could he do something like that? How could he be so stupid as to let them trick him into signing that damn piece of paper? Putus, how many times have I told you that I don't trust those white people? Them a devil! Them a viper! Them a two face! Them a murderers! They murder our men, women, and children! And Cudjoe gone and signed treaty with them?" she exploded, clasping her hips with her hands. "What's wrong with that boy? Is he drinking puss piss or something and it made him mad? Lawd oh! Lawd oh!" she cried aloud. "Look what I have lived to see; my own flesh and blood has sold us out to the white devils! Lawd have mercy on him!"

Then she began humming an old Ashanti grieving song that Putus had not heard for a very long time. She took a piece of black cloth and tied it around her head as she walked around in circles for hours; humming one mournful song after another.

That night Mada Kuzo appeared to her in a dream.

"I am here my chile! I see that you're angry," Mada Kuzo greeted her with a smile.

"Thanks Massa God that you've come Mada Kuzo. You're the only one who understands how I feel," Nanny said with delight.

"So you think that what Cudjoe did was wrong chile?" Mada Kuzo asked.

"I don't think so Mada Kuzo, I know that it was a big mistake and we're going to suffer for it down the road. Mada Kuzo, tell me that I'm right and Cudjoe is wrong," Nanny pleaded, searching her face desperately for approval.

"My pet, you're both right."

"But how can both of us be right?" Nanny asked, looking puzzled.

"It is like looking at the two different sides of the same coin. You're looking at the situation from the present while Cudjoe was looking at it from the future. You see my pet, you're feeling the pain right now and you want to kill it, cut it out right now, which is fine; but on the other side, Cudjoe was thinking that the British people were not going anywhere soon and he was getting old and tired, along with his people. Both of you want the British out, yes?" she nodded, followed by Nanny. "So you say, 'fight them with weapons and warriors, but Cudjoe said, 'Let me fight them with diplomacy.' Two approaches, same problem. Now the question is which approach has the better chance of winning and surviving in the long run? Is it yours my chile, with your: aging warriors, shortage of weapons and ammunition, shortage of new recruits, shortage of food and a respectable living standard, living in the shadows, travelling only at nights, like duppy, not daring to show your beautiful faces in the daylight for fear of being shot by a soldier or worse, a militia's musket? Or Cudjoe's approach which was to make peace with the British because: he was tired of the fighting, his men were also tired of the fighting, their weapons were old, ammunition was in short supply, and above all, they were nearly starving and were living like rats in a hole. He knew that it was just a matter of time before they would be defeated and put back in chains.

That was the option as far as Cudjoe was concerned. So his plan my chile was to milk the British for all they're worth. The Governor was under pressure from all levels of government in England to solve the violence problem. Jamaica's sugar industry was their cash cow, their pride and joy; and this senseless violence was causing them to lose a lot of money. So from the king's palace in England to the politicians, down to the Governor of Jamaica, everybody was fed up with the violence and needed it to be fixed as soon as possible, so that they could get back to raking in the tons of money. But what was stopping them? As far as they were concerned, just a little bunch of hungry, half naked, runaway slaves in the mountains, running around without a plan or purpose," she said with a cynical look. "So the lawmakers in England put heavy pressure on the Governor of Jamaica to solve the problem quickly, by any means necessary. As a result, the Colonel approached Cudjoe and offered him much more than he even wanted in exchange for peace. Consequently, the boy in a stroke of genius took them for all its worth. What would you have done if you were in the boy's position my chile?" Mada Kuzo asked flashing her familiar toothy smile.

"But some of the agreements in the treaty are terrible Mada Kuzo, terrible!" Nanny cried.

"Remember my pet, in negotiations you never get everything that you ask for and you have to take some things that you don't necessarily like. The question you should be asking yourself is; is it something that I can live with, yes or no?"

"I don't think that I could live with it," Nanny said shaking her head in disapproval.

"I understand my pet," Mada Kuzo said softly. "Which one of the rules are you talking about?"

"'The one that says that the Maroons agreed not to harbor any new runaway slaves, and to help the British to catch these slaves for a price. That is ungodly Mada Kuzo, ungodly! How could any of us, knowing where we're coming from, agree to a rule like that? It is wicked, unconscionable and I will not accept it, not now, not ever!" she said defiantly.

"Calm down my pet, I heard you and I agree with you."

"You agree with me, Mada Kuzo? You're not just saying that to make me feel good?"

"Have I ever deceived you my pet?" Mada Kuzo asked directly.

"No Mada Kuzo, sorry Mada Kuzo, I got carried away," Nanny apologized. "I know that you're the only person I can really trust to tell me the truth."

"As I said before my pet, Cudjoe believed that he could live with that one but obviously you can't; but don't throw out the baby with the bath water. There are some good things in the treaty, for example the one listed that said that the Maroons would be given large amounts of lands and would not have to pay any taxes on it forever. My pet that is great news! Great news! It might not mean anything to you right now, but after you're dead and gone, generations to come will be thankful for it. They will call you and Cudjoe geniuses. The British are a tight fisted bunch, and you people have actually pried their hands open and made this deal. What a deal! Pure genius!"

"So what must I do now Mada Kuzo?"

"Follow your heart my pet, follow your heart," is all she said, and then she was gone.

The following morning Nanny arose early, before everyone, and with her mug of coffee in hand she thought long and hard on what Mada Kuzo had said. Just thinking about returning runaway slaves made her feel sick to her stomach, and to get paid for that was even worst, disgusting! It was immoral and she didn't want any part of it.

Later in the morning at a meeting with Putus and Quao, she told them of her decision.

"I agree with you Chief," Putus said. "If that law was in when we were on the Plantation, we might still be there today."

"But the treaty has been signed Sis," Quao said. "What can we do?"

"If a law is unjust, you shouldn't have to obey it," Nanny snapped back. "What are we here for, but to care for the weak and protect them from the strong?"

"And where does it say that we're the guardians of all African people?" Quao asked sarcastically.

"Chief," Putus butted in to change the subject and avoid an argument. "We have to go; the ladies are outside waiting on us to go up into the forest and pick herbs."

"Oh I wish you would see it differently Quao," Nanny said, as she left with Putus.

A week later an English gentleman on a horse came into the town looking for Nanny. He introduced himself as a government agent and said that he was there to talk with her about the treaty.

Nanny kept very quiet during the entire presentation and at the end he asked her if she had any questions.

"What if I don't want to sign this treaty?" Nanny asked bluntly.

"What do you mean?" the gentleman inquired, looking rather puzzled. "Is there something that you don't understand?"

"I understand everything," Nanny shot back. "Do I look like I'm stupid?"

"No, no, Chief," the man replied, trying desperately to look humble. "But all the other Chiefs have signed," he said, wiping beads of sweat from his forehead with his handkerchief.

"I am not them, I am my own person and I'm not happy with some of the rules, if you would like to know."

"Which rule is that Chief," the gentleman asked cautiously.

"I don't like a lot of them, but the main one is the one about; let me have a look at the paper again." Nanny ran her fingers down the list then she stopped.

"This one here which states that, 'the Maroons agreed not to harbor any new runaway slaves, but rather to help the British to catch them and return them; and Maroons will be paid adequately to return the runaway slaves.' I can't with a clear conscience agree to a thing like that. I believe that slaves have a god given right to choose their destiny, and if it means running away, then we should be here to give them a start, not throw them back into the fire. Where is the compassion in that? Suppose the table was turned, would we want that to happen to us? Of course not! Then why would we want to put such a heavy burden upon these new runaway slaves? Evil! Evil! Pure evil! And as Massa God is my witness, I will not be a part of it, not now, not ever!" she said defiantly.

Nanny dreamed of the day when she and her people would not have to fight the British. She was well aware that her people were tired of the fighting and wanted peace so that they could put down permanent roots, but this was not the time. There was so much more work to be done.

The government agent stood silent, not saying a word. He had heard about this little woman, the sister of Chief Cudjoe in St. James.

'Oh, she is so different from him,' he observed. 'He is calm and together, someone you can reason with. But she, oh boy! She is so bloody opinionated, tough, stubborn and feisty. The boss was right. That was the reason why he said to leave her for the last. What she needs is a good flogging to put her in her place,' he said to himself.

"What other rules do you disagree with Chief," he asked politely, but just wishing that she would shut up so that he could be on his way.

"Let me show you which one. Yes, this one! This one! Read it for yourself. It states that, 'the Maroons agreed not to revolt against the British.' What I would like to add is, unless they are provoked by the soldiers or the militia. That would make it fairer, don't you think?" Nanny asked.

The gentleman did not respond to Nanny's proposal but merely asked if there were any more rules that she did not agree with.

"Well, the funniest one of all is this one down here which states that, 'the Maroons agreed to fight for the British in case of an attack by the French or the Spanish.' That there is a big joke! A big joke! Why do you believe that we would ever lift one finger to help you British if you were attacked? Personally, I believe that we Maroons are closer to the Spanish, than to you British. We trust the Spanish more than we trust you British any day."
The man looked away seemingly uncomfortable.
"Listen to what I'm saying now Mister whatever your name is," Nanny began,

"Campbell," the man offered. "Campbell."

"Yes Mr. Campbell, as I stand here today, the way you British are treating us I wouldn't lift a finger to help you if you were attacked, especially if it was by the Spanish. How can you expect us to help you fight your battles and die for you when you treat us like dogs?"
The agent bit his lips and refused to say a word.
"You British people need to look into yourselves and decide if you want us Maroons as equal partners or you want us as slaves. The choice is yours."

'This little woman is bright,' the agent thought to himself. Who is she really? Where did she get all this knowledge? And that British accent, amazing! I can't believe that it is coming from an African woman. She sounds just like a teacher at one of our British schools. I could listen to her talk for hours, although I don't like how she keeps scolding us. She speaks with so much authority and conviction. Some of these Africans are really brilliant!'

"Mister Government man, sir," Nanny said, "Go back to your superiors and tell them what I've said and come back with something that we can work with."

As he left, he tipped his hat and bid farewell. He felt as if he was in the presence of greatness. He would cherish this moment for the rest of his life.

Chapter 40

Nanny was certain that she had made the right decision not to sign the Peace Treaty. The government agent had not brought back anything new to the table when he returned.

"I will not sign that treaty as it is written," she told him sternly. Finally they agreed to a kind of a truce so that both sides could get some relief from the fighting; postponing the debate for a later date. Nanny was guardedly excited with her decision. Although she didn't get what she wanted, but neither did the British. The only thing that happened was that they had kicked the can down the road for another day.

"At least you didn't 'sellout' to the British, Chief," Putus said.

"I will fight them day and night until they give us the justice that we're due," Nanny insisted. "In fact, the only reason why I'm even considering it is because of my people; they're tired of the fighting and living from day to day in conflict. They deserve a break Putus. Believe you me, if it wasn't for them, I would tell the British where to go with their Peace Treaty. Me and you know that this is all a big sham."

On the day of the signing, the government agent arrived bright and early with his entourage. Nanny invited them into the reception area that was specially prepared for the occasion. After the customary greetings and formalities, it was time for the signing. Everyone held their collective breath. The government agent was especially anxious. Would she go through with it?

'This is one crazy and unpredictable African woman,' he thought to himself. 'I hope that she will sign it so that I can get out of here.' Nanny calmly picked up the quill pen, with its brightly colored feathers, signed her name, and gave it to the agent for him to sign too. Not many words were exchanged.

After the signing, Nanny thought that she would have some fun at the soldiers' expense.

She casually strolled over to the soldiers and politely asked them if they would care to shoot at her with their muskets, for fun.

At first her request was met with puzzling looks. They did not quite understand what she was asking. They looked at each other and wondered if she was serious or she just wanted to let them look like fools in front of her people. They politely declined but Nanny insisted.

"Come on gentlemen," she coerced them. "What are you afraid of? Get your muskets and fire at me. I will take full responsibility if anything goes wrong. My people here are my witnesses."

The soldiers considered the challenge carefully for some time, and not wanting to offend Nanny and her people, decided to accept.

Everyone stood silent as the soldiers raised their muskets to fire. Nanny appeared overly calm and confident as she watched the soldiers sweating under their collars.

The order came loud and clear from the commanding officer, "Ready! Aim! Fire!"

In a flash, Nanny spun around several times, bent down, then straightened up. Suddenly she stopped abruptly and faced the firing squad. She slowly walked towards the soldiers smiling, and with outstretched hands returned all their bullets.

"There is peace," she said calmly, and then pointing to the sky she reminded them, "Only Him alone can kill me. Only Him alone can take me when He's ready."

As Nanny and the villagers waved goodbye to the British, Putus commented, "Chief, you had them baffled. Did you see how their eyes nearly popped out of their heads when you gave them back their bullets? To tell you the truth Chief, I nearly wet myself."

"I just love to confuse the British chile, because they think that they know everything about African people," Nanny said, with a mischievous smile.

"They think that we are puppets on a string which they can play however they wish. So I like to do things that they don't expect and then leave them to figure it out."

"I don't think that they're going to figure out that one for a long, long time," Putus said to laughter.

Days later, Nanny got a notice that the Governor, in fulfilling his promise, had signed a Land Patent Agreement, granting Nanny and all her people a parcel of land of about 500 acres near Moore Town. Nanny was extremely happy because it meant extra acreage for her people to cultivate as Pumpkin Hill was quickly running out of fertile lands.

Later that day at the planning meeting Quao caught everyone by surprise.

"What! You're not serious Quao?" Putus shrieked. "What do you mean that you're not coming with us?"

"Sorry Sis and you too Putus," Quao began in a trembling voice. "I love you two a lot, but I think that it's time for me to move out on my own and stand up on my two feet. You two have been more than mothers to me and I really appreciate everything that you've done for me; but this is something that I have to do for myself."

"So where are you planning to move to?" Nanny asked.

"I was thinking of moving closer to the sea coast," Quao replied.

"What's so special about the sea coast?" Putus asked with a questionable look on her face.

"I always liked the sea coast," Quao replied, flashing a toothy smile. "I always found the sea coast interesting. There are so many more things to do down there. Mark you, I still love the hills but I believe that my future is near the sea coast."

"So Quao, tell me what you're thinking; what's your dream? Tell me so that I can figure out how best to help you," Nanny said, noting how determined he was to venture out on his own.

"I was thinking Sis, now that we're planning to move to this new place that would be the perfect time for me to move out on my own. We could ask the people if anyone would like to come with me and then we could take it from there. So on moving day we would all leave at the same time, you travelling across to Moore Town and me and my group travelling down to the little fishing village on the coast."

"Sounds like you've given this thing a lot of thought and you have everything worked out," Nanny said. "I'm so proud of you little brother, you have certainly paid your dues here and deserve to launch out on your own. Take whatever you need. Massa God go with you."

Part Four

The Motherland

Chapter 41

"Mada Nanny, are you sleeping? Don't sleep now Mada Nanny," the children pleaded.

"Tell us more!" one little boy begged.

"What happened next, tell us Mada Nanny," a little girl in a brightly colored dress implored.

"Come back tomorrow, and I will tell you how the story ends," Nanny promised, looking rather old and tired. "Now run along and play children and let the old lady rest," Nanny urged with a weak, friendly smile.

"Come, come children, go and play and let Mada Nanny rest, she's tired," a neatly dressed young lady in dreadlocks said, ushering out the kids. "Come back tomorrow, but not too early, and Mada Nanny will continue the story."

Nanny flashed a weak smile and slowly nodded her head in appreciation. God knows that she was grateful for this young lady. The girl had stuck to her like glue from the first day she arrived. She was a distant relative but she could well have been her own daughter. She had literally moved in with Nanny on the very first day; taking over the cooking and cleaning and being at her beck and call all day long. Mada Kuzo had really picked a good person for her. But then again, this was not surprising, she always delivered on her promises.

Nanny can still remember the look on Mada Kuzo's face when she told her that she had nothing more to offer the people of Jamaica. They were on their way toward nationhood, and so she wanted to go back home.

"Home chile? What do you mean? I thought that this was your home?" Mada Kuzo said, looking visibly confused. "My pet, do you really know what you're saying? Africa has changed a lot since you left. What will you do down there, an old woman, like you?"

"I don't know Mada Kuzo, but what I do know is that I want to be buried back in my homeland. This is not my homeland Mada Kuzo; my adopted land yes, and I love it dearly, but it is not my homeland. I want to go back down there one last time to feel the sun on my face and eat the good fresh African foods again before I come to join you. Going back home is like completing the circle Mada Kuzo. I've given all my youth to Jamaica to make it better for everyone, both Africans and the British; so it is my time now to do something for myself. It might sound selfish Mada Kuzo, but I think I deserve that break."

Mada Kuzo stared down at her in silence for some time, and then between clenched teeth said, "Why you refuse to take the easy road, I will never know.' Alright then, if that is what you really want to do then here is what I will do for you. I'll prepare everything for you down there including a house keeper, a nice young girl from your father's side of the family. Nice girl, she will make sure that you are well taken care of."

"Thanks Mada Kuzo, I don't know what I would do without you," Nanny said, with a warm smile.

* *

The next day, the children couldn't wait to visit Nanny. Some of them waited for over an hour before Nanny came out of her hut to greet them. She soon sat comfortably in her favorite chair under the big shade tree and then addressed the eager eyeballs staring back at her.

"Children are you ready to hear the rest of the story?"

"Yes Mada Nanny!" they shouted with joy.

"So where did we stop the last time?" she asked.

"The part where you and your younger brother Quao split up," a little boy blurted out.

"That's right," Nanny said with a broad smile. "I see you were paying attention."

"Of course Mada Nanny!" they all shouted with delight.

"Well let's get started then,".... And for the next couple of hours she relived her experience back in Jamaica, leaving nothing out; to the amazement of the children.

* * * * * * * * * * * * * * * * * *

It was nearly five years since Nanny had moved over to Moore Town and Quao had moved down near Crawford Town by the sea coast, Nanny's story unfolded. Many positive changes had taken place. The folks continued to cultivate pumpkins as their main crop along with other crops including: yams, bananas, plantains, potatoes, fruits and vegetables. Clashes between the British soldiers and the Maroons were becoming very rare; in fact it was down to its lowest since they signed the truce. More and more people had put down their weapons and secured plots of land to grow cash crops for the market. Others were actively involved in buying and selling at the market and business was good. The population was coming into its own, becoming more prosperous and contented citizens.

But for Nanny, this was a mixed blessing. She lost her husband Adou one year and her best friend Putus the following year. This was a very sad time for Nanny as she was now without her two best friends. The two people who understood her, made her laugh and made her happy, were now gone leaving a big hole in her heart. She could still hear Putus' voice in her head, laughing happily, telling her this and telling her that. Nanny really missed her best friend.

Although she carried out her duties as the Chief competently, the magic was wearing thin. She did not feel the excitement of past years, waking up at the crack of dawn roaring with enthusiasm to meet the challenges of the day. Rather, everything was becoming routine and predictable.

The town was also changing. The people were becoming more independent and were branching out into many new types of business ventures. Nanny found herself working more and more in the background, providing support and acting as a mentor to the young and upcoming leaders.

It was around this time that she suddenly felt homesick for Africa. It started like a mere ripple, and then it developed into a giant wave of desire. She just longed to set her feet back on the shores of the Motherland. This was surprising because she had always thought of Jamaica as home. She tried to shrug off the feeling but it just would not go away.

At nights, she dreamt of happier times during her childhood with all her family. The hut was filled with joy and laughter. It was so much fun, and she could not wait to get back there.

'What more can I do here for these people?' she mulled over in her mind. She had brought them to this land safely and helped them to become independent human beings again. She inspired them to dream again, to reach for the stars and chart their own destiny. She had done her job. She had given them back their confidence to get back up and try again, even when the odds were against them; she had done her job. She had impressed upon them the notion that black is beautiful. She had provided them with the tools to earn a living and to take care of their families. She had done her job. She had replaced hopelessness with a promise of a brighter future. She

331

had done her job. She had taught them to be respectful of their families, and for that matter, all human beings, regardless of race or color. She had done her job. She had put back the fire in their bellies to fight for what they believed in and not to be discouraged by what other people said. She had done her job.

Epilogue

Nanny returned to Jamaica after spending eighteen months in her tiny village in Africa. She believed that she would've been happy back there but she was mistaken. Everybody whom she knew and loved was in Jamaica. She also did not want to be separated from the world that she had grown to love. Most of all, she wanted to spend her last remaining days among her people.

By now her health was failing rapidly. Many family members and close friends kept a constant vigil at her bedside. The entire community waited patiently outside, quietly humming old African songs and giving thanks to Massa God, because that's what Chief would have wanted. Nobody wanted this beautiful human being to be alone at this time.

Nanny's frail heart bubbled over with emotion. She felt the love and warmth emanating from her people.

The nurses, most of whom she had trained, tried their best to make her as comfortable as possible.

A spirit of peace and serenity engulfed Nanny and the entire town. She was happy that she had returned.

As Nanny looked over to her left, her old, tired, fading eyes caught a glimpse of a bright light slowly coming towards her from way in the distance. Suddenly appearing in the light was her good friend Putus! Then Adou! Then Cudjoe! Then Mada Puko! Then her mother and father and a host of other souls who had gone on before her, all smiling with joy.

She knew that her time was drawing very near and she was pleased.

But suddenly she realized that someone was missing! She looked around desperately but couldn't find Mada Kuzo!

'Where could she be?' she mumbled in her head. 'Everybody is here except her!'

All of a sudden, out stepped a smiling Mada Kuzo offering her hand.

"Come my pet, take my hand! You've done well. We're all here waiting for you."

Sources:

1. www.scholars.library.miami.edu/slaves/individual_essays/howard.html
2. History of the West Indian Peoples: Book 111 - By E. H. Carter, G. W. Digby and R. N. Murray
3. www.wikipedia.org/wiki/nanny_of_the_maroons – Nanny of the Maroons
4. www.jamaica.com - Jamaica's true Queen: Nanny of the Maroons by Deborah Gabriel.
5. www.jnht.com/site_nanny_town.php
6. www.jnht.com/site_moore_town.php

Nanny visits the British General.

ABOUT THE AUTHOR

Colin Reid was born in the Parish of Clarendon, Jamaica and migrated to Canada with his family. He now resides in Toronto and teaches at a public elementary school. The Legend of Nanny is his first novel and was inspired by his love of History and the need to document the struggles of people of the Diaspora. Visit him online at: www.colincreid.ca and follow him on Facebook and Twitter @ColinCReid54.